Just Saying

Just Saying

By Denise McDonald

Copyright

JEBWizard Publishing
Books with Character

Table of Contents

Dedication

For Chris

Dedicated to my son, Luke

Chapter I   Juicy Fruit

There's a hole in the window.

While staring out the paned frame, lost in his thoughts about living in this room, Smike's eyes focus like seeing a holographic image. There, but not there.

No longer staring *out* the window but *at* the window, his attention shifts to a small hole. Myriad thoughts, questions, and random memories rush in that he cannot quite consciously harness.

How did that hole get there? How long has it been there? Like maybe when dad lived in this room as a child. Maybe it was from a slingshot or BB gun? Dad had both, but surely wouldn't have told Paps about accidentally shooting a hole in the window because that would have certainly resulted in a terrible beating. He didn't remember seeing it as a child when he and his parents and younger sisters visited. He almost always stayed in this room or sometimes downstairs in the family room on the couch or in a sleeping bag in front of the only TV in the house.

The room hasn't really changed since those childhood visits. Also, it couldn't have been there that long either, surely not. Well, not decades with no one noticing and not doing anything about it. Grandma Nettie would have noticed for sure. She was meticulous around the house and would have had Paps fix it at once, that's for certain. The hole must be new. Maybe some neighborhood kid was playing around and caused it. Again, it must be recent, like within the year or so; otherwise, Grandma Nettie would have done something about it.

Suddenly, Paps interrupts Smike's temporary trance.

"Ya can stay heeah in yaw fahthah's ole room. Some of yaw ahnt's ole toys and junk ah in the closet. Grammar Nettie moved those items from across the hall to make space faw hah sewin' and crafts stuff. Move anythin outta theyah faw whatevah and what not. The dressah draw is empty faw yaw clothes."

Smike, young man of slender build with a full beard and long dark hair tied in a bun, and Paps, his thin, balding, stubbly, and crotchety grandfather are in a small upstairs bedroom of a timeworn two-story house built in the 1950s, but owned by Paps since the early 1970s. Standing by the foot of a single bed, while still holding one of his bags, Smike looks solemnly out the only window in this room. To his right, with the window between them, his grandfather leans on his cane, gazing down, while noticeably smacking gum.

After awkward silence, Paps looks up and says to Smike, "Did ya heeah me Michael? I'm the one with the heeahin problem, not you! Ansah! Anythin ya wanna say aw ask me?"

Paps never addresses Smike by his nickname, won't even call him Mike. He always calls him Michael and when upset, addresses him as Michael Alan and when really pissed, its Michael Alan Schrod. And ultimate anger is expressed through, Shit, shit, SHIT, Michael Alan Schrod! Weird too, because Paps refers to Smike's dad as Jim or Jimmy when his proper name is James. Always seems to take a tougher, more formal stance with Smike in many ways. In the past, when he stayed for extended summer visits as a child, Smike received Paps' corporal hardline punishment for minor, normal childhood offenses. Compared to his father's stories, perhaps not as hard-hitting as what his dad experienced. Paps is an old man now but still outwardly mean. Smike knows his grandfather loves him, but this physically declining curmudgeon must still always be in control through harsh directives. All family members submit to his absolute authority.

Looking across at Paps, Smike quietly points up between them toward the window and says, "There's a hole in the window."

Paps looks at the hole, stares at it for a couple of seconds, takes out the wad of gum that has probably lost its flavor at this point from his incessant chewing, and plugs it into the window gap.

Then, turning back to Smike, straight-faced, he asks, "What hole?"

Speechless, Smike just gapes at him. No response to provide. No comment to make. Smike knows the history. Family never questions, they just accept Paps for what he says and what he does. Period. The notion is, just deal with him the best you can. Surprised that Paps didn't go looking for duct tape to temporarily fix the hole, which is his normal all-around, go-to fix-it material, Smike guesses the gum was just handy at that moment.

He then silently watches as Paps hangs his cane on his pants pocket and reaches in to grab a pack of gum from the other pocket.

Paps gestures to Smike with the gum pack extended and offers, "Joocee Fruit?"

Smike shakes his head and mildly responds, "No thanks."

"Suit yawself" Paps states flatly as he unwraps a fresh piece of gum, sticks it in his mouth, and starts chewing, leaving the gum wrapper to fall to the floor. He then limps past Smike toward the door and out of the room while informing him in a by-the-way fashion that the upstairs bathroom toilet is not working.

Once Paps exits, Smike gently drops his bag on the floor and thinks to himself, *Well ain't that the shit.* He then picks up the gum wrapper and throws it in the trash.

Chapter II Knight in Shining Armor

In his typical routine, Paps drives to some store each morning, usually the discount grocery store, a dollar store or the nearby hardware store; oftentimes, he would stop at all three. In the afternoons after lunch, first thing he did was check his mail. During mild weather, he would later walk to the local variety store for small perishable or indiscriminate items. This was his daily ritual that really hadn't changed since his retirement, even after Nettie's passing. He was a tinkerer who always had some home projects going on all the time that required a random item or two, for which he would impulsively head off to a store to find. Basically, he just really couldn't sit still for very long, even with his knee inflicting pain with each step. The cane offered only a small semblance of stability.

This afternoon, the day before Michael was scheduled to arrive, it's chilly but nice enough for a walk to the store. Actually, temperate enough for a long walk, first time in a while. Grabbing his cane, he dons his warm beanie, jacket, and gloves to head out. During his walks, he chews gum, head always facing down, and never really notices anything around him, as he focuses on his internal, rambling ideas. On this day's walk, his thoughts are filled with apprehension about his grandson living with him for a while, apparently to 'help' him after knee surgery.

He didn't think that he needed any assistance and wasn't exactly thrilled about having a close family member invade his space and perhaps mess with his routine and lifestyle. He had his schedule and meal choices down pat. Didn't like the idea of changes in his life that were going to occur as a result of Michael moving in. Plus, he's not convinced that he will even go through with the knee surgery.

Family members saw their living together differently though; thought it was a solid, temporary fix for both of them and encouraged their short-term union. Paps' son Jimmy, Michael's father, said that it would be good for the pair, that this was convenient for both of them, really, since Michael quit his job, sold his condo, and was transitioning into a music career and Paps was facing surgery that would make him immobile for a period of time and in need of assistance. However, he just didn't see the practicality of the co-habitation plan in the same way and felt some resentment for being cornered, or rather coerced, into this living arrangement.

He loves his grandson and is proud of him for graduating with a degree in chemical engineering; first one in the family to finish college, and he has made a very good living as a professional the past eight years. In his way of thinking, though, he just couldn't grasp *why* his grandson would give up a solid six-figure salary and career to write music. He's concerned that income in the arts and entertainment business is happenstance at best. His grandson's reasoning in shifting from a secure income and steady lifelong employment, to not knowing if or when the next paycheck was coming, was plain wacky to him. He couldn't help but feel negatively judgmental of his grandson's career change and subsequent decisions.

As Paps chews on this pending situation, he arrives at the variety store. Even though he needs only two items, cream for his coffee and chewing gum, he walks up and down every aisle, eyeing all the items. It's a sacred process, a steadfast routine, and for some strange reason, comforting for him to check out everything in the store.

All of a sudden, he hears a young woman call out, "Sir Sid, I see you have your sword with you today to ward off dragons in the Kingdom!"

Paps turns and recognizes the woman; it's Susan, Jeanne's granddaughter, currently living with her. He knows that Susan has some sort of, what Jeanne calls, *mental issue controlled through medication*, but not sure of her actual, formal diagnosis. Doesn't matter. She's a nice girl who, for whatever reason, has attached herself to him. Jeanne told him that Susan just likes him, plain and simple; she calls him her *knight in shining armor*. Where that notion came from, he was clueless, but always played along since there was no harm in it.

Keeping with the illusion, Paps responds "Lady Susan, so lovely to see ya. Wayuh is Queen Jeanne?"

"Why, she is attending to Princess Sadie at our castle" Susan replies.

Continuing this improvisation, Paps responds "I doan know this new membah of yaw royal household."

Although not showing his concern, Paps is slightly uneasy about Jeanne not being nearby, doesn't seem right.

Susan beams with pride, "Sadie is the most lovely and extraordinary baby throughout the entire kingdom! You must meet her soon. We will have a grand, formal gathering at the castle vestibule during the new moon. Please attend."

"Of cawse, Lady Susan, it will be my pleashuah!" he responds, accepting her fictional invitation.

Paps contemplates calling Jeanne after he returns home to make sure all is well with her and Susan. Perhaps Susan missed a dose of her medication or something.

"I must tend to my task and search for food and other needed fundamental items Sir Sid. It is my foraging quest today!" she says, then directs him "Continue fighting the ogres and dragons to keep us all safe!"

Abruptly, Susan turns around and heads back down the aisle in the opposite direction.

As she leaves, Paps calls out behind her, "Give Queen Jeanne my fondest greetins!" but doubts Susan heard him.

He consciously tries to remind himself to call Jeanne later.

Returning to his store tour, Paps completes each aisle review, collecting both needed items, and then resolutely saunters to the checkout line. It is a rather long line for this time of the day, and he's a little ticked off, spurred by his impatience waiting for anything. Unfortunately, while in this pissed state, behind him is a young worn-down looking woman with three children: one infant in her arms, and two rambunctious pre-school aged children jumping around like wild animals. At first, he tries to ignore them and just faces forward, but that doesn't work. The oldest nags him asking about his cane. The other younger one starts pulling on his pants to get his attention. The mother appears profusely apologetic but is barely able to hold onto the infant while pushing the shopping cart through the line, let alone deal with these two fledgling hooligans.

Just Saying

Not sure from where this thought emerges, perhaps out of desperation from his threadbare nerves, but Paps comes up with an idea.

Turning around, with contrived enthusiasm, he offers the kids a deal, "Hey kiddos, ya wanna be in a contest?"

They both explode with, "Yeah!" and "What is it?" "Is there a prize?"

Paps explains, "Oh yes, itsah competition that yaw muhthah has to approve."

He looks at the mom who nods with unspoken anguish *anything you can do would be appreciated!*

Paps then puts his items on the conveyor belt, grabs two packs of gum from the stand next to the checkout lane, and says, "Let's see who can balance a pack of gum on theyah head the longest!"

They both yell out, "Me!" "Me!" over and over again while jumping up and down.

"Okay, yah've gotta settle so I can place the gum on top of yaw heads. If, and this is a big if, if ya can balance it to the point that yaw muhthah has *completed* checkin out awl of hah food items, ya will receive the gum as a rewahd. BUT, and this is an impahtant but, ya cannot chew any of the gum until ahfta ya retawn home and yaw mah gives it to ya, got it?"

"Yes, yes, YES!" they both squeal loudly.

"One moah thing," Paps cautions "Ya must also walk safely and in the best, ohdahly mannah possible back to yaw cah and listen to evahythin yaw muhthah tells ya, Okay? Uhthahwise, the deal's off!"

"Yeah, we wanna play!!!" the oldest yells.

Paps then stations them next to each other, having them stand perfectly still like soldiers at attention, and gently places the gum packs on their heads. He looks back at the mom who mouths, *thank you* in total appreciation for this brief break he has provided from the kid-conjured chaos.

Noticing his strategy, and equally grateful, the checkout lady softly says to him, "You're a genius!"

Paps winks and smiles at her. He then tells the clerk to add the price of the two packs of gum to his ticket. He pays and turns to see the boys softly giggling with gum packs precariously balanced on their heads. Chewing his gum, Paps turns back to the cashier and claims, "Nah, no Einstein. Pahhaps just a wise ole man who cayhries a big stick; howevah, sum mistake me as a knight in shinin ahmah!"

He then swings his cane up and thrusts it forward in a jousting manner before repositioning it on the ground and hobbling out the store carrying his purchased items.

Chapter III Breadcrumbs

At least Smike's long drive from Texas to his final destination had many scenic views to appreciate along the way, but trepidation of living with his grandfather plagues him. It's not that he doesn't love the old man, it's just that he wants quiet, alone time to write his music. Pretty confident that Paps will distract him or not approve of his musical endeavors; and of course, harass him about it. However, he had already planned to move from Beaumont; anywhere else would work, just needed to get away. Up North was fine. And his grandparents' home always had a familiar comfortableness to it. It will be different though, with Grandma Nettie not there. She always kept Paps on an even keel and tempered his mood. He could be a real pain without her corralling his negativity and caustic comments.

Grandma Nettie once explained to Smike that his grandfather wasn't *always* rough around the edges. She would tell him that after Paps came back from Vietnam, he just wasn't the same person; that he had lost some of his good nature from the war experience. Grandma Nettie became pregnant with Smike's father around the same time that Paps was drafted in early 1965 and his father was born later that year during Paps' first deployment; so, Smike's father didn't know Paps' previous, more agreeable self. Grandma Nettie would advise Smike to be patient and kind with Paps. Seemed a strange approach at the time because Paps was the grown-up, not Smike; and Paps himself was rarely patient and kind, quite the opposite actually. Smike resolved himself to reality. He just needed to find positive notions about the arrangement his father had engineered and mediated for him cohabitating with his grandfather.

First positive, he would be able to help his grandfather and the entire family would appreciate that, even if Paps didn't. Second constructive point, it would be a semi-fresh start for him in a new location to pull inspiration for crafting lyrics. Third reason to be upbeat is that he would have somewhat uninterrupted time to write his songs since he no longer had responsibilities aligned with a regular nine-to-five, five-days-a-week job. Lastly, and most importantly, this situation was *temporary*. He needed to remember and keep that last point at the forefront of his thinking. If he stays optimistic, he can make the best out of the not-so-perfect circumstance.

He suspected that his father wasn't just thinking about what was best for Paps; he wanted Smike to take time to more fully grieve and get out of his depressed slump. Smike had only recently acknowledged his troublesome state. Louisa passed over a year and a half ago and he still hurt from the loss. A few months previously, he made some tough decisions to quit his job, sell his place, scale back on possessions, and move. Anywhere. Just move away. He had a nest egg saved that would give him a couple of years committed to just writing music and playing songs. He knew how to live on a shoestring budget. Did that in college. There was no financial hardship in this decision, and he would not be a burden to anyone. He also didn't have that many friends that he would be leaving behind in Texas. Since childhood, he had been somewhat of a loner. The handful of friends he had in Beaumont was couple's friends; but with Louisa gone, getting together was heartbreakingly awkward for everyone.

Surprisingly, his father supported his decision to quit the engineering position and work on his musical career. In fact, after his condo sold in Beaumont so quickly, Smike temporarily moved in with his parents, returning to his childhood home in a middle-class neighborhood south of Houston, away from the hustle and bustle of major city life, and a distance away from chemical plants and other industrial sites. The return home was an appreciated short-term respite; however, the intent was to take a little time to plan moving close to Austin and gain footing in the music scene of that area.

Then news came of Paps' knee surgery with no family member available to assist him. Or perhaps, no family member *willing* to volunteer their time and services; that is, for taking on the tiresome and unappreciated task of dealing with a very demanding, difficult to deal with, bad-tempered, aging individual, who was very much stuck in his ways! That's when his father got the notion of a tradeoff deal. Smike could stay with Paps and support his recovery from knee surgery before making a permanent move to the Austin area. So, although he wasn't moving to Austin at this time, the roundabout detour to Massachusetts could provide a quasi-fresh start; even if that meant being around a stale, cranky old soul like Paps.

In some ways, he looked forward to experiencing seasonal changes of the northeast. That was another positive! The summer would not be so sweltering as in Texas, fall would yield the splendor of autumn foliage and the changing colors of tree leaves. If he stayed through the winter, snow would be soothing to watch. He already knew that arriving in early spring would involve assisting Paps in planting a garden, which he always had a patch of vegetables sprouting every year. Smike inherently appreciated plants and gardens. He and Paps possessed that trait of nature loving. This was the only common attribute he could think they shared between them; both had green thumbs. The difference, the entire family recognized; Paps was acutely better at spreading manure. It's late April and he wonders if Paps has conducted any preparation for the garden yet. Doubt it, as the area recently had a freeze and light snow. Weather is definitely different in Massachusetts.

Unexpectedly, he has a funny thought and wonders if there would be gum wrappers all around the house. He remembered Grandma Nettie constantly picking them up and following after Paps as he dropped them on the floor. There was one instance when Smike was visiting as a young boy, and he asked Grandma Nettie where he could find his grandfather.

In a joking manner, she said, "Just follow da Juicy Fruit wrappers like Ansel and Gretel's dropped breadcrumbs."

That memory stuck with him. She had a funny way of explaining things that made sense to him and her peculiar reasoning always seemed to fit the situation. Also, Grandma Nettie's French-Canadian accent, where she couldn't say her "h's" endeared him. Smike admired and respected his grandmother. Despite her destitute upbringing and lack of educational opportunities, she was the most socially astute and creative person he ever knew. He always believed that he got his love of music from *her* because of all the tunes she would play for him on her stereo during summer visits.

Lovingly reminiscing about her impact on his life, a comforting memory arose how Grandma Nettie so wanted to come to Louisa's memorial service, but her health prohibited traveling. Paps couldn't leave her alone, so neither could make the small family gathering to honor Louisa. He understood. They both loved Louisa and would tease her about how much they were looking forward to being great-grandparents for the first time. In this moment, Smike's emotional pain and sorrow returns with a vengeance; his loss is immeasurable. Even fond

Just Saying

memories stir mental and emotional anguish that punish every
fiber of his being.

Chapter IV Kielbasa Bologna

It's midday when Smike drives up to Paps' house. He sees the old Plymouth parked in the driveway, but close to the road entrance, not pulled all the way up to the shed, so he can't park behind it. He wonders why Paps did that. He knew about him arriving this afternoon. Smike decides to park his Prius at the front gate. That will actually be easier for unloading his things anyway.

While Smike removes items from his car, Paps sees him out of the family room bay window, comes to the front door wearing his favorite green plaid, flannel shirt and while leaning on his cane, yells, "Michael, jeet ahready? Cause, I'm makin kielbasar faw suppah."

Smike loudly replies, "I'm not hungry right now, but that sounds good Paps, thanks."

He wasn't much of a meat eater but knew this was one of Paps' staple meals. Kielbasa bologna on soft white bread or sometimes toasted rye, slathered in mustard, usually topped with sliced yellow, Vidalia onions. Smike guessed that after a lifetime of ingesting greasy sausage, Paps' cholesterol was exorbitant; however, it didn't seem to slow the old man down.

Paps returns inside and Smike unloads his remaining boxes, bags, and keyboard, leaving his bike on the rack attached to the back of his car. Trying to gain entry to the front yard, the old gate stubbornly sticks. He fights with it for a bit until finally able to jar it open. After moving several loads to the front door, Smike places all of his possessions just inside the house entranceway, because he was not clear where Paps wanted him to put everything.

Just Saying

Paps comes up to Smike at the entrance and gives him a side hug that is reciprocated. Pointing to the family room, which Paps calls the *pahlah*, Paps kindly commands Smike to come over, sit down on the *sofer*, and rest for a bit.

Paps then heads to his lounger and Smike to the couch, as Paps, while chewing gum, asks, "So how was yaw trip?"

"Best that can be expected. Fortunately, had good weather" he replies.

"But, what? Ya couldn't make yaw bahba appointment and get yaw hayuh cut befoah ya left? And ya lost yaw razah, too?" Paps asks in a resentful, bitter tone.

And here it starts, little digs that are common shots of criticism, marginally cloaked in Paps' perception of social decency during what is normally considered everyday conversation. Smike knew to expect this, but had barely sat down; and was therefore, caught off guard. Anticipating Paps' repulsion to his long hair, he deliberately tied it back into a bun for it to be less obvious. He already knew that his hair would be Paps' first strike, but figured that he might have waited a little until after some settling in. *Should have known*, he thought. Smike actually wasn't a big fan of kielbasa bologna, but even more so, he hated the typical baloney spewed from Paps' lips. He was getting both within the first few minutes after arriving.

In contrast to Paps' aggressive style, Smike's modus operandi was to quietly take Paps' punches, absorb the blows, and virtually throw his hands up in defeat. He never struck back. Just stayed silent long enough for the verbal hostility to pass. Besides, Paps never asked him *why* he was growing his hair out. So, Smike didn't feel that he owed him any explanation and decided to just let Paps wallow in his own false assumptions, whatever they may be. Paps grunts, something like *shoulda known*. He too had accumulated expectations for how his grandson interacted with him. Couldn't understand why Michael would never stand up for himself. More than the long hair, it disappointed Paps that Michael was so passive and unresponsive to challenges thrown at him. He hated that Michael acted like a wimp. Schrods were *not* cut from a docile, submissive cloth. They were fighters! Michael always took the path of least resistance, never fought for anything that Paps could see. This bothered and frustrated him about Michael, and he didn't know what to do about it either.

Neither one says anything to each other for a few minutes. Then Paps, grabbing his cane, gets up.

"Checkin on the kielbasar" he informs Smike.

Smike says, "Okay, let me move some of my stuff out of the way."

Paps barks, "No, leave evahythin until ahfta we eat. Just follah me to the kitchen."

At which, Smike customarily follows his order.

Once in the kitchen, Paps turns the stove off under the pot of boiling water in which the bologna is cooking and asks, "Wanna beeah aw soder?"

Smike tells him that water is fine. He then monotonously assists his grandfather with placing plates, utensils, and condiments on the table. Paps forks the kielbasa out of the pot, places it on a platter, and brings it over to the table while Smike automatically grabs a beer from the refrigerator for his grandfather and gets a glass of water for himself.

After they sit down, Paps removes his gum and sticks it on his beer can (apparently, saving if for an after-meal treat). He then shares that he got special, fresh hoagie buns for them to try out, blesses himself, and they begin eating without saying much to each other, with the exception of Paps asking Smike if he likes the hoagie rolls and kielbasa. With an indifferent manner, Smike provides a lukewarm endorsement.

Finishing their meal, Paps takes his last sip of beer, sticks the gum back in his mouth, and while smacking, says, "Let's go upstayuhs so ya can see wayuh ya'll be stayin."

Smike responds, "Okay, let me grab some of my things."

Paps clutches his cane, Smike snatches a bag and a couple other items by the entranceway, and they head up the stairwell; neither one expressing too much excitement about the state of their new union.

Chapter V Small Corner

After Paps cautions him about the non-functioning upstairs toilet and leaves the bedroom, Smike looks around. It's a simple room; nightstand next to one side of the single bed, small trash can on the other side, desk with a chair pressed against one wall, dresser drawer next to it, some shelving on another wall housing a few books and pictures, and near one corner of the room, a rather tiny closet.

He starts arranging belongings that he brought upstairs; placing his journal, harmonica, and cell phone on the nightstand, as these are a few of his most valuable possessions. The desk looks like a solid location for his keyboard; stretches his arms out to measure surface area to be about the right size. Once he retrieves it from downstairs, it will be mounted there. The dresser drawer is empty, just like Paps said, and there is plenty of space for most of his clothes. He had given many clothing items away, mainly his professional-style shirts, suits, and ties. Kept his favorite set of dress clothes and one suit for special occasions and will hang those in the closet.

He then goes to the closet, opens it, and on the built-in shelf finds an old tin doll house filled with plastic furniture, some vintage troll dolls strewn about, and a kid's old plastic bank shaped like a sad hound dog. To make space, he will move these items across the hall to the craft room. Might keep one troll and place it on the nightstand for fun and nostalgic reasons. On the floor of the closet are some worn out, old-fashioned girl's shoes and what appears to be either a suitcase or some type of storage case textured in brown, fake alligator material. He pulls it out, sets it flat on the floor, sits down cross-legged in front of it, and unlatches the flaps to open it up. Lifting the case lid, he finds a small, bright red accordion. What an unexpected discovery!

Immediately excited and eager to play this ultra-cool, old-timey instrument, he gently removes it from the case. Underneath, on the bottom of the case, are musical scores for beginners, as well as information about the keys which play the melody; and the bass accompaniment, which are the chord buttons. He already knows how to play the keys but will have to learn about positions of the buttons for performing the bass. What a startling find in this unassuming closet.

As he's trying on the child-size accordion, it's too tight and he has to loosen the straps. Obviously sized for his aunt when she was a young girl, he adjusts the straps, slips it on again, and plays around producing sounds.

In heaven, he revels in the bellowing sounds echoing through this small room and is totally consumed in the moment. Something new will now be added to his musical repertoire. He would never have guessed such an enchanting surprise would be hidden away in this closet, in this room, in this house. He now has a little hope that perhaps, if not right now, perhaps later, by adopting this forgotten instrument, he can make a small corner of this room his own, which is exactly where he prominently places the accordion in full view.

Chapter VI Old, Ongoing Testament

Waking up the next morning, Smike's surprised that he actually had a deep, relaxing sleep his first night at Paps' house. He gets out of bed, walks over to the window, looks out, and taps the hardened gum on the hole. Paps' car is still in the driveway, so he hasn't left to go anywhere yet. And, no rumblings are heard from downstairs, which is Paps' wakeup call for anyone in the house; mainly his way of saying, *I'm up, so ya need to be up.* So, Smike throws on his warm running suit and shoes and heads down the stairs and out the door for a quick three-mile run. He remembered the area well enough to run a path around the surrounding neighborhood.

Smike was looking forward to establishing his new routine: Run first thing in the morning (weather permitting), shower, fix breakfast for both of them, then work on writing lyrics and playing music, break for lunch, return to his music in the afternoon or run errands when needed, make dinner for both of them, spend some early evening time watching a movie, game show, sports or the news with Paps, and lastly, return to his music endeavors before bed. This was a general schedule that, in Smike's mind, could support what he envisioned would meet both of their needs.

However, he imagined that Paps could, at any time, throw a monkey wrench into any routine he might try to establish. Even though Paps had his own daily schedule, his impulses often took over, without any forethought or planning, he would respond to random thoughts that would jump into his head about something he needed or something he wanted to work on. Thus, multiple, often needless treks to local stores would consume Paps' mornings and frequently drag into afternoon store visits as well. Only exceptions were scheduled doctor visits. They took priority; however, Smike remembered that Paps almost always stopped at some store afterwards, even if he didn't need anything. Essentially, Paps was a restless soul who rarely relaxed, with the exception of when he hunkered down to watch television and enjoy a couple of beers late in the day.

On his run, Smike notices it's a little cooler, crisper weather than he expected; next time he will remember to wear gloves. Fortunately, before he knew it, his run was over, the gate was ajar, and he's walking up the porch stairs to the house. He sees that Paps' car is gone. Likely left for one of his early morning store visits. Unfortunately, when he tries to enter the house, the front door is locked. Paps didn't know that Smike was up already and had headed out for a run, so he locked the front door behind him.

After cursing under his breath, thinking that he could feasibly be locked out for several hours in the cool air, Smike luckily remembered that a house key was hidden in the back yard for the back door entrance. He jogs back, retrieves the key (hidden under a plant pot where it has always been stored), opens the door, and goes upstairs for his shower. Slogging up the stairs, Smike mentally reminds himself to ask his grandfather for a house key.

Once in his room, he grabs some clean clothes and enters the upstairs bathroom. When he turns on the showerhead, water just drizzles out. There's no water pressure, at all. Smike grabs a white towel hanging on the holder and heads downstairs to use Paps' bathroom shower.

He finds that the shower downstairs works just fine, so he indulges in a warm rinse to clean up, unwind, and relax his leg muscles. Exiting the shower, he dries off and wraps the towel below his waist. He looks in the mirror and reaches his arm behind his back, straining to touch the end of his long, wavy hair behind him. Not there, not just yet. But close.

Out of the blue, he's startled with Paps at the bathroom door, holding a bag and loudly yelling at him, "JEEZUS CHRIST!!!"

Jolted, Smike responds, "WHAT?!?" not sure why Paps is barking at him.

"I mean, look at ya, long hayuh, full beeahd, scrawny, ribs showin, with loin cloth wrapped round ya, ya look just like Jeezus!" While shouting, Paps adds in a harsh and cutting pitch, "And what ah ya dooin yoosin my showah anyway?"

Here again, Paps shoots a sarcastic shot at Smike. And here yet again, Paps critiques him without full information of the situation. Assumptions about circumstances, before asking questions or gathering data, were frequently made by his grandfather. It was annoying, irritating, downright frustrating to deal with, especially on an ongoing basis. Plus, who was Paps, a bony, gaunt-looking old fossil, to call *him* scrawny?

Smike calmly, but more loudly and forcefully than usual, responds, "The shower upstairs doesn't work. The problem may be related to the toilet issue."

"Well shit, we'll hafta fix that!" Paps says, surprisingly flipping to a more pleasant, gleeful demeanor as he hands the bag he is holding to Smike.

Just Saying

Smike scans it and sees a toilet valve assembly package. A woeful look comes over his face. Paps loved projects and reveled in those that he and Smike could work on together; especially those of which he was *in charge*. Smike knew that collaborative endeavors around the house typically involved Paps dictating to and hawking over his designated minion or minions. There were never joint collaborations or any sense of teamwork with Paps. He controlled every turn of the screwdriver, specific to his directions and demand for all handiwork around the house. Additionally, more often than not, the work ended up being a Band-Aid job, a temporary, shabby fix. Paps was all into getting things done quickly and moving on. A crushing sense of dread gripped Smike; he was not looking forward to fixing the shitter with Paps because he would also have to deal with Paps' shit.

Paps exits the bathroom while barking at Smike to get dressed. He was taking him to breakfast. Smike knew this meant going to a local greasy spoon, which most likely would present huge, hearty meals of mostly fried staples. Paps rarely ate out unless it was a special event, or the restaurant provided large meals at cheap prices. This dive must be one of his favorites.

Smike gets dressed, runs back upstairs to grab his wallet, car keys, and jacket, and joins Paps impatiently waiting downstairs by the front door, while smacking his gum and leaning on his cane.

"Let's go, slow poke, need my breffis, I'm stahvin" Paps urges.

"Okay Paps, are you driving, or am I?" Smike asks.

"I'm driving; ya doan know wayuh to go" Paps snaps curtly.

While leaving, Paps locks the door and Smike remembers being locked out earlier.

Walking to the car Smike mentions to Paps, "By the way, I'll need a house key."

"Will give ya Nettie's key set when we get back" Paps replies.

Paps unlocks the car, throws his cane in the back seat, and they both get in. After letting the car warm up, Paps backs his vehicle out of the driveway onto the street. Smike notices very quickly that Paps uses his right foot for pressing on the gas only and uses his left foot for the brake. The pressure in hitting the brakes must cause pain in Paps' damaged knee. Smike knows not to mention this observation, not at this time at least. Paps would get incensed and bitch at him not to worry about it; so, he keeps his mouth shut.

Chapter VII Blue Skies

As a passenger on this surprisingly lovely and pleasingly quiet drive, Smike soaks in the scenery and beautiful blue sky; all of which lull him into pleasant thoughts about writing music later in the day. His reverie is soon disrupted as they arrive at the home-style country cooking restaurant. Very eager to get in, sit down, and order his typical meal, Paps marches to the entrance. As they enter, the attending waitress knows Paps as a regular and seats them quickly.

Once settled, she hands them menus and asks Paps, "Same order as usual Sid?"

"Yeah, seenyah supah special, and whatevah my grandson wants. Need to fatten him up" Paps replies.

Smike isn't given any time to look over the menu as Paps glares at him to hurry, so he orders off the top of his head a poached egg, wheat toast, and a small bowl of oatmeal. The waitress asks if he wants coffee.

He replies, "Hot tea and water, but would like a little cream on the side for the oatmeal."

"Ya got it, Sid's grandson!" she mocks with emphasis since Paps failed to introduce the two of them.

Smike jumps in, "I'm Smike, nice to meet you . . ." and pauses for her to share her name.

"Skye, as in blue sky" she shares.

"Oh, like the song *Blue Skies*" Smike speculates.

Beaming, Skye says, "Yeah, EXACTLY, my mother named me after that song. She said the lyrics made her happy, just like her having me!"

"Lovely name, after a lovely song" Smike states with kindness.

Skye, smiling, turns and says to Paps, "I like your grandson, Sid. Takes after Nettie, I see" she adds with sarcasm.

"Hmmph, intrahductions ovah, need my cuppa Joe" Paps barks in a complaining and brusque tone.

"Coming right up" Skye confirms while turning away.

Obviously bothered by what Paps perceives as unnecessary conversation, that is, the niceties of social interactions; he attempts to shut down discourse unless, of course, he is the one controlling the dialogic exchanges. Smike noticed Paps demonstrates *a little* more civility with strangers and others outside of the family. So, he must have some sense of his arrogant and pushy personality to somewhat subdue it with others. Just not sure to what degree he is aware or not. Probably not. From what Smike has seen, Paps is not a very insightful or self-reflective individual. Or perhaps, he just doesn't care.

Skye soon returns with the coffee, tea, and water. Smike and Paps sit there for a few moments not talking, just drinking their beverages and waiting for their meals. As there is a continuously looming dark cloud around Paps, Smike gazes out the restaurant window and consciously retreats to ephemeral gratitude for the scenic view and blue sky.

Chapter VIII Old Pair

"Hey stranger!" Jean yells out across the restaurant directed to Paps as she grabs the friend she is with and hurries towards him.

Paps, scowling, says under his breath, but loud enough for Smike to barely hear him, "A couplah Nettie's friends who drive me crazy. Ole dungahrees ah chattah boxes."

Not sure he heard Paps correctly, Smike didn't quite understand what he meant.

The two elderly ladies come up to the table where Paps and Smike are seated. Jean reintroduces herself to Smike.

"You probably don't remember me, Michael. We met at your grandmother's memorial service when I gave a loving speech about her. I'm Jean Krachec. Nettie and I were good friends."

The other senior woman exclaims, "I was Nettie's friend as well. I'm Jeanne McNeal but spell my first name with an added 'ne' just to clarify so you don't mix us up."

Smike immediately knows he will not mix them up; one lady is tall and thin, craggy face, with dyed jet-black hair, even though it's obvious from her roots that her natural hair color is pasty white. The other lady is chubby with considerable rolls around her middle, soft curls of graying reddish hair, and dentures that slip when she speaks. Besides, all he has to do is call each one Jean. Name sounds exactly the same. They both appear affable and kind-hearted. He quickly surmises they must be, since they were Grandma Nettie's friends.

Jean interjects a request, "May we join ya? We've already eaten but would love to visit for a bit."

Smike nods, "Sure!" and gets up to pull the chairs out for each of them to sit down.

Both ladies grin in appreciation as Jeanne says, "How gallant of you Michael, thank you!"

Paps appears tacitly resistant to them joining their table. Chuckling inside, Smike has little doubt that these two talkative ladies joining them for breakfast grates on his grandfather's nerves; however, surprisingly, Paps starts the conversation.

"Jeanne, I saw Susan at the stoah the uhthah day without ya and she said that theyah's a new membah of yaw household, a baby?" Paps asks inquisitively.

"Oh, you didn't know Sid. I haven't seen you for such a long time, since just after Nettie passed. And I haven't seen you at church or you haven't been coming lately. Not Christmas and not even at Easter. You know, you don't have to kneel when you come to church" Jeanne prefaces her explanation.

"Anyway, Susan had a beautiful baby girl! She named her Sadie. They are both living with me. I'm now a great-grandmother! Isn't that great?" she exclaims with exuberance.

In the background, her friend Jean grabs Paps' arm to get his attention and confirm as well as impress upon him how the baby is gorgeous with beautiful blue eyes and a perfect disposition. Paps mostly ignores her, while earnestly listening to Jeanne.

"Congratulations Jeanne!" Smike shares.

Just Saying

Unusually courteous, Paps says, "That's good news Jeanne. I wasn't shuah if Susan was imaginin a child aw not. She was in hah princess state-of-mind and ya wuhrn't with hah, so I was a little conceahned."

"Oh no, all is fine! Susan is taking her medication and is a fabulous mother! She is so in love with Sadie! And I watch the baby when she occasionally runs to the store" Jeanne explains.

"Well, good! Good to heeah" Paps responds.

He actually seems a little relieved.

Smike, however, is clueless about the situation and what they are discussing about Jeanne's granddaughter's *state-of-mind*. Obviously, this is not the time or place to ask about specifics or possibly intrusive details into Jeanne's private situation, so he quietly listens. However, he thinks Jeanne sounds a little naïve for her senior years.

Jean abruptly changes the subject, with what appears to be her original intent in talking with Paps.

"Ya know Sid, we are so glad to run into you. The Saturday Night Bingo Game for the church needs an announcer. Chuck has laryngitis and we need a replacement. You have such a loud voice; it would be great if you could volunteer. Will reward you with a case of beer, your favorite brand, and all the pizza you can eat! Whatja think?"

"Well, I doan know Jean, Michael just arrived, and we have sum things to do" he responds with indifference.

Paps and Jean begin bantering back and forth about the request while Jeanne leans toward Smike and quietly says in private, "You look so much like your grandfather, but your manner, your way of being, is much more like your grandmother" and after a slight pause with a smirk, adds, "Good thing, huh?"

Smike smiles, nodding his head in agreement.

During their side conversation, Jeanne then adds, "Nettie used to say Sid was contrary, which we all know he is, but she also told us of his sweet way of courting her when they first met. Apparently, he won her over by serenading her late at night by her window."

Very much surprised by this anecdote of Paps' apparent sensitive side, Smike doesn't remember Paps ever singing, so he skeptically asks, "My grandfather sang to her?"

Jeanne begins her reply "There is more than one way to serenade Michael . . ." when they are interrupted by Jean asking them a question.

Apparently, the debate between Jean and Paps reached a crescendo and now Jean, through a socially coercive tactic, strategically sought to tilt the final decision in her favor.

"So, Michael, Jeanne, don't ya think Sid should be the announcer at Bingo this Saturday? Wouldn't he be great?" Jean pushes for confirmation.

What an ironic and unexpected opportunity for Smike to turn the tables on his grandfather who initially tried to use *him* as an excuse to turn down Jean's request; so, he takes it.

Just Saying

"Paps, I think it would be great for you to help out in this situation. You have always told me that service to the church is important" Smike says while grinning broadly.

The added bonus in his maneuver, he actually uses Paps' own words about church service to solidify the point.

Now cornered and desperate for a logical plea to get out of this forced commitment, Paps glares at him in a disapproving grimace.

"Well, I'm not really able to drive too fah because of my knee. May have knee sahjahry soon" Paps counters with a lame excuse.

Smike offers a solution, "Oh, I can take you Paps. Will drop you off and pick you up. Plus, you have always told me to never refuse free beer or food!"

He sneaks in another one of Paps' platitudes to hammer the final nail in this Bingo coffin.

Jean quickly seals the deal, "Good! Better show up Sid! Will see you on Saturday, before five, at the church conference hall! Michael, please feel free to stay and join in on the festivities."

Smike thanks her as Skye arrives with breakfast. Paps' spread is a mammoth amount of food on what seems like endless plates being set in front of him. They all gawk at what is laid out. Jean feels compelled to make a comment.

"Ya know Sid, everyone knew what a good cook Nettie was and how much food she would make for you every day. Always wondered why you didn't weigh three hundred pounds!"

Paps utters under his breath, "That's cause half the naybuhhood felt free to stop by owah house at any time to eat most of the food she made faw me."

Not hearing or perhaps ignoring him, Jean continues while eyeing his seemingly limitless meal, "Never understood how you stayed so skinny. Guess it's your metabolism. Not everyone can eat like a horse and stay thin."

Getting up from her seat, she then adds, "Well, we'll be on our way and let the two of you enjoy your breakfast."

The two ladies button their coats, put on their gloves, and unceremoniously leave while waving good-bye.

After the pair exits, Paps vents in a huff "Shit, Michael Alan, whyja do that? Ya could tell I didn't wanna be involved in that Bingo shit!"

Sputtering, he catches his breath, then continues to grumble, "And ya remembahed my advice 'bout chawch, 'bout beeah, 'bout food, but nevah listen when I say to get a hayuhcut! Just doan get ya."

Smike confidently declares, "Well, I think this Bingo service would be a good thing for you to do, that's all."

"So, ya side with those raggedy, ole, wawn-out payah of jeans?" Paps snaps.

Smike, a little surprised, laughs under his breath at Paps' comical phrase of *raggedy, old, worn-out pair of jeans* used to describe these ladies and prods for clarification.

Just Saying

"Is that what you call them? You don't like them? I thought they were Grandma Nettie's good friends?" Smike questions.

"They ah raggedy, ole, and wayuh me out. It's not that I doan like 'em cause they wuhr good to yaw grandmuhthah. Theyah just a payah, ya know? Nettie would laugh when I called 'em that and would say that evahyone likes a payah of ole comfahtable jeans" Paps explicates, ending in some veneer of civility.

He then removes his gum, places it on his coffee saucer, blesses himself, and gruffly dictates, "Let's eat befoah owah food gets cold!"

Chapter IX Routine

Paps had already visited his favorite shopping spot earlier that morning when he purchased the toilet flush valve assembly at the local hardware store. Smike wasn't sure if this product would solve the issue with the upstairs toilet. However, this was Paps' routine, his approach to randomly, sometimes blindly, address pressing issues, just how he operates, how he functions; which from Smike's perspective was rather dysfunctional and not efficient. After breakfast, the rest of the morning involved Paps driving them to his other two preferred retailers; a dollar store and a discount grocery store.

At the dollar store, Paps loaded up on toilet paper, even though he has a year's supply in the basement. Smike remembered the family side joke; behind his back, they all call Paps the *Toilet Paper Hoarder.* Grinning, while quietly thinking about this, Smike places the packs of toilet paper in the trunk. They then head off to the grocery store where Paps gets some fresh lettuce, tomatoes, and apples. He asks Smike if he wants or needs anything. Smike picks out some herbal teas and offers cash to cover the expense. Paps refuses his offer and pays for all items at the counter.

As they leave the grocery store and walk back to the car, Smike notices Paps limping more distinctly, each step appears guarded, as if he is in more pain. This has been a long morning of outings and errands for his grandfather, and he has done a lot of walking. Smike suspects that his grandfather is hurting but doesn't want to admit that to him. As they place the groceries in the car, Smike asks Paps if he can drive his car home. He rationalizes this request with a faked reason; that he needs to get to know the area and roads and there is no better way to do that than to drive around. Remarkably, Paps acquiesces and tosses the keys to Smike. This is quite surprising because Paps rarely delegates driving to anyone else.

Paps says, "Well ya should know the way back, since I drove ya heeah."

It's clear to Smike that his grandfather's daily routine is becoming more difficult for him because of his knee pain. Smike wants to ask him about his next doctor visit but feels this is not the time. Paps would get angry and infer that Smike is condescending about him being somewhat disabled. He decides to wait to ask him at a later time, as he has only been in town less than two days.

Once they return home, Smike pulls all the way up to the shed. He suggests to Paps that this will give him room to pull his own car into the driveway rather than leave it parked on the street. Paps quickly and curtly corrects him; Smike is told that it is called *doah yahd*, not *driveway*. Smike thinks to himself *whatever* and blows off Paps' minor rebuke, knowing that these types of talking-down-to scolding lectures will be ongoing, regular reactions from the crusty and crass old fart. Smike should expect them.

They both exit the car, each carrying items purchased that morning and enter through the back door as Paps says, "Havin subs faw lunch. I have moah hoagie rolls, some ham, and just got fresh lettis and t'maydahs."

"That works Paps. I can fix the sandwiches and if I remember correctly, you like mustard and mayo on it. Do you want sliced onions as well?" Smike asks.

"Yeah, just bring to the pahlah when ready. I'm tyuhd. Wanna watch a little TV and relax" Paps responds.

Smike says, "Sure thing!"

"Also, doan fawget the beeah" Paps orders.

"You got it" Smike responds.

Paps leaves all items he was carrying by the back door and as he hobbles to the family room, directs Smike, "Take the tahlet paypah down cellah."

Soon after, Smike hears the TV blaring as he carries the toilet paper downstairs to the basement and brings all the groceries into the kitchen.

From this outing, Smike's early morning thoughts of his possible routine have already been tossed. He can work around Paps' set morning schedule, which he is confident was the whole purpose of how Paps scheduled the morning activities; that is, so Smike would know what Paps expected and where he wanted to go each morning on most days. Smike could adjust his music writing to afternoons and early evenings. He may just have to skip watching the news and game shows with Paps. No great loss, since Smike generally didn't watch much television anyway.

Smike yells from the kitchen, across to Paps in the family room, "Want it toasted?"

Silence, no response. Smike figures Paps can't hear a thing with the TV so loud, so he runs into the family room while delivering his beer.

Just Saying

"Do you want your sub toasted?" Smike asks as he hands the beer to Paps.

"Ya know, that sounds good!" Paps responds, taking his gum out to drink his beer.

Smike returns to the kitchen, finishes fixing their lunch, and delivers it on trays to the family room. In ritualistic fashion, Paps removes the gum, places it on the beer can, blesses himself, and then takes a huge bite out of his sandwich. They sit together quietly eating while watching one of Paps' favorite game shows.

Chapter X Project Interruptus

After quickly devouring his sandwich, in like three bites, and lapping down his beer, Paps turns the TV off, throws a new piece of gum in his mouth, and says, "Let's fix the golden throne" as he gets up, leaning on his cane, and proceeds towards the stairs.

Smike, in between bites, is only halfway finished with his sandwich, but Paps appears oblivious. Smike knows that he is expected to put everything down and follow his grandfather upstairs. Looks like his afternoon will not be spent writing music. A different agenda item has taken priority.

Holding onto the rail with one hand, cane in his other, Paps moves slowly up the stairs. Smike follows behind. At the top of the stairs, just behind the craft room and kitty corner to Smike's room, they enter the bathroom. The valve assembly is on the floor next to the toilet where Smike left it earlier. Paps says, "The tahlet bowl doan fill up with wotta" and directs Smike to take the cover off the toilet tank, which he obediently does.

Paps then commands him to turn the water valve off below the tank. Again, Smike follows his grandfather's directions, gets down on his knees to reach behind the toilet and turn off the water valve.

Suddenly, while squirming around, Paps announces with urgency, "Uh, oh, oooh, I gotta crap. Goin downstayuhs. May take a while, so doan do anythin mayjah until I retawn" then turns around and quickly leaves.

Smike is on his knees, straddling the toilet with his arms around the seat, when an unexpected memory emerges. The last time he was in this position in front of a toilet was with Louisa. He remembers vividly, like it was yesterday, when she called him into the bathroom, sitting on the toilet, arms on her lap, with tears in her eyes.

He emphatically asks her *"What? What is it?"*

She lifts a pregnancy tester from her lap and while gently weeping says, "We're having a baby!"

He remembers dropping to his knees in front of her, completely overwhelmed and ecstatic with this unexpected but highly anticipated, welcomed news. It was the happiest, most exhilarating moment of his entire life!

Looking deeply into her tear-drenched face; he grabs her shoulders and pleads, "So, *now* will you marry me?"

They fall into each other's arms, tightly squeezing each other while crying with joy.

Between sobs, she tenderly says, "Of course, I was *always* going to marry you!"

Smike tears up and begins to sob softly. His soul is aching; he feels empty. He can't even work on a toilet without thinking about her. His life with Louisa, his rapture of bliss, was senselessly ripped away from him. Everything else is meaningless. Being here feels hollow. Fixing this toilet is inconsequential. Nothing makes sense. What the fuck is he doing? Smike then sits on the bathroom floor with his legs crossed, head down, hands propping his forehead covering his eyes and cries uncontrollably. Out of nowhere, fond but heart-wrenching memories trigger this emotional torment.

After a few minutes, Paps returns, unaware of Smike's emotional condition, and states with a sense of elation, "My deed faw the day is done! So wayuh ah we on this prahject?"

Smike covertly wipes his eyes avoiding direct eye contact, gets up and walks swiftly past Paps and out of the bathroom.

"I need a break. I'll be in my room."

Paps complains, "Hey, ya can't just stop in the middle ova job! All the pahts ah lyin on the floah."

"I'll get to it later" Smike responds tersely while going into his room and shutting the door.

Paps doesn't remember his grandson acting this way before. Not exactly belligerent, but deliberately dismissing his commands. He senses, though, that he needs to let whatever this is, go; and therefore, returns downstairs to watch TV.

Chapter XI Catching Breaths

Smike lies on the bed, grabs his harmonica, and starts playing. With each breath of air expressed, tender melodies materialize and cursorily calm his wretched emotional state. Breathing in and out is more purposeful than just staying alive. Each breath creates something new, a fresh unique sound, a different series of tones; novel music that resonates with his longing psyche, his marred essence, his incomplete being, his spiritual void. He feels that this self-designed therapy, through music, is cathartic for healing his damaged soul; although, Smike does not believe he will *ever* be completely healed or whole again. Too much scarring has accumulated for him to fully function as the propitious individual of his past self. Death and the depth of his loss irretrievably changed his life trajectory into an unknown path and hopeless abyss. Music was saving his life, but in his deepest introspection, he's not sure it's worth saving. However, Louisa always thought more of him.

In her frail state, he remembers Louisa trying to comfort him by saying, *Just breathe, keep breathing, each breath means more than you can imagine.*

From this poignant memory, Smike stops playing, pulls his harmonica away from his mouth, and starts crying again. In her deathbed, weak and a mere shadow of her former being, Louisa exuded more strength and inspirational conviction about the simple beauty of life and humanity than he could ever imagine. After Louisa's death, her unyielding spirit continues to guide and encourage him. He feels her celestial reassurance with every breath, to create, and contribute something of substance to the world. She wanted him to move beyond just numbly going through the mechanical motions of living; and question, the commonly unquestioned banality of life. She believed in him more than he believed in himself. However, she also believed, through music, he could, in time, believe in himself and his gifted potential.

He returns the harmonica to his mouth and starts playing again. This magnificent instrument, comprised of many holes, presents endless possibilities, for breathing in and out and creating something beautiful. He easily teases out melodies, giving life to his music, but doubts anything he creates could ever be worthy of her memory . . . her essence . . . her beauty . . . her being.

His memories of Louisa were an oxymoronic bondage. A bondage to the sublime bliss of loving one so deeply, but equally bonded to the horrific gutting of his soul through the loss of someone so intimately dear to him. He would never be released, and he didn't want to be. He would never give up these memories to shed his torment. He would never give up Louisa.

Losing her created a hopeless hole, desperate spirit, and seemingly insurmountable loss in his life. Smike doubted that he could fill a hole this massive through any actions taken. However, early on during her treatment internment, Louisa encouraged him to follow his love of music. She wisely expressed to him that *holes are not just empty; they serve as catalysts for change.* She reminded him that his harmonica has many holes, each one making a different sound; collectively, an array of melodies. *The possibilities are endless! How glorious!* she would say.

Louisa believed and assuredly proclaimed that his music would reverberate out to the world and resonate with others as absolute testimony to his talent and life purpose. He never quite believed that, as *his* faith was experienced solely through *her*, and now she was gone. Louisa lived virtuously, knowing that life's cacophony of events often produces dissonance, but occasionally harmony arises; and one should seek harmony. Therefore, his resolve could only be to live to produce harmony; to express *and* catch his breaths through his music, as a tribute to Louisa.

Smike has been in this room, on this bed, for several hours now. He's not hungry and figures that Paps can fix his own dinner; for this evening, anyway. Emotionally exhausted, he falls asleep.

Chapter XII Good Morning Sunshine

Getting up the next morning, earlier than the day before, Smike decides to make Paps breakfast before his run. He remembers his favorite: two fried eggs, a sausage patty, buttered toast, and coffee with cream and artificial sweetener, so he goes downstairs and begins preparing it. Fixing breakfast is also a way for him to indirectly apologize for abruptly leaving their commode project the day before. He's not sure when he will return to tackling the toilet, but not today. He hopes Paps doesn't ask or pester him about it. Doesn't want to explain anything and would prefer to just let it go for now.

Of course, in this small house, Paps smells breakfast being made, enters the kitchen smiling, and says, "Well good mawnin sunshine, somethin smells good!"

Then, placing a ring of keys on the kitchen table he adds, "These ah faw you. Doan want ya to get locked out aw anythin."

The gesture appears to be some form of thoughtful, unspoken support extended to Smike. Funny thing is that Paps had no idea that Smike was actually locked out the day before.

"Thanks Paps! Please sit down and enjoy" Smike says while placing the prepared food on the table.

Paps sits, blesses himself, and begins eating while Smike joins him and sips a hot cup of tea. They don't say anything to each other for a few minutes, while Paps devours his breakfast.

Paps notices that Smike is in his running gear and asks, "So, what ah yaw plans tudday? Ah ya gonna run?"

Just Saying

"Yeah, wanted to make you breakfast first. Hope it's the way you like it" Smike responds.

"Yeah, good. Just fry the eggs a little hahdah next time" Paps replies while engulfing a huge bite.

"Sure" Smike responds plainly.

Even Paps' compliments often involved a form of critique in some way.

"Anythin else ya plan to do? Did ya finish the tahlet last night?" Paps asks somewhat hesitantly.

"No. I do plan to work on it, but not today. Was thinking about driving around the area to gain a sense of the surroundings. You want to be my tour guide?" Smike asks, not quite understanding why he tagged on this impulsive offer because he really wanted to get away and be alone.

Perhaps the tail-end invitation was just a courteous reflex. Crossing his fingers; he's hoping Paps will decline.

"That's a good idear and I'd be happy to show ya the area. Maybe we can drive through Methuen and go as fah nawth as Hayvrill. I met yaw grandmuhthah in Hayvrill. On the way back, we can eat hot dawgs aw ambahgahs faw lunch at Chauncey's. Yaw fahthah likes that joint" Paps replies with an enthusiasm rarely seen.

Paps' response wasn't what he expected, but the idea of driving to other nearby cities sounded interesting.

Smike graciously replies, "Sounds like a plan. Give me an hour to clean up the kitchen, get my run in, and shower."

"Go ahead and *run, Michael, run*, I'll take cayah of the dishes" Paps offers tongue-in-cheek.

Lightly laughing, Smike thanks him, plugs in his ear buds, exits the kitchen, and heads out the door. He looks forward to listening to music for a longer run this morning. During good runs, he'd bask in the solitude of his own thoughts and free flowing ideas for lyrics inspired by splendorous memories of Louisa.

The sun was shining brightly, and the run was exceptional. Arriving back home, Smike takes a quick shower, gets dressed, and is ready to head out in less than an hour. Of course, irascible Paps, already at the front door, implores him to hurry up! He would have been in the car already, but they were going in Smike's car, so he was forced to wait.

Chapter XIII Directions at Every Turn

One thing left to do, Smike asks Paps if he can store his bike, which is currently on the rack behind his car, in the shed.

Paps, frustrated with this minor delay says, "If ya can find room!"

"Pretty sure that I can make it work" Smike replies.

"Ya will need the key mahked with an 'S' on Nettie's key chain to get in" Paps informs him.

"Thanks" Smike says. He figures the 'S' stands for 'shed.'

Smike unlocks his car and let's Paps sit there while removing his bike from the rack and rolling it to the shed in the backyard. He unlocks the shed, and although crowded with junk, easily adjusts the array of random objects to make room for his bike. He notices a twelve-foot ladder hanging horizontally on the side wall and remembered that Paps used it to paint his house. One painting project he observed was funny, but also a scary event as Paps precariously perched on top of the ladder, swayed while swinging his arms as if he was going to fall backwards. Of course, he didn't fall, but looked like he was going to. Smike's father called Paps *Mr. Magoo* with all of his near disasters that occurred over the years. Locating the ladder was good to note since he will need it when he fixes the upstairs bedroom window with the hole in it. He also spots Paps' tool box and a work table that has other devices he may need. After placing his bike in the shed, he returns to his car and gets in.

"Quick check, Paps. Just say 'check' after each item named, okay?" Smike horses around with a process that Paps used with him as a child but embellishes a tad.

Paps seems somewhat amused and remembers their routine.

Smike starts "Keys?"

"Smahtass, check" Paps says grudgingly.

"Wallet?" Smike asks.

"Check" Paps replies while muttering some indiscernible comments under his breath about always needing money.

"What about reading glasses?" Smike queries.

"The beddah to see ya with asshole" Paps jests.

Smike then *whispers*, "Hearing aids?"

"WHAT?" Paps yells.

Normal voice, Smike repeats, "Hearing aids?"

Adamantly, Paps claims, "Ya know, I doan have heeahin aids and doan wanem! Look like cashews stuck in yaw eeahs."

Smike chuckles, then sarcastically inquires, "Now, most important . . . gum?"

Paps growls, "Dammit, let's go!"

Just Saying

Laughing, Smike backs his car out of the driveway. Paps immediately directs him where to go, providing more detailed directions than a Global Positioning System. *Tawn heeah, stop at the flashin light, this next arear is a speed trap, so slow down, theyah's a fawk in the road comin up, watch out faw staties*, etc. This was Paps' way of controlling when he wasn't driving. Everyone in the family hated driving Paps anywhere, just all-around irritating.

Within a few minutes of their drive, they traverse beyond the outskirts of Lowell. Most of this strip of road to Methuen parallels a river. Some areas are rustic and quite nice. They arrive within twenty minutes. It is a smaller town than Lowell and Paps just wants him to drive around the town and see a few things that he points out. They don't even stop anywhere. Apparently, Paps had already planned to spend more time in Haverhill before heading back home for lunch at the hamburger and hot dog joint. So, they continue on and venture north.

Haverhill is larger than Methuen but smaller than Lowell. Paps has him drive around multiple streets of housing before stopping at one older, three-story home.

"This triple deckah is wayuh yaw Grandmar Nettie lived when she wawked as a nanny and cook faw a doctah that was sponsawin hah citizenship. Theyah wuhr a lot of French Canadians in this town. Probbly still ah, doan know" Paps shares.

He then points to a window on the second floor and says, "That was hah room up theyah."

"You met her through a family friend, right?" Smike asks for clarification.

Providing details in his response, Paps clarifies, "A lady I met from chawch was a distant cuzzin of yaw grandmuhthah. She intrahduced us."

Smike jokingly recalls, "Grandma Nettie told me that when she first saw you, she thought you were good looking. She said this was *before* she was prescribed eye glasses for her visual impairment."

Ignoring Smike's jesting jab, Paps tumbles into his own train of thought.

"Annette Quellette. Loved that hah name rhymed. Yah've seen pictuahs of yaw grandmuhthah when she was youngah. She looked like a movie stah! I was just a lucky bum" Paps admits with candor.

He then continues, "Had to help hah lahn English. She would call a buddahfly a bahd. It was funny."

"Yeah, that is funny! *You* teaching Grandma Nettie English, how to say *bahd* and *buddahfly*!" Smike kids, distinctly noting and imitating Paps' strong Boston accent.

Smike thought it was funnier that Grandma Nettie, with her French-Canadian accent, would say "ting" for "thing" and combined with Paps' dialect, anyone visiting the household had to have genius-level linguistic deciphering skills to understand their communicative exchanges.

"Ahnuf jokin. Let's go to Chauncey's. It's past noon and I'm gettin hungry" Paps orders.

Just Saying

They drive back to Lowell and arrive at the restaurant just as the bulk of the main clientele are finishing their meals and leaving.

Paps is happy about that because he says, "The line is always long and I hate waitin, but the dawgs ah the best and the buns ah soft."

Paps orders a hot dog with all the fixings and some onion rings. Paps strongly encourages Smike to try a burger. He grudgingly complies but orders a small one with a side salad. Surprisingly, the burger is probably the best he's ever had, and he tells Paps so.

Paps says, "See, I toldja!" as if he's always right.

From their drive, Smike took mental notes of where they travelled and spotted several stores he planned to visit without Paps. He wanted to get materials at the hardware store to fix the window. Had to do this covertly; otherwise, Paps would interfere and try to supervise everything or worse, go cheaply with the fix. He wasn't going to follow his directions on this project. Simple things became a juggling act around Paps.

Chapter XIV Hardware Store

The next day, Smike planned his clandestine visit to the local hardware store. He wanted to get supplies to fix the window pane in the upstairs bedroom and needed to wait until Paps left for his typical morning trip to the dollar store, which Smike would deliberately decline in joining him with some made-up reason. Then he would slip out while Paps was gone, purchase the needed materials, and keep them in the back of his car. The gum in the window hole no longer served as an effective plug. Plus, it was nasty. Paps' Bingo service on Saturday would give him a few hours to secretly complete this project with no interference or push back from the old man.

Once Paps left for his morning store trip, Smike locks up, gets in his car, and drives to the hardware store. He enters, grabs a cart, goes directly to the glass section, and once there, gives the attendant the thickness and dimensions of the piece of glass he needs cut for the window pane. After the glass order is made, he roams around searching for a few other needed items.

Two store workers, donned in typical business logo-shrouded utility aprons and caps, are spotted at the end of the aisle talking with each other. One worker is a very tall woman and the other a man of short stature and bushy beard wearing shorts and working boots. Smike is somewhat amused at the man stretching his neck and looking up about forty-five degrees to talk with his female work mate.

After motioning to get their attention, he walks up to them and asks, "Where can I find caulk?"

Just Saying

The man turns his head sharply to his work partner with a huge smile and faintly says to her, "See, I toldja this was gonna to be a good day!"

Facing straight ahead at Smike, the female worker doesn't hesitate with her expressionless response, "Go past the *wood*, and the *hoses*, and make a left at the *pipes*."

Her partner laughs as he says to Smike, "Come on, I'll take ya to that item."

A little baffled by the woman's response and the guy's laugh, Smike suddenly realizes what his question sounded like he was asking about and how this woman made fun of him with her response. Escorted to the location, he finds the item, and selects the appropriate type of caulk needed for the job.

Smike thanks the store worker for his assistance, who responds in an animated, flirty tone, while winking "Anytime! Just let me know what ya *need*."

Smike then picks up the cut glass, gathers a couple more minor items, and heads to the checkout line. He finds himself behind a distraught mother who is trying to manage three young children while purchasing items. It appears the two oldest are boys around three to five years old, jumping around, smacking each other, and bumping into the mother and shopping cart, all while the mother simultaneously holds a young girl in one arm while scanning products with the other. She stops several times to calm the boys down and seems totally overwhelmed. Smike moves in front of his cart, kneels down to the boys' eye level, cups his hands as if trying to warm them, and starts blowing air between his thumbs to make a whistle sound.

The boys notice, stop their ruckus, come closer to him, and slowly start mimicking what they see Smike doing. Having successfully caught their interest, Smike smiles at them. The oldest boy notices Smike's gold tooth, points to the star in the middle and of course, asks about it. Smike redirects him by demonstrating how to hold their hands and blow to make a whistle sound. Completely captivated, these actions keep both the boys busy while their mother finishes scanning items. She looks toward Smike and gives an appreciative nod while mouthing, *thank you*!

Smike's assistance in temporarily distracting the unruly children speeds up the wait in the checkout line since the mother now quickly completes the scanning process and exits. The boys follow their mother while continuing attempts to replicate the whistle sound through their cupped hands. Smike smiles thinking the gimmick worked, but probably for only a short time. Kids have short attention spans.

He scans his items, leaves the store, loads up the back of his car (because he doesn't want nosey Paps to accidentally see the materials and ask about them), gets on his phone, calls in a take-out order at a local Greek restaurant he spotted earlier, and detours to pick it up. Smike thinks that if Paps returns home before he does, there will be questions about where he went. Telling Paps that he ran out to pick up lunch as a treat will go unquestioned because Paps never complains when someone else foots the bill for a meal.

Chapter XV Baby Goulash

As he suspected, Paps beats him home. Smike walks in carrying lunch.

Looking up from his lounge chair, Paps asks, "So what do we have heeah?"

Smike responds, "I brought lunch. Will set this in the kitchen and bring you a plate."

Paps complains, "I doan recognize da smell. Hope it isn't some of yaw vejahtayeeuhn stuff."

"I know your food preferences Paps. Got you a Gyro sandwich with extra meat. Think you will like it."

Smike lays the bags on the kitchen table and gets some paper plates and plastic utensils. He fixes his own plate and then makes Paps' plate with the Gyro and scoops out a dollop of baba ganoush and also hummus, adding one falafel on the side as well.

From the kitchen, he calls out to Paps, "You will want to try some of these other side items to let me know if you like them."

Walking into the family room, Smike lays the plate on Paps' dinner tray and says, "Hope you like it!"

Paps eyes the food while Smike settles down next to him to eat and watch Paps' selected game show for the day.

While pointing to each item, Paps quizzes Smike, "What's this, and this, and this? Some of this stuff looks like mush."

Smike informs him that there is hummus made of garbanzo beans, a falafel patty made of chick peas, and baba ganoush made of eggplant.

"You like beans, and peas, and eggplant, so you might as well try them" Smike urges.

Paps removes his gum, blesses himself, then reluctantly tries the hummus and quickly spits it out while moaning. Smike reflexively responds with a very disappointing look. First taste trial is a failure.

Paps then tries the falafel and seems to like it, but says, "This is okay, but rathah dry. Gonna need a glass of wotta."

He then dips the last bite of the falafel into the baba ganoush and throws it into his mouth.

"Hey, this baby goulash is pretty good! I'll have sum moah if theyah's any left. Get my box of hahd pretzels from the kitchen as well, and a glass of wotta."

Enthused with Paps' interest in trying something different, which is way out of his comfort zone, Smike grabs a glass of water, gets the container of baba ganoush from the kitchen table, snatches the pretzels, and returns to the family room. Paps quickly grabs the items from Smike and starts dipping hard pretzels in the baba ganoush as what appears to be his new-found favorite dip.

Paps often unknowingly or sometimes deliberately used comical malapropisms for new terms to his vocabulary, so Smike hesitantly corrects him, "It's called baba ganoush, Paps, not baby goulash."

Just Saying

"Whatevah, it's goulash to me" Paps snaps harshly.

Smike quietly watches as Paps appears to enjoy eating this strange combination of food. As usual, Paps crunches down hard on the pretzels. Smike has, to no avail, previously warned him before about how this can damage his teeth but feels compelled to caution him again.

"Paps, those pretzels will crack your teeth, especially as you get older. Perhaps I can fix you a soft pretzel baked in the oven?" he offers as an alternative option.

"Doan wawhy 'bout it! I've been eatin' these way befoah even yaw fahthah was bon. Nevah hawt me befoah. Yaw a wawhy waht Michael!"

With a scowl on his face, Paps continues crunching his pretzels and finishes the entire container of pureed eggplant.

Smike reluctantly accepts this partial victory getting Paps to try something new. He knows he can't change all of Paps' bad habits and has settled on accepting some baby step successes, even through *baby goulash*.

Chapter XVI Bowl of Boogers

It is lightly raining the next morning, so Smike skips his run and decides that since he is up early, he will make a healthy breakfast for Paps; that is, before Paps gets up, notices, and squashes his efforts. Smike found some success the day before, introducing Paps to Greek food; therefore, bolstered to try again. Along with coffee, the menu is comprised of oatmeal and wheat toast (buttered with margarine rather than butter), with a side of turkey sausage (although Paps will not be informed that the sausage is made from fowl that Smike covertly picked up earlier). Paps, red meat kind-of-guy, universally rejects healthier options, often before even trying them.

Paps smells the coffee, enters the kitchen in his skivvies, and says "So, whatahya fixin this mawnin *Julia Child?*"

Without answering, as Paps sits down, Smike places the bowl of oatmeal and plate of buttered toast and sausage in front of him. He steps back to wait for what he expects will be a raging refusal. And it comes.

"I doan eat boogahs! No flavah! Shitty texcha. Just a big bowl of boogahs, get it away from me" Paps shouts.

Grandma Nettie once told Smike that Paps didn't like oatmeal and barley. He would complain that they all had the texture of boogers and no flavor. Her response *Well how would you know Sid unless you ate your own boogers before?* She could always shut him up. Had her funny way of putting him in his place with how she humorously phrased retorts or comments.

Channeling Grandma Nettie, Smike smartly responds, "I wouldn't know. Have never eaten boogers."

Just Saying

Frowning, Paps snaps, "Smahtass!"

Ignoring his affront, Smike suggests, "Just thought you might like to try something different. Can sprinkle in some raisins if that will make it more palatable."

"No, shit, Shit, SHIT, just take it away. I'll eat the sausage and toast. Bring me my cawfee" he snaps.

Paps is pissed. Michael is already trying to change what he eats.

Not too upset with Paps' rejection of the oatmeal, it won't be wasted because Smike will eat it, even if Paps won't. Also, he is pleasantly surprised that his grandfather has not noticed the exchange of margarine for butter on the toast, and that the sausage is not his usual brand of pork. So, he retrieves the bowl of oatmeal and quietly enjoys it while watching Paps devour the sausage and toast in a couple of bites. Mini victory. Grandma Nettie would be proud.

"Bring me anuhthah sausage link" Paps bitterly commands.

Smike obliges and then starts cleaning up. Paps informs Smike that because of the weather, he won't be going anywhere this morning. Smike lets him know that after he cleans up, he will be upstairs most of the day writing music.

Paps shuffles to the family room, plops down on his lounge chair, turns on the TV, and flips through the channels. Nothing worth watching, so he decides to play a video of an old war classic; one he has seen many times before. At some point in the viewing, he starts snoring and falls into a deep sleep.

Sid bitches, "Damn, tyuhd of the mush they give us in these field rations. What is this Sahjent Kahn, sum kinda puddin? No flavah. Has the texcha of boogahs."

Kahn replies, "Not sure, but will gladly trade my ham and lima beans shit for your booger pudding."

"That's right, Jooz doan eat pawk" Sid lightly jibes.

"And Schrod, good Catholic, always blesses himself before eating" Kahn kids back.

"Hey, I'm thankful to gawd for evahy meal" Sid replies with a serious emphasis.

Kahn rebounds under his breath, "Just not boogers."

Caldwell interjects, "Hey, nobody likes that ham concoction. I'd claim to be Jewish too if I got out of eating it" then adds, "I'd give my left nut for a slice of my blessed mother's apple pie right now."

Sid quickly suggests, "Ask the Medics."

Perturbed, Caldwell asks, "How the fuck are Medics going to get my ma's apple pie?"

"Naw, no pie, but they can help ya find yaw left nut faw removal with theyah magnifyin glass" Sid jokes.

Soldiers sitting around eating rations all laugh.

"Schrod, you think you're so funny. Just an irritating asshole" Caldwell loathingly replies.

Just Saying

"I've been called wawse" Sid cracks.

Sergeant Kahn, as squad leader, switches to more serious discussion, "So, heads up, the Huey will pick us up for clearing an area a few klicks north of here. Be ready to depart by fourteen hundred. Schrod, Martinez, Long, Hatfield, and Pender, we are heading out. Gonna be an all-nighter, so pack what you'll need for scouting the area. Caldwell, you'll stay behind with Thomas and Romanoli."

Pender asks, "Can we have a little entertainment before departing?"

Romanoli jokingly adds, "Yeah, Schrod can put all of his hot air to good use!"

Kahn replies, "That's up to him."

Sid responds, "Be happy to" and straightaway starts whistling the uplifting song 'Daydream.'

Everyone enjoys his musical performance. Some even start singing along the words to this song.

"Damn, you're a good whistler Schrod! Could become professional. Do you sing too or just whistle?" Long asks.

"Oh no, I doan sing. Ya doan wanna heeah my voice. It's pretty bad. Actually, contacted the Pentagon to considah recawdin me singing and then broadcast to the Viet Cong. They would awl throw theyah hands up, covah theyah eeahs, and sahrendah immediately just to stop the aggravatin noise" he jests.

The group laughs while gathering supplies, loading the Huey, and getting in. They soon launch and after a short ride, land at the target site. Schrod, leaning out the open side door, sees a missile coming toward the helicopter and screams, "Incoming!!!"

Smike tries waking Paps, lightly shaking his shoulder, asking, "Are you alright?"

Anxious from what he observed, Smike shares, "You were yelling in your sleep, like having a nightmare. Afraid you might take a swing at me while trying to wake you up."

Totally disoriented, Paps comes out of his tormenting slumber realizing he's at home and his grandson is rousing him.

Groggy, but quickly gaining his composure, he snaps, "I'm alright. Doan wawhy 'bout it!"

Decidedly concerned, Smike wasn't sure what he could do to calm Paps. He sits on the couch and waits.

After about a minute, Paps yells at him, "Go back upstayuhs and write yaw music. I'm fine!"

Smike indulges his grandfather's order, but he's now aware that something is troubling his grandfather. He wonders how he will question him about it since Paps resists nearly all probes of a personal nature.

Paps is doubly upset over what has happened; obviously, his recurring nightmares are terrifying and immobilizing, but now his grandson witnessed one of his frightening fits. He hopes that no questions are asked about this incident and will act as if it never happened.

Chapter XVII   Bingo

It is now Saturday, mid-afternoon, and Smike plans to drop Paps off at the church a little early for the Bingo Night event. He has all the supplies to clandestinely fix the window pane upstairs and will do that when he returns.

Smike plops down on the couch next to Paps sitting on his lounger and asks, "You about ready to go?"

"Tryin to get rid of me? It's too eahly. Doan have to leave til fah-thahty to get theyah on time" Paps replies.

"Jean said that they would feed you pizza. Thought you might want to go a little early to eat a piece, in peace, before having to call the numbers" Smike suggests.

"Actually, that's a good idear. I like theyah pizzer. Okay, gimme a few minutes to get ready" Paps states in agreement.

"Sure Paps" Smike replies as he watches his grandfather lean on his cane to get up from his lounge chair and go to his bedroom.

The strategy, to leave a little early, worked. This pleases Smike because it gives him an extra hour or so of daylight to finish the window job.

Paps returns fairly quickly and says, "Hey, I like havin a chauffah! Let's go *Kato*. Ya know the way to chawch."

"Sure do!" he replies, knowing that it doesn't matter that he knows the way because Paps will annoyingly tell him each turn to take anyway.

After a short (twenty minutes), but arduous drive (that is, dealing with following the maddening dictation of Paps' unnecessary directions), they arrive at Parish Hall. Upon his grandfather's urging, Smike decides to walk in with him and meet the Bingo crew. The 'pair' is already in the kitchen preparing pizzas and other food goods sold at the event. Apparently, this once-a-month business affair is a solid money-maker for the church.

Jean spots them and calls out, "Sid, you made it and you're early!"

The other Jeanne adds, "Sit down and we'll bake a pizza for you. Michael, you wanna slice too, right?"

Smike replies, "Actually, I need to take care of a few things, but thank you for your generosity, ladies!"

"The boy doan wanna be round ole folks" Paps replies snidely as he sits at the work table.

"Speak for yourself Sid, I'm in my prime" Jean mocks regarding the elderly reference.

Speaking to Smike, Jeanne suggests, "Well, if you're going straight home Michael, you can take the case of beer with you now."

"I can do that" Smike replies.

"Doan hafta wawhy 'bout him drinkin it, so that's fine with me" Paps confirms.

Jeanne asks Smike, "What? You aren't a beer drinker like your grandfather?"

Just Saying

"No, not really, except for when doing yard work on a hot day" Smike replies.

"I'll believe it when I see it" Paps comments with a defiant tone since he has never seen Michael drink a beer.

Jeanne directs Smike, "Follow me to the cooler."

Smike follows, grabs the case of beer from the large, built-in refrigerator and heads back to the work table. He then says his good-byes and leaves. The ladies and Sid conduct small talk while waiting for the pizza to bake. Once ready, Jeanne pulls it out of the oven and cuts it into slices. They all grab a slice. Sid removes his gum, blesses himself, and takes a gigantic bite of pizza.

"Pretty good, huh Sid?" Jean asks.

"Yeah, damn good!" catching himself, he chases the comment with "Guess I shouldn't swayah in chawch" he says while chuckling.

Jeanne adds, "All I know is my blood sugar was dropping and I needed something in my system."

"Aren't we all falling apart, with diabetes, high cholesterol, heart conditions, arthritis, dysfunctional knees. Guess we are old Sid, you're right!" Jean proclaims.

"Speak faw yawself Jean, I'm in my prime" Sid jokes.

They all laugh and continue eating.

Jeanne adds out of concern, "I do worry about my health and age being questioned. Don't wanna lose guardianship of

Susan and Sadie. They don't have anyone else, and I don't either."

As a true friend, Jean reassuringly replies, "You will always have me. Ya know that!"

Jeanne smiles at her with deep appreciation and love.

Other volunteers start straggling in, grabbing slices, and joining them at the table. It will be a rather long evening for Sid, but surprisingly, he's enjoying the company.

Chapter XVIII   Hole No More

Smike returns home, places two six-packs from the case in the fridge, and takes the other two six-packs to the basement. He then retrieves all the window repair items from the back of his car and takes them upstairs. Next, he heads to the shed for the ladder and moves it to the front of the house. He returns to the shed and scours the tool box to locate a putty knife and hammer. Grabbing these items, he returns to the kitchen where he already knows there is duct tape and snatches it.

Now upstairs, Smike tapes an 'X' with the duct tape on the window pane with the hole and hits the glass with the end of the hammer. The glass easily breaks but the tape keeps most of the pieces in tack. Ironically, he notices that the gum stays put in the hole. He discards the glass and cleans up the edges of the pane. Once cleaned, Smike knows the hard part will be inserting the glass replacement from outside and caulking around it while on top of the ladder. He grabs all needed materials, places them in a bag, swings the bag over his shoulder, heads downstairs, and goes outside.

Ensuring the ladder is secure; he takes careful steps to the top of the ladder, and easily reaches the window. Gingerly, he grabs the glass from the bag on his shoulder and places it in the frame. He then begins caulking.

A voice from the street calls out, "Hey young man, whatja doing up there?"

This is not a moment for him to stop what he is doing, turn around, look down, and cordially explain his actions. He needs to finish the current bead of caulking.

While staying focused and without turning around, he responds loudly, in a typical direct response, "Fixing a window pane."

"Well, looks like you could use a spotter" the voice responds.

Before Smike could decline the offer, the man was bracing the ladder for him. Smike actually felt a little more secure, even with a stranger assisting him. Finishing the caulking, he uses the putty knife to clean up excess material. He looks down and the man holding the ladder grins up at him.

"Glad to see that it's you and not Sid on top of this ladder" the man says with a chuckle, and then adds, "That would be a disaster waiting to happen."

As Smike descends, he asks the man, "So, you know my grandfather?"

"Oh yeah, stubborn old coot! He rarely accepts help from anyone. My boys and me tried to shovel snow for him, but he wouldn't have it" the man shares.

Smike thinks that this sounds just like Paps. Stepping off the ladder, he introduces himself.

The middle-aged man jovially returns the introduction with, "I'm David, Sid's neighbor from down the corner. Nice to meetja."

"Nice to meet you too, David" he replies.

Smike suddenly gets a little worried that this neighbor, now a witness to what he hoped to complete in secret, may indiscriminately or unintentionally tell Paps about what he observed.

"Well, David, I could use some assistance, rather a favor. Unlike my grandfather, I'm not afraid to ask for help" Smike poses.

"Sure, whatja need?" David asks.

"Please don't mention to my grandfather what you saw me doing today. He'll just give me a hard time about it" Smike pleads.

David releases a loud belly laugh and says, "I getja man. Looks good whatja did, but he probably won't notice. Better he not, notice. I'll keep my trap shut. He's a proud old man."

"Yeah, so you *do* know my grandfather!" Smike replies.

"Also big-hearted. Always gives me tomatoes from his garden. So proud of them. And Nettie, God rest her soul, made the best pies ever!" David adds.

Smike, cheered by David's comments, suddenly offers, "Would you like a beer?"

He thinks this is the least he can do for his new acquaintance that held the ladder for him and promises to keep his secret.

"Now that's something Sid rarely shares" David chortles.

"Come on in, I'll grab one for you" Smike says.

Inside, Smike hands David a beer and they both sit at the kitchen table. David opens up by questioning Smike, like a classic nosey neighbor who wants the skinny on what's going on.

"Here for a short visit?" David asks while pulling the beer tab before taking a sip.

"Well, not exactly a brief stay. Hopefully, Paps will have knee surgery soon and I am here to help him out. Of course, he doesn't think he needs any help. Contrary, you know?" Smike says in an uncustomary elongated response.

"Saw he still uses his cane. I thought he was supposed to have surgery before Nettie passed" David replies.

"He was taking care of her near the end. Guess he didn't want to be immobile while she was ailing" Smike surmises.

"My ma played cards with your grandmother. She told me that Sid was really good to Nettie. This house used to be busy with visitors. Everyone loved Nettie. We were all worried about Sid feeling lonely. Glad you're here. By the way, where is he?" David asks.

"He volunteered to call numbers for Bingo Night at the church. And that reminds me; I need to leave in a couple of minutes to pick him up" Smike responds.

"Good for him! And good for you to help out your grandfather. Guess being good-hearted runs in the family" David states.

Just Saying

David finishes his beer, they exchange niceties, and as he gets ready to leave, he warns Smike, "Better replace that beer because Sid will notice and ask about it."

David *does* know his grandfather and glad he cautioned him.

Chapter XIX Totus Toilet

Living with Paps over a week now, Smike decides it's time to finish fixing that toilet. Just tired of running downstairs to take a pee. The shower is a different issue; will probably need a plumber to check out the low water pressure upstairs. For now, he is stuck taking showers in Paps' bathroom.

As he walks into the upstairs bathroom, the valve assembly materials are still how he left them; on the floor. He inspects the tank and sees the flapper is warped and that is probably what caused the issue, so he determines what equipment will be needed to exchange all the parts. He descends downstairs and heads to the shed to gather the necessary tools. Paps sees him exit but doesn't say anything. Smike soon returns carrying a tool bag and that's when Paps says something.

"Whatja dooin with the tools *Handyman Hank?*"

Smike responds, "Fixing the toilet."

"Finally! Was wondahin when ya'd get off yaw keestah. Tyuhd of yoosin my crappah, huh?" Paps comments.

"Yep!" Smike replies succinctly and goes upstairs, hoping that Paps doesn't follow him to oversee the work.

After a short period of time, he completes the project and the toilet works. Well, the water is now collecting in the tank, but *very* slowly. There is a water pressure issue for sure. At least now, he can cross the hall for trips to the bathroom rather than using Paps' toilet downstairs. This will also mean fewer interactions with Paps, which is a good thing. Smike gathers all the tools and returns them to the shed outside. Upon reentering the house, Paps calls him into the family room.

"Is evahythin wawkin now, *Bob Vila*?" Paps asks.

"It is" Smike replies.

"Thought that kit would fix it. I'm right again!" Paps brags.

Smike thinks that all they really needed was a new flapper, which would have been cheaper but replacing all the other parts with new pieces is a preventative action.

"Yes, right again Paps" Smike falsely agrees.

"Hava few uhthah prahjects that need tendin to when ya can get round to it" Paps states.

"Just let me know" Smike offers.

"Will need the laddah faw one of 'em" Paps says.

Staying quiet, he hopes Paps is not referring to the window upstairs that he already fixed.

Paps adds, "The guttahs need cleanin. But ya can wait till it gets a little wahmah."

First week in the crapper; now, sometime in the near future, he will be in the gutter. Paps has his way of throwing him into messy crevasses to descend into and rise out of, never unscathed.

Chapter XX Runs in the Family

Other than fixing the toilet, Smike's visit so far has been relatively uneventful. He has somewhat settled into a routine and carved out some time for his music. Typically, he runs early in the morning, showers, fixes breakfast for Paps, sometimes drives Paps around on needed errands, prepares a small lunch when they return, and then they both go their separate ways and do their own thing in the afternoons. Usually, Smike plays his instruments and writes lyrics or crafts scores. Paps piddles on trivial projects, watches TV, naps, and sometimes walks to the local convenience store. The evenings were humdrum. For dinner, Smike would either make or pick up some food. They would share their evening meal together. Then Paps, while drinking beer, would watch television in the family room and Smike would depart to his room upstairs.

However, although the routine worked on some level, Smike was growing restless, and he noticed his music writing slowed down. Monotony left him uninspired. More concerning, there was no discussion about future plans for Paps' knee surgery and this made Smike even more restless. He starts thinking that he is more like his grandfather than he realized. Guess restlessness runs in the family.

This evening, after cleaning the dishes, Smike decides to join his grandfather in the family room for a short period of time and covertly slip in a question about his next doctor visit.

Paps looks at Smike entering the room and quips, "So, ya will grace me with yaw presence this evenin?"

"Thought we could watch the news together" Smike states, acting innocent to his true intention.

Just Saying

"Doan watch the news anymoah. All gahbidge! Haven't ya noticed? All shit, 'specially the political shit. These politicians on AWL sides, ah cahrupt, self-sahvin liahs and thieves!" he vehemently gripes.

"Can't and won't disagree" Smike replies.

Half muttering, Paps says, "Of cawse ya woan."

Paps continues his sour tirade, "*None* of 'em can run the govahnment. Too busy polishin theyah poles! And, not tokkin 'bout populahrity polls eithah, no, tokkin 'bout the ones between theyah legs!"

In the middle of taking a sip of water, Smike chokes, getting caught by surprise with Paps' crass but comical phrase. He thinks to himself, *where does he come up with these lewd sayings?*

Then more civilly, Paps adds, "Can read the local paypah faw news if ya want" as he picks it up from the side table and tosses it to Smike.

Smike has national news at his fingertips on his cell phone and laptop, so he places the paper by his side and ignoring Paps' comment, redirects the conversation to ask, "So, what is your choice of shows to watch this evening?"

Paps answers, "Family game show. Can't believe how stupid some of these contestants ah. My guesses ah beddah than awl of 'em!"

Inviting himself into the game, Smike poses, "Well that's a bold claim! Will have to watch you in action and perhaps make a few conjectures myself."

While smacking his gum, Paps eagerly accepts his challenge with, "Oooh, yoosin big collahj wawds! Let's see how ya do against the mastah."

He then takes a sip of his beer and says, "Let's go!"

Smike figures that at some point during this faux game simulation, perhaps during a commercial, he will have an opportunity to ask Paps about his next doctor's visit. He needs to go soon and Smike must be there with him to find out details about the procedure and post-surgery therapy. However, he is very surprised how pumped-up the old man is getting about the two of them watching and playing this game show together. He knows that Paps is competitive and enjoys games, but he seems viscerally voracious about going head-to-head with him. Although Smike's intent in participating is different than Paps, this might be fun on some base level; especially, if he experiences triumphant moments of sticking it to him with victorious responses.

Watching the show, both are enjoying just calling out intuitive answers to the questions posed. Cranking up his cranky nature, Paps revels in generating snide comments to Smike's responses. Smike picks up the play and slings a few worthy comebacks. Definitely in his element, Paps actually seems happy for the first time since Smike's arrival.

During a commercial, Paps asks Smike to get him another beer and the box of hard pretzels.

Smike complies and while handing him the box of pretzels, again counsels Paps, "You know, hard pretzels hurt your teeth and can cause dental damage."

Just Saying

"Mind yaw own bizness, willya?" Paps replies as he crunches down hard on the pretzel.

"Well, just saying . . . don't want you to crack a tooth" Smike responds more lightheartedly.

This set of commercials runs long and Smike thinks it's a good time to ask about Paps' next doctor's appointment.

"On a different subject Paps, I was wondering when you're scheduled for your next visit with the orthopedic surgeon" he asks.

"I cancelled it this week. Rescheduled faw next Tuesdee mawnin" Paps meekly responds.

"Great, would like to join you. Can drive if you like" Smike offers.

"Okay, ya can come, but keep yaw mouth shut at the doctahs. Doan offah any opinions" Paps orders.

"Whatever you say Paps" Smike replies with feigned obedience, although he's thinking that he may need to privately ask the doctor some important questions.

After the game show is over and his purpose in asking about the appointment is completed, Smike bids goodnight to Paps and retreats upstairs with the local paper that Paps tossed him earlier.

He plops down on his bed, opens the paper to the local want ads and job openings, when he serendipitously notices a posting that reads,

Denise McDonald

Keyboardist needed for local retro band. Call (978) 555-3808 to schedule an audition.

Chapter XXI Healthy as a Horse

Tuesday morning rolls around and Smike is in the doctor's office with Paps while he receives an examination and consultation.

"Other than your previous history of high cholesterol, currently treated and controlled by statins, all tests, blood work, urine samples, etcetera, indicate that for your age, you are healthy as a horse and can easily handle the knee surgery and rehabilitation" Dr. Brandt states in a confirming tone.

"But, will I be inna wheel chayah ahfta?" Paps asks.

"That is a slight possibility, but probably not. Therapy and your response to treatment will dictate your recovery. More likely, you will use a walker for a short period of time. Again, much of your recovery will depend on your efforts to rehabilitate" the doctor replies.

"I doan wanna be in a wheel chayah and doan wanna walkah. Those contraptions will make me look *ole*" Paps complains.

"After surgery, getting around may require some form of assistance, again, temporarily" the doctor counters.

The doctor then looks down at his clipboard of notes, flips back a few pages, looks back up at Paps, and while gazing over his glasses in a deliberate, forceful stare says, "And, according to my records, you will be seventy-seven on your next birthday" nailing the punch line that, well, Paps *is* old.

"I doan know if I even wan this sahjahry" Paps refutes, obviously in denial on this aspect of his health. So, the doctor decides to approach the argument for surgery from a different angle.

"Tell me about your pain, Mr. Schrod. On a scale of one to ten, how would you rate it?"

"While sittin, zero to two. Walkin with a cane, round seven. Any presshah down aw weight on just this leg, ten plus" Paps answers honestly.

The doctor then manipulates Paps' right leg to test resistance and his response to pain.

"So, from what you have shared already, the cane doesn't appear to be helping you get around that well or alleviate discomfort. Can you live with this pain?" the doctor asks seriously.

"No, I doan wanna live with the pain, but I also doan wanna be incapacitated faw months ahfta sahjahry" Paps growls.

"Well, again, recovery depends on how you follow-thru with the therapy. I do recommend you have the surgery, but the decision is up to you. Do you have family who can assistance you, post-surgery or perhaps a service provider? Is that why your grandson is here?"

"Yeah, my grandson can help" Paps stingily shares.

Smike, standing quietly in the corner, acknowledges his assent to the doctor with a nod.

Dr. Brandt replies, "Okay, let me know your decision soon. If you decide to go through with the surgery, it will need to be scheduled soon, understand?"

"Yeah" Paps grunts.

"Just want to add that any remaining shrapnel from your original injury may have exacerbated arthritis in your knee. Quite frankly, not sure how you have gone this long without surgery. Will leave a pain medication prescription with the receptionist. Take as needed" Dr. Brandt informs him.

The doctor adds, while looking directly at Smike as if to get him to take care of one troubling issue, "And, I noticed that your toe nails need clipping. Not doing so will not only impede your mobility but could also result in an ingrown toenail and infection."

Smike glares at Paps' gnarly toenails and gags. He is repulsed and does not want to go anywhere near those repellent knobs of nasty digits. This is not something he signed up for. Will need to figure out an alternative option.

"You can get dressed now and before you leave, talk to the receptionist about scheduling your surgery. If not today, please take our business card so you can set a day and time for the procedure once you make an affirmative decision" Dr. Brandt advises and then leaves the room.

Paps commands Smike, "Leave while I get dressed. Wait outside faw me."

Smike leaves the room, pulls out his cell phone, and once out of earshot, calls his father.

"Paps is resisting surgery. I don't know if he will schedule it today or wait or perhaps decide he doesn't want to do it at all. Doctor said he is healthy as a horse" Smike informs his father.

After his father responds, Smike adds, "Yeah, well from what I have seen, he is healthy as a horse's ass if he doesn't have this surgery. Paps is mulishly denying how his knee pain is limiting mobility. Of course, I will encourage him to go through with it. I mean, I'll try, but you know how that goes. Still up to him. Will let you know once I know his decision. Give my love to mom."

Smike then hangs up and waits for Paps to exit the examination room.

Obviously, Paps needs the surgery and will eventually agree to have it done, but he is dragging out *when* it will occur. Smike ponders that he may be staying in Massachusetts longer than expected. This also means that he needs to add some activity to his routine and nail clipping is *not* going to be one of those undertakings.

Paps hobbles out of the examination room and heads to the receptionist's desk where Smike joins him. Paps informs the receptionist that he wants to "Book the sahjahry fah the fahst week in Septembah. Gonna be busy this summah tendin to my gahden" Paps explains.

Smike didn't think about the timing of Paps' garden, and how his dedication to growing tomatoes would place a priority on his schedule. Surgery set in September means at least a four-month extension on his stay in Lowell. He will definitely have to follow-through on setting up additional activities to fill his time.

Just Saying

Smike texts his father, *Good news—Paps scheduled his surgery. Bad news—Not till the beginning of September! Crossing fingers he doesn't cancel or reschedule for a later date.*

Chapter XXII   Blooming Garden
            Variety Idiot

Smike knew the garden work was pending after overhearing his grandfather at the doctor's office. In fact, the very next day Paps informs him that he wants to get garden materials, as well as some juvenile plants in preparation for his plot in the backyard. He plans to plant a variety of vegetables, but fewer this year: eight tomato plants, four pepper plants, as well as loose leaf lettuce, basil, green onions, carrots, and cucumbers. A significantly smaller version compared to his past garden missions.

Shortly after breakfast, they leave to shop for everything needed for the garden. They will make two stops. One at the hardware store and another at a local nursery.

Paps wants Smike to drive the Plymouth, "It has moah room faw stuff" he claims.

Smike agrees and they take off for the first stop at the hardware store.

After arriving, they walk in and Paps goes to the shopping cart area, saying to Smike, "Gonna get a cahrij faw all the stuff I need."

Smike didn't think that they were getting many items here but guesses that the shopping cart will stabilize Paps as he walks around the store and that's why he really wanted one. They are greeted by the same worker who previously helped Smike find caulking material.

Just Saying

"Well, you're back I see! What can I help you with?" the worker asks.

Selectively hard of hearing; Paps rarely misses communications not intended for him. Catching the worker's comment, he unobtrusively asks, "What did he mean 'yaw back'? Ya came heeah without me? What faw? When?"

Smike thinks, *Well shit! Never easy duping Paps! Need a viable excuse.*

Lying, Smike murmurs, "I think he's mixing me up with someone else."

"Doan seem like it" Paps says, but lets it go.

Paps tells the worker everything he wants and is guided around the store to pick up each item. He notices the worker occasionally looking over and smiling at Smike.

After they acquire all items on Paps' mental list and head to the checkout line, the worker says directly to Smike, "Again, if you ever need anything, just let me know" and heads back to the entrance of the store.

Paps pokes, "Hey, I think that guy is sweet on ya. Hope he's mistaken ya faw someone else" and chuckles.

Smike doesn't respond. He's just glad that Paps doesn't realize he came to the store before. And, surprisingly, Paps has not yet noticed that the window pane of glass has been replaced. Of course, he rarely comes upstairs to visit his room, so this may be why. Hopefully, he has forgotten all about it.

They pay for the supplies and then drive to the nursery. After arriving, Smike notices the expansive layout of the nursery what looks like a significant amount of walking on uneven ground. He suggests to his grandfather to stay in the car and he will get all the items needed. Paps unexpectedly agrees and dictates to get adolescent tomato plants, must be either Beefsteak or Big Boy variety.

Smike grabs a cart and easily locates the plants and seeds. Within a few minutes, he loads everything in the back of the Plymouth and they drive home. Upon arrival, Smike unloads materials as Paps quickly directs Smike to clean up the garden area.

"Ya can dig holes faw the plants befoah lunch. Plenny a time. Remembah, at least eight-inch holes faw the t'maydah plants and round two feet apaht. Will bloom beddah, last longah, and get moah vejtibles. Also, plant basil between the rows of t'maydahs. That'll keep those hawrible, green hawnwawms away. Get stahted!" he commands.

Paps limps to the back door entrance and enters the house. Smike heads to the shed and grabs some gloves, a rake, and shovel to start cleaning the garden area. He remembers the garden layout as a child from many years of summer visits. Paps would have him pull weeds and water plants to earn some loose change. Smike would use the payment to buy treats when he and his grandfather would later walk to the convenience store. It was a sweet deal for both of them.

Smike smiles as he notices Paps' two-foot angel sculpture dubbed his '*Gahdenin* Angel' (another one of his malapropisms) still in the same spot overlooking the plot. Paps claimed it protected his plants. Smike flashes back to when he was six years old and watched his grandfather talk to his tomato plants while pouring beer on them.

"Theyah ah vitaminz in beeah my friends that'll help ya grow biggah! And the Gahdenin Angel will look ovah ya too!" Paps claimed.

Of course, Smike now realizes that was all bullshit. The beer was either a little flat or warm, but Paps didn't want to completely waste it, so in his warped way of thinking, he thought the plants would benefit from something he loved.

Working in the garden is relaxing for Smike and breaks up the tedium of dealing with Paps' other daily demands and irritating interactions. He can easily finish planting today. Needs to. Has other plans for the next couple of days to prepare for an event scheduled on Saturday morning. Intends to fully immerse himself in practicing songs on both his keyboard and harmonica. Excited about trying something new, but nervous about delving into something somewhat out of his comfort zone; however, he thinks to himself, *I'd be an idiot not to just go for it.*

Chapter XXIII   Impressions

Smike arrives at a community bar early Saturday morning to conduct an informal audition with several hometown musicians, all members of a local band called *Knead Naked*. The band's obvious manager and only female, Violet, sports a plum beret over her pixie haircut with sweeping long bangs that partially cover her right eye. Multiple piercings are central to her intended image. She is the twenty-something lead vocalist who also plays the fiddle. The group's guitarist and back-up singer, Mitch, is an antsy, wiry young man with sleeve tattoos on both arms whose demeanor subtly exudes working-class values and a likeable manner. Smike is later told that Mitch and Violet are high school chums who have performed together for over a decade. Denny, oldest of the group, early thirties, is the drummer of bi-racial heritage with dreadlocks and a toned physique. He is also a back-up singer for the band. At this gathering he appears detached, lost in his own thoughts while looking down and lightly tapping straws on glass mugs, coasters, and any other object on the table, which conveniently serve as his pseudo drum set.

The bar owner, Fred, an older man of few words with heavy crescent sagging bags below his eyes, is the only other person in the bar at this time. He inconspicuously rummages around in the background, clicking glasses, preparing for the day. Fred is responsible for graciously providing the group access and space for the keyboardist try out. After brief handshake introductions and name exchanges, Smike sets up his keyboard and plays a few well known, classic tunes that are well received by the band members. Unexpectedly, he then pulls his harmonica from his top shirt pocket and jams. A little surprised, but clearly impressed by Smike's instrumental trial, each band member claps in approval and individually imparts some form of positive recognition for his skills.

Mitch then questions him, "So, what bands have you played in?"

"Does a high school garage band count?" Smike asks.

Mitch replies, "Depends, did you get paid?"

Smike owns up, "Uh, no, just riffs with friends for laughs."

Surprised, Violet nudges for clarification, "Really, never played in a band before?"

"No. Play for myself mostly."

Mitch adds, "Virgin! Cool beans!"

Violet, then falls into a hyper-focused, serious stance to deliver an instructive overview of the group.

"We are a retro cover band that plays sixties, seventies, eighties, and nineties hit songs across multiple musical genres. Mostly soft rock, pop, blues, couple of country songs, R and B, soul, even punk; basically, we tailor song selection to the job and client preference. Jobs include weddings, birthday bashes, retirement parties, and various gigs at local bars. Occasionally, we flex our talents at small concerts in town or in Boston."

Mitch interrupts, "Hub hoodsies there!"

Violet rolls her eyes and continues, "Also, we play here at Fred's Tavern weekly on Friday nights for our neighborhood followers. Through other gigs, have as many as three shows a week. We each play at least one instrumental solo during our two-hour performance, with a thirty-minute break between sessions. It's all for fun and the love of music as pay is barely pocket change, which we split evenly by the way. Some patrons tip as well. Music is our Meta. Our regular daytime jobs pay the bills, get it?"

Smike nods in acknowledgement as Violet continues, "One non-negotiable—NO freebies for family or friends."

Mitch interrupts again, "Many in my family are moochers, so you get what she is saying."

After a brief expression of annoyance towards Mitch's obvious attention-deficit affliction of continually interjecting his thoughts, which appears to be habitual, Violet continues "with the exception of Memorial Day and Veterans Day at the Veterans of Foreign Wars Hall that is the local VFW, down the road. Those are twice-a-year courtesy performances to honor soldiers."

Mitch adds, "Dedicated fans, the military."

Violet confirms and continues, "And Rudy lets us sometimes practice in the Veterans Hall on some Sunday mornings or other times when it's not in use. The hall has great acoustics! Quid pro quo type of thing. Last point, no booze or recreationals while playing. Basics."

Mitch adds, "Just so you know, most of our practices are at Granny Mabel's garage on Sunday mornings. She's Denny's grandmother."

Violet shakes her head and darts a castigating look at Mitch for habitually interrupting.

She then endorses Smike's audition with enthused praise, "Your keyboarding skills are solid and your harmonica playing is WICKED PISSA!"

Not sure what that phrase means, but it sounds like a strong compliment to Smike.

Mitch, yet again, jumps in, "We never had a harmonica player in our band before, like it."

Violet turns and gives Mitch a scowl to quiet himself and stop interrupting her conversational flow.

She then turns back to Smike and states, "You probably have questions, but we'll start with a few for you, about you, your song preferences as well as knowledge of classics from the bygone decades of music we honor in our performances."

Looking directly at Violet, Smike replies, "Sure, hit it."

Violet first probes on a personal level, "So, howdja get your name Smike?"

To glibly bait the group to welcome him as a band member, Smike says with a smirk, "I'll share that story after I get to know you all better, like after a couple of gigs."

Mitch, catching the humor, snorts a laughing "humph!"

With a soft giggle, Violet says, "Fair enough."

She continues, "So, what is your all-time favorite song?"

With no hesitation and expressed through an air of reverence, Smike responds, "*Hallelujah.*"

Mitch quickly validates Smike's response with "For sure!" and solicits more information, "But which artist's version?"

With assertion, Smike turns to Mitch and claims, "Buckley, hands down. Real vocals. Relatable on every human level. Primal."

Mitch validates, "Agree man!"

Violet then poses, "What about best song by a *female* artist?"

Smike thoughtfully responds, "*Me and Bobby McGee* by Joplin. Raw, authentic voice. On point rhythm. Simply stellar lyrics."

Smiling, Violet then asks, "Is she your favorite female singer as well?"

With heartfelt sincerity, Smike says, "Actually no, Eva Cassidy. Deeply expressive, soulful voice. She captured hope and passion with every note. Her songs move me emotionally."

Violet tenderly whispers under her breath, *I'm in love*, as if to herself, but in direct response to Smike's reply.

After fleeting silence, she continues "So, who wouldja choose as the top male vocalist?"

"Okay, so, I will do this by decade because there are several I totally appreciate. Going way back to the sixties, this singer pre-dates all of us, and maybe even our parents, has to be Sam Cooke with his rendition of *A Change is Gonna Come*. Have to chase that with Otis Redding's *Sitting on the Dock of the Bay*" and then adds, "I love playing that song on my harmonica."

Just Saying

Denny, who remained silent to this point, while fully engaged in his virtual drum rendition of *Wipe Out*, suddenly looks up directly into Smike's eyes and shouts *"Transcendent!"*

Denny then returns to his straw tapping while mumbling something about *two of Granny Mabel's favorite singers.*

Smike continues, "For the seventies, Marvin Gaye for *You're All I Need to Get By* and *Let's Get it On.* Natural melodic soul."

After a short pause, he then adds, "Also gotta mention, Freddy Mercury. Ultimate musical icon! Vocals, hellava range. *Bohemian Rhapsody,* classic in its own class."

All agree.

Smike resumes acknowledgments with, "The eighties, that's tough. I would have to say a toss-up between Prince and George Michael. Prince for his lyrical interpretations and expressive vocalization throughout all of his songs and George Michael for purity of his voice."

Smike finishes, "And lastly, Kurt Cobain from the nineties. Most notably for his tender version of *And I Love Her.*"

Mitch, missing this touching nostalgic moment to pause during Smike's sharing of principal singers, quickly and annoyingly interjects, "So, what about best guitarist?"

Somewhat startled, Smike circles back to Mitch and focusing on his question replies, "Of course, all-time greatest is Henricks. Unadulterated genius and intensity. However, Stevie Ray Vaughan, profound blues guitarist, is my absolute favorite."

In support, Mitch returns, "Again, agree! Both role models for all six stringers!" then adds "I deeply admire Beck, Clapton, May, and Page as well, but Santana's *my* favorite."

As an admonishment, Violet snaps, "Well, this isn't about your opinion Mitch. Keep that to yourself for now, okay?"

Mitch seems unfazed by her reprimand.

Violet continues to probe, "What about greatest keyboardist?"

"I can't say he is the greatest, but Leon Russell is definitely my favorite. He had a unique, quirky style on the keys and was a fantastic song writer as well" Smike responds.

Denny shares "We play two of his songs *Tightrope* and *Masquerade* that are popular with our fans" and then adds, "Masterpieces in my opinion."

Smike nods in agreement.

Violet then asks, "So which harmonica player inspired you?"

"Easy, Toots Thielemans! Belgian jazz musician who also played other instruments like the accordion and he was a skilled whistler. You need to hear his rendition of the *Midnight Cowboy* theme song. Sorrowfully moving!" Smike responds with zeal.

While still beating straws on the table, and never looking up, Denny then asks, "So who would you say is the all-time greatest drummer?"

Just Saying

Pausing, Smike realizes his hesitancy will not be well received by Denny, but answers honestly, "I don't really know."

Denny stops tapping his straws, looks directly at Smike with a questioning glare, and assertively prods, "Ah, come on man, give up a name."

After a short pause, Smike replies, "Okay, Zeppelin's John Bonham."

Denny gives an assenting signal raising one straw in the air like a drum stick and defiantly bringing it down, returns to his straw tapping with a kindly comment, "You're an old soul Smike."

Smike shares, "My parents' and grandparents' choice of music was a big influence on me."

Suddenly Mitch bellows, "Hey, wait, wait a minute, it just hit me, all the musical stars he named are dead!"

The group thinks about it for a second and then laughs in awkward discomfort.

Mitch continues, "Yeah, and most of 'em died young . . . like around our ages."

They all get quiet and temporarily slide into a more somber consciousness about their conversation.

Smike breaks the silence by declaring, "Lost geniuses in their prime. Makes them more memorable, really."

Uplifted, Violet says, "Absolutely!"

Then she mockingly asks, "But do you have any current favorite bands? With members still living, that is?"

Thinking he's clever, Smike responds, "Well, *Knead Naked* is rockin'!"

Everyone chuckles, knowing he never heard them perform.

Violet pushes, "No really, tell us your favorite band from any era."

Smike takes in a deep breath, slowly exhales to say with confidence and emphasis, "You might not know this band, kind of understated, but *Big Head Todd and the Monsters.*"

After pausing, he adds "love the lyrics and the jazzy, bluesy vibe of their songs."

Denny quietly confirms, "See, legit. Old soul!"

Mitch interjects, "Well, I thought for sure he was gonna say *Lynyrd Skynyrd.*"

They all stare at Mitch.

With a repulsed look on her face Violet cracks, "You're one sick puppy Mitch!"

In a submissive fashion, he responds "Was just joking. Trying to stay with the *all-dead* pattern."

Violet then pointedly asks Smike, "Just curious, what's your preferred music genre?"

Just Saying

Unsolicited, Denny, more involved now, utters a guess, "Bet bro loves the blues."

Smike confirms, "Yes, blues and ballads mostly. I like to write bluesy ballads" and then adds, "I must say the musician that started it all for me, my appreciation for the Blues that is, and influenced many of the legends I mentioned, is Muddy Waters. Just didn't want to leave him out."

Denny reiterates, "See? Old man soul, man."

Mitch then asks, "So, what about your favorite song writer?"

Smike shares with assurance, "Nilssen. He had a range of styles but *Without You* is his most inspirational song. Both his lyrics and music made me want to be a song writer."

Mitch, in deadpan response, "He's dead too, just didn't die young."

At first, everyone just stares at Mitch and then they all break out in light laughter, while Violet throws her hands in the air, shakes her head, and poses a questioning look like *what is with him*?

Fred, who has been quietly watching and listening while prepping for the day, spontaneously asks in a single word, "Balladeers?"

"Thanks for asking! My top three favorite balladeers are Marty Robbins, Gordon Lightfoot, and Don McLean" Smike replies with an added nod to Fred for asking a key question that highlights and parallels with his songwriting interests.

Fred returns Smike's nod with a kinked smile.

Violet shifts the questioning to make a request, "Now we wanna hear your voice Smike. Sing a song for us."

Smike replies, "I don't sing. Just play music and write songs."

Violet counters, "All members must sing in our band. With up to three gigs a week, my voice gives out, so we share a lot of the vocal work."

Smike echoes in profound disappointment, "Really, I don't sing."

Suddenly, Mitch and Denny both start gabbing over each other, blurting out songs that they sing and duets they performed in the past. As their exchanges escalate, Denny accuses Mitch of only wanting to sing songs with sexual innuendos like *My Sharona* and *Pearl Necklace*. Mitch unreservedly agrees and comes back with *but, those are the only ones worth singing*. They ramble on for a while.

As the talking-over-each-other blathering between the two of them becomes inaudible, Violet, looking deeply saddened, asserts, "Well, you heard it, we all sing in this band. Guess this just won't work."

Smike silently looks around the bar, not knowing what to say or how to convince them that he would be a complementary addition to the band. It's clear; none of the members indicates that they will budge on this condition. He then spots the bar keeper's plaid trapper hat with ear flaps hanging over a jacket on the coat rack.

Just Saying

Smike suddenly stands up and asks "Fred, can I borrow your cap?"

Fred shrugs his shoulders and with an indifferent expression gives grudging consent.

Smike goes over to the coat rack, grabs the cap, haphazardly throws it on, and starts swinging his elbows out in awkward, alternating animated movements, while singing a cappella in an *Elmer Fudd* voice,

I'm widin' in yowa cawa

As he continues, Violet, Mitch, and Denny are bowled over and explode with laughter, totally glued to his silly act. Smike's comedic portrayal of the song *Fire* by the Pointer Sisters catches them completely off guard! Noticing their interest captured, he continues his impersonation.

Inspired, Violet quickly composes herself, stands up, and in her own voice starts singing with him in unison the next stanza. Their impromptu duet has Mitch and Denny slapping their knees and cheering them on in unabashed appreciation.

Smike then stops his arm movements, turns, and lightly grabs Violet's hands bringing them up to his chest, pulling her close. She picks up on the gesture as they look into each other's eyes with feigned affection and continue to sing the subsequent verses.

Wewwa, Womeo and Juwiet
Samson and Dewiwah . . .

Mitch and Denny are howling as Smike and Violet complete the song.

Through this unplanned, impromptu performance, Smike unquestionably galvanizes his place as a new member in the band. They all enjoy an extended laugh while Fred watches, shaking his head in puzzlement.

Mitch shouts, "Jeezsum crow!!! Ya AWA FIWA Smike! That was hilarious! You killed it! Thought you said you couldn't sing."

Smike corrects him, "No, I said, I *don't* sing. Never in my own voice, that is, but I do impressions."

Denny adds a personal endorsement, "Either way, you do YOU!"

Violet bolsters their collective opinion of Smike's unique musical prowess, "Guess we need to add a comedy element to our act now. What other impressions do you do?"

Smike responds, "*Kung Foo Fighting* as Mike Tyson, *California Dreaming* as Arnold Schwarzenegger" pauses, then tongue-in-cheek adds, "Also, *Sounds of Silence* as Helen Keller."

Without any forethought, Mitch quickly questions, "Wait, you do *women's* voices TOO?"

With a cynical jab, Violet corrects him, "She was a deaf-mute writer from mid-last century. He's joking, ya boob!"

Mitch looks dumbfounded, until swiftly realizing his gaffe with a look like *Oh, yeah, right!*

Smike clarifies, "Actually, I sign the song. Guess I am musically dyslexic. Can sign, but not sing."

Just Saying

Denny compliments him with, "That's funny! Love the irony on all levels, brilliant man!"

Regaining entry in the discussion, Mitch quizzes, "So, what the hell gotcha started doing these hilarious impressions?"

"Just to make my girl laugh" Smike simply and warmly replies.

Everyone is quietly grinning when Violet, glancing at Denny and Mitch with a questioning expression and raised eyebrow, solicits nonverbal agreement on their group decision.

Wholeheartedly signaled through Mitch's affirmative nod and Denny's thumbs-up, she says, "Welcome to our band Smike! Other than keyboards, be ready to do one 'impression' song and a harmonica solo for each performance."

Completely surprised by the quirky series of events, Smike responds with sincere gratitude, "Great, thanks!"

He then asks, "So, now I have a question for all of you. How did you come up with your band's name *Knead Naked*?"

Smirking, Mitch replies, "We'll tell ya at another time; that is, when we get to know you better, maybe after a few gigs."

They all share another laugh as Smike, smiling broadly, shakes each new bandmate's hand to finalize the agreement, and says, "Fair enough!"

Chapter XXIV   Jamming Crew

The first practice session, conducted the next day in Granny Mabel's garage, felt rewarding to Smike in voluminous ways. He enjoyed playing his instruments, relished practicing and performing songs with others who equally appreciated music, and he got to know them all a little better. They just clicked.

Violet, apparently a workaholic, operates a floral shop Monday through most Saturday afternoons (Smike noted the ironic parallel of her name and occupation) and sings in the band up to three times a week. And Sunday mornings are always reserved for band practice.

Her boyfriend, Beau, a medical supply sales representative, travels a lot. His schedule is just as rigorous as hers. Not yet officially engaged, they are unofficially planning and saving for a big wedding. Violet comes from a huge family and all the siblings have names that represent colors. Her mother obviously has a sense of humor. The story goes that because their last name is Green, her mother thought it would be funny to give her children color names, so she started off with Sage, the oldest son, then Jade, the oldest girl, then Emerald, the next daughter, and by the time she was expecting her fourth child, she had run out of names complementary to Green, but stuck with colors. So, the fourth child was named Scarlett. The fifth and sixth children, both girls, were named after flowers that also represented colors; Rose, and then Violet. Her seventh and last child, a boy, was named Indigo. Violet told Smike that she often dons shades of purple clothing and accessories when performing (as this represents her first name). She also admitted an affinity for unique head coverings like berets, scarves, and top hats.

Regarding Mitch, during the week, he works for his dad's plumbing business. The youngest in his family, he currently lives in a room above his parent's garage. Like Violet, he too often works on Saturdays, usually mornings. Mitch didn't mention anything about a girlfriend or partner. He kind of comes off as a player, but not really. This may just be his swaggering façade. The most unique of the three band members, he seems really smart in a lot of ways (word play, trivia knowledge, musical prowess) but goofy, a little attention deficit, and somewhat clueless about certain social clues. However, Smike views him as an outgoing and very likeable guy.

Denny has a regular job as a physical therapist. Although he didn't provide specifics why, he shared that he moved in with Granny Mabel when he was twelve years old. She worked as an administrator at the local police station at the time but now retired. Basically, she raised him, encouraged him in his schooling, and helped him with college expenses. Mostly, though, his tuition was paid by waiting tables throughout college. Three years ago, he married Cecile. She is also a physical therapist. That's how they met; at work. They live in a condominium not far from Granny Mabel and visit her often, almost daily.

Violet, Mitch, and Denny, all have tatts. Mitch has the most with both arms completely covered. Violet and Denny have a couple sentimental ones that aren't as obviously displayed. Smike doesn't have any tattoos, but he has a gold overlay on his front top right lateral incisor with a star cutout that reveals tooth enamel underneath. He got this in memory of Louisa, so that every time he smiled, the tooth represented his love for her. She was the star in his life. They all commented how they liked it, but surprisingly didn't ask him about the meaning behind it.

They probably assumed it was a type of grill for an aesthetic effect. He was just grateful that no one asked.

Regarding himself, Smike shared with them how his parents married very young. His father started his own successful back-up power supply and battery business and his mother worked as a librarian assistant for over twenty years. Neither finished college, although his dad had a baseball scholarship that he partied away. Smike and one of his two sisters completed their degrees. The youngest sister is dragging out her coursework but expected to graduate next spring. When she finishes, his mom will call this her kids' college trifecta. Fortunately, all three siblings had partial or full scholarships. Smike shared with band members that he quit his chemical engineering position to pursue music but did not mention Louisa. They all seemed surprised that he would give up a high paying salary, but in credit to all of them, no one pushed for more explanation of his decision. They all get why he loves music and have all quickly recognized his talent. Last thing he told them was that he was living in Lowell to take care of his grandfather. He shared what he felt comfortable imparting, nothing more.

All band members, like Smike, come from working-class families. Other than their shared love of music, their similar economic background is another aspect of how their lives overlap and serve as a connecting force. Curiously though, these four individuals, ages mid-twenties to early thirties, are not typical oldies music lovers. Smike had mentioned previously during the audition how much his parents' and grandparents' musical choices impacted his love for classical pieces. Always felt that he was peculiar in this regard in comparison with his peers' musical interests; therefore, he wondered why *they* too, liked older tunes. Violet mentioned that the band's previous keyboardist was a woman in her late fifties, much older than the rest of them, who recently became a grandmother and just didn't have the time to perform any more. They figured that because they were a 'retro' band, whoever applied for the keyboardist position would be older like her. So, they were pleasantly surprised to see someone in their own age group.

Each one gave different reasons for loving oldies. Denny revealed he was definitely influenced by Granny Mabel; especially, when he first moved in with her and was introduced to the rhythm and blues music she listened to. He felt comforted by those songs, which resonated with the troubling transition he was going through at that time. Mitch disclosed that his father taught him the guitar and the tunes he learned were all from his father's rock and roll generation or earlier. His parents had him when they were in their forties, so there was an even greater generational gap in music he was exposed to during his formative years compared to his peers. However, he unquestionably connected with the melodies of the seventies' era. Violet shared that being the next to the youngest in a gaggle of kids left her feeling lost, isolated, ignored, and forgotten. At around eight years old, she began wandering to her great-aunt's house down the block from her home to spend time with the lonely widower, who eagerly welcomed Violet's company. Violet relished their nearly daily rendezvous of listening to music together. She appreciated the connection formed with her loving great-aunt and the songs played on her old-timey stereo she inherited and cherishes to this day. She mentioned that her favorite female singers are Patsy Cline, Roberta Flack, Stevie Nicks, Whitney Houston, Blondie, Gloria Estefan, and Annie Lennox. Their songs are the ones she performs most often. One significant difference between all of the band members is that Smike is the only song writer.

Their first session and the easy conversations throughout the afternoon convinced Smike that they are undeniably a jamming crew, a genuine ensemble, and he feels comforted in the musical bond they have quickly constructed. Everyone is looking forward to their first performance at Fred's Tavern this coming Friday, less than a week away. Stepping out of his comfort zone by joining this band appears to be a very good decision for Smike at this time.

Chapter XXV   Nice Weather

Mid-May now, warming weather is conducive to longer runs and garden work. After the first few challenging weeks with his grandfather, things are going more smoothly for Smike. He tells Paps about gaining a position in a band, playing part-time, and will have his first performance this coming Friday. Paps declines the invitation to observe him play.

He argues, "I doan wanna pay FIVE dollahs faw a beeah!"

Sounds like Paps; however, critique of Smike's musical efforts *being a waste of time* as an excuse is excluded from rejecting the invitation. Smike wonders if his grandfather is softening up a little. Like the spring thawing of frozen ground. Apparently, nice weather sprouts more than just fruit-bearing plants.

As Smike leaves for his gig early Friday evening, Paps encouragingly calls out to him, "Have fun with yaw music. I'll be enjoyin the weathah in the backyahd while watchin my gahden grow."

From this comment, a silly memory surfaces from one of Smike's summer stays when he was a young child. Paps told him that they were going to the movies. This excited Smike because Paps rarely spent that kind of money; going to the movies was frivolous and expensive from Paps' perspective of things. He would, however, rent movies (and would often make illegal VHS copies of the ones he liked best).

Smike remembers one summer when he was ten years old. Paps ran several connected extensions cords through the back door, well into the back yard, and then plugged in his dated TV propped up on a weathered picnic table. He placed a couple of lawn chairs in front of it. Paps told Smike that once it got dark, this was just like going to the drive-in movies and they could watch a show in the backyard while eating popcorn. It wasn't quite how Smike imagined them going to the movies, but the arrangement was unique and actually fun. Only down side was mosquitoes. The citronella candles didn't do much to keep them away.

Paps always enjoyed sitting in the back yard, and relished nice weather, in solitude. Smike understood how Paps would choose sitting alone, taking in the beauty of his small plot of nature, over going into a crowded barroom, dodging elbow jabs, and waiting in long lines for the commode in the tavern.

Chapter XXVI   Hot Mess Exchange

The bar crowd was rather heavy and the jam-packed room, sweltering. After an hour of well received songs by the audience, the band takes a break. During the interlude, Violet, Mitch, and Denny visit with fans by the stage as Smike goes to the band's designated table to drink some ice water and cool off. He reflects on how pleasantly relieved he is at how well their session has transpired so far, and they were just half way through their performance at this point.

Unexpectedly, an attractive woman, with perhaps a tad too much makeup, plops down next to him and flirts, "Violet tells me you are a wicked harmonica player, and I can't wait to hear your solo!"

Taken aback, Smike hasn't met this woman before and seems startled by her boldness.

"So, you know Violet and I know Violet, but I don't know you" he replies.

"I'm Scarlett, Violet's sister. Attend her gigs when I'm not modeling" she covertly brags.

"Nice to meet you Scarlett" Smike states with a somewhat forced smile and extended hand.

Scarlett eagerly shakes his hand while asking, "So, howdja get the name Smike?"

"Did Violet put you up to asking this question?" he queries.

"Nah, I just wanna know. It's a unique name, must have a story behind it, right?"

"I'll tell you *how* I got my name in an exchange of information. I want to know how the band got its name."

This piques Scarlett's gossipy disposition, so she revels in the opportunity to share the mysterious background story.

"Okay, deal. It's kind of a convoluted story, but here goes. Violet and Mitch were high school friends who started playing at a local pastry and coffee shop for tips and complimentary treats the summer before their junior year of high school. The owner was the grandmother of a high school buddy of theirs who suggested this venue as it would enhance both budding businesses. Earnings were slim, so Mitch made a sign that read 'Need Tips' which several customers mistakenly assumed was their group name. At some point, a long-time regular customer suggested they change their band name to 'Knead Tips' as a play on words and an ironic twist since they were performing where people ate baked goods. Violet and Mitch thought it was clever and kept the name for a while, until their high school friend openly shared with them a story that his grandmother was an insomniac who often baked in the middle of the night scantily dressed. See, she lived in the apartment loft above the shop. They joked about the image of this large grandmother making rolls while displaying her 'rolls.' They thought this was so funny; Mitch was inspired to modify the name to *Knead Naked*. The band name was solidified when Mitch noted that the two words were anagrams. Ya see, Mitch may sometimes act like an idiot, but he is really sharp! And he's like a brother to Violet, so she can criticize him, but no one else. She will defend him like a mother tiger!"

"I gotta say that is a great story Scarlett and memorable!" Smike replies.

Just Saying

"Okay, so now tell me how you got your name?" Scarlett asks in eager anticipation.

"Louisa gave it to me as a nickname" he coyly responds.

"Wait, that tells me who gave you the name, but doesn't tell me anything about how that name came about. And who's Louisa?" Scarlett responds in disappointment and then nippily adds "That's not fair! Come on, give me the story behind your name, that's our deal" she lamented.

"Our deal was *how* I got the name and I told you" Smike teased, holding back to passively push her button.

Scarlett snapped, "You know that I wanna know how the name came about. That's just not right, you playing me like this."

Walking by, Mitch overhears the tail end of the conversation and snidely comments, "Hey, many guys have *played* Scarlett, if you know what I mean."

She quickly counters, "Well not you!"

Mitch laughs and with sly confidence responds, "Not yet."

Scarlett glares back with no response.

The band members start returning to the stage. Smike sees his exit and apologizes to Scarlett that he has to leave.

She says, "But wait, I wanna find out more about your name and about your gold tooth too, Smike."

Trifling, she adds, "For that story, I'll exchange information on when I'm available for a night out next week, how about that deal?"

Ignoring her obvious flirtatious invitation, Smike says "My harmonica solo is coming up. Hope you enjoy it!"

Effectively deflecting her offer, he smiles at her, turns away, and heads to the stage.

When he reaches the platform, Mitch whispers in his ear "Scarlett's a hot mess, but Violet protects her at every turn. You know how family is, can't throw shade or you'll get burned."

Chapter XXVII   Downright Fabulous

The following Sunday morning, the band meets early to practice at the VFW Hall in preparation for the gratuitous Memorial Day event to honor veterans the following week. Band members gather at the main door with their musical equipment and gear in tow as Rudy arrives to let them in. Just by how their light conversation reverberates throughout the room while walking in, Smike thinks, *Violet was right, this hall has great acoustics.*

The one major song request that must be included in the act for this upcoming event is Lynyrd Skynyrd's *Free Bird*. Denny appears jazzed to be the vocalist and Mitch decidedly stoked to serve as lead guitarist for this song, but they really need someone to play rhythm with a slide guitar. Smike has no idea how they were planning to address this limitation, when shortly after they set up, an older man walks in lugging a guitar. Smike watches as Mitch strides over and escorts this fellow to the band set up area. Violet goes up to the man and gives him a warm family-member-type-of-embrace.   Denny   shakes   the gentleman's hand while pulling him in for a manly hug. Mitch then turns and introduces Smike.

"This is my father, Mister Monroe, but he likes to be addressed by his first name, Curtis. He's gonna accompany us with the *Free Bird* song" Mitch proudly shares.

Shaking his hand, Smike says, "Wow, great to meet you sir, I mean, Curtis, and very much appreciate you joining us."

Smike thought that Mitch's dad was a plumber; didn't realize he was a musician. Mitch only mentioned learning a few guitar songs from his father. He clearly sees a strong familiarity to Mitch.

A modest man of apparently few words, Curtis replies, "Hey" acknowledging Smike while barely making any eye contact. He then silently straps on his guitar.

After basically no preparatory discussion, Violet directs the start of the *Free Bird* song, counting off *one, two, three*, and they all begin playing. Curtis performs as if he has been part of the band for years, intuitively complementing everyone's musical parts. Curtis' rhythmical adeptness impresses Smike. Before he knows it, the lengthy song is over. Smike sucks in his breath and thinks, *this was amazing!*

Curtis then nonchalantly removes the guitar and says "Taking mother to church. See you all next week."

He waves good bye and quickly departs.

After he leaves, Smike asks, "So, that's the only song he'll play with us?"

Violet replies, "Yep. Every year he plays just that song but stays for the full event."

"He is such an impressive guitarist. I mean, I was in awe watching him shred those strings! Has he played professionally Mitch?" Smike asks.

"Nah, don't like attention. Self-taught, by the way. Exemplary role model for me, huh?"

"Absolutely, my man!" Smike replies.

Just Saying

Over the next two hours, the band practices all the other favorite veteran songs they planned to play, including *Spirit in the Sky* with Mitch as lead vocalist and Violet as back-up and Smike's harmonica instrumental for *Sitting on the Dock of the Bay* paired with light drum beats from Denny and guitar strumming by Mitch. Also, Violet tenderly sings her solo *Leaving on a Jet Plane.* Lastly, they finish up with Denny, away from his drums and center stage, singing *God Bless America.* Violet poignantly accompanies him with her violin. The entire set presents powerfully emotional renditions of classics. Beyond impressed, Smike felt quite moved. Violet shared with him that the audience starts singing along with the last song, often shedding tears. He has no doubt about that.

Wrapping up the session, Violet adds, "Okay, see you on Friday and we will meet here again next Sunday, same time. The following day we play in this hall starting at seven. Try to get here around six fifteen or earlier. We perform for a little over an hour and a half. The veterans like an early evening."

Mitch suggests, "You should bring your grandfather, Smike. Can bait him to join us with the one-dollar beer for veterans."

"Great idea! Will try that approach, but he is one tough nut. I wouldn't bet on him showing up" Smike shares in discouragement.

Denny adds, "This is my favorite place to play, and we get to perform some of our best songs! We sound downright fabulous in this hall! Too bad if he doesn't come. He's gonna miss a great show."

Smike agrees and wishes Paps will make this performance, but doubts it based on his grandfather's past pattern and habit of thoughtlessly declining invitations that he doesn't deem worthy.

After assembling their gear, they all share farewells and leave.

Chapter XXVIII   In the Gutter

Smike arrives home after the session to find Paps in the front yard, sitting on his lawn chair and working on a flower bed by the front porch.

While exiting his car, he calls out, "Hey Paps, I can do that. I know your knee is hurting. You shouldn't be weeding."

Paps responds, "It looked bad. Thought I'd wawk on it cause the weathah is nice. Nevah know when we might have company."

"You should have added it to my project list" Smike replies.

"Well, thought I could wawk down low onda flahwah beds and ya could wawk up high and clean the guttahs tudday" Paps shares, pointedly reminding Smike of a previous project that he had not yet completed.

"Damn! Right! Let me take my gear upstairs, change, and I'll get on it right away" Smike sheepishly responds.

"Bring me a beeah on yaw way back" Paps requests.

"Will do!" Smike says as he heads inside with his keyboard.

Smike soon returns, hands the beer to Paps, and asks, "So, are you expecting visitors?"

"My friend Jonathan usually visits the end of May aw eahly June. Want the place to look good, ya know?" Paps divulges.

Lightly joking, Smike says, "What? You have a friend?"

Paps snarls, "Shitass! He's an ole friend. Ya met him befoah when ya wuhr a kid and know him as Mistah Kahn. He's the guy with the eyepatch. We see each uhthah a couplah times a yeeah" and then caustically grumbles "So do *ya* have any friends, *Mr. Lonely*? Nevah have anyone ovah. Live like a hahmit, stayin awl to yawself."

Smike thinks, *well, that sounds like the proverbial pot calling the kettle black*, but doesn't respond. He leaves to get the ladder from the shed, grabs some garbage bags from the kitchen, and begins cleaning the gutters.

Chapter XXIX   Rejection

The next day Smike tentatively poses an invitation to Paps.

"I have a Memorial Day gig at the VFW hall next Monday starting at seven in the evening. They offer one-dollar beer for veterans. Not free, but cheap! And, you could meet some of my friends that you claim I don't have. Would you like to come?"

"Well, I doan know. Doan really like beein round a lot of people" Paps replies.

Smike counters, "Attendees will be mostly vets. The performance will conclude early, so we'll be home by nine. And I remember that you and Grandma Nettie used to go there sometimes. You took me a couple of times when I stayed with you over the summer, remember?"

"I remembah, just doan go out much to those kinda places anymoah. Nevah get comfahtable round some of those goobahs yakkin theyah heads off. Nettie was the social one" Paps gruffs.

Very much disappointed, Smike wants Paps to hear him play. However, Paps doesn't seem at all interested in Smike's music or performances; just not a priority for him.

Although feeling dejected, Smike shrugs it off and to appease Paps' own interests asks, "Okay, so, what projects do we have for today and the rest of the week Paps?"

"Kind of a long list. Wanna finish the flahwah beds out front, scrub the downstayuhs bahthroom, tidy up the pahlah, and wash the kitchen floah" Paps rattles off.

Smike responds, "Spiffing up the place sounds like you want to impress your pending visitor."

"Place hasn't been quite the same faw awhile. Nettie would be embahassed from the high heavens!" he discloses in heartfelt guilt.

"I am on it, Paps. Please don't do too much to irritate your knee. It must be painful. I can do it all" then jests, "I just don't do windows."

As soon as his last comment sprang from his mouth, Smike cringed. He may not clean windows, but recently fixed one upstairs and surely doesn't want to inadvertently bring that to his grandfather's attention.

Chapter XXX　　　Ordinary to Exceptional

Smike spent the week addressing the project list, focusing on one ordinary task a day. For the most part, Paps stayed unexpectedly out of his way and did not micromanage his work, except for organizing the front room. Everything needed to stay where Paps wanted things, even if it looked a little messy and muddled. Of course, nearly all of the tasks were cleaning duties and not technical in nature, so that is probably why Paps was relatively absent from watching over him and offering intrusive directives. By Friday, the house looked spick and span by Paps' standards, and he seemed content with what Smike completed.

Smike's breather would be Friday's regular performance at Fred's Tavern. In the evenings, he had practiced some of the new songs for the Memorial Day event and knew that the band would trial a couple of them that night. He felt excited that the band came together so quickly, more than he ever imagined or expected.

And, of course, Friday's session *was* exceptional. Fans loved the songs they introduced and added to their play list. As a result, Violet, Mitch, Denny, and Smike swelled in anticipation for Monday's Memorial Day gig. Pumped up, Smike could barely contain his excitement. Monday could not come soon enough! Their second Sunday rehearsal at the Veterans Hall only confirmed their anticipation for an excellent performance the following day.

When Smike arrived that Monday evening at the Veterans Hall, nearly an hour early, no parking spaces existed within several blocks. This required parking farther away than expected and towing his equipment a good distance. Totally energized, he was completely oblivious to the physical effort extended.

Finally reaching the venue, he walks in, overwhelmed by the massive crowd; at least two hundred people in attendance already. This is the real deal! Powerful positive energy gushes over him! Fred's gig of thirty to forty patrons definitely pales in comparison. He has been with the band a very short period of time, actually just two performances at Fred's Tavern so far, and really had no preconceived notion of how joining this band would evolve so quickly. Nervous anticipation sets in and he's eager to start playing to release his irrepressible mixed feelings of tension and exhilaration. He wonders, *why have I waited so long to channel and express my spirit as a musician?*

Violet arrives soon after Smike, then Denny, with Mitch and his father arriving last. The crowd cheers while the band sets up. Once settled and ready, Violet introduces everyone. Curtis receives the loudest roars of appreciative applause as he humbly acknowledges the crowd.

The band members feel completely consumed in extreme satisfaction from the audience's gratitude for and involvement in their music. The whole time, Smike thinks this is one of the most satisfying experiences of his life. A bonus confirmation emerges at the end of their performance with a standing ovation from the veterans and their guests. Beaming, Smike and his bandmates wave and bow to the crowd.

Still riding high as he gathers his musical equipment to leave, an older gentleman comes up to him.

"Heard during introductions your name is Schrod. Are you related to Sid?" the man asks.

Just Saying

"Yes sir, he's my grandfather" Smike happily replies.

"Haven't seen him here in a while. He used to come here twice a month with his wife during dollar beer nights. How's he doing?"

Smike responds, "Well, we lost my grandmother over a year ago. Guess he stopped coming after she passed."

"Sorry to hear that son. Please share my condolences with him and tell him that Andy Schatzer asked about him and I look forward to talking about baseball and sharing a beer with him again soon."

"Will do, Mr. Schatzer" Smike confirms.

"Please, call me Andy. By the way, exceptional performance young man! We are thankful to your band doing this for us on this special day."

"Our pleasure!" Smike replies with genuine pride.

The grateful audience found pleasure in their performance, but the pleasure was unquestionably mutual. For Smike, performing at this venue, with these bandmates, and the welcoming audience, generated multiple gratifying layers of satisfaction for the entire experience.

Chapter XXXI　　　Not Quite Enough

After a mentally invigorating and delightfully rewarding Memorial Day gig, the previous week was rather mundane, a letdown. Basically, other than playing with the band, morning runs and a little music writing, Monday through Friday, Smike mostly just tended to Paps' house projects, cleaning, and light garden work during the day. Although productive, he felt stuck and a little bored.

Smike has been in Lowell a little over a month now and was still looking for something else to fill his days throughout the summer. He wants more . . . has to keep busy.

Randomly scanning the reliable local paper provides another job lead.

Part-time driver needed for local shredding company. Contact Vic Frette at (978) 555-0212 for information on the position and to schedule an interview.

This is something he can easily do that would consume some of his boring down-time and help him stay out of Paps' way. If this job isn't a good fit or doesn't work out, no harm in trying. He calls, fills out an online application, and schedules an interview.

Chapter XXXII   Don't Fret It

Dressed in gothic-style clothing, with heavy dark make-up, black lipstick, and straight, pitch-black hair, the woman sitting at the shredding company's welcoming desk looks up and in a monotone voice asks, "Are you here for an interview?"

Smike responds simply, "Yes."

"Sit over there" she states while pointing to a couch, then adds "The owner will meet with you soon."

The receptionist gets on the phone to inform who Smike guesses to be the owner that the interviewee has arrived. Hanging up, she points and directs Smike to go through the door to the left.

"You don't need to knock" she adds.

Smike enters the office and sees a thick-setted, middle-aged African American woman. She stands up and reaches out her hand to greet him.

"Hi Smike, I am Vicki Frette, thanks for coming in."

He shakes her firm grip but seems surprised. With the first name Vic on the ad, he thought the owner was going to be a man.

She appears to recognize he was not expecting a woman owner and explains, "Yes, I am a female, minority, business owner, and professionally shortened my name from Vicki to Vic, to get an edge in the field. Started out twelve years ago with two trucks and three employees. Need all the angles I can get, if you know what I mean."

"Totally get it" he returns while affirmatively nodding his head.

Vicki jumps right into the interview.

"First, I am very impressed that you received a full athletic and academic scholarship at the University of Texas. Surprised that someone with your skills would apply for this position. So, this morning, I called your reference, former supervisor Chris Boden. He spoke highly of you. Said you were sharp, although modest about your intelligence, reliable to a fault, and had what he thought was a significant future as a chemical engineer at the plant. He was very surprised when I called though, thought you were headed to Austin to pursue a music career."

She deliberately pauses and gives him a questioning look as if to explain his previous employment history and how his apparent new goal as a musician is very different than driving a truck part-time. Smike picks up on this opening to discuss his interest in the job.

"I am a musician and song writer. Recently moved here to assist my grandfather with his pending knee surgery" he explains in the shortest, simplest response.

Then adds, "Part-time work will keep me busy, give me a little income, and fits with attending to my grandfather's scheduled medical needs, as well as my musical gigs at night and over the weekend."

Vicki acknowledges "That is definitely inspiring, ambitious, and selfless."

Just Saying

She then quickly cuts-to-the-chase, "Here is what you need to know about me Smike . . . I am a direct person, so let me get this straight and ask you candidly. First, you quit what I am guessing was a high paying job to pursue music, right? Are you any good at it because Lowell is a long way from Nashville, Los Angeles, or Austin?"

Without hesitation he confidently retorts, "Yes, ma'am, I am good. Actually, think I'm better than good. Music is my passion, so decided to finally go for it. Musicians find inspiration everywhere and Lowell is a unique, smaller town setting, rich with creative sources that motivate artists."

"Got it. But more pointedly, what I am wondering is, how long do you plan to be in this area?" she asks.

Smike replies, "I think anywhere from six to eight months. It depends on when my grandfather's surgery actually occurs, his recovery pace, and how quickly I can create my musical portfolio and land an agent."

"I appreciate your honest response Smike. And something else you need to know about me, I believe in supporting employees' ambitions beyond working at the shredding company. Usually, these individual employees are working on a degree part-time or developing a trade. You have a degree and a budding trade but seems like you need a little cushion of time to realize your dream and musical ambition. Sounds like this part-time position will work for both of us and will *harmonize* both our goals" and then adds, "Sorry, couldn't resist the pun" Vicki asserts with a wide smile.

Smike chuckles.

She adds one request, "Will you play at our company Christmas party if still around?"

"Absolutely!" Smike happily replies.

With no additional fanfare, Vicki directs him, "Okay, go back to the front desk and Shannon will give you additional forms to fill out. We will order a couple of business shirts and hats for you as well. Wear khakis, not jeans, so you may need to purchase a few pairs. Also, I have no issue with your hair, but for safety reasons, please keep it in a bun or ponytail tucked under your hat. You will be assigned a locker as well. Your schedule will be Monday, Wednesday, and Friday from eight to five. You will start after the business shirts and hats arrive. Shannon will contact you, probably via a text message. Also, if you don't have one already, be sure to get a Massachusetts driver's license as soon as you can."

Vicki was not kidding. She *is* direct and speedily got to the main purpose of the meeting. He quickly realizes that he landed the job and stands up to shake her hand in appreciation.

"Thank you for this opportunity, Ms. Frette!"

"Don't fret it Smike!" she snickers.

"Our business slogan by the way is, *Fret it? Just Shred it!* A clever play on my last name. Get it?"

Smike laughs in response.

Exiting for the lobby, he shares "I am happy to be part of your team of drivers."

Vicki waves him on.

Just Saying

Smike walks up to Shannon at the front desk and she already has a packet ready for him to fill out. Expressionless, she tells him that he can complete the documents and return them to her the next day or so. At that time, she will give him a key to his locker and will provide his pick-up schedule with addresses and directions to all customer locations.

Chapter XXXIII   No Saturday Night
          Dance

Wisps of clouds lightly brush the sky as a gentle breeze relaxes Paps while he lovingly labors in his cherished garden. Enthused anticipation instantly jars him this morning as he proudly notices that some plants already had buds on them and he couldn't wait until the loose-leaf lettuce can be cut for a home-grown salad. In a state of comfortable contentment, he leisurely picks some weeds and waters his plants. Around noon, while sitting in his lawn chair admiring the patch of budding plants, Paps noshes on a bologna sandwich and sips ice water. *Doan get moah relaxin than this* he thinks. Feeling a little tired, he goes inside and reclines on his lounger. After a few minutes, he falls into a deep sleep.

What the fuck happened? Dazed, Sid finds himself thrown from the blazing Huey. He shakes himself into consciousness and tries to get up, but an injury impairs him. He feels tremendous pain and sees a huge gash on his right knee with shrapnel imbedded, torn skin, and bone clearly visible.

Grabbing a nearby rifle, he leans on it to pull himself up and look around. Their helicopter had been hit and was in flames. Several of his comrades are unmistakably dead, trapped in the downed and burning Huey. He now remembers seeing the missile coming at them and remembers yelling, then jumping out of the side opening.

Gaining his bearing, he knows where the missile was fired from and needs to get out of the opening to a more sheltered area. The jungle nearby would be his best chance. Looking around, he spots Hatfield, immobile on the ground, who also appears to have been thrown from the explosive hit. He hobbles over to him. Hatfield is dead. Looks like a broken neck. He then hears Kahn calling for help from the other side of the wreckage, lying on his back, holding his face in anguish from pain. Relying on the rifle as a crutch, Sid limps over to him and drops to the ground next to Kahn. The whole left side of his face is bloodied, with a gaping hole where his eye used to be. Sid tries to calm him, quickly removes his own shirt fatigue and tears it into strips to serve as a makeshift bandage for Kahn's head wound. Cognizant of Sid's assistance, Kahn consciously calms himself to receive aid.

After bandaging the wound, Sid frantically says, "We gotta get outta heeah man! I saw wayuh the missile was launched. Ya know they will be heeah soon to kill off any sahvivahs. Can ya get up?"

"Damn, I'm hurt, bad. Just go. Get out of here!" Kahn orders.

"No way, we ah goin togethah! You can help me walk and I'll guide ya wayuh we need to go. Just get up!" Sid pleads.

Somehow Kahn musters the strength to get up, helps Sid rise with use of the rifle, and they clamber, as best that they can, into the jungle brush less than fifty yards away.

Once deeper into the brush and not visible to the source that downed them, Sid explains to Kahn, "Hatfield is dead, broken neck. Looks like Martinez, Long, Pender, and the pilot wuhr stuck in the choppah. Doan hava radio, no food or wotta, just this rifle. Doan know if Viet Cong saw us. If they did, they will look faw us, so we gotta keep movin."

Kahn moves his improvised bandage slightly away from the injury and asks, "How bad is it Schrod?"

Trying not to noticeably recoil from the horrific injury, Sid says, "Well, ya woan get a date faw Sattahdee night's dance, but I woan be dancin eithah!"

Sid adds, "Yaw alive, I'm alive, let's keep movin and find sum sheltah."

Using a compass pulled from Kahn's pocket, they continue through the jungle toward what they believe is the direction of their home base. Starting to get dark, they look for a spot to hunker down for the evening.

Trying to console Sid, as well as himself, Kahn says, "Our troops will be sent to the assault site. Once they realize we escaped the wreckage, they'll look for us."

Feeling defeated and beaten, Sid counters his point, "They may think that the Viet Cong captuahd us. May not sahch."

Smike, high-spiritedly enters the house late in the afternoon, excited about his new job.

Not noticing his grandfather snoozing, he calls out with high energy and enthusiasm, "Hey Paps, going to make a celebratory spaghetti meal tonight. Got a part-time job driving a truck!"

Hearing Smike's voice, Paps rouses from his nightmare, irritated and visibly shaken. Smike quickly realizes his grandfather was asleep and apologizes for waking him. He assumes his grandfather's agitation is from being awakened from his nap; doesn't fathom it's a reaction to the mental state he was in mid-dream.

Seeing his grandfather's aggravation, Smike meekly goes to the kitchen and sets the bags of groceries down. Better to not say anything else; will docilely prepare and deliver a plate of food on a TV tray and wait for his grandfather to calm down. Never easy reading and responding to Paps' shifting moods.

After dinner, short of any conversation with Paps, Smike goes upstairs and texts Mitch about getting together the next evening. He has an idea for adding a new song to their performances and wants to run it by him. Mitch is available, so they decide to meet at Fred's Tavern and talk about it over drinks. He then fills out an online document for a Massachusetts driver's license, then searches for men's clothing stores nearby, and ends his evening playing a new song on the accordion.

Chapter XXXIV   Morning Talk

Up early to fix breakfast, Smike wants to tell Paps about his new job before he runs. Soon joining him in the kitchen, Paps says he only wants coffee this morning.

"What? You don't want *anything* to eat?" Smike asks, very surprised at Paps refusal of food.

"Upset stomach" he shares.

"Wonder what that's from? Was it the spaghetti I made yesterday? Do you need something from the pharmacy to help settle it?" Smike questions.

"Nah, the pahster was good. Somethin else. Took Pepto already. Should kick in soon" Paps replies.

Paps suspected, but didn't share, that his tummy distress was more likely due to his disturbing afternoon nightmare the previous day.

"Okay, just let me know if you need anything. And, by the way, not sure if you heard me about the news yesterday. Got a job driving a shredding truck three days-a-week. Looks like I will start next week. Just have to get a Massachusetts driver's license" Smike informs him.

"Between the band and this job, yaw gonna get busy. Hope ya can continue to help me in the gahden. Needs weedin, ya know, *Mr. Green Jeans*" Paps replies.

Smike has no idea of the Mr. Green Jeans reference, but it does not appear to be negative, which is a first.

Just Saying

Paps then adds, "Guess yaw gettin tyuhd of my puss, huh?"

"No Paps, that's not it" Smike says, providing a white lie, then adds a relatable rationale, "Like you, I gotta stay busy."

"Just remembah the gahden, that's impahtant" Paps states.

"Of course!" Smike willingly replies.

He then gets up to go for his run.

As he is leaving, he shares, "After I get back and shower, will be going to the Registry of Motor Vehicles and won't be home for lunch. Have some shopping to do. If your appetite picks up, lunch is made already and is in the fridge. I'll be home briefly this afternoon. Should have enough time to tend to the garden and make dinner for you, but plan to meet Mitch this evening at Fred's Tavern."

"Grab a rack a beeah while yaw out. Will help settle my stomach" Paps requests as he finishes his coffee and pops a piece of gum in his mouth.

"Don't think beer will help your gastro issues Paps" he replies, waiting for a comeback line or some made up reason how the yeast in beer is medicinal, but it doesn't come.

Paps stays silent; he really must be feeling badly.

Chapter XXXV　　Running and Remembering

Absolutely stellar weather this morning for his run. The pounding of each step on the path pacifies his racing mind. Louisa's face flashes before him with a loving memory.

"You are always smiling Michael! Why are you always smiling?" Louisa asks him while sporting an equally distinctive smile on her face.

Lovingly gazing at her and stroking her hair, he responds "How could I not smile when looking at the most beautiful woman in the world?"

Louisa blushes and says, "You are my smiling Michael. My smiling Mike! My Smike! That's what I'll call you from now on, Smike! My affectionate nickname for you. This will be just between us, our own private code."

"You can call me whatever you want. I will always answer you" he says, while pulling her closer and softly kissing her lips.

One of his most recurring and cherished memories emerges; one of the most beautiful. He remembers her long, flowing strawberry blonde hair. Her stunning hazel eyes that lit up every time she smiled and laughed. Lit up when she was angry too, but in a different way. Didn't matter, he loved the light in her eyes. It warmed his heart. He also loved her freckles, that she hated, but he loved every one of them. Tried counting each one on her face with a kiss. She would try to stop him, but he would persist until they both started laughing.

Just Saying

She gave him his nickname. It meant everything to him. This was the moment he realized that she loved him as much as he loved her. He was Smike to her and he wanted to continue to be Smike to the world. He saw himself through her love for him.

Chapter XXXVI   Stuff to Do

After a refreshing run and quick shower, Smike dresses and heads out to take care of errands. He quickly learns that some things are pretty much the same no matter where you go; whether it is the Department of Motor Vehicles in Texas or the Registry of Motor Vehicles in Massachusetts. You become a number and need to go through procedural motions. He completed the online application the night before. Should only have to pay the fee and get a new picture. Too bad you aren't supposed to smile anymore for the picture; he won't be able to show off his gold tooth. The process goes faster than expected, but he's thinking the whole time that *at some point I need to officially change my name from Michael to Smike.*

After securing his license, he goes shopping for khaki pants, grabs a quick veggie sandwich for lunch, and texts Mitch to confirm their scheduled meeting later in the day. He will have enough time in the afternoon to do some light gardening. The plants probably need watering. He decided to make chicken noodle soup to help with Paps' stomach issue. To save some cooking time, he picks up a roasted chicken on his way home. Right before returning, he suddenly remembers Paps' request for beer and stops at a convenience store.

When Smike pulls into the driveway, he sees Paps in the backyard, already watering the plants. He grabs the purchased items and exits his car. Paps looks like he is feeling much better.

Walking toward the back door, Smike yells out, "Making chicken noodle soup for dinner. Picked up a six-pack and a fresh loaf of bread."

Just Saying

"Bless ya *Shaggy*! Feelin beddah from just tokkin to my plants" Paps replies.

"That's great" Smike responds, and then after entering the house, drops his newly purchased khakis off in the laundry room before taking the food staples and beer to the kitchen.

It doesn't take long for him to whip up the soup and even less time for them to eat it. Paps loves soups and stews and heavily douses them with ground pepper. Smike can't help but stare in amazement, watching Paps shake the pepper shaker to create a perfect black blanket on the soup's surface. Smike thought that chicken soup would soothe his grandfather's stomach, but now realizes it doesn't matter what he fixes, his grandfather can sabotage any good effort.

"Tasty soup Michael" Paps says between slurps.

Wondering if he can taste anything other than black pepper, Smike replies "Glad you like it, Paps!"

"Yeah, just needed to add a little peppah" Paps says, adjusting his compliment.

Smike then remembered the older gentleman he met at the Memorial Day event.

"Hey Paps, met a man at the VFW named Andy Schatzer. He told me that he's sorry to hear about Grandma Nettie's passing and hopes to see you soon to share a beer and talk about baseball."

Paps replies, "He's one of those goobahs who can tok yaw eeah off, specially 'bout spawts."

"Just wanted to pass on his message to you Paps" Smike responds and then lets the conversation stop without asking any questions about the gentleman.

Smike surmises that Paps' knee pain factors into limiting his socialization and that's why he makes up excuses for not going to places he used to frequent.

Smike finishes his soup and starts cleaning up the kitchen. Paps gets up, grabs a beer, and leans on his cane to walk to the family room and watch television.

Since Paps completed the garden work, Smike uses the time to write some lyrics and play a few songs before leaving to meet Mitch for their get-together. Smike found the day especially inspirational for lyric writing and falls totally in sync with his harmonica while lying on his back in the tiny bed; consequently, he gets lost in the moment and loses his sense of time.

Suddenly realizing it's getting late, Smike jolts up out of his bed thinking, *damn, gotta leave now to meet Mitch!*

Chapter XXXVII   Fawning Fan

Mitch and Smike arrive at Fred's Tavern about the same time; find a table and sit, while waiting for a waitress to take their order.

Mitch starts the conversation, "So, what are ya thinking Smike?"

"Well, I've been playing around with my aunt's accordion and have taught myself how to play the bass part. You know, the buttons" Smike shares.

"Cool man! So, you wanna play it in the band? Super idea! Funny though, cause if you shaved your beard and slipped on some large glasses from the seventies, you'd look just like Weird Al Yankovic with the accordion strapped on!" Mitch jokingly responds, and then after a slight pause asks, "What song are ya thinking we could play?"

"Actually, I want to first confirm your willingness to be the lead vocalist for the song. Was thinking *Squeeze Box* by The Who. Hoping the band would be receptive to adding it to our play list" he shares.

"Hilarious! That would be fun! And yeah, would be happy to sing it and get the chance to play my banjo. I'm all in!" Mitch confirms.

Smike explains, "Listen man, I just didn't want to step on anyone's toes. Figured you would be on board, but how will Violet and Denny respond? I mean, I haven't been part of the band for very long to make suggestions to the song list."

"Hey, you are a full band member now, so can freely share all of your ideas with everyone. Denny will laugh and say this is definitely a song for me to sing. Violet will appreciate the vocal break and will love your idea for adding the accordion. You keep surprising us with your talents. Also, glad you felt you could come to me first. But, really, don't need to" Mitch explains.

"Okay, just wanted to make sure. So, do you wanna get together maybe some time on Saturday to practice the song a bit before we pitch it to Violet and Denny during Sunday's practice session?" Smike asks.

"Can ya come over to my place? I won't get home until around three-thirty, but we can have dinner with my family" Mitch suggests.

Smike replies, "That sounds like a plan! Just text me your address."

During a break in their conversation, as they wait to place their drink order, Mitch scans the bar and notices three ladies at a table to his right. One appears to be staring directly at Smike.

Mitch says, "Looks like ya have an attractive young lady interested in you. She is to your left and staring at you like she would like to meetja, but don't turn around."

"Aw, come on, don't mess with me. No one is looking at me" Smike disputes.

"Listen, have to tell ya about my hypothesis regarding women—when you meet them, if they retain a constant stare with locked eyes with you for three seconds or longer, *without talking*, they are attracted to and interested in you" Mitch shares in a seriously informative manner.

"You're probably right and it has probably been scientifically proven already. I know you know random facts and trivia" Smike chuckles.

At this time, the waitress comes to their table and takes their order. While doing so, she smiles at Smike while mostly ignoring and dismissing Mitch. She then returns to the bar.

Suddenly, Mitch starts getting excited as he spies activity across the room and says under his breath, "Holy crap! Don't look now. That hottie is heading over here. She has a laser focus on you. Don't look. Just stay cool!"

Smike appears unaffected by Mitch's heightened anticipation.

The woman arrives to the table and asks Smike, "Aren't you the new keyboardist and harmonica player for *Knead Naked*?"

"Indeed, I am" Smike responds with a formal tone.

"I'm Rebecca and I love listening to you play the harmonica. Such an awesome sound!" she says.

"Well thank you!" Smike replies with modesty, then trying to divert attention away from himself, adds, "And sitting with me is our guitarist, Mitch."

Without even looking at him as her eyes are locked on Smike, Rebecca half-heartedly states, "Hey Mitch." Then directed to Smike, she flirts, "I look forward to your next performance."

Rebecca then turns and consciously, as well as in a deliberately slow pace, sashays back to the table where her friends are seated.

Soon after, the waitress arrives, serves the beverages, and states while pointing to Rebecca who just left their table, "She paid for your drinks."

Smike waves an acknowledged *thank you* to Rebecca. She seductively smiles back at him.

Laughing, Mitch says, "I need to come out with you more often man! And, she stared *intensely* at you for like one full minute! Definitely into you. You now have your first band fan my friend! Guarantee she will be at our gig tomorrow night."

"She was just being nice and wanted to share a compliment. You all have fans, right?" Smike counters.

"Not any wanting me to squeeze their box" Mitch teases.

Laughing, Smike replies, "Now THAT's why YOU are the one to sing this song Mitch! You get the innuendo within the lyrics."

"What? Come on, pretty obvious double entendre in the lyrics. Everyone gets it" Mitch claims.

Switching to a different topic, Smike shares personal news.

"Wanted to tell you that I just landed a part-time day job as a truck driver. Start next week. Actually, got a text that my hats and shirts are in, so will start on Monday."

"Great man! You're gonna get busy now. How does your grandfather feel about it?" Mitch asks.

"I tried to tell him yesterday afternoon, but he was just waking from a nap, was grumpy, and didn't really acknowledge what I was saying during dinner. So, told him again this morning and he was fine with it as long as I continued to help him with the garden. He seems to understand that I just need something more to do" Smike replies.

"Well, if you need anything *more* to do, you could start dating. Looks like you have a waiting line between the waitress, your new friend Rebecca, and others like Violet's sister Scarlett. That'll keep ya busy. Just saying" Mitch snickers.

Smike confides, "Want to keep my life simple right now. Not looking for a relationship to complicate things and doubt that I will be around the area that much longer anyway."

"Never know. You could find Lowell a good place to settle. And, you already have friends with me and the other band members, as well as your growing fan club!" Mitch argues with good-humor.

Smike laughs as the two spend time talking about future band gigs and his song writing ideas, when Mitch casually slips in, "So, how'd ya get your name?"

"Trying to be sneaky? I'll give you only a hint at this time. It's an abbreviation for two longer words melded together" Smike shares with deliberate ambiguity.

"First word must be smartass" Mitch jokes.

Mitch is a humorous, good guy, who can be somewhat forward with his comments, but he's *not* pushy. Smike appreciates his style and knows he now has a new friend.

Chapter XXXVIII   Hearth and Home

Friday's session at Fred's was solid and just like Mitch predicted, Rebecca showed up, front row and center stage. Also, Smike's new comedic act of impersonating Willy Nelson singing the song *My Ding-A-Ling* proved to be a huge hit as patrons totally chimed in with the bawdy chorus.

The only down side of the whole evening occurred prior to the session as he left the house, when Paps, spying his braided hair and headband (for the Willy Nelson impersonation), made the snide comment, "When ah ya gonna get yaw head scalped Pocahontas?"

Saturday afternoon, Smike pulls up to Mitch's home where he is outside sitting on the porch waiting for him. Mitch waves for Smike to follow him to what looks like a two-story garage next to the house. Smike grabs the accordion from the back seat and trails behind Mitch. They enter the garage through a side door and Mitch immediately points out a partitioned-off back room with a small kitchen, fully supplied with stove, sink, and fridge on one end, and through another door on the other end, a shower and toilet.

"My father built this. He's a gifted builder, all self-taught. Wait till you see my room upstairs" Mitch proudly states.

"Your father is gifted on many levels and across multiple skills. Very talented" Smike confirms.

They exit the back room and by the far wall go up a narrow set of stairs to a door for entering the second floor.

Just Saying

Mitch opens the door and exclaims, "Welcome to my hearth and home!"

The space looks like a cushy, fully furnished studio apartment with bed, desk, couch, television, and entertainment system that includes a VCR and stereo with speakers. There are even windows; one on the far side wall and another at the back that overlooks the backyard. Of course, Smike spies unique decorative items strewn about that fully depict Mitch's personality, such as a three-foot tall gargoyle figure in the corner. Most notably, tons of books fill shelves, boxes, and appear scattered in random piles all over the room. Highlighted in the most prominent section of the loft, three guitars, a ukulele, and a banjo capture attention as Mitch's most valued belongings.

Impressed, Smike shares "This is really cool Mitch. It's like the ideal bachelor's pad."

"I know. Just don't have any girlfriends right now to enjoy it" he despondently replies, and then confides "Had a two-year 'significant other' relationship that ended over a year ago."

"Well damn, sorry to hear that Mitch" Smike responds, trying to be supportive.

Mitch then reveals unsolicited details, "She fell in love with someone else. No hard feelings though cause she was good for me and she is a good person."

"Her loss, my friend" Smike states.

Mitch responds, "Guess some things aren't meant to be. Anyway, done moping" then asks, "What about you Smike, left any lady friends back in Texas?"

Caught off guard, Smike feels close enough to confide in Mitch, but not ready to share about losing Louisa. Not at this time, anyway; as intimate emotions could emerge that would change the course of their purpose in meeting.

He decides to deflect, "We'll talk about that another time. Would like to play around with our music before enjoying your mother's fabulous dinner" Smike answers.

"Okay, but have to warn you, not sure that you will find my mother's meatloaf that great. Let's just say, I pile on the catsup to give it flavor" Mitch jokes.

Chuckling, Smike retorts, "I'm sure it will be fine."

Grabbing one of his guitars, Mitch jests, "Then, let's play. Working up an appetite will help make the meal more palatable."

Smike hands the music sheets to Mitch, gets out the accordion, and they start playing for a while. Thoroughly enjoying their session, when suddenly interrupted by a blinking red light on the wall in the middle of the room.

Smike asks, "What's that?"

Mitch replies, "My mother doesn't like coming out here and going up and down the stairs all the time just to let me know when dinner is ready or if they need something from me. Before cell phones, my father put in the light as a signal. Tried a buzzer first, but I couldn't always hear it when jamming or playing my CDs. He's really sharp. Can solve any problem."

"Impressive! Look forward to meeting your mom and having dinner with both of your parents" Smike replies.

"Regarding the meatloaf, you're a braver man than me *Gunga Din*. Wantcha to know that indigestion will follow" Mitch kids.

Placing their instruments down, they leave the room and head over to share a meal with Mitch's parents.

Chapter XXXIX   Can't Refuse

Sunday morning's practice was great! Violet and Denny loved the idea of adding the accordion to the performance and thought Mitch's and Smike's version of *Squeeze Box* rocked.

Before Smike knew it, Monday rolled around and he started his new part-time job. And, just like he expected, it was a straightforward position: arrive on time, check in, drive to designated locations on his schedule, pick up materials, return to the work site, unload, and check out.

At the end of his first day driving, Smike walks to his assigned locker to change some of his clothes. Pleasant weather that day; so, he rode his bike to work, but now needed to get back home quickly to fix dinner. The ride is a good forty minutes, depending on traffic and the route.

A Hispanic co-worker, around his age, probably a little older, comes up to him and introduces himself.

Extending his hand, he says, "Hi man, welcome to the company. I'm Rally."

"Nice to meet you Rally, I'm Smike" he replies while rolling up his clothes and stuffing them into his backpack before slinging it across his shoulder.

Rally adds to the conversation, "I noticed your bike out front. Hate to tell you but a rain shower is predicted to hit within the hour or sooner. I'm thinkin sooner. Perhaps you would like a lift home? I drive a truck. You can put your bike in the bed."

"Thanks, but don't think that will be necessary. Again, thanks for the offer" Smike graciously declines.

"What? You don't think it's gonna rain? I'll betcha twenty dollars *that I don't have*, that it'll rain in the next twenty minutes. Where on the road will you be at that time? Don't wanna get drenched, do ya?" Rally rambles a rationale to convince Smike to accept his friendly proposition.

"So, Rally, you're making this offer but have no idea where I live. You may have to drive an hour out of your way" Smike counters to test Rally's altruism.

"I drive all day long. What's an extra hour? Besides, if you lived an hour away driving, how long would that take you to bike here? The odds are that you live fairly close. And, I'll betcha an additional twenty dollars *that I don't have*, that I will drop you off at your home in less than thirty minutes after we leave the site" Rally challenges.

Humored, Smike queries, "So, you're a non-betting, betting man Rally?"

"I'm good with the odds, but don't have the finances or collateral to dive into any real gambling. And, my wife would crucify me if I even tried. We are saving for a house" Rally explains.

Conceding, he says, "I get that. You have solid priorities of wife and home. You know what, I will accept the lift and agree to your fictional bet, but mostly because I want to test your claims that it will rain in the next twenty minutes and that you can get me home in thirty minutes."

"Cool, we can get to know each other during the ride. I enjoy company and rarely have time to talk with anyone. Warning you now, I'm a talker" Rally responds.

Smike has already figured this out. And from his actions, he also surmises that Rally is an outgoing, high-energy, good-natured guy.

Smike gets his bike and follows Rally to his truck. After placing his bike in the bed of the truck, they jump in and drive off. Smike starts the timer on his Fitbit, deliberately demonstrating to Rally that he has clicked it to begin logging. He then gives him Paps' address. Rally says that this location is actually on his way home and he needs no other directions.

Rally starts his extended monologue by saying that Vicki is the best boss he has ever worked for and he has been with her for five years.

"Vicki is fair and generous. In fact, do ya know that she lets me leave early to go to classes? Very flexible about my hours. Believes in my schooling. And, she really doesn't have to do this, but she will give me a fifty-dollar bonus for each 'A' earned and twenty-five dollars for each 'B.' Of course, I always strive for 'As' and show her my grades like you would show parents your report card" Rally shares.

"So, you're taking college classes?" Smike asks.

With enthusiasm and pride, Rally shares, "Yeah, working on a degree in social work. My last semester of classes is this coming fall and I have Internship next spring. Then, I graduate! First one in my family, ever! My parents never even went to high school."

Just Saying

Praising his work and effort, Smike states, "That's fantastic Rally! Very noble profession."

"Well, I've gotta give back, ya know? I've been fortunate. Things could've gone very badly after my mom passed away when I was sixteen. My father left a full decade before her passing, so she was basically a single mother that whole time. I was six and my younger brother was just a little over a year old when he left. We think he went back to Puerto Rico, so Marco doesn't remember our dad at all. Anyway, we have no idea where he went. Probably back to Puerto Rico, like I said, but really don't know for sure. He could be dead for all we know. Anyway, my mother moved from Boston to Lowell after he left. Thought it was a better place to raise boys. We lived here for ten years before my younger brother Marco and I were orphaned and placed in the state system. Tina, our social worker, helped me tremendously. She sponsored me to join the Army at seventeen. And when I turned eighteen, she assisted me in gaining legal guardianship of my brother. He was thirteen at the time. Four years later, he joined the Army as well and around that time, I met my wife, Marciella. She was in the Army too. She is a year older and I hate to admit that she outranked me. Anyway, we married and within a year had our son Pablo. He will be eleven in a few weeks. Real smart kid and I'm not just bragging. He's in the gifted program at his school."

Rally warned him that he was a talker. This was evident through the sharing of his full life history in a very short period of time. Although rambling and difficult to keep up with details shared because he was such a fast talker, Smike became so captivated by Rally's story that he didn't notice the weather change, but Rally did.

Rally suddenly blurts out, "Hey, I won the first part of the bet. It's raining! What time is on your Fitbit?" bragging as he questions Smike.

Smike reads the time, "Eighteen minutes and twenty-three seconds. You're good Rally! But for the second part of the bet, not sure if you can get me home in less than the twelve remaining minutes."

"Ya don't know the area, do ya? We're around seven minutes away" Rally counters and then resumes his historical narrative.

"So, I have a few more minutes to fill ya in. Anyway, thank goodness for the GI Bill! And I am grateful to Tina, my social worker. She's the inspiration for me going into the field. I can really help people who most need help. My wife is in the service field as well. She is a Licensed Practical Nurse but taking classes to be a Registered Nurse. Both of us served ten years in the Army and decided to get out when our son was five and ready to go to school. We figured that we would be transferred many times and he would have to move to different schools with each transfer. Just wanted him to have a stable environment. So, we got out of the military and moved back to where I was raised. Brought Marciella's mom with us. Families of Mexican heritage stay tight. It's tough though with all of us in a two-bedroom apartment. Pablo and Abuelita Maria have to share a room. That's why we're looking to get a small house soon. Need the space. My son is getting too old to share a room with his Abuelita. Most likely, we won't be able to get a house until after my internship because I won't be able to drive a truck that whole semester. Less income" Rally expounded.

Smike couldn't get a word in but preferred to listen anyway.

Rally continues, "So, not sure if your biking thing is for health or environmental reasons. Both are great! But, if biking to work is due more to the impact on our environment, we could carpool if you're interested. I mean, the weather is good until around October but then it gets cold through March or early April. Snows can hit pretty hard too and riding your bike just won't cut it in a blizzard. Carpooling would also save on gas money, that is, if ya ever plan to drive to work. For me, I am all for the environment, but more so, need to save money for our house. Whatja think about carpooling?" Rally asks.

Smike thinks carpooling would definitely be a solid measure for when the colder winter weather kicks in.

"Sounds like a good idea . . ." he begins to respond when Rally interrupts.

"The thing is I would have to drive each day during the school year. I often drop Pablo off at his friend's house before school starts in the mornings. Wouldn't wantcha to have to do that as part of this arrangement. And, if something happens in the middle of the day at school, I need to be able to leave to get him. If you drive, I wouldn't have that option. School is out now, but Pablo is going to some gifted program this summer for a few weeks. So, similar type of situation. But, if you could contribute gas money, that would be very helpful for me. For you, ya get to enjoy the ride and hear my stories. Plus, carpooling supports the environment. An offer you can't refuse, right?"

Smike thinks carpooling would work especially well on Fridays since he has to get home quickly before his band gigs on those days.

He responds, "Yes, can't refuse. However, there may be some days that I want to ride my bike. I am happy to contribute to the gas expense. Just let me know what would be a fair amount."

Rally seems to suffer from monkey-brain, with his thoughts swinging from one topic to the next, when he says, "We are pulling into your neighborhood right now. It's really nice. My wife would love to live in one of these houses. Hey, check your Fitbit. We arrived way under thirty minutes, right?"

Looking at his wrist, Smike confirms, "Yes! Well then, looks like I lost both non-committed bets."

"Okay, so how about twenty dollars per week to cover your part of gas? That is round trip for three days each week. Vicki told me that you'll drive on Monday, Wednesday, and Friday. This works great for me because my classes this summer are on Tuesday and Thursday nights and I go straight to class from work. And now, I know where you live. Pick you up Wednesday morning?" Rally wraps up as he pulls in front of Paps' house to drop him off.

"That will work. Sounds like you figured this all out before we even met. One thing, I would like to add a complimentary coffee or tea to my tab. If you know of a good coffee shop or café on the way to work, my treat" Smike adds.

Clearly excited, Rally responds with enthusiasm, "You're my new best friend Smike! Howdja know that I love coffee in the mornings? Know the best place to go, too. They don't have a drive-thru but make the best lattes. I haven't had any lately cause they're pricey. Ya know, saving for that house. So, you're a coffee drinker too?"

Just Saying

Smike assumed that Rally enjoyed his coffee. From his hyperactivity, he appeared to have had several cups already. Of course, this could just be Rally's personality.

"Actually, I like a good Chai tea" Smike responds.

Without acknowledging Smike's response, Rally adds, "This'll sound strange, but coffee actually calms me. I read somewhere that coffee does that for those suffering from hyperactivity. I've always been a little hyper."

With Rally, what you see is what you get. He is hyper, he is a talker, but Smike also sees an individual in front of him with a huge heart, clear goals, strong work ethic, and someone who possesses a cup-half-full world view, always seeing the positive side of things, although he obviously experienced hardships as a youngster. His hardiness and optimism have clearly been shaped as experiential survival strategies and are honorable traits.

Upon stopping his vehicle, Smike exits Rally's truck to quickly retrieve his bike in the light rain shower and states, "Let's exchange phone numbers in case either of us has last minute change-of-plans."

"Right! And sorry, didn't get to hear anything about you. I tend to dominate conversations but working on that. So, do ya live by yourself?" Rally shares as a last-minute question.

"With my grandfather. You'll have to meet him. He's a veteran too! Thanks for the lift, Rally" Smike responds while rolling his bike up the driveway.

He then directs Rally to type in his phone number as he calls it out and adds, "text me so that I can save your number."

They wave to each other as Rally leaves.

Guess I have another new friend now he thinks. Just couldn't refuse Rally's offer and glad he didn't.

Just Saying

Chapter XL Early Morning Coffee

Wednesday morning rolls around and Rally arrives right on time. Soon, they are in front of the esteemed coffee shop called *More Please Café* for what Rally claims are the best lattes ever.

Smike hops out and reviews Rally's order, "So you want a medium breve latte, right?"

"Yeah, unsweetened. Gotta keep my figure" Rally comically replies, as he taps an obvious roll around his middle.

Smike thinks Rally's comment and action of tapping his tummy are funny because cream added to coffee is just as fattening than sugar added, but replies simply "Got it, back in a bit" while turning toward the café entrance.

In the time it takes for him to reach the front door, Smike notices two men outside the shop by the main window. One standing, the other sitting directly on the concrete with his legs crossed. Fleetingly, Smike thinks the man sitting is likely homeless.

Rally, from his view, also notices the two men in front of the store. He thinks that he has seen these two before and has similar thoughts about the one man being homeless. He notices the tall man standing; a nicely dressed senior African American, who is talking to the one sitting. The one sitting appears disheveled in appearance but coherent and listening to the other man.

Once inside, Smike orders the latte and Chai tea and then impulsively asks the barista, "Can you tell me anything about the two men outside?"

The barista replies, "The tall black man is JoJo; he has been a regular for years. Well at least as long as I have worked here, so around four years or longer. Each morning, he stops to talk to Slim, the homeless guy, before coming in and eating his breakfast. Well, we all call him Slim, and we think he is homeless, but no one knows his name and he doesn't talk. When JoJo finishes his meal, he buys coffee and a snack for Slim before he leaves. During good weather, JoJo stays outside and talks to Slim as he gulps down his coffee and food. Slim is harmless and doesn't solicit from customers. He has become an accepted local fixture the last couple of years. The owner will not call police on him since he causes no issues."

"Well, that's a story! What does JoJo get for breakfast and what does he order for Slim? I'm assuming he hasn't eaten yet since he's outside talking to Slim. I would like to purchase their coffee and breakfast this morning" Smike generously offers.

"Nice of you! JoJo has a large black coffee with sugar and picks one of five breakfast sandwiches. This is Wednesday, so he'll have the sausage, egg, and cheese. He gets Slim a sweetened latte and a sticky bun. Apparently Slim loves the sweets" the Barista replies.

"Done, do it!" Smike completes his order.

In a short period of time, with the order ready, he walks out with the drinks and meals for JoJo and Slim, as well as the two drinks for him and Rally. Rally watches as Smike exits the store, stops and talks to the man standing while handing him the breakfast foods and drinks. He sees the man act surprised and appreciative; smiling, while accepting the goods. Then Smike heads toward the truck.

Just Saying

"Hey man, saw that ya bought breakfast for those guys outside the café. That was very kind of ya! You're a generous dude" Rally acknowledges.

"Interesting story, Rally. The man sitting is Slim. Well, they call him that, but don't know his real name because he's mute. The tall guy standing is a regular customer, JoJo, who has befriended Slim. Apparently, Slim is a good listener and JoJo talks to him each morning. JoJo also buys Slim breakfast, but this morning, I took care of coffee and breakfast for them" Smike expounds.

"Ya definitely made a couple of new friends on this morning's coffee break. One good deed done for the day, my friend. If I had twenty dollars, I would've bought 'em breakfast, too" Rally confirms.

"I know you would Rally. You look after others. I have already figured that out about you" Smike replies.

Rally then asks, "Hey man, didja notice the large silver belt buckle that the JoJo guy was wearing?"

"No, not really" Smike responds.

"Well, it stands out like a winning medal of some sort. If he's wearing it next time you see him, ask about it, will ya?" Rally asks.

"Remind me and I will" Smike replies.

Guess Rally is a little nosey about things he observes.

The rest of the trip to work, they enjoy their drinks over conversation. This time though, Rally shared a little less about himself and instead asked Smike direct questions about why he moved to Lowell and his plans for the future. Smike shared how he would be taking care of his grandfather while writing music. He also mentioned his band gigs. Rally acknowledged what Smike shared and then informed him that if he ever wanted to drive full time, this coming January, he would be leaving the company and Smike could step in. Smike listened but thought that was very unlikely. The current part-time schedule would work until he moved back to Texas, probably mid-spring of next year or sooner. However, he did not share his tentative plans with Rally.

Chapter XLI Cards Dealt

Paps and his trusted military friend, Jonathan, finish eating sandwiches while sitting at the kitchen table drinking coffee and enjoying light conversation. It was ritualistic for them to get together several times a year. These were cathartic visits as they both suffered from residual trauma regarding their shared Vietnam experience. A tight emotional bond had formed over the past half-century. Paps didn't really have another close friend or relationship like this, so he valued his time with Jonathan. For these visits, sometimes Paps would drive to Jonathan's home in Albany, New York. This happened when Nettie was alive as she enjoyed the trip and adored Jonathan's wife. Other times, Jonathan would come to Lowell with his wife or he would be dropped off by his granddaughter Abby, an artist, who occasionally had some art shows at a co-op gallery in Haverhill, a short jaunt north. For this visit, Abby dropped her grandfather off in the morning and reminded him that she would pick him up a little after six to get back home before too late in the evening. Paps appreciated that this visit was at his home because right now, although he wouldn't admit it, he couldn't drive three hours by himself. He also relished the fact that they could quietly converse *alone*. That rarely happened. It was a little after five in the afternoon when Paps shifts the conversation to a more personally troubling and burdensome subject.

"We should nevah have been theyah, I still doan undahstand it" Paps laments.

Jonathan knew where the discussion was headed. He also knew that this was an opportunity for him to shoot a couple of key questions to Paps and from his responses, he could evaluate his mental state. Through their lifelong friendship, Jonathan had the ability to tilt Paps' negative thoughts away from self-loathing, or at least neutralize potentially explosive emotional qualms that have plagued Paps since Vietnam.

"Listen Sid, we survived, had beautiful, productive children, and now enjoy retirement, our grandchildren, and please remember that we have always done our best" Jonathan replies.

"Well, ya did pretty dahn good with collahj, a prahfessional job as a phahmaceutical resahchah, and a big, cozy house! Nettie always enjoyed stayin at yaw house, thought it was beautiful. I could nevah give hah that as a postal wawkah" he whined.

Jonathan retorted, "Stop it! The two of you loved each other and that's all that counts, you know that! Regarding Nettie, how are you doing? Last time we talked, you were missing her deeply."

"Of course, I still miss hah, will always miss hah, but grateful faw the fifty-five yeeahs we had togethah. She had a good, long life. I need to remembah that. She told me to remembah that!" Paps shares in confidence.

"Yes, very positive way to look at things Sid. By the way, the house looks kept up and I thought you might have a little trouble since she did all of the cooking and cleaning."

"My grandson Michael has been living heeah faw a while and he's a neat freak like Nettie. Drives me crazy, but he's okay to have round, I guess. He helps" Paps relinquishes half-hearted praise.

"What a talented, smart young man. Thought he was a chemical engineer in Texas, what changed?" Jonathan asks.

"I doan really undahstand it, but he quit his job makin great money. Sold his place and gave most of his belongins away to sum chahity. Says he wants to write music like *Jayry Gahcia* aw sumthin wee-id like that. And my son Jimmy comes in with this cockamamie idear faw him to stay with me faw a while to help out. I doan need any help and Michael can write his music anywayuh, doan have to be heeah in Masserchoosits. Besides, ahfta beein heeah just a couplah weeks, he goes out and gets a job playin in a band sevahal nights and then laytah lands anuhthah job drivin a truck a few days a week. Not heeah that much anyway" Paps explains.

"I'm guessing him being here has to do with your pending knee surgery" Jonathan deduces.

Paps snaps, "It's scheduled, but may not even have that procedjah. Dooin just fine. Doan undahstand all the hullaballoo evahyone is makin 'bout it."

"Well, you do have this regular need for a cane now, I notice. Used it only occasionally before. And, you really don't want to wait until you're too old for the surgery to be effective. You see how long I have been using a cane due to arthritis. I hate it. Was losing the damn thing all the time, until Abby wrapped some pink fluorescent duct tape around the top so I could find it more easily. Got a little upset with her, but it works. Remember Sid, family help out even when you don't want their help or think you don't need it" Jonathan shares in an extended explanation.

"Ya kept losin the cane cause ya have only ONE eye, ya blind idiot!" Paps mocks while chuckling.

Jonathan responds in laughter at Paps's affectionate taunting. They would commonly chuck one-liners back and forth with no intention of hurting each other's feelings. Their brotherhood formed and solidified through this type of benign, non-serious, sarcastic exchanges. Since Jonathan's Vietnam injury, Paps has referred to him as One-Eyed Jack; and in a rebuttal fashion, Jonathan has referred to Paps as Joker. It's fitting. They tease that neither of them operates with a full deck and they must play the cards they have been dealt with in life.

Jonathan then seriously asks, "Are you sleeping, okay? Any disturbing dreams?" in reference to Paps' recurrence of nightmares that, other than Nettie, only Jonathan knew about.

"A few" he replies.

Jonathan queries Paps for more detail, "How bad?"

"Michael woke me up dawin one 'bout gettin hit in the Huey. A second one was roughah. Was ahfta we got hit. And I keep relivin the rescue attempt when owah kind Samahitan was assaulted" Paps solemnly shares.

"I keep telling you, that was *not* your fault, Sid! If anything, I am just as much to blame. Please go back to the Veteran Administration for counseling" Jonathan advises.

He then adds, "Bad experiences, and the reliving of them, are processed through our subconscious. Your nightmares are a reaction to that traumatic experience."

Paps retorts, "VA counselahs doan know shit! And ya sound just like 'em. From what I've seen, most of those psych doctoahs ah young punks who have no battlefield expahience and no idear of what goes on in wah."

Jonathan attempts to persuade him, "You're probably right about their inexperience, but counselors will listen to you like I listen to you. They may even offer some helpful suggestions. You need to trust someone other than just me because a couple of visits a year with me just aren't enough therapy, my friend. You are one tough guy Sid, but avoiding or trying to deny your anguish and failing to get help will eventually wear you down emotionally and mentally. Don't be so fucking stubborn and accept help for once, will you?"

Trying to deflect, Paps argues, "Hey, we both know, what doan kill ya makes ya strongah!"

Jonathan instantly quips, "Except taxes, taxes will kill you. *Or*, they will financially maim you for the rest of your life!"

"Now, that's the truth!" Sid confirms as they share a hearty laugh.

Jonathan had a way of adding humor during serious discussions, but always returned to the main point.

"Really, just get your ass in for a counseling session. Promise me!"

Chapter XLII   Fraise Pie

Suddenly, before Paps could answer, Smike, returning from work after Rally dropped him off, comes bolting through the front door. He sees Mr. Kahn sitting at the kitchen table and recognizes him from previous interactions over the years, but had no idea that he would be visiting this day. He quickly heads straight over to him.

"Good to see you, sir" he states while delivering a strong grip and sturdy hand shake.

"Great to see you too, Michael. Your look has changed since I last saw you at Nettie's funeral" Jonathan responds.

Paps interjects, "That's somethin else, I doan get why he has to let his hayuh grow like *Rapunzel*."

And there it is; Paps again throws a negative comment at him, but this time with an audience to witness.

In a diverted comment, Paps shares that the oven should have reached four hundred and fifty degrees and directs Smike to get the pie out of the freezer, remove the covering, and place it in the oven.

Jonathan asks, "Is this Nettie's famous fraise pie?"

"Yeah, last one left. Thought the three of us could enjoy it togethah" Paps shares with reverence to this special treat.

As Smike follows Paps' instruction, he finds this act touching, that Paps wants to share the pie with his friend and with him as well. It's an amazing pie that everyone relished and would fight over for the largest slice.

After he places the pie in the center of the oven, Jonathan calls Smike over to join them at the table. Smike gladly obliges. He wanted to ask about their friendship. Didn't know how two, such dissimilar individuals, one Catholic, one Jewish, from different stations in life, and divergent world views, could be such close friends.

Once seated, Smike asks, "Actually, I'd like to hear more about how the two of you have been such good friends all these years because you seem so different."

Paps quickly and cynically responds, "That's simple, who wouldn't wanna be *my* friend?"

More seriously, Jonathan poignantly states, "We shared an impactful life event, which was a bonding experience. Basically, we saved each other. Differences dissolve when you face potential death and together survive the failings of humanity."

Paps looks down at his coffee. He appears uncomfortable as a grave look engulfs his face.

"You mean in Vietnam?" Smike probes.

Paps abruptly attempts to redirect where the questioning could lead, proposing a more benign topic of discussion.

"Didja know that Jonathan's nickname in the Mahreen Cawr was *Dahrantay*" and then directs Jonathan to turn sideways.

Paps continues, "Just look at that schnozzola! Evahyone in the platoon, not just owah squad, figahed that his nose would be the Viet Cong's main tahget. They couldn't miss, right?"

Pointing to his patch, Jonathan adds, "They were aiming for my nose and got my eye!"

Laughing, Paps augments discussion, "He was called Dahrantay until he got wawd that he was receivin a battlefield commission from enlisted Sahjent to offisah faw his brayvahry and leadahship. He was owah squad leadah and was gonna be a Fahst Lieutenant. Ahfta that, we joked that we would call him *Fahst Lieutenant Mustang.* He was goin to be the only mustangah among us."

Jonathan clarifies, "Michael, a soldier promoted from enlisted to officer rank is called Mustang. That never officially happened to me. I was nominated before our last excursion but discharged due to my injury. Your grandfather would have received a commission nomination as well; he just didn't have his high school diploma at that time. That is the only reason I outranked him, and that was only for a very short period of time during the end of our tour."

"So, you knew Mr. Kahn as your squad leader since you were a Corporal, right?" Smike asks.

"Yeah, he was my squad leadah, a great leadah" Paps confirms with a serious inflection.

"I thought that the military frowned upon fraternization between squad leaders and troops, how could you be friends?" Smike queries.

Ignoring the premise of the question, Jonathan assertively responds, "Your grandfather was the *bravest* and *most humane* individual I have ever known. He stood up for me in tough situations. He's a genuine friend, who I love as a brother."

Although he didn't show it, Smike seemed surprised, never really thought of Paps being described as humane.

Jonathan continues, "Before assignment as squad leader, there were a few guys in the platoon who would harass me, call me Jew boy. Sometimes they would get aggressive and push me around. Your grandfather, skinny as a rail, always had my back. He really didn't have the muscle to physically put some of these guys in their place, but he had the smarts and the mouth. Boy, he had the mouth. Still does. Anyway, he could shut them all up with one cutting statement. Make them look like idiots. They didn't like it, so they stopped bothering me."

Smike remembered his father telling him about how Paps was poor growing up in Boston and at fifteen years old had to quit school to work and make some money to help his family. He also said that Paps was teased and hassled by neighborhood boys for being so thin and poor. They didn't like that he was smarter than they were either. He was an easy target for the bullies. However, his grandfather had vocal talent and the intelligence to strike back at assaults by his tormentors through his verbal prowess. That mouth of his probably developed as a survival skill.

During his own childhood, Smike observed Paps defend, support, and assist marginalized individuals in the neighborhood and some from church as well. Ironically, though, regarding his own family, Paps was not so sympathetic; quite the opposite actually, with relentless browbeating for minor infractions. Smike fleetingly wondered if Paps bullied family members to make them tough; tough like him, tough like he expected them to be in an ostensibly malevolent world.

Chapter XLIII   Mother

Paps again looks down at his coffee, seemingly concerned that his diversionary tactic didn't work and that emotionally deep sharing in front of his grandson will expose his vulnerability and feelings. He was not comfortable with these questions and potential responses, too deep, too revealing.

Jonathan picks up on Paps' uneasiness and follows Paps' deflection strategy by sharing, "Guess what your grandfather's moniker was in the Corps Michael?" Jonathan poses.

"I have no idea. Perhaps *Killjoy*?" Smike responds, thinking about harsh possible nicknames that could be applied to both Paps' personality and the havoc of war.

"No, it was *Mother*" Jonathan shares with a smile while looking at Paps, trying to get him to look up.

"Oh, I get it! *Mother*, for *Mother Fucker*!" Smike snickers.

Jonathan corrects him, "No, *Whistler*'s."

"Whistler's? As in *Whistler's Mother*? That doesn't make any sense" Smike responds in confusion.

Jonathan begins to explain with, "What? You didn't know that your grandfather . . ." when Paps quickly looks up, stares sharply at Jonathan to stop, and simultaneously commands a directive to Smike with, "Michael, check on the pie, doan want it to bawn."

Jonathan stops, squints, and looks apologetically at him. Paps just stares back, slightly shaking his head like *doan go there.* Smike, still confused, sits there for a second and then, as directed, gets up to check on the pie.

The pie appears ready; so donning oven mitts, Smike pulls it out and sets it on a trivet to cool down. Removing the mitts, he then pulls out some plates from the cabinet, gathers utensils from the drawer, and brings the items over to the table. This preparation time allows for the temporary and tacit tension in the room to dissipate. Putting the mitts back on, he carries the pie over to the table and places it in the center as they quietly stare at the magnificent pastry that they all long to dive into.

Chapter XLIV — To Nettie, Last of the Best

Inspired, Smike tells a story about his grandmother and the history of the wild strawberries known as fraise.

"Grandma Nettie and Paps would go to New Brunswick, Canada every summer to visit her siblings and cousins. They took me a couple of times. I especially remember the first time, when I was around eight years old. It was great! There was this beautiful cabin near a lake. And, the food was fabulous and plentiful . . ." he was in the middle of the story when Paps interrupts.

"Beeah was pretty good too" he says with a laugh.

Smike continues, "Even though I didn't speak or understand French, had so much fun with cousins my age, because they could speak broken English. I was sad when told it was time to leave; plus, I wasn't looking forward to the long drive back. As we crossed the border over this bridge to go stateside, Grandma Nettie told Paps that they needed to stop at her fraise place on the other side. She had this spot near Fort Kent, Maine. It was away from the town, a long walk from the country road where we parked. And for several hours, well it seemed like hours, we would pick these tiny, sweet, wild strawberries. I started eating as many as I could gather, while occasionally putting some in the plastic container. She would complain and tell me that the more I ate, the less there would be for the pies. So, of course, I stopped eating them and just picked as many as I could to fill the container. Considering the time it took, you would think that we would have enough berries to fill an entire truck, but they were a fairly rare delicacy. Grandma

Nettie told me that what we picked was enough for just a couple jars of preserves and two to three pies. So, they were very special."

Jonathan, and even Paps, enjoys the telling of this story when Paps adds, "Nettie couldn't pick any strawbahries the last few yeeahs. Just couldn't make the trek from the ole road to hah secret spot of strawbahries. So, hah nieces would take hah and let hah sit in the cah while they picked the bahries faw hah. That's how she could still make the pies."

The three of them sit for a while smiling in appreciation, watching steam rise from the pie, relishing and fully taking in the satisfying smell of wild berries, when Smike grabs a large knife and starts cutting slices, asking Jonathan and Paps how large a piece they wanted. He then gently serves slices onto their respective plates, as well as his own. They all revel in the sweet aroma of the best homemade pie ever and appreciably knew that this was the last of the best.

Jonathan starts first, grabs his fork, digs into his slice, raises it in a toast fashion manner and says, "To Nettie!"

Smike and Paps follow, raise their forks, and nearly in unison say, "To Nettie!" "To Grandma Nettie!"

Silently, they enjoy each delicious bite, slowly savoring every crumble of tender dough and sweet berries. Only the clicking of their utensils on the plate can be heard.

As they're finishing their treat, there's a knock on the door. Smike quickly licks his fork and gets up to answer. It's Abby. In denim overalls with her auburn hair tied up in a bun on the top of her head and trellis wisps of hair loosely hanging down, framing her face; she looks appealingly worn out. They may have met before, but he doesn't quite remember. It doesn't seem that she remembers him either. They were probably young children when, and if, they met. Anyway, he greets her and escorts her to the kitchen.

"Would you like a piece of strawberry pie?" Smike asks.

"Can I get it to go?" she responds.

Smike says, "Sure, let me wrap it up."

He goes to the pantry closet to get a plastic container and a small bag, never expecting what would come next.

Jonathan and Paps harshly correct Smike and explain to Abby that it is *fraise* pie made from wild strawberries personally foraged in the most northern part of Maine by Grandma Nettie. They confirm that it is very rare to have this delicacy.

As he's packaging the pie, Smike thinks that he should have called it fraise and explain where it came from because it *wasn't just* strawberry pie. He failed to honor his grandmother with this oversight and was rightfully corrected by his elders.

Abby reminds Jonathan, "We gotta go grandpa! It's going to be a three-hour drive and that's not counting stops for restroom breaks."

Jonathan responds, "And my old bladder is just not what it used to be!"

Paps laughs and confirms with, "I heeah that ole man!"

Jonathan then gets up, leaning on his cane with one hand and the chair with the other. Paps gets up as well, nearly identical procedure with his own cane. Everyone slowly heads to the door.

As Abby and Jonathan exit, Jonathan turns around and says, "See you soon my friend!"

Paps shouts out, "Said the one-eyed man!"

Walking toward the car parked at the front of the house and while never turning around, Jonathan slips his hand behind his back and flips Paps the finger.

Grinning, Paps acknowledges the gesture and says, "Now, theyah's the love!"

Chapter XLV   Woodstock for the Not-So-Stocky

Fred's Tavern was crammed on Friday! To Smike, it looked like in addition to regulars, a higher number of younger patrons, appeared present, many standing outside waiting to get in. He didn't know if this was normal or not. Smike speculated that the surge of twenty-something attendees could be an end-of-the-semester school year phenomenon that comes in waves; again, he just didn't know what to account for the increase of bar customers. Really didn't matter much though, since he and his band mates became highly fueled by the energy in the room and that helped make their performance a great act.

The following Sunday morning, the band meets for their practice session conducted in Granny Mabel's garage. Violet reminds everyone that they have an upcoming Woodstock theme gig the following Saturday that is a regular event for resident Baby Boomers. Band members are directed to dress in late sixties, early seventies retro-fashion clothing; that is, bell bottoms, flower-printed polyester shirts, handkerchief headbands, long strands of wooden beads, flip flops, and anything else that flashes the Flower Power image of that era. Violet points out that Smike's long hair and full beard are perfect and with a few accessories, he'll fit in great! This sounded like fun, but Smike wasn't sure where he could find that type of clothing and quickly wondered if there were any local vintage resale stores. He figured that he had some homework to do to prepare for this event.

Granny Mabel enters the garage carrying a tray of freshly made lemonade. Thanking her, band members eagerly down the tart, cold, and refreshing drink as they wrapped up a very energizing jam session. Getting ready to leave, Violet hands everyone the final list of songs that they will perform. Smike grabs the list, says his good-byes, loads up his keyboard, and heads home.

Carrying his musical equipment, he raucously enters the house, unintentionally banging stuff against the door. Paps, in his underwear, sitting in the lounge chair with the TV blaring, doesn't even notice Smike; he appears to be dozing, which is not uncommon for his mid-day routine. Smike is relieved about that. He doesn't feel like exchanging pleasantries or rather customary *non*-pleasantries with Paps and quickly heads upstairs to put his instruments and gear away. Once in his room, he grabs his journal and lays on the bed to jot down new thoughts for songs. Lying there, he remembers that Paps told him Grandma Nettie had placed some of his dad's and aunt's old clothing in the other upstairs bedroom that she converted into her craft room. He thinks there might be something in that room he can use for the Woodstock gig since his dad sort of grew up during that era. His father certainly had a stouter build than he did, as Smike was built more like Paps, and much leaner. But even if the clothes are a little large, at least he has something with which he could work.

He gets up to take a look throughout the adjacent room, rummages around, and notices that in the closet there is a box marked 'Jimmy's clothes' so he pulls it out and eagerly starts digging through it. On the very top, Grandma Nettie had neatly folded several polyester shirts. Smike spies one that will work perfectly with its fluorescent green paisley design. He wonders about the era and how people at that time thought this was 'cool' looking. How times have changed! Regardless, he's thrilled with this find and quickly tries it on. Of course, like he expected, it's a little loose on his slim frame, but he figures he can pleat fold it in the back and tuck it into his pants. Continuing through this treasure trove of outmoded clothing, he pulls out the grand prize: a pair of antiquated, faded and worn to perfection, bell bottom jeans! He has hit the jackpot! Excitedly unfolding it, his mood instantly shifts to dejection as he notices a large hole in the pants' back pocket.

"Fuck!" he verbalizes out loud while thrusting his entire hand through the gaping hole! Fortunately, the hole is along the pocket seam and he quickly thinks this is salvageable. He can stitch it up, if only for a temporary fix. Grandma Nettie's dated sewing machine is in this room, flush against the back wall. He finds her sewing kit next to it and searches for blue thread, confident that he can thread the machine since it is an older model and shouldn't be too complicated to figure out. After briefly fumbling with the thread, he plugs in the machine and tests his stitching skills on a scrap piece of material from the sewing kit. Eyeing his handiwork, he determines the machine functions well enough. With high concentration, he then aligns the jeans onto the sewing area, folding the torn part of the pants against the pocket seam and tentatively presses his foot down on the pedal while holding the material and guiding it through for a clean and even stitch.

Suddenly, with no forewarning, Paps is at the doorway behind him leaning against his cane while sarcastically yelling, "What ah ya dooin *Betsy Ross*?"

Of course, Paps could see what Smike was doing, and of course, he had to make some snide remark and apply yet another character label on Smike to jibe him. This was Paps' caustic approach to fabricate some sense of engagement with Smike by instigating conflict through nearly every interaction he had with him.

Continuing to sew without looking up, Smike responds with a disinterested tone, "There were no sewing machines when Betsy Ross was alive."

While smacking his gum, Paps promptly delivers a more modern rejoinder, "Okay, so what ah ya dooin *Mahtha Stewaht?*"

Have to give him credit. Paps still has quick wit, even at his age.

While finishing the stitch, Smike, simply and lacking affect, replies, "I'm sewing up a hole in a pair of dad's old jeans."

After a minute or so, while still at the door, Paps then snaps an unexpected directive, "Hey Michael, tawn round, have somethin I wanna show ya."

Smike halfway turns, just looking over his shoulder for a side view, observes his grandfather, underwear pulled down, mooning him with hands spreading his cheeks as he jokingly says, "How 'bout ya sew up this hole?"

Mildly disgusted, but not surprised, he turns back to his project and mumbles under his breath, "Just give me a wad of gum large enough and I'll stuff that hole!"

Paps doesn't hear his reply and continues chuckling while he pulls up his underwear, leaves the room, and hobbles back downstairs.

Chapter XLVI   Tie One On

After being repulsed by the mooning event several hours earlier, Smike later traipses downstairs, dreading having to ask Paps for anything. Even simple interactions with this old codger would often explode into major episodes of negative banter and totally unsolicited critical comments as well as incessant questioning. However, Smike thought one of Paps' old neckties would be an ideal addition, as a headband, to his ensemble for the Woodstock show. As usual, Paps was in the family room watching TV. Playing was an old war movie on his VHS that surprisingly still worked. Paps was fully reclined with his feet up and a heating pad laying across his bum knee. Disrupting him from his relaxed state would result in grudging hesitation, verbal strikes, and probable cursing. A simple request always sparked reluctance from his grandfather, and he was rarely willingly helpful. Just one of Paps' control strategies. Smike always tried to keep questions and requests as simple as possible to limit his grandfather's range of adverse responses.

"Paps, could I borrow one of your ties?" he asks.

"What? Hold on. Let me pause my movie."

After fumbling with the remote, Paps questions, "Ya wanna bahrah a tie? Ya doan have any of yaw own? Aw, ah ya an admiah of my fashion sense?"

Paps often ended responses to questions with a wisecrack.

"I have ties but need a classic one from the nineteen seventies" Smike explains.

Again, he made sure to keep the request simple and direct.

"Dammit, I need to get up now and look through my closet" Paps snaps at Smike.

Smike tries to reassure him that he doesn't want to cause any inconvenience.

"That's okay, I'll go in your closet and look through them. You don't need to get up" he says.

Paps barks, "I doan wantcha in my room gettin in my things! Ya know that!"

At this point, Paps throws the heating pad off his knee, moves the recliner to the upright position, grabs his cane, and clumsily gets up.

Huffing past Smike towards his bedroom down the hall, he angrily mumbles, "Just follah me ya fuckin *sphinctah Chawlee hawse.*"

Smike, astonished, wonders, *What did he say? Did he call me a sphincter Charlie horse? What the heck is that?*

As if Paps could read Smike's mind, he clarifies more loudly, "Yaw such a pain in the ass!"

Every day there was a unique insult spewed from Paps' mouth, created from his troubled mind and acidic thoughts of always being some sort of victim or on the shitty end of the stick in life. Beaten down, yet again, Smike follows his grandfather to his bedroom. Actually, he had rarely been in this room, mostly viewed from just outside the doorway. They get to the closet and Paps moves his shirts to the left to reveal a special hanger that held his ties. Sure enough, there were several dated ones that could work with what Smike imagined for his outfit.

"So, which one of these dooyah wanna use?" Paps questions in a more subdued tone.

Smike picks one out, pulls it from the hanger, and says, "This will work, thanks!"

Paps bitingly remarks, "Return it the way ya received it, clean and eyeined."

"Of course, Paps! Again, thanks" he replies.

Smike notices that some of Grandma Nettie's clothes were still hanging in the closet but doesn't say anything about it. As they exit the bedroom, walking parallel to each other, Smike observes a picture on Grandma Nettie's dresser drawer of him with Louisa. Paps detects Smike's observation of the photo and stops.

He then picks up the picture, gazes at it, and says in a softness Smike never witnessed before, "Yaw Grammar Nettie loved hah, ya know?"

Caught off guard with this rare temporary moment of tenderness from his grandfather, he simply responds, "Yes, I know."

It was always a fucking roller coaster ride of sentiments interrelating with Paps, from disgust and disappointment, to this brief loving connection. No emotionally stable person can easily deal with these types of exchanges without shifting to feeling a little unhinged. Once out of the room, Paps returns to his recliner and his beer, while Smike walks back upstairs.

Chapter XLVII — Historic Affair

Again, the band's gig at Fred's Tavern on Friday evening proved to be a very positive turnout! Apparently, their popularity as a band was flourishing because Violet mentioned how she received more frequent than normal calls for scheduling private shows.

Saturday morning arrives and Smike starts getting dressed for the Woodstock gig. His father's jeans are a little baggy. Fortunately, as a teenager his dad was thinner and this is not an issue that a belt doesn't easily fix. He dons the vintage shirt, carefully folding the sides to the back and tucks into his pants. He buttons only a few at the bottom of the shirt, leaving his chest somewhat visible to capture the image of the era. He had dug through his aunt's old jewelry box that was in Grandma Nettie's craft room and serendipitously found a tear-drop shaped peace sign necklace. He throws this around his neck and then slips on a pair of flip flops that he brought with him from Texas. Lastly, with his hair fully down, he wraps Paps' tie around his head covering his forehead, knotting it in the back, and throws the ends behind him. He then goes into the bathroom to check out his look. Staring at the image, he believes he has nailed it. Definitely looks like a hippie. Returning to his room, he gathers his keyboard, harmonica, and music sheets and waits for Mitch's text for when he arrives outside to pick him up. Mitch offered to give him a lift since the performance is out of town at a farming home and probably would be difficult for Smike to find. The cool thing is that they will perform in a renovated barn. Invigorated, Smike thinks this will be such an awesome and exciting experience for him.

Just Saying

Text received, he grabs his stuff, and heads downstairs. As he reaches the front door, he waves good-bye to his grandfather.

Paps sees him in full attire and yells, "Hey, what protest ah ya goin to *Abbie Hoffman*?"

In typical fashion, Paps slews another quasi put-down; of course, thinking that he is funny.

Paps' comment doesn't warrant a response, but Smike offers a straightforward statement in his standard style.

"This is for the all-day band performance I told you about. Thought you might enjoy this one with people around your age in the audience."

"Doan like dressin up and doan wanna pay high dollah faw beeah" Paps responds.

He continues, "But hey, doan get me wrong, I *dig ya* man! Ya ah *groovy*! *Tie one on* faw me, *Tiny Tim*, but *tiptoe through the tulips* and stay away from that *wacky tabacky*" while laughing and holding up his coffee cup in a toasting gesture.

Smike leaves slightly disheartened, not sure when Paps will ever decide to hear him perform, but eager to get out of there.

After jumping in Mitch's car, Mitch says to Smike, "Ya look rockin'! Love it, man! You will enjoy this gig even more than the Memorial Day event. Lotsa old folks, like over four hundred show up over the course of the day and they always tip extra. Wanna warn ya though; you will smell wafts of the seventies. These seniors know how to party! It's a historic affair!"

"I've been looking forward to it!" Smike replies with jubilance.

"So, your grandfather doesn't wanna join us?" Mitch asks.

"No, and that is probably for the best anyway. He has been having a harder time getting around these days. But you will have to meet him soon. Quite a character. When you meet him, that event will be a different type of historic affair" Smike answers.

"Looking forward to it" Mitch responds, while handing Smike a case of CDs.

He adds, "Pick a favorite, unless you wanna hear me sing the whole trip there."

Flipping through his selection, Smike calls out, "I got it! Perfect choice!"

He selects Doobie Brothers and plays the first song *Listen to the Music*.

Mitch says, "Oh yeah man, stellar selection!"

They both jam the entire jaunt to the farm house.

Chapter XLVIII Hair Due

The Woodstock gig was amazing! Smike *now* confidently knows he has found his calling. He has also decided it's time for a slight change.

Smike arrives at a nearby hair salon for his appointment. Earlier in the week, he tested his hair length, which had grown a full inch since his arrival at Paps, and he could now easily reach the tip of his hair with his arm behind his mid-back, so was due for a cut. Would be at least a ten-inch pony tail.

He scheduled with a hair dresser named Ellis, a young Asian man, who cuts men's hair exclusively. Checking in with a kindly, middle-aged Asian woman, he notices that pedicures are conducted at this salon as well. That is good to note since his grandfather has overgrown, contorted toenails that is not a task he wants to tackle. Unfortunately, he doubts Paps would ever consider coming into a business that he would view as a woman's frou-frou shop. Alternative options ruminate in his mind when the hair dresser comes over and introduces himself.

Ellis asks him about the cut and style that he would like. Smike explains that he wants it short, almost shaven on the sides and longer on the top.

Ellis says, "Okay, so an edgy, hipstah type of look" and then pulls a magazine with pictures for Smike to pick out an image to confirm the desired cut.

Guided to the back for a shampoo, Smike is told Ellis' sister, Elsye, will handle washing his hair.

Elsye shows up, introduces herself, and says, "Wow, you have beautiful hair, please tell me you're just getting a trim" as she starts rinsing his hair.

Smike immediately notices her bright eyes and gentle smile. Inexplicitly, he senses a trusting nature about her and believes he can openly share his intent.

"Actually, getting a short cut, but want the long pony tail donated to *Loving Locks*" he asserts.

Complimenting him, she elatedly shares, "That's lovely! The wig makers will appreciate the quality and amount of hair you provide!"

The rest of the shampooing is completed with no discussion, with Smike's eyes closed as he enjoys this rare luxurious moment that includes a scalp massage. Elsye, on the other hand, soaks in his handsome face, kind eyes, and striking smile, which displays a unique gold tooth. Plus, she conjectures that his hair contribution to an organization, which supports individuals going through cancer treatment and hair loss, indicates he must be a sympathetic and thoughtful guy. She completes the final rinse, lightly dries his hair, and wraps the towel around his head. Elsye directs him back to Ellis for the cut and then goes to a nearby pedicure station to perform services for her next scheduled client.

As directed, Ellis ties Smike's hair into a pony tail, cuts it, and sets it to the side. During the rest of the haircut, surface-level conversation occurs between them. Nearby, Elsye listens closely. Smike has drawn her interest and attention. He seems like a decent, likeable guy, and there are so few and far in between like him. Not to mention that he is a fine-looking man.

Just Saying

Ellis finishes the cut, brushes excess hair off his shoulders, and hands Smike the mirror to conduct a three-hundred sixty-degree view of the style. He grins with appreciation for his new, polished look.

Ellis adds, "Your tight haircut doesn't match your long, unruly beard. Suggest you trim it back as a finishing touch to your overall professional look."

"That sounds great; can you trim it for me?" Smike asks.

"I don't do beards; again, need to send you back to my sister. Hopefully, she will have time between clients" he tentatively offers.

Elsye has been covertly listening the entire time and thrilled to hear this exchange but doesn't want to appear as if she has been eavesdropping, so she stays quiet.

Ellis asks her loudly, "How close are you to finishing up your pedicure Elsye? Can you do a beard trim in the next couple of minutes?"

Elsye replies, "Finished. My customer's nails just need to dry. I can do a trim in five minutes after I clean up here."

"Great!" Smike says.

Instructed to stay at the station, Elsye soon arrives with an electric shaver, comb, scissors, and other utensils. She begins the trim, but unfortunately, he can't converse while she works on his beard; however, she can continue to appreciate his attractive facial features. Once the trim is completed, she pats his face with toner and has him inspect to admire the final look in the mirror. He states that he is equally appreciative of both the beard trim and haircut. After handing Elsye a hefty tip, he gets up to tip Ellis, and then pays the station attendant for both services.

Smike asks, "So, it's my understanding that the salon can mail in the hair donation for me, right?"

While in the middle of cutting another customer's hair nearby, Ellis confirms, "Absolutely! We have your residence address in our files for the organization to send you an acknowledgement letter. The pony tail is in front of you at my work station on the counter. Elsye will mail it in."

Smike grabs the pony tail from the counter and hands it to Elsye, who takes this moment to say, "Many would say that your cut and trim are wicked pissa!"

"You know, I have heard that phrase before and still not sure what it means but guessing that you think it looks good" He responds.

"Oh yeah, ultimate compliment" she says with subtle flirtatiousness.

He thanks her and then asks if she does at-home pedicures for the elderly. She explains she hasn't done that before but would consider it. She tells him to just call the salon for a day and time, specifically asking for her. She again immediately thinks what a compassionate person he is to take care of a parent, grandparent, older family member or friend. As he exits the salon, Smike says that he will call soon.

Elsye watches him leave and through the store front window sees him outside briefly talking to a couple as they walk by with their dog. She notices him kneeling down to pet the puppy. She thinks, *Wow, he's an animal lover too! Definitely a keeper!* But she feels that she's not likely to see him soon or possibly ever again.

Holding the ponytail, which is still wet, she finds a plastic bag and slips it in, but doesn't seal it so the hair can properly dry. She then gets a large manila mailing envelope as Ellis gives her the *Loving Locks* address for mailing.

She starts writing Smike's residential address on the return portion of the envelope and asks Ellis, "How do you spell his name, is it *S-m-i-k-e* or *S-m-y-k-e* or *S-m-i-e-k*?"

"I don't know, just list the return name as 'S. Schrod.' That will get an appreciation receipt letter sent to him" Ellis impatiently instructs her.

So, she does as directed and hopes Smike will call to schedule that at-home pedicure, but doubts that will ever happen. Besides, he probably already has a partner. Good guys like that usually do.

Chapter XLIX   Big Foot

As he struts in the front door, Smike displays his new haircut, proud of the look, but prouder for donating his hair to a worthy cause.

Paps, reclined in his lounger, sees him sporting his polished appearance and shouts, "Hey, *Tom Cruise*, what ah ya dooin in my house and what have ya done with *Big Foot*?"

Smike smiles and asks, "So, you like it?"

"Looks shahp, finally!" Paps states.

"Well, now we just need to work on you Paps. Talking about *Big Foot*, gotta take care of those nasty toenails!" Smike says.

"Mind yaw own beeswax youngstah" Paps retorts.

"Just saying. You don't want to get an infection. You know, you can have a pedicurist come over and trim them for you right here in the family room. Will massage your feet as well. You will feel great!" Smike tells him.

"I doan wan stranjahs in my house. And doan wan anyone touchin my feet" he snaps.

"I don't want to touch your feet either, trust me. But a professional can do it right. You heard what the doctor said about why it's important for you to trim those nails. And since you don't own a chainsaw for handling those protruding branches out of your toes, gotta get something done" Smike argues.

"My nahbuh David, from aroun the conna, has a chainsaw. Will bahrah from him" Paps jests to deflect.

Smike surmises that Paps will not concede to having a pedicure. Not now, anyway. Will have to pitch the idea again in the near future. Timing has to be just right with him, which is rare.

He responds to Paps' joke, "I look forward to meeting your neighbor David and any help he can provide."

"Well, now that yaw presentable, an intrahduction can happen" Paps retorts.

Paps has no idea that Smike has already met David. He's fairly sure that David will keep his confidence about them meeting previously. After two months in Lowell, he has met a few acquaintances, like Mr. Schatzer, but only three of Paps' friends other than David; Mr. Kahn, and the other two, Jean and Jeanne, who were actually Grandma Nettie's companions. He wonders if Paps has any other buddies. Seems like a loner. Smike himself is a loner, but not lonely. Paps may be a loner who is lonely. The house was always bustling with visitors when Grandma Nettie was alive. His grandfather constantly complained about it. Not anything like that now. No one, other than Mr. Kahn, has stopped by to visit. Paps doesn't draw the social interactions that Grandma Nettie did. Everyone misses her. Paps must miss her too, but he rarely talks about her.

One thing Smike has noticed is that his grandfather still enjoys his garden. His plants are his friends and Paps talks to them with kindness reserved for vegetation only.

Chapter L   Growing Friendship

Mondays, Wednesdays, and Fridays continue as carpooling days. Only exceptions were a few good weather days when Smike chose to bike to work. Usually, during their drive, Rally dominates the conversation. He loves to talk about his family, his classes, and his prospective profession. Smike believes that once he graduates, Rally will be an exceptional contributor to social services in the community. Rally shared that he will need to continue for a master's degree in social work, an MSW, to be most impactful, but that is dependent on forthcoming financial factors. Smike has heard his complete plans for the future regarding his professional goals and supporting his family. Through observing all of his actions, Smike respects Rally's principled nature and the values he lives by every day. Their friendship has grown over a short period of time.

This morning, as Smike jumps into the truck, Rally just stares at him and teasingly asks, "Do I know you, sir? I'm not an Uber driver. Just here to pick up my good friend Smike."

"So, it's that drastic of a change, huh?" he queries.

"Man, ya look GQ, I mean, not that you weren't good looking before, but this is a helluva transformation my friend" Rally responds with highest compliment.

"Paps likes it too but shouldn't get used to it. I'll let my hair grow out again" Smike explains.

"What about the beard, willya let that grow out too?" Rally asks.

"Probably not right now. Will continue to trim it or shave it completely if it gets hot this summer. Come colder weather, will let it grow out a little" he replies.

"It's like you're a chameleon. Ya look very different, but somehow pull off both the grunge and professional look equally well" Rally comments.

"Well, thank you my good friend! I appreciate that!" Smike responds.

They pull up to the café and as usual see JoJo and Slim out front. Smike waves to them going in and as he comes out, hands them both their coffee and breakfast. This act has become a charitable routine. Rally notices him stop to talk a little longer with them than his previous visits.

When he returns to the truck and hands him his coffee, Rally asks, "I'm nosey, so what didja talk with 'em about today? Ya know, I have to know" urging Smike to share.

"JoJo complimented me on my hair cut and said he noticed that I came by most Mondays, Wednesdays, and Fridays, but never on Tuesday or Thursday. He has figured out my schedule. Told me that they now wait for me to show up three days a week. Said they very much appreciate my generosity."

"That's nice. The two of them seem like they're friends. Even if Slim don't talk, it's similar to the two of us. You aren't exactly silent, but I do most of the talking. Guess we just understand each other. Real friends understand each other" Rally says.

"Insightfully stated my friend!" Smike confirms.

"Of course, you can always tell me to shut up, ya know? Won't hurt my feelings" Rally says.

"I enjoy listening to you Rally. You inspire me" Smike states sincerely.

Feigning affect, Rally jokes "Now, don't make me cry man, I mean, don't wanna make my coffee salty with tears. Would spoil it!"

They both laugh and quickly arrive at the work site.

Chapter LI Band's Reaction

This Friday evening, Smike arrived a little early for their gig at Fred's Tavern. As he walks in, no one seems to recognize him. Well, not initially anyway.

Mitch is the first to notice and runs over exclaiming, "Are you a shedder? Lost your mane, huh?"

"It was time, that's all" Smike explains, limiting the reasoning behind the change.

Violet comes up to them and asks, "Smike, is that you? Wondered what you looked like under all that hair" she kidded.

Denny, on the other hand, doesn't say anything and acts like there's nothing different worth noting.

Violet asks, "What's this transformation about? Did the shredding company require a haircut?"

"No, personal choice. Will let it grow out again" he explains.

"Well, it looks good! Although, now I won't get the chance to French braid your hair" Violet says jokingly.

"Bottom line is my hair cut will have no impact on playing the harmonica, keyboards or accordion" Smike retorts.

In a direct but casual tone, Mitch poses, "More importantly, will the ladies like it better?"

Violet states, "Clearly, he already has a female fan following, you know that! He could be bald and covered in warts and the ladies would still love him."

Mitch argues, "Well don't know about the warts, that's taking it a little too far regarding the love of his fanship."

Violet explains, "Nah, not taking it too far. Fred says the female clientele attendance has increased exponentially, by a rate never seen before in such a short time. He thinks the ladies like Smike, and he's happy about it, because with more ladies showing up, guys follow, and of course, sales increase."

Smike just doesn't see what Violet and Mitch infer regarding his appeal with the female fans and laughs off their comments.

After another successful performance that evening, the band briefly meets to confirm rehearsal on Sunday. They have several major gigs coming up, including an outdoor Fourth of July session at the community park and the following Saturday a wedding gig; they need to run-through their song list and practice some newer, recently added songs.

Chapter LII Pure Coincidence

Restless and still a little bored, even after adding the job of driving a shredding truck a few days a week, Smike finds himself running more frequently than normal. Other than Tuesday and Thursday mornings, he adds afternoon runs on his days off from driving and most Saturdays as well. Being cooped up with Paps, even for a short period of time during the day, is also an influencing factor on his choice to increase how often he runs. These runs get him out of the house and serve as a great de-stressor. Constantly looking for new paths, he checks out the park where the band will conduct their Fourth of July session. Luckily, it is fairly nearby with several different routes of running and bike trails, so quite a serendipitous find. His runs also generate budding song lyrics as his meditative state rouses reflections and memories of Louisa. This new running path in the park, plush with soothing sights of many different types of trees, a charming pond, and local wildlife, easily spawn fond reminiscences of his time with her since they often walked in local parks.

Fully enthralled in his thoughts, until unexpectedly interrupted when he spots a young Asian girl, with a large Bloodhound pulling her, waving like she knows him. He slows down and removes his ear buds.

"Hey, I know you! Smike, right?" she claims.

Smike looks closely and remembers her from his hair cut appointment over a week earlier.

"Yes, and you're Ellie? Right?" he responds.

"It's Elsye, but you were close. Pretty good memory" she clarifies, then adds "a coincidence to run into you."

"And who is this old boy dragging you around the park?" Smike asks.

"This is Beauregard. Actually, Colonel Beauregard demoted from General after an egregious infraction for chewing up my favorite pair of shoes" she complains.

Smike laughs, bends over to pet his head, and says, "Well, although a naughty boy, your Beauregard is a handsome specimen!"

Elsye corrects him, "He's not mine. I wish! I dog walk and dog babysit for family and friends. My apartment doesn't allow pets. This is how I get my 'pet fix' since I can't have a dog of my own right now."

"I get that. Miss having a pet myself. Love dogs and cats equally. They provide comfort and accept you unconditionally" he shares with sincerity.

Elsye's previous perception of Smike being a kind individual is reinforced from this chance meeting and exchange. Surprisingly struck mute, kind of stymied, she's not sure what to say. Wants to say *I would comfort and provide you unconditional acceptance.* But of course, that would be totally and boldly inappropriate; definitely not her style.

She opts for a somewhat modified and abbreviated response, "Animals sense caring people and they attach themselves" she says, and then goes silent.

While putting his ear buds back in, Smike says, "Well it was great seeing you Elsye, and nice to meet Beauregard, your *borrowed* pet" as he waves and returns to his run.

Elsye lamely responds, "Yeah, great seeing you too!" and waves as he runs off.

Damn, she felt like she missed an opportunity to engage in lengthier conversation with him. She should have asked about the home pedicure he inquired about at the salon, but that would have just brought business into the brief discussion. Hopefully, she will see him again on the trail. She walks it two to three times a week.

As Smike returns to his run, he suddenly thinks that he should have asked Elsye about the home pedicure and inform her that he's working on getting his grandfather to agree to having it done. But it wouldn't have done much good right now anyway since Paps is adamant about not having anyone touch his feet.

Chapter LIII Party Invitation

During their next drive to work that Monday, Rally invites Smike to his son's eleventh birthday party to be held at a roller-skating rink at a nearby location the following Sunday. He tells Smike that this will be a chance for him to meet his family and see some of their co-workers in a different light as they often cut up with one another when together in an informal setting. Also, his mother-in-law, Abuelita Maria, would be making her famous tres leches that everyone loved! Rally tells Smike, he knows that he doesn't eat a lot of sweets, but he has to try at least one bite of this infamously delicious cake.

Rally adds, "Everyone skates. Gotta, cause I'll be videotaping the event to capture some hilarious moments for a montage that I create each year played at the company Christmas party. You will not believe how Vicki can get around the rink. Impressive, really."

Smike tells him that he would be honored to attend and even though he hasn't skated in years, he would strap on a pair and take a spin around the rink. He then asks what his son Pablo is into, so he can get him an appropriate gift that he would like and enjoy.

Rally responds, "Pablo is interested in many things and would appreciate anything you give him; it's his mother Marciella who has conditions—nothing large, since we don't have much space in our apartment."

Smike responds, "Got it. Will get him something that can fit in his pocket, how about that?"

"Great man, I appreciate it!"

Just Saying

Smike has already figured out what he will get Pablo. He received his first harmonica at age ten and even though he hadn't met Pablo yet, he thinks this would be a solid gift for him, even if he doesn't like music. Surprisingly, since arriving in Lowell, he hadn't checked out any local music stores, so this will be something fun to do this week.

Chapter LIV Personal Passions

Smike had plans for Tuesday. After his morning run, he would work on the garden. Paps said there was some weeding down low near the stems that needed to be done, which was too difficult for him to reach. So, Smike fully anticipated tending to that task. Then, in the afternoon, he meant to check out a nearby music store; which, for him, was like a kid going to a candy store. A real treat for him with a built-in purpose to buy a harmonica for Pablo.

During breakfast, Smike informs his grandfather of his schedule for the day.

Elated about his garden, Paps replies, "Wait til ya see the t'maydahs this mawnin! Theyah growin like crazy. Peppah plants are bloomin nicely as well!"

Smike had been so busy lately; he hadn't done much with the backyard patch. He sensed that Paps' passion for his plants is equivalent to his own love of music. It was nice to see him cheerful about something. And, as rarely as his grandfather's happiness occurred and then rapidly dissipated, Smike wanted to support this fleeting incidence of pleasure. He also enjoyed watching Paps' momentary satisfaction and delight with his prized garden.

After breakfast, they exited the back door so that Paps could show off and highlight new plant growth.

Bragging, Paps shares "Will have moah vejtibles than we can eat this summah; so, wanna give sum to naybuhs, friends at chawch, and yaw friends too, Michael."

Just Saying

With enthusiasm, Smike replies, "That's great Paps. Granny Mabel will love it! She's Denny's grandmother and houses our Sunday band practices. Always makes us a little something to snack on, so now I'll give something back. And Rally loves anything that's free!"

Paps then adds, "Michael, I'm gonna invite David, my naybuh, ovah this ahftanoon. Need faw ya to pick sum vejtibles and fill this containah faw him. Would be nice if ya wuhr heeah to finally meet him."

Smike responds, "I won't be gone long this afternoon. Just going to the music store for a bit."

"Good! Ya know, haven't seen David in a while. Could always count on him if I evah needed somethin. His muhthah played cahd games with yaw grandmuhthah and when he dropped hah off, he would stick round and we'd tok. He's a decent man. Drove Nettie to the hospital when she got sick" Paps shares this unexpected note.

"I didn't know that" Smike replies somberly.

Paps sadly confesses, "Yeah, I was too upset to drive. When I stayed with yaw grandmuhthah in the hospital, he took care of the house until yaw fahthah could fly home. A good naybuh, ya know?"

"Sounds like it" Smike says, while quietly gaining additional appreciation for the man who, unsolicited, braced a ladder for him while he was fixing the upstairs window.

More light-heartedly, Paps adds, "And the guy makes the best pickles from the cucumbahs I give him. He'll bring me jahs of 'em."

Smike replies, "I look forward to meeting him."

As their conversation ends, Paps goes inside and Smike begins picking weeds to make his grandfather proud. He wants the garden to look well-tended. And, as always, the gardening work relaxes him.

After he finishes weeding, making sure to pick the best vegetables for David, he cleans up, and drives to the music retailer. Totally in his element upon entering the store, his whole body responds like being zapped with electric energy. He could stay for hours but picks out a harmonica and leaves rather quickly; vowing to return soon for a longer visit. He needs to arrive home in time to *meet* David, although Paps doesn't know that they met before.

Chapter LV Not the First Meeting

David and Paps are sitting in the family room drinking beer when Smike returns. David gets up and introduces himself like they never met before. Funny, this unspoken secret between them. Paps seems pleased that the two of them 'finally' meet and appears to have real respect for David.

Showing off the large basket over flowing with vegetables, David offers them both a genuine compliment.

"Love your vegetables! You grow the juiciest tomatoes and my wife and boys love 'em!"

Paps interjects to inform Smike, "David has three boys. Awl wawk hawses like theyah fahthah!"

Smike swiftly realizes why Paps likes David. He views him as a hard worker. Probably the number one characteristic his grandfather values in others. Smike enjoys seeing Paps appreciative of someone like he appears to be of David. Something new he's learned about his grandfather, that he actually *likes* someone. That is, other than Mr. Kahn.

Smike asks, "So what do you do David?"

"Home construction. Sometimes sixty-hour weeks. My boys work part-time when not in school. Like in the summer and over weekends" David responds.

Paps interrupts, "Yeah, and he has evahy tool evah made, I'm tellin ya! Need a special socket, he's got it."

With intentional sarcasm, Smike asks, "Own a chainsaw?"

"Yeah, I do. Why, need some trees trimmed?" David asks.

"Nah, just Paps' toenails!" Smike teases.

Paps grunts, "Not funny, smahtass!"

David looks at both of them, not really sure about the family side joke, but chuckles along with Smike anyway.

Chapter LVI Habit-Forming, Habits Forming

After two months with Paps, Smike acquired two jobs that keeps him fairly busy, established a running routine, familiarized himself with the lay of the land in Lowell, carved out specific time to write music, regularly nurtured his spirit in the garden to relax and wind down, and resourcefully addressed Paps' ongoing needs and requests. He has formed some productive and satisfying habits.

Similar to what he noticed about Paps' positive demeanor demonstrated earlier this week, he too is happier. Most importantly, his music writing flow rolls more effortlessly than expected, spurring joy in his soul and contentment in his heart. Inspiration seems to be all around him; especially through the intriguing people he interacts with and meets. His world has expanded with varied, stimulating activities and engagement with a diversity of individuals. Life is different . . . and good. Actually, very good!

Friday's band session at Fred's Tavern felt especially rewarding this week. The crowd was huge and multiple requests were made for several of Smike's impression songs and harmonica solos. He finds his confidence growing as a musician and performer. Never knew before about the reciprocity of energy exchanged with audience members while playing his music. It's a fulfilling feeling, emotionally powerful, addictive, and before these new, recent events playing music to others, totally unimagined in his mind of limited experiences. His world is growing and for the first time, he's welcoming it.

He thinks of Louisa. He thanks Louisa. She envisioned this life for him. He just never knew.

Chapter LVII   Lovely Long Day

The band met at Granny Mabel's garage for practice early Sunday morning. Per Paps' suggestion, Smike brings a basket of fresh vegetables from their garden, including loose leaf lettuce. After he arrives, he hands the overflowing cornucopia to her.

Very grateful, she tells him, "Why, you are so thoughtful Smike! This is perfect for the salad I'm making for lunch today. Thank you."

Smike responds, "Sorry that I won't be able to stay for lunch but have to leave a little early for a friend's party."

Granny Mabel radiates an understanding smile.

As they prepare to practice, everyone gabs in shared pleasure about last Friday's session and how their band following seems to be growing. They all compliment Smike about his contributions and express sincere gratitude for how he seems to bring out the best in each of them and has expanded their repertoire of songs. Smike humbly thanks them but doubts he has had that much of an impact. He's just thrilled to be part of this dynamic band.

Before they begin their practice session, Violet explains that many of the songs played for the Memorial Day bash at the VFW can be recycled for their outdoor Fourth of July session, so they don't have to spend much time practicing those songs.

The following Saturday wedding gig, though, requires a handful of requests that are new to the band. They will spend most of their practice session on these new songs. She notes that the bride and groom are in their late fifties, so this nuptial is like a second time around for both of them.

Violet shares, "The one song on the list that I love the most is *At Last*. Musically easy for all of you to pick up even though we never played it before."

Mitch replies, "Oh yeah, Violet, you will wail that one!"

Smike adds, "I used to listen to Etta James' version over and over again. And loved her rendering of *I'd Rather Go Blind*, too. Timeless! She absolutely defined soul music."

Denny says, "Yeah, the epitome of soul! And, another one of Granny Mabel's favorite songs, too!"

"Not to mention a great song for slow dancing. This will be the one the couple dances to. Okay, so have some music sheets for all of you. Let's play!" Violet says as she directs them to get started.

Two other new songs added to their playlist include *Truly Madly Deeply* that Violet and Mitch will perform as a duet and *Everything I Do, I Do It For You* will be sung by Denny. Smike thinks this will be the band's most romantic play of songs, several of which are tear-jerkers. They end their practice session, emotionally inflated and elated, Smike personally acknowledges being a soft-touch for sappy songs. Extending his regrets for not sharing lunch with them, he leaves early to make Pablo's birthday party.

Smike arrives at the rink with little trouble finding it. Walking inside, he suddenly swells with pleasant memories of when he skated as a kid; always had fun, enjoyed being with the few close friends he had doing silly stuff, and of course, skating to music. Immediately, he spots Rally across the rink, with a huge grin on his face while waving his arms to get Smike's attention to come over. He easily spots a large crowd of children, lots of mothers, several of his work mates, and Rally's wife, son, and mother-in-law all hanging around a large birthday banner, with streamers, balloons, and food spread across a table. Smike heads over. Once there, Rally straightaway introduces him to his wife Marciella, a lovely woman with a calmly confident demeanor. She thanks him for coming as he hands her the packaged gift. Rally then introduces him to his mother-in-law who smiles and gives him an unexpected introductory hug and kiss on the cheek.

Pablo, a very outgoing young man, doesn't wait for his father to introduce them.

He comes right up to him and says, "It is very nice to meet you Mr. Smike. My dad talks about you all the time and says that you are super smart."

Smike replies, "Well, not sure if I am super smart, but very confident that you are! Your dad tells me that you make the honor roll every semester and you love math and history."

"Yep, love number games and reading about people from the past. My dad says I'm a geek, but not really; otherwise, I wouldn't have so many friends here, right?" Pablo claims with self-assurance.

Smike affirmatively responds, "That sounds right Pablo" and then adds, "I see that you are talkative and sociable like your dad, too, huh?"

"Yeah, but I got my smarts from my mom and Abuelita. Did you know that I speak two languages?"

He then asks Smike, "¿Hablas español?"

Smike replies, "Si, hablo un poquito español, pero es muy mal."

Pablo laughs and says, "Not bad, I can understand you."

Suddenly, Pablo's friends urge him to join them as they're getting their skates.

He says, "Excuse me Mr. Smike; I am going to skate with my friends now. Hope you can stay for cake."

"Of course, Pablo, so nice to meet you."

This kid's genuine pleasantness warms his heart. He definitely takes after Rally in many ways and Smike clearly understands Rally's pride in his mature-mannered, friendly, and bright son.

Looking around, Smike notices that many of his work mates showed up and he compliments Rally about the turnout.

Rally notes, "Yeah, the only one who couldn't make it is Shannon. One of her kids is sick."

Surprised, Smike responds, "I didn't even know she had any kids."

"Yeah, *three* of them!" Rally clarifies while holding up three fingers, and then adds "all under six years old, too! Has her hands full and probably why she looks so gloomy all the time."

Just Saying

Somewhat stunned to hear that, Smike makes a mental note about this information.

Rally soon calls everyone over to sing *Happy Birthday* so Pablo can start unwrapping presents. He smiles broadly as he opens the present from Smike and sees it's a harmonica. Pablo immediately starts blowing in it to play sounds. Smike tells him that free music lessons come with the present. The entire family shares their appreciation.

Unwrapping of presents continues, when Smike quietly tells Rally that he will skate for a few laps to build up an appetite for the tres leche birthday cake. He goes to the main skating center, rents a pair of skates, sits down on a bench to put them on, and then heads to the rink to get in a few laps. It has been a while since he last skated and he's hoping that he doesn't make a fool of himself.

Chapter LVIII   Brand New Key

After he starts to skate, the song *Brand New Key* by Melanie comes on. It's a fun, uplifting tune that allows Smike to enjoy the moment. He makes about one lap when, peripherally, he notices someone of short stature skate up beside him, uninvitedly grab his hand, and begin to synchronously skate with him. It's Elsye.

"I promise, I'm not stalking you!" she says while lightly laughing.

Startled, he looks and realizes he knows her.

Smiling while continuing to hold her hand, he says, "Guess you can tell I need assistance to get around the rink. I haven't done this in years. Feel free to stalk me if you promise not to laugh when I fall on my ass!"

"Looks like you are doing just fine! Glad to see someone closer to my age acting goofy" she replies.

They continue skating until a new song comes on, *How Do You Mend a Broken Heart*, by the Bee Gees, at which time they skate to the bench area. Both sitting down, they begin removing their skates while enjoying good-humored conversation.

Unexpectedly, Smike asks, "Would you like to grab a cup of coffee or tea? My treat. I know a cool place called *More Please Café*."

Elsye, thrilled with his invite, agrees to meet at the café. She knows the place and will meet him there in a few minutes. They exchange phone numbers and Elsye leaves. Smike grabs the skates, returns them, and scouts the rink for Rally, to extend his farewell.

He spots Rally at the birthday table engulfing a huge bite of cake.

Rally sees Smike coming toward him and with a full mouth, mumbles, "Ya gotta try this cake man, it's the bomb!"

"Absolutely! Need to get it to go though, if that's alright with you!" Smike replies.

"Sure, but what's the hurry?" Rally asks.

"No hurry, just going to grab some tea with a nice young lady" Smike says.

"Ya dawg, go for it!" Rally teases.

"It's not like that. She's a lovely person who I enjoy talking to" Smike explains.

"Just glad ya could make the party man! Be sure to say your good-byes to everyone. Otherwise, they'll wonder where ya went. Oh, and by the way, don't think that you weren't caught on film. Marciella videotaped your skating proficiency. Not too shabby my friend" Rally snickers.

Abuelita Maria prepares a plate of the tres leche for Smike as he says his good byes. He thanks her and then leaves.

Marciella whispers to Rally, "I am not sure, but I believe that the young lady he's meeting for tea is Ms. Kim."

"What, ya mean Pablo's teacher?" Rally asks in astonishment.

"Yes, that's who he was skating with but they seemed to know each other" she responds.

"Interesting!" he says with a curious tone.

Marciella censures him, "Now don't go interfering or asking him questions about her. Just mind your own business. As a friend, he will talk about her when he feels like it."

She then cautions him by adding, "I really mean it Rally!"

"Okay, my lips are sealed. My mouth glued shut on the topic" he professes while motioning a twist with his fingers around his pursed lips.

"Better be!" she warns.

Chapter LIX Coffee, Tea, Or Something Else?

Elsye is already at the café by the time Smike arrives. While entering, he spots Slim sitting in his spot and waves to him. It's later in the day, so JoJo isn't around.

Once inside, he goes over to Elsye and asks, "So what would you like to drink?"

"Would love a Chai tea; that is my favorite drink here" she shares.

"Me too! They make a good one, huh?" he responds.

"I mean, I love a good coffee, but at this time of the day, tea is better. Very soothing" she clarifies.

Smiling, Smike nods and goes to the counter to make the order. Returning with their drinks, they begin light discussion. Smike doesn't remember the last time he had an interesting conversation with a woman. It was refreshing. And, she's really smart! Very articulate. She works in a salon and from their verbal exchanges, seems capable of doing more than pedicures. However, he doesn't judge her. That surely isn't his place. And he, more than many others, knows what it means to follow your own path of fulfillment. He thinks *judgment of others should never come into play regarding individual personal and professional decisions.*

After a two-hour conversation, they discover several things they share in common: a fondness for animals, dedication to family and friends, a love of music (Elsye plays the flute), appreciation for the *Far Side* cartoon (both wish Gary Larson would come out of retirement), and enjoyment of quirky films. The quirky film thing was not that they really *like* oddball B-rated or C-rated films, they just enjoy making fun of them while watching by adding commentaries, inserting new lines in the dialogue that would make the movies funnier, and just being creatively engaged in enhancing subpar movies. Actually, the weaker the film, the greater the opportunity to add seemingly unrelated, morbid, silly, and crude lines.

"You know, I just can't help myself when I see a funny movie or picture. Almost always have to add comments or a line. And, will make a picture or an illustration into a meme" Elsye shares.

Suddenly animated, Smike endorses her comment by sharing a short personal vignette.

"Me too! My family had a contest a few years back. My grandfather sent everyone a picture of him sitting in a lawn chair in his back yard, in front of the shed, with a huge cabbage from his garden plopped on his lap. No one quite understood why he sent this picture to us. Guess he was proud of what was grown in his garden. Anyway, my aunt asked everyone to send her their ideas for a funny caption. Through a family vote, the best caption would be printed under the scanned picture onto T-shirts as a Christmas present from her. Everyone's responses were hilarious. Although my suggestion did not make the final cut—*Leaf through this*, my aunt and sister had the best lines. My aunt's line was —*You think this cabbage is huge, you should see my zucchini!* My youngest sister won though, with the line—*It took one working hoe to get that head up!*"

Elsye laughs loudly and says, "That is SO hilarious! Love your family's sense of humor!"

Just Saying

"Yeah, well, we were kind of making fun of Paps, as he is the bane of our family's existence, so he never saw the T-shirt. But really, it was all done affectionately. Sort of like comic relief too though. He is a tough old codger" Smike confesses.

Solid connection made; Elsye thinks this is a great moment to suggest another rendezvous.

"I have an idea. Let's get together and watch *Cabin Boy*. I have an old copy we can watch at my apartment. You bring dinner and I'll supply the wine" she suggests.

"Sounds great! Super pick of a movie. Ripe for blasting stream of consciousness reactions and one-liners. Generally, I am free Sunday through Thursday evenings; however, this week I have a Fourth of July band performance on Wednesday at the park, a gig on Friday at a local bar, and one this coming Saturday afternoon" he shares.

"Let's go for this Thursday around six. Will text you my address" she responds, and then adds, "Would love to see you play sometime, too."

"Of course, will share our performance schedule; I could use a fan in the audience" he jokes and then asks, "And, what do you want for dinner?"

"Surprise me" she responds with a smile.

They hug good bye and leave the café. Elsye thinks what an unexpected and delightful afternoon and early evening. Smike considers the same thoughts.

Chapter LX Lips Sealed, Sort of

Monday morning, Rally picks Smike up for work and finds himself chomping at the bit to ask about the woman he left the party with to spend some time. He promised his wife to keep his mouth shut. Thought he might be able to let Smike speak more freely and naturally through open-ended questions related to his life in general. He decides to wait until after they picked up coffee to ask questions.

Rally watches Smike give JoJo and Slim their coffee and pastries, speak with them for a few minutes, and head back to the truck.

Once inside and seated in the truck, he asks him, "So, still haven't met your Paps. What are some things you do with him?"

"Goodness, Paps? Hmmm, well his garden is his major focus right now. It's progressing well, so he's happy about that. I help out. Actually, I love gardening as well" Smike replies, a little surprised as Rally doesn't often ask him many questions about himself; however, he knows Rally is a curious, nosey kind of guy.

"See? I didn't know that about you. Should ask you more questions about yourself. I mean, you know everything about me cause I can't keep my mouth shut. I know little about you. Wanna learn more" Rally argues.

"Actually, you have more in common with my grandfather than I do. He served in the Marine Corps during Vietnam" Smike shares.

"Did he see any action?" Rally prods.

"Yeah, pretty sure, but he doesn't talk about it. And I am not encouraged to ask, so I don't" Smike replies, and then adds, "Did you see any action Rally?"

"Fortunately, no! Grateful for that. Had buddies who did though and it was rough. Psychologically, emotionally, and mentally tortured, not to mention those that ended up with physical injuries. To tell ya the truth, don't know if I could ever pull a trigger" Rally replies and then quickly catches himself to divert back to asking Smike questions.

"Does Paps like your music?" Rally pointedly asks.

"He has never really heard me play. I mean, not as an adult" Smike replies.

"What? Really? How come? I mean, doesn't he hear you play at home? I mean, ya gotta practice, right?" Rally probes.

"Well, first, I only play upstairs and he rarely comes up there because of his bad knee. Secondly, he is hard of hearing and mostly watches TV with the sound blaring, so he can't hear me practice" Smike shares.

"Do ya offer to play for him? Just wondering" Rally continues.

"Have invited him to several gigs, but he just isn't interested" Smike glumly shares.

"Ya know what? I would like to come to one of your shows with Marciella" Rally suggests, as he feels a little sad that his friend doesn't seem supported regarding his musical endeavors.

"Well, we have a Wednesday evening Fourth of July performance at the park. It's a free event, sponsored by local vendors. Bet your whole family will enjoy it. Also, every Friday evening, Fred's Tavern, from eight to ten-thirty. We also have a daytime gig this coming Saturday as well, but it's for a wedding reception. You can't crash that one, my friend!" Smike laughs.

"Wednesday evening at the park sounds great; however, I will be studying for one of my summer class finals. In fact, won't be at work at all that day. Meant to tell ya, that you will need to drive yourself or ride your bike. However, pretty sure Marciella can take Pablo and Abuelita to the park and that will leave the apartment quiet for my studying. Will tell her about it. The bar gig sounds good too but can't make this Friday as we have something already planned, maybe another Friday would work. Marciella will love it; she likes to dance after a few drinks! And, we haven't been out to a bar in quite a while. Also, just wondering . . . have any groupies? I mean, ladies love musicians, right?" after this elongated reply, Rally slips in a calculated question at the end in anticipation of a meaty response.

"No groupies. Not that kind of band and I haven't been part of the band long enough to draw a following. There is a neighborhood fan club for the band itself though" he modestly responds.

They arrive at the work site without Rally finding out specific information he was aiming for; however, he discovered quite a lot about Smike that he didn't know prior to this discussion. And, he kept his word to his wife. Didn't ask Smike anything about his new female friend. However, he senses that more personal conversations will occur during their carpooling jaunts. The door has been opened and Smike appears receptive to providing personal responses.

Chapter LXI Fourth of July

Again, Smike offers Paps an invitation to see him perform at the Fourth of July bash. And again, Paps declines. His argument this time is the distance having to walk to the park's outdoor venue, although he walks nearly every afternoon to the convenience store. Paps also complains that he would get home too late. Exhausted and disheartened from another one of Paps' recurrent rejections, Smike doesn't push it; just lets the *old napping dog lie.*

At the event, Smike finds the outdoor venue less intimate and much more intimidating than the other settings in which the band previously performed; however, the opportunity to expand performance settings provides needed experiences to add to his portfolio. Also, from Smike's perspective, another professional benefit involves watching several bands play before and after their session as well as meeting other local musicians. The event parallels what he imagines would happen when he moves to Austin in that well-established music scene. Unexpectedly, numerous musicians from other bands came up to him after the performance to compliment his skills. He felt validated by and welcomed into this growing music world.

The highlight of the evening though was when he spotted Marciella, Pablo, and Abuelita push their way to the front of the crowd just before *Knead Naked* began their session. He saw Pablo grinning and waving his arms like crazy to get Smike's attention. He waved back at them thinking that this is the first time that people he knows have actually come to see him perform. Warmed his heart. To cap it all off, the fireworks of the evening captured his explosion of emotions for the day! Brilliant and bright!

Chapter LXII   Alone Together

Paps sat in his lounger, TV turned off, just sipping a beer. It's early in the evening and he didn't care to partake in watching any national holiday festivities. He's tired from garden work all day, missed his afternoon nap, and just wants to rest. After the sun sets, he looks out the bay window and views the skyline filled with stars as he falls into a profound slumber.

Kahn and Sid move deeper into the bush to seek shelter. They travel while there is still daylight, until they find an area suitable for creating coverage and serving as a safe space for sleeping the night. Both exhausted and in pain from their wounds, they hunker down to catch a few hours of sleep. Sid takes the first watch while Kahn drowses. He worries how they will get out of this mess; especially, since both are incapacitated, still losing blood, and becoming weaker with each passing hour. He thinks of Nettie and his newborn child he may never see and begins to softly weep. Sid curses his fate. The war is bullshit. Being in this situation is bullshit. The world is fucked up and in the big scheme of things; he and his comrades are inconsequential, collateral damage. Just not right. However, alone but together, he and Kahn are still alive and at least have a nominal shot at returning to camp or being rescued by others in his platoon. As his thoughts shift from an ominous state to a more hopeful outcome, he glimpses through the trees at a small patch of sky which reveals countless brilliant stars. Everyone in Vietnam, the Viet Cong, villagers, and U.S. soldiers, can view this same wondrous scene of exquisite beauty from their own perspective. In this small corner of the world, does the sky look the same to everyone? Is it appreciated by all? Sid wonders, why do mere humans take the marvels of life for granted? Why are lives so easily disregarded and tossed aside as negligible pawns in this stupid, power play of an unexplainable and devastating war? As he gazes up at the sky, he consciously notes to never take life for granted and gains some comfort at how the beauty of the interstellar sight remains unmarred by the ugliness of the world in which he finds himself. He wonders for a while, staying vigilant for any movement around them. After several hours, no longer able to keep his eyes open, he wakes Kahn for his stint at keeping watch. Sid then quickly falls into a deep sleep. Kahn stays awake for a short period of time before his injury causes him to pass out.

Loud fireworks in the neighborhood wake Paps from his dream state of absurd contradictions: nature's splendor overshadowed within man's atrocities. Viewing the colorful lights in the dark sky through his bay window, he can't help thinking how these celebratory fireworks represent canons and shells bursting in the air; replicating and representing images of war's destruction. The world is a paradox that angers and pains him.

Chapter LXIII   Roosevelt

Smike shows up Thursday evening with chicken tacos, chips, and homemade salsa (from tomatoes, onions, and peppers grown in Paps' garden). A slobbering Basset Hound, pushing up against Elsye, greets him at the door.

"Who's this?" Smikes asks looking down at the hound clambering his leg.

"This is Roosevelt. Watching him for a couple hours this evening. Don't tell my landlord" Elsye pretentiously pleads.

She then adds, "Just kidding, this is my landlord's dog."

"So, the first hound was named after a military officer and this one is named after a President?" Smike surmises.

"Actually, no, named after Eleanor" grabbing her jowls and pulling them down, making a sad face, Elsye says, "Get it?"

"Ha ha, yeah, that's funny!" he responds to her humor, hands her the bags of food, and starts petting Roosevelt.

They both head over to the couch where Elsye has two glasses and a bottle of red wine on the end table. Plates, utensils, and napkins are set to the side. She pours the wine and he places tacos and chips on plates. They toast to new friendships and she starts the movie. The commentary between them begins immediately, like kindred spirits razzing silly remarks and creative one-liners throughout the entire show. It's a very satisfying, comfortable tryst filled with laughter.

Just Saying

After the movie, they decide to get together again soon. Smike invites her to his gig coming up, but she can't make the Friday night session because she doggy sits Beauregard almost every Friday evening, so probably won't be able to catch any of his performances at the Tavern. As an alternative, Smike offers her to come to his place this coming Saturday evening after his wedding gig, and he will play some of his music for her.

She loves this idea and quickly accepts the offer, then adds, "So, I'll get to meet your grandfather. Have visions in my head of what he's like from your description and stories you have told me."

"What I've shared so far just doesn't fully do justice to the simple complexity or perhaps complex simplicity of his character" Smike joshes.

"So, you're saying, he's an oxymoron?" she quips with a question.

"Brilliant! Yes Elsye, he is, with an emphasis on the moron part. Just be warned, meeting him may scar you for life!" Smike teasingly responds as they hug before he leaves her apartment.

Chapter LXIV   Yin and Yang

The week was filled with highly successful and rewarding band performances that included the Fourth celebration in the middle of the week and then a double-header weekend performing both Friday and Saturday. Friday evening, the band rocked at Fred's Tavern. With a discernibly growing crowd, Fred brought in some extra tables and chairs stationed outside the bar and even ran additional speakers outside as well. The wedding gig on Saturday went exceptionally well; earning the highest tip amount from this session than any others previously.

After the wedding performance, Smike radiated an emotional high when he picked Elsye up at her apartment early in the evening. He enthusiastically tells her all about the week's band events as they drive to Paps' house. He proudly shares with her how his friend Rally couldn't make the Fourth event, but his family showed up and cheered him on. Rally told him on their drive to work Friday morning how much his family loved the music and now he can't wait to hear him play. Because Elsye hasn't known Smike that long, she refrains from telling him that she knows the family as Pablo's teacher. She just doesn't want him learning about her through a secondhand source; so, she quietly listens and discloses nothing about already knowing Rally on a professional level. Smike adds how huge the Friday crowd was at Fred's and how the band's wedding performance was their best ever. At this point, Elsye responds with eagerness to hear him play a few songs for her.

As Smike and Elsye enter, they notice Paps sitting in his lounge chair, drinking a beer, and watching a vintage TV game show. Fortunately, this particular evening, he is fully clothed.

Just Saying

Smike greets his grandfather with a brief *hello* and notices him click his remote to silent, which he never does.

Curiously, eyeing Elsye, Paps mockingly questions "So, who do we have *heeah*?"

Smike supplies an introduction.

"This is my friend Elsye. Elsye, this is my grandfather."

Paps loudly responds directly to Elsye, "Well, 'Elsye' doan sound like a Vietnamese name."

Smike looks toward Elsye with an expression like *I warned you about him and now you are his newest target and victim of verbal assaults and insults.*

But she just stares straight ahead at Paps and with a quick, no-nonsense quip replies, "Perhaps that's because I'm American."

Paps lightly snickers and returns with a second volley, "Well, ya know what I mean." (Which of course she did, she was quietly thinking he was a racist bastard.)

After a brief pause, Paps knits his brow as if in deep thought and adds, "And Elsye is the name of a cow. Now, who would name theyah daughtah ahfta a cow?"

Smike barely holds back from audibly expressing his loathing frustration of Paps' socially inept interactions just long enough for Elsye to go toe-to-toe with the old junk yard dog by employing her subtle but serious and well-honed repartee ability.

In a tacitly false respectful manner, Elsye asks, "So, how would you like for me to address you? As Mr. Schrod, Sidney, Sid, Paps, or perhaps something else?"

Paps cynically queries, "Well, what's *yaw prahfahence* in how ya would like to address me, *Elsye*?"

In a deadpan fashion, Elsye replies, "Um, let's see . . . how about, *asshole*?"

Pleasingly surprised by Elsye's comeback, Smike just gleams. He should have known better. Never should have underestimated that Elsye could not hold her own, even with this cantankerous old coot. Caught off guard, Paps didn't expect an equally sardonic soul to cut him down to size.

Paps howls and slaps his knee! "I've been called wawse!"

Smike thinks, *Yeah, even by some of your own family members.*

Then, after barely acknowledging Elsye's response, he turns to Smike and says with emphasis, "I *like* hah!"

Elsye just won Paps' favor by giving him the tit-for-tat exchange he tries to goad from others, most often resulting in disappointing verbal swaps below his standard of sarcasm. Paps applies this bantering test to most new individuals he meets. Up to this point, Smike had *never* seen *anyone* give it to Paps in equally measured verbal tradeoffs. She clearly passed his test.

Smike nods and softly confirms, "I like her too."

Out of some sense of obligation, he then dismissively shares his agenda.

Just Saying

"We're going upstairs Paps. You can return to enjoying your show."

Paps jumps at the chance to throw another zinger.

"This is a fahst! Yah've *nevah* brought a friend ovah befoah!"

Sporting a wide Cheshire grin, he then continues with a final derisive and juvenile jab, "Wondah what this *means*?"

Not responding and slightly embarrassed, Smike turns away and gently guides Elsye up the stairs. Once in his room, he floods Elsye with praise for how she handled the uncomfortable situation by putting Paps in his rightful place.

In response, Elsye proceeds to lecture him with her insight.

"Smike, you just don't get it. Your grandfather . . ."

Cut short, Smike interjects and clarifies with a laugh, "You mean asshole?"

Elsye continues, "Yeah, asshole, right! Well, his disposition is combative, pure and simple. Brandishing bravado is his shtick *and* he's gotten away with inappropriate behavior for a long time, so his whole routine *is* routine. I'm guessing that you always defer to his dominance and your path of least resistance persona only fortifies his authority over you."

Smike knew that he regularly backed away from confrontations with Paps, but only because of his sense of respect for him being his grandfather, and also how he was brought up to honor elders. However, there *were* a handful of instances when he stood his ground where Paps would grudgingly concede. In retrospect, those were most likely instances of little importance to his grandfather.

Before Smike could supply a partial argument based on these points, Elsye punches her point.

"Together, you and Paps are like oil and water, light and dark, day and night, piss and vinegar, fire and ice . . . you are the Yin to his Yang, don't you see? His harassing comments to anyone are just invitations to joust. I don't even think his intentions are mean either. He just thinks that he's funny. Anyway, sling back raw comments just like he does and maybe, sometimes, not only will he back down, he may appreciate your direct, honest retorts and respect you for acknowledging him through heated verbal exchanges. Lukewarm, subdued interactions just don't cut it with him."

Smike pointedly questions Elsye, "So, how'd you get so insightful figuring him out in just a couple of minutes?"

"Well, first, you've told me about several of your not-so-pleasant interactions with him, and also, I've gotten to know you and see what a gentle introvert you are. Bottom line is you don't *think* like him, at all, and he definitely doesn't *think* like you. It's easy for me to see your relational dynamics because I'm an outsider" she soundly responds.

Smike argues, "Well, you're no longer an outsider. Just scored major points with him *and* it seems like the two of you connected on some level, am I right?"

"Yeah, we definitely connected. And it will be fun lobbing snarky remarks at him, but you two need to work out your relationship. Just saying."

Chapter LXV   The Journal

Elsye looks around his room and comments, "You haven't quite made this your own space yet, huh?"

"Won't be here long enough to put forth the effort. Mostly depends on the old man's recovery from knee surgery and me finishing my song portfolio" he replies.

Elsye then spots his journal on the nightstand, goes over to pick it up, and asks, "So, is this your song journal?"

"Yes, for lyrics mostly. A few stream-of-consciousness thoughts as well" he confirms and clarifies.

"May I?" she requests permission to read his work.

Sanctioning her review, he preps with "These are drafts, nothing finalized, but sure."

Elsye plops down on his bed in a prone position with knees bent and feet dangling in the air. Smike moves some stuff around his room before joining her on the bed. Lying on his back next to her, he pulls out his harmonica and softly plays some tunes while Elsye immerses herself in reading his prose.

After a few minutes she shares, "Damn Smike, this is really poignant and powerful, actually spellbinding. Central theme across most pieces seems to be longing for a forlorn love. You capture deep pain, sadness, and vulnerability expressed in the words and prose" she construes.

Guessing, Elsye adds, "Sounds like a stunning woman inspired your poetry . . . not just physically beautiful, but heart and soul as well."

Smike confirms, "Yes, beauty beyond any conceivable standard, boundary, or comparison. Love of my life."

Assuming this woman was no longer with him; she continues and hesitantly prompts for more information.

"What happened?" she cautiously queries.

Somberly, he responds, "Lost her. The entire world lost her."

Smike's deep emotional cut from loving this woman and still grieving her loss was clearly palpable to Elsye. She saw splendor in the intensity of the love he experienced but didn't know how to tell him what a rarity this was and despite the depth of his pain and suffering in his loss, there should be gratitude for having known her and the close, deep tangible connection he had shared with her.

Elsye kindly responds, "Your words honor her Smike. She is an exquisite muse for your music. You are blessed to have known and loved each other."

Smike tears up and continues softly playing his harmonica. They lay quietly on the bed. No other words exchanged for a brief period of time.

Chapter LXVI   Capote

Elsye decides to engage in this rare opportunity to possibly crack open Smike's protective shell and asks, "So, how did you know that *she* was the one?"

Smike is taken aback. Although he freely talks about how his music is personally important and allows him to express his feelings, Elsye asked a more direct and private question about Louisa and his relationship with her. He hasn't really talked much about Louisa since she passed. Just too painful, still.

He says softly, "Louisa. Louisa was her name."

Intrigued, Elsye encourages him to continue "I would love to hear about Louisa."

Slightly pausing, he shares "In college, I took a literature class. We all had to select a novelist to research and read at least one of their pieces to try and understand their writing style, what they chose to write about, and why they were writers."

Elsye guesses that Smike must have met Louisa in this literature class. She waits to hear more to confirm her thinking.

"Anyway, I picked Truman Capote because he was a unique character, wrote *Breakfast at Tiffany's*, which was also a song by the same title that I liked. *Deep Blue Something* sang it. The lyrics and music resonated with me. Also, he died on the day of my birthday, so thought I would go with checking him out" he explains.

She didn't know that much about Capote, other than he was a writer, but definitely knew the song he referenced and it was

~ 241 ~

about a relationship. Smike exposes his tender heart; a romantic at his core. She loved that about him. Her natural instinct is to prod for details with questions, but she continues to lie there quietly waiting with heavy anticipation to hear more. And he delivers.

"So, I'm reading about him and he really was extravagant! He lived a fascinating life; especially as a gay man during a time when there was strong discrimination against individuals outside the social margins. Definitely an outlier in many ways, but I think that he lived his life mostly on his own terms."

At this point, salivating to hear more with every syllable he utters, Elsye's interest is completely aroused.

Smike continues, "What grabbed my interest about him was his response to an interview question about his work. The question was something about when he knew his writing was right or completed. For absoluteness or finality, and I am paraphrasing here, he supplied a metaphor about an orange. How nature made an orange *just right*."

Not emitting a peep, Elsye finds herself totally immersed in what he shares.

Smike continues, "What Capote said rang true to how I viewed my music and writing lyrics. Also, I thought about how the image of *just right* applied to relationships as well. I mean, I was very much a loner in high school. Really didn't have too many friends. Basically, just worked diligently on my homework and classes. Stayed to myself. Ran cross-country, which allowed me to ruminate on my thoughts with no one around. Song writing expressed my personal thoughts, my genuine identity, captured intense feelings I experienced, relationships, and I see now, my hopes in life. No interruptions from others around me. No one else, somehow, had access to distort what I was thinking. And, like Capote knew when his writing was completed, I knew when a song was final, when it was perfect, for me, that is."

Dumbfounded, Elsye finds herself completely speechless; a very rare occurrence for her, but one that evoked penetratingly thrilling feelings.

She really wanted to hold him and kiss him all over, but breaks from her silence and surmises by asking, "So Louisa was your orange?"

"Yes. We met at a mutual friend's party a couple years after college. I just landed a position at a chemical company in Beaumont. She just completed her master's degree as a child counselor. I am not one to go up to a woman, but she was stunningly beautiful" he shares in adoration.

Again, pausing briefly, he then continues, "There was this fruit bowl at the party that she was standing next to. I faked going over there to get a small serving. She looked at me, smiled, forked out a slice of orange, and offered it to me. Her heart was just as breathtakingly lovely."

Elsye tenderly says, very softly, "Oh my."

"That was it! I took the bite. We talked all night long. I never felt so connected to anyone else, ever. She was perfect for me. We lived together for nearly four years and got engaged" he openly shares.

Smike couldn't go into more details about Louisa's pregnancy, miscarriage or her illness and tragic death. He stopped talking hoping that Elsye understood enough from what he said. She did. Elsye had this gift of keen insight about individual emotions and she picked up from what and how he talked about his true love, that he wasn't going to go further. Not now, anyway.

Chapter LXVII   Forced Bond

While Smike was still upstairs, Elsye stops downstairs and seeing Paps still reclined in his lounger, snaps at him.

"Give me your cell phone" she orders.

Surprised, Paps replies, "I doan have a cell phone. Costs too much. Have a regulah phone."

He then asks, "Why do ya wan my phone anyway?"

"Smike says that you need a toe nail trim. I'm going to give you my number so you can call me and we will schedule a time to do that" Elsye graciously, but grudgingly offers.

"No, I doan need a toe nail trim. He's a wawhy waht" Paps replies with adamant resistance.

Forcefully, Elsye barks, "Dammit, old man, just give me your address book!"

With a sustained surprised look while totally complying, Paps reaches over on his side table, grabs the address book, and hands it to Elsye.

"Need a pen too" she demands.

Yielding to her directive, Paps reaches over, grabs one, and hands it to her. She quickly writes her name and number in his book.

"Listen asshole, if you ever change your mind, you now have my number" she impatiently yaps at him and places the address book and pen on the end table.

Paps just grins. He likes Elsye's style and energy. She's a direct, no-nonsense, domineering individual. He can relate to her. She asserts and expects respect and action from others. From Paps' perspective, Elsye is a breath of fresh air compared to other young women from her era, which seem too complacent and boring.

Paps playfully asks, "Can I call ya if I need beeah picked up from the packie?"

"Only if you share" she insipidly responds.

Paps laughs.

Scrambling down the stairs, Smike catches just the end of the conversation and asks, "What is Paps asked to share?"

"His sacred beer" Elsye said.

Smike spiritedly replies, "Well if he shares his beer, he really does like you!"

"Yippee for me!" Elsye mockingly responds while holding her hand up and twirling her pointer finger in contrived excitement.

Directed to Smike, Paps openly confides, "She's a keepah Michael. Gotta lot of fiah and fight in hah."

Smike then walks Elsye out to his car to take her home. During the drive, they talk about getting together next week on a Saturday afternoon to watch a classic 1950s movie that Elsye has never seen before, *Seven Samurai*. Since the dialogue of this movie is in Japanese, they will insert phrases they think the actors are saying. Should be fun.

Chapter LXVIII Shed Surprise

After a very brief band practice Sunday morning, Smike mentally gears up for helping Paps clean out and reorganize his shed in the afternoon. Grandma Nettie was basically the main keeper of the shed, but the last few years of her life, she couldn't do much with it and Paps just threw shit around in there. It was pretty messy at this point, making it difficult to find anything.

When Smike pulls into the driveway around noon, he spots Paps in the backyard, sitting in a lawn chair while holding a running water hose to hydrate the plants. He looks mighty proud of his produce. And Smike admits to himself, it is a grand yield of vegetables this year. As he exits his car, Paps calls out to him, "Ya ready to tackle the shed? May be a two-day prahject and ya only have half a day left tudday."

Walking toward the back door, Smike replies "Going to fix lunch first. Have anything in particular that you would like?"

"Yeah, wanna chicken salad sub, con on the cob, and some fried b'daydahs. Peeled and sliced the b'daydahs already. Ya just need to fry 'em up. The fresh con is shucked already, too" Paps assertively states while commanding his meal order.

"You got it Paps" Smike responds while entering the house through the back door.

He thinks *Paps is really hungry this afternoon.*

Within a half hour, the food is prepared and Smike delivers it outside, placing it on the picnic table. Paps comes over and sits down.

Just Saying

Spying the meal layout, Paps barks "Need catsup for the b'daydahs and some ice wotta."

Smike then returns to the house to retrieve the condiment and glass of water.

While eating, Paps offers clear directives.

"Ya ah gonna hafta pull out awl the boxes and plastic containahs. Check faw dead rodents ah uhthah vahmintz when sweepin it out. The tools need to be ahganized, too."

What he said is pretty much how Smike imagined the process and key elements of the task.

Paps finishes his meal and tells Smike he's heading inside to watch a show. Smike assumes that his grandfather needs a nap as well; so hopefully, he won't be micromanaging Smike while he declutters the shambles in the shed. That is, for a little while at least.

Smike unlocks the shed and starts removing objects blocking the entrance, out and away from the door. There are at least thirty some boxes and containers. Most aren't too heavy, probably old clothes in them and other small items. He empties the entire shed, sweeps it out, and then mops it down with cleansing liquid. It looks like a totally new storage space and smells a lot better, too. While waiting for the floor to dry, he checks out the boxes for placing them back in the shed. He wants to reorganize placement of the boxes by the sizes and types of materials in the containers. Regardless, he needs to look in each box because some are marked and others are not. Also, the markings may not accurately align with or be correctly labeled by what is actually packed inside the cartons. Paps would often chaotically throw stuff together.

He comes to one large, taped up plastic container marked 'military' that doesn't appear to have been unsealed in years. Removing the tape and opening it up, he finds an old Marine Corp uniform, including a jacket with metals pinned on it, some covers and caps, a pair of boots, random military items, and a large manilla folder filled with pictures. Removing the folder, he carries it to the picnic table to look through the photos, which appear to be of Paps when he was a young soldier. Some pictures look like when he was stationed stateside, but a few others appear to be actual sites in Vietnam with comrades. From these photos, Smike notes that Paps clearly was a good-looking man when he was younger. And, in several of the pictures, he's sporting a smile of genuine happiness. Rare images, for sure. Feeling compelled to ask Paps about these vintage photos, he goes inside with the envelope to question him and perhaps hear a little history about his grandfather's military experience.

Smike walks into the family room. Paps is watching television, not napping.

"Hey Paps, found this envelope with pictures of when you were in the military. They are great! Would love to hear about your experience in Vietnam" he innocently requests.

Paps' sudden movement, and the rage in his eyes, catches Smike by surprise. Paps snatches the envelope from his hand "Stay outta my stuff and mind yaw own bizness!"

Shocked, Smike freezes. He doesn't understand Paps' reaction and has no clue what to say to him. So, he just quietly stands there while Paps scrambles out of his lounger and storms off to his bedroom.

Returning outside to complete his work efforts on the shed, Smike bears deep concern about upsetting his grandfather. That surely was not his intention and he's not sure what he can do to make amends. For now, he will have to let it go. Besides, he's had such a tremendous week with performances, can't let this one episode with Paps (of many others) spoil it.

In his bedroom, Paps forlornly looks over the pictures in the envelope. He had not seen them in years. Viewing them is a painful process and emotionally tiring. He rests his head down and soon falls asleep.

Chapter LXIX   You Are Hurt ... Come With Me

Around sunrise, both Sid and Kahn are startled by an older Vietnamese woman chattering to them "Bạn bị tổn thương . . . đi với tôi" and moving her arms as if motioning for them to get up. Both their bodies immediately bolt upright into a defensive stance with Sid grabbing his rifle and pointing it at her. They have no idea what she repeatedly shouts to them.

Kahn says softly in distress, "She may be Viet Cong or a sympathizer."

Just as apprehensive, Sid senses though that this woman wants to help them. When spotting them sleeping, she could have hit them over the head or called for others to capture them, but she didn't.

"We would've been dead already. I trust hah" Sid says while lowering his rifle.

Both strained to get up and lean on each other for assistance as they struggled to intuitively follow the woman deeper into the bush. Within a few minutes, they are at what appears to be her hut. As they enter, the woman makes comfortable spaces for them to rest. Somewhat relieved, they plop down on mats covering the ground.

The woman gives each of them a cup of hot liquid, then goes to another location in the hut and grabs worn material that she starts ripping into strips. She then pours water into a wooden bowl and brings all materials over to the two injured soldiers. This welcomed Good Samaritan begins examining and tending to their wounds. She starts with Sid, tears off the lower part of his pants fatigues near his injured knee and cleans his wound. She then gets up and grabs some age-old container holding a greasy substance. She begins lathering the balm on Sid's knee wound before wrapping it tightly with the ripped strips of material.

Weak, but appreciative of her tending to his injury, Sid gazes at her like she is an angel sent from heaven while sipping on what he believes is the best tea he ever drank.

The woman then goes to Kahn, removes the wretched bandage from his gruesome facial wound and starts muttering with an easily interpreted tone of distinct concern that transcends any language barrier, "điều này là xấu" repeating over and over again. She follows a similar nursing process with Kahn by cleaning his wound, applying the homemade salve, and wrapping his injury in clean strips of cloth. Kahn takes another sip of the hot liquid and soon passes out.

Chapter LXX   Noticeable Shift

Monday morning, while getting in Rally's truck, Smike hands him a basket of vegetables from his grandfather's garden.

Very appreciative for the vegetables, Rally acknowledges, "Abuelita is gonna love these!"

On the drive to the café, Rally quickly notices that this morning differs from others. Smike is the one dominating the conversation, completely swelled in enthusiastic jabbering. Rather surprised in his persona shift, Rally happily listens.

Arriving at the café, Smike jumps out, and follows the same established routine: pick up the order, deliver to JoJo and Slim, talk with those two for a short time, and then return to the truck with their hot brews.

Returning to Rally's truck, still in his highly energetic mood, he rambles, "So, found out about JoJo's belt buckle that you wanted to know about. It was a retirement present from the business he worked for as a technician. Had forty-two years with this company and is very proud of the buckle. Says it is one of his most prized possessions. I complimented him about it and said that you noticed it as well."

Without a break in talking, but swinging to a different topic, he continues, "The band is way beyond what I expected, so satisfying to play with Violet, Mitch, and Denny. They are true musicians. We had a fabulous week and I am so motivated with my music and song writing. Last week's experiences were inspiring! Getting a lot of new ideas for my music and solidifying a few pieces as well. Right now, my only regret is not doing this sooner. I mean, what was I waiting for?"

Just Saying

Rally sits quietly, wondering and hoping Smike will talk about who he assumes is a new lady in his life. He guesses that part of Smike's enthusiasm must be related to meeting this woman. Rally, such a personally prying kind of guy, can barely contain himself, but must keep his promise to not directly ask about Ms. Kim. Must be patient but can prod him to share more through indirect questions that might trigger discussion about her. Smike's openly talkative disposition right now is rare and he doesn't want to miss this opportunity to find out more.

Rally furtively queries, "Marciella said that there were tons of young ladies at the Fourth celebration who seemed totally smitten with ya. Meet up with any afterwards?"

"No, but I was absolutely energized by the crowd! Wish you were there; it was utterly awesome! And our other gigs, Friday night at Fred's and the wedding bash were exceptional as well!" Smike shares.

Rally thinks, *Damn, can't get Smike to talk about his love life.*

He tries another approach by asking, "So, no down time for relaxing?"

Smike, matter-of-factly, responds, "Not really. Busy all week. In between events and band practice yesterday morning, started cleaning out Paps' shed. And there's always light work on the garden. You have received some fruits of that labor. Actually, I take that back, garden work is calming for me, so that would be my best down time. Definitely worth the time spent on that plot of vegetables."

Well, he tried, but certainly wasn't going to hear any news about his friend's potential relationship with Ms. Kim. Not today, anyway. Smike continues his uncharacteristic blathering. Rally wonders if this is how he sounds to Smike when on his own tangential, one-way chats. They had shifted roles this day.

Chapter LXXI   Rabbit's Foot

Smike made breakfast for Paps before his run Tuesday morning. When he got back, he decided to finish organizing the shed and would take a shower afterward. He was getting tired of using Paps' shower though. It was time to get the upstairs shower fixed and he decided to call Mitch to schedule a day for him and his father to check out the low water pressure. He wasn't going to tell Paps about this right now though, for several reasons. He would have to think this through for it to have a successful outcome. Besides, they hadn't talked much since Sunday. In fact, neither Smike nor Paps mentioned anything about the blow up over the old photos. Basically, both acted like it never happened.

Later in the evening, Smike calls Mitch for his availability on examining the plumbing issue. After checking with his father, Mitch confirms that Saturday morning is open to inspect the problem. They then briefly discuss their upcoming Friday gig.

Mitch jokingly says, "I'm not superstitious or anything, but our gig falls on Friday the thirteenth. So, we all wear a rabbit foot or lucky hat or anything to ward off bad luck but just to be silly. You may want to consider what you will do."

Smike laughs. He's not superstitious either but gets the gag and remembers seeing a four-leaf clover medallion in his aunt's old jewelry box. He'll wear that, just for fun.

Mitch then adds, "Well, will finally get to meet your Paps this weekend."

Smike cautions, "Just keep your rabbit foot close by when you come over!" They both laugh.

Chapter LXXII   Draining

Using the downstairs bathroom across from Paps' bedroom has not just been inconvenient, but also an uncomfortable privacy issue for both of them. Of course, he knows that Paps will have pushback in hiring anyone to fix something in his home and a bigger barrier is the cost, as he will vociferously complain and resist that as well. Smike decides to prep Paps with an innocuous lie. He will tell him that whatever the cost, he will receive a significant Veteran's discount for the services and parts. Smike figures that will break down Paps' resistance a little to the expense.

Grudgingly, Paps agrees to the arrangement to review and possibly address the low water pressure issue, but mandates that he must fully supervise their work. Smike has experienced Paps' *hawking over* almost everything he does for him around the house. It is *very* annoying and *extremely* difficult to follow his directives while in the throes of repairing a previous messy patchwork job Paps might have thrown together in his commonly sloppy, uninformed attempts at handiwork. Smike makes sure to warn Mitch what will happen with Paps trying to direct their work and also makes a pre-emptive deal that neither Mitch nor his father talks to Paps about the expense. Smike plans to covertly pay for half of whatever the total cost comes to, just to get it done. And, if Paps argues that the doctored cost is still too much, he will then offer to pay for half of that amount just to win his grandfather over and get everything fixed. So, really, Paps' final bill will be about a quarter of what anyone else would pay; he just doesn't need to know that.

Mitch and his father arrive mid-morning on Saturday with full working belts strapped on. Smike leads them upstairs. Paps, who has been in the kitchen drinking his coffee, clumsily follows, giving them history of when the problem started, what he thinks happened, and how he already tried to fix it. Mitch is genial to Paps, while Mitch's father doesn't say much and just nods his head as if he's listening to Paps, but Smike doubts he's paying attention to anything Paps says. Mitch's father, Curtis, appears serious in just surveying the plumbing issue.

Once upstairs, Paps goes to the craft room and grabs a chair that he brings over to the bathroom door entrance. He plops down on it and starts observing their work. Mitch, with a knowing look, tacitly motions to Smike that everything is fine. He's got it from here with *both* problems; the plumbing and the obsessively controlling old fogey.

With doubting confidence, Smike leaves the bathroom and goes to his room to tap new ideas for lyrics. He slips on ear buds and falls into an enjoyable rhythm with his creative thoughts.

Over an hour passes with no incident, when Mitch comes to Smike's bedroom door and says, "We have identified the problem as very old clogged pipes, but wanna take a lunch break in a few minutes. You okay with that?"

Smike suggests, "How about I order a pizza? You can eat here. Have some beer as well. How does that sound?"

Mitch replies, "That'll work! Dad likes meat on his pizza. I eat anything" and then leaves Smike's room.

Smike remembers that Elsye is coming over later in the afternoon to watch the movie classic *Seven Samurai* and later listen to some of his new tunes. He decides to call her and ask her to join them for lunch. She lives near the pizza place and can pick it up on her way over. That could work great for everyone. Smike calls Elsye to ask her if she is agreeable to this modified plan. She consents, actually very happy with the change in their schedule. Smike then calls the pizza parlor, makes the order for a large pizza, and returns to his journaling.

Meanwhile, across the hall, Mitch and his father continue to work on setting up the plumbing repair and start compiling a list of parts that will be needed. Paps peppers them with questions about prices for parts and labor and how long repairs will take. He makes sure to complain about his limited fixed-budget as a retiree. Mitch acknowledges his comments, which seems to only slightly appease Paps, but no expense total is provided. Mitch's father stresses how from what he can tell, the pipes are nearly seventy years old and clogged. They need to be replaced, period. Looks like a minimum of two days of labor needs to be scheduled for next week.

A little time passes when Mitch's father says, "I need for ya to check the downstairs bathroom, Mitch."

Paps responds, "It's dahrectly below this one, right across from my bedroom."

So, Mitch heads downstairs.

While just outside the downstairs bathroom entrance, Mitch notices Elsye coming to the front door with a large pizza.

He yells up the stairwell, "Hey Smike, the pizza delivery girl is here."

Elsye hears him, opens the door, and enters the front room. Mitch is surprised that this delivery person would just walk into someone's house like that and he marches over to her. Smike, scrambling down the stairs, quickly moves past Mitch and greets Elsye with a kiss on the cheek while grabbing the pizza box.

Eyeing Mitch with disdain, Elsye sarcastically comments, "Your plumber here assumes I'm a pizza delivery girl."

With an equally disturbed look on his face, Mitch quickly scowls, "Well, hey Smike, Ms. Hypocritical here, thinks I'm your plumber!"

With immediate tension already established between them, Smike attempts an awkward introduction.

"Elsye, this is Mitch, my bandmate and friend, who, with his father, is checking out the upstairs plumbing problem."

Mitch grins, moving his chin in an upward jerky motion like *See, I'm his <u>friend</u>*.

"Hmmph" she snorts with skepticism like *You don't seem like someone Smike would be friends with.*

Smike continues, "Mitch, this is my friend Elsye. I asked her to pick up our pizza on her way over to watch a movie with me this afternoon."

Elsye breaks into this huge smile like *See, I am his friend, <u>not</u> just a delivery girl, you idiot.*

Surprisingly, Mitch grins broadly while squinting his eyes, wondering if she is more than just a friend.

Smike says affirmatively, "Okay, let's eat" as his lame bid to break this unexpected and brewing friction fails.

He yells upstairs to Paps and Curtis to come down for pizza, places the pizza on the kitchen table, and hurriedly grabs an extra chair from the family room.

Elsye turns away from Mitch so he can't read her lips or hear her, grabs Smike's arm, pulls him closer, and in reference to Mitch, meanly whispers, "I don't like him."

Smike leans toward her ear and softly says, "He's really a good guy, trust me."

With sternness, Elsye shakes her head and stomps to the kitchen table. Mitch then grabs Smike's other arm and pulls him back away from the entrance to the kitchen.

He quietly asks, "So, are ya friends or *more* than just friends?"

Smike replies, "We are more than just friends, but *not* in the way you think."

Mitch happily responds, "Good, cause I *like* her. She's feisty!"

As everyone gathers in the kitchen, Smike gets out paper plates, napkins, beer, and water. They all sit down and start fixing their plates.

While chewing his first sloppy bite, Mitch throws a criticizing comment to Elsye.

Just Saying

"If ya really are Smike's friend, I would've met ya at one of the shows already."

Smike quickly becomes uncomfortable and braces for Elsye's backlash.

"Well, you haven't seen me because I *work* all of the time; however, I have the benefit of hearing his music in *private* performances" she sneers with a huge, exaggerated smirk.

Smike's discomfort is growing while Paps, conversely, perks up watching these two engage in what he anticipates as a good sparring match.

Elsye then retorts, "If you are Smike's friend, how come I haven't heard about you?"

Loudly chomping his food with pizza sauce dripping down the side of his mouth, Mitch says, "Well if ya really *knew* Smike, ya would know that he don't share much about his personal life. Ya have to beat it out of him" Mitch revels in this temporary touché moment.

Smike has had enough and in a loud voice says, "Stop, you are both draining me!"

Paps then counters, "Actually, I'm enjoyin this and want 'em to go on. Would've assumed that Elsye would've chewed him up and spit him out by now, but Mitch is a clevah monkey and holdin his own with hah. Fun to watch!"

"Thankya Mister Schrod, I appreciate that" Mitch says in humble gratitude.

Of course, Paps then tamps down the compliment with, "Yeah, thought ya wuhr just anuhthah chump but ya ah actually smahtah than the avahage bayah Mitch."

Thin on patience, discouraged and disgusted with this three-ring circus, Smike, not saying a word, grabs his plate, hurriedly leaves the kitchen, and goes to the family room to finish his meal in peace. He seems completely frustrated that two of his favorite people appear to despise each other. No one follows him or says anything as they all continue eating quietly.

Except for Paps; he chuckles and mumbles, "Michael doan like confrontations."

Chapter LXXIII   Swords Drawn

After Mitch and his father leave, Elsye and Smike settle in the front room to watch *Seven Samurai*. Invited to join them, Paps, instead, calls Smike into the kitchen to talk.

"How much is allah this plumbin wawk gonna cost? Doan want 'em to get stahted and the expense to accumulate to sum ungawdly amount! We can do most of the wawk owahselves aw I can ask David to help" Paps tetchily questions, setting up to quarrel with his grandson.

Smike calmly responds, "I'll talk with Mitch before they start next week, but you have to trust that their rates will be fair and they will complete it all in the best professional manner. Curtis is a highly skilled plumber. And, you know, this has to get done. If those pipes just start to crumble or burst, you'll have a bigger mess and greater expenses to deal with. And, David works sixty-plus hours a week. You don't want to impose on him to help out. He's got his own life."

Paps swears loudly at Smike, "Shit, shit, *SHIT*, Michael Schrod, this is *my* house. *My* decision."

From his fervent bitching, Smike knows Pap is pissed and agitated. Paps doesn't like not being in full control. He must always be in charge of everything. Paps dashed the optimistic mood for enjoying a classic movie with Elsye through his stubborn, narrow-visioned perspective. Smike thinks *why can't Paps listen, agree, and get along, just for once?* Paps thinks *Michael should mind his own bizness. He's not payin faw it, I am!*

Elsye hears their argument from the front room and interrupts with a suggestion.

"Can the details of this decision be worked out at another time?" she asks.

Smike makes an urgent plea by swinging the pre-planned affordable option to Paps.

"I will pay for *half* of all expenses Paps. I'm living here, the repair is for the shower that I will be using, so that's only fair. Will you agree to that?" he asks.

Grumbling, Paps grudgingly replies, "Doan want eithah of us spendin too much money."

"Okay, I will talk with Mitch about us doing some of the sheet rock work on the walls they have to rip out and the repair painting. We can do that together. Does this compromise sound workable?" Smike suggests.

"Yeah, okay, and David aw his boys can help us with the wall wawk. But, ya havta let *me* make all the final decisions. Undahstand?" Paps counters.

Of course, Smike understands. And of course, he knows that Paps' tight-fisted nature with money may drag out the work where the final results could end up half-assed. For now, he appeases his grandfather.

Smike yields, "Yes Paps, I understand. So, now will you watch the movie with us? It's one of your favorites."

"Yeah, but I need a beeah" he gruffly replies.

Smike wonders if any Samurai ever faced and dueled with such a formidable foe as his grandfather. He doubts it.

Chapter LXXIV   Drive in the Country

After band practice Sunday morning, Smike asks Mitch if they can talk about the pending plumbing work timeline and expenses, since he needs to give Paps some answers. Mitch suggests they take a short road trip to talk about it; he has something he wants to show Smike out in the country. Smike agrees and Mitch follows him home so he can drop his car off and they can ride to the countryside together.

After jumping in Mitch's car, Smike asks, "So where are you taking me?"

"You should wait to see it before I tell ya about it, okay?" Mitch says.

"Sure, in the meantime, give me some numbers on expenses for the plumbing work. I have to massage the final total a bit so that Paps doesn't balk at getting this all done. So tired of using his shower" Smike laments.

On the drive, they discuss the expenses, which Smike finds totally reasonable and knows now he can easily cut the number down and cover much of it himself (without informing Paps of the actual full expense). Mitch also tells him that he and his father expect to work on the pipes a minimum of two days. It may run into a third day. So, they were thinking about starting on Tuesday and finishing by Wednesday evening or sometime on Thursday. To Smike, this is a workable plan.

Now driving on a gravelly road that appears to be in the middle of nowhere, Mitch passes an orchard of apple trees as he pulls up to an abandoned old farm house near a broken-down barn. He stops in front of the house.

"We are here!" Mitch says beaming.

Looking around, Smike responds, "Pretty cool place. Why did you want to show this to me?"

Mitch replies with pride, "I'm buying it. A fixer-upper. Got six acres of land and so much history. The house is way over a hundred years old! Gonna raise lots of animals like chickens, maybe a cow and some pigs, and will have cats to prey on varmints like mice."

Smike is not sure if Mitch is serious or hopeful, like something he wishes could happen, like a longing for a dream location to live on his own or a future desire for renovating a home.

Mitch continues, "Been saving since I was a teenager. Living with my parents, never had any expenses except for my tatts and guitars. My father is gonna help me put in a new bathroom and kitchen. Plan to have it livable by next summer. Will spend the fall gutting the insides."

Realizing that this is not a whimsical aspiration, but rather a real and earnest endeavor that Mitch shares with him, Smike exclaims, "Wow, Mitch, I'm impressed! Who else knows about it? I mean, this is exciting!"

Mitch responds, "Paperwork should be final by the end of this week. Put a hefty down payment on it. My father made me co-owner of the plumbing business, so this gives me collateral with the bank. He is sixty-five now and plans to retire in five years, so the business will go to me then, anyway. Haven't told anyone yet cause wasn't sure if the sale would go through. Violet will love it though. She knows that I've always wanted to refurbish an old farm house."

Excitedly, Smike replies, "Well this certainly calls for a celebration! You're now going to be a home owner! Or is this considered a homestead?"

"My true hearth and home, not the loft over my parents' garage. That space will be transformed into a playroom for my sister's kids" Mitch proudly replies.

They walk around the area as Mitch points out a dilapidated chicken coop and how he's looking forward to fresh eggs. He says the barn is the grand prize as he plans to renovate it into a musical studio. He and his father will also eventually build a two-car garage next to the house once it's upgraded and completely remodeled.

Invigorated by Mitch's confidence and optimistic energy, Smike offers his assistance.

"Anything I can do to help Mitch; I am happy to lend a hand. This is a very worthy undertaking. I am thrilled for you" Smike says with sincerity.

Before finishing the tour, Mitch picks a couple apples from a nearby tree and hands one to Smike.

"Looking forward to growing my own fruits and vegetables too!" Mitch announces.

While munching on the fresh and perfectly ripe apples, they get in Mitch's car. On their drive back, Mitch slips in a CD by Wet Willie and plays the song *Keep on Smilin*. He notes the harmonica instrumental part and suggests this is a great song for Smike to learn. Smike agrees and thinks about how happy he is for his friend.

Chapter LXXV   Lucky Pennies

Monday morning, Rally and Smike share updates on their weekend activities. Their conversational exchanges are equally balanced; actually, first time since they have known each other. Smike hears that Pablo is practicing his harmonica. Rally finds it interesting that Paps has agreed to the plumbing repairs that Smike coordinated. As part of their drive-share routine, they stop to pick up coffee and Smike hops out.

Returning to the truck with their order, Smike, as usual, stops to give JoJo and Slim their breakfast and coffee. Rally notices JoJo hand Smike some small objects from his pocket. He sees Smike smile and nod to JoJo as a *thank you* and then heads back to the truck.

Rally queries, "Saw JoJo give you something. What is it?"

Handing Rally one of the items, Smike says, "He gave me two wheat pennies. One for you and one for me. Said they are lucky pennies and will bring good luck to kind people. He also said that they are worth a little money, so keep them safe. Paps has an old coin collection. I'm going to share this with him and find out what he knows about them."

Rally asks, "Can ya see the date on 'em?"

"Looks like both are nineteen-forty. Think he said they were minted the year he was born" Smike replies.

"Well, our day started out lucky with this gift. And Pablo loves history, so he'll be researching to find out all about it" Rally adds.

Putting the pennies safely away, they return to their conversation.

Smike says, "You know, thinking about it, I could ask Paps about his coin collection. If I share this coin with him and show interest in his collection, he may pull it out and start working on it. Apparently, he has this large jug filled with old coins that he keeps in his bedroom that haven't been sorted yet. This could keep him distracted from bugging Mitch and his father while they're working on the plumbing this week."

"Great idea! Hope that works, cause you've told me how he can hound ya while working" Rally responds.

Smike cleverly replies, "Guess I'll just have to rub this lucky penny to test its magic."

They both laugh while pulling into work.

Chapter LXXVI   Repair Despair

Returning home from work and hoping to pique Paps' interest, Smike hands the penny to Paps and asks him about it. His grandfather barks at him to go to the kitchen drawer and get his magnifying glass. Looks like his curiosity is sparked.

Supplying the magnifying glass, Paps quickly grabs it from Smike and examines the coin.

"It's in mint condition, faw shuah. Nineteen-fawty is not too ole. Doan have a mint mawk, so made in Philly. Nice penny" Paps reports.

Not because he really wants to know, but rather to keep Paps engaged, Smike asks, "Is it worth much?"

Paps replies, "Not shuah, will havta resahch it."

Smike questions further, "Don't you have a coin collection Paps?" and then requests, "Would love to see it."

"Oh yeah, have a great collection in my bedroom closet. I can bring it out but would need to place it on the kitchen table. Need room to lay 'em out" Paps responds with a willingness rarely seen.

Smike adds, "Thought you had a large jug or barrel full of coins you still need to sort. Perhaps I can help you go through them and you can teach me about coins."

Paps retorts, "Ahrn't the plumbahs comin t'mawrah? Doan wan my valuables out wayuh they can see them. Really, doan wan them heeah at awl."

Thinking quickly, Smike responds, "I can set up a work table in your bedroom for the coin sorting. That will give you free space that won't be bothered with, by anyone other than you. Just close the door and they won't even see what you're doing."

Paps finds this suggestion a little suspicious.

He snaps, "Then who exactly will be watchin ovah theyah wawk t'mawrah?"

Smike responds with a practical suggestion.

"Listen, you don't want to be going up and down the stairs all day. How about you watch them get started in the morning and later in the afternoon before they leave, you conduct a full inspection. That limits the trips upstairs and will prevent your knee from aching" Smike says in a straightforward manner.

Smike then adds with sincerity, "Plus, you and I can focus on your coins. This will give us some time together on something that I am interested in learning about from you."

Paps intuitively realizes that Michael probably wants to keep him out of the way of the workers, and he truly was worried about his knee pain attempting multiple flights of stairs, but he's highly attracted to the idea of sharing his knowledge about coins with his grandson.

"Okay, that'll wawk. Ya need to get the extra table outta the shed and clean it up. Can set it in my room in the mawnin" Paps concedes.

Smike feels triumphant. Mitch and Curtis can work with nearly no interruptions from Paps. And, he will be able to spend some quality time with his grandfather. He truly is interested in coins and what his grandfather can teach him about the collection. Just needs to remember to keep his mouth shut other than asking questions about specific coins and their history. Letting Paps be in full control will make the day, and hopefully, the rest of the week, go smoothly.

Chapter LXXVII   Rare Wonders

Rally could barely control his excitement when he picked Smike up on Wednesday.

"Did ya know that the pennies JoJo gave us could be worth as much as a thousand dollars? Not saying they are that valuable, but hey, ya never know. Pablo checked it out online and he was so energized about it. Wants to start collecting coins now!"

"Yeah, some of them are worth quite a bit. Spent most of yesterday going through Paps' coin collection. We sorted through hundreds of old coins that he had in this jug. I actually learned a lot. And believe it or not, we had a nice time together. Just hoping that he stays in his room today with the coins and leaves Mitch and Curtis to complete their work" Smike responds.

As they pull up to the café, Rally requests, "Be sure to thank JoJo for me. They really are lucky pennies."

Smike replies, "Will do!"

Smike's driving day went exceptionally well Wednesday and was over before he knew it. Even better, after arriving home he found out that Paps apparently stayed fully focused on his coins all day; remaining out of Mitch's and Curtis' hair.

That evening, Paps eagerly showed Smike what he finished sorting and pulled out a few special coins that he thought were worth the most. He mentioned that they could go to a coin shop the next day after Mitch and Curtis finish up some final touches on the plumbing job in the morning. He wanted to get some of the coins appraised for value and condition. Paps also said that he had a lot of duplicate coins and would place some in a bag to give to his friend's son, since now the boy wanted to be a coin collector. Smike wonders about his grandfather. The old man really did have exceptional moments when he was a genuinely thoughtful guy.

Besides completion of the plumbing with Smike now being able to shower upstairs, the great event of the day on Thursday was Paps finding out that one of his coins appraised at fifty dollars. He decided to celebrate by taking Smike to lunch, which like the appraised coin, was very rare!

Chapter LXXVIII   Just Like Any Other
Day

Plumbing work completed and coins sorted, Paps returns to his normal daily activities on Friday. That afternoon, in his skivvies, Paps watched his regularly scheduled late afternoon game shows while enjoying a beer and some hard pretzels; just like any other day. Crunching down on the salty treat, he suddenly feels a very uncomfortable crack as a sharp pain shoots through the lower left side of his jaw. *Shit*, he thinks. He may have cracked a tooth. Grabbing his cane from the side of the lounger, he gets up and walks to the bathroom to examine the dental damage in the mirror. Opening his mouth, he sees that a back molar is cracked and there is a loose section. He lifts the broken piece out of his mouth, looks at it, and then throws it in the sink.

"Shit, shit, SHIT" he mutters, and then thinks, *Michael can't know 'bout this. Will nevah heeah the end of it.*

Many times, Smike warned his grandfather about how hard pretzels could possibly harm his teeth or dental work. Bothered by his grandson's intrusive counseling on his well-being, Paps would angrily dismiss Michael as a worry wart. Although he would never acknowledge that perhaps he should have listened to Michael, he fleetingly thought about it in this moment.

Paps returns to his lounge chair, mutes the TV, pulls out his address book on the side table, picks up the phone, and makes a call.

Just Saying

"This is Mistah Asshole. Couldja come ovah? I need some assistance with somethin" Paps says with reluctance over the phone to the person on the other end.

Paps doesn't want to ask anyone for a favor because he doesn't want to be perceived as needy, disabled, or an incapacitated invalid. However, most relevant to his concern regarding this situation is Michael finding out. The person on the other end of the phone asks about his grandson's availability to help, so he feigns an excuse based on factual information.

"Michael is drivin the shreddin truck tudday and then goes straight to his show at Fred's Tavahn. I doan wanna pull him away from eithah job. Would appreciate yaw help" Paps pleads with sincerity.

The person on the other end of the phone confirms that they can come over right after they get off from work in a few minutes.

Paps responds, "I auw ya, thanks!" and hangs up.

Meanwhile, he gets back up and returns to the bathroom to rinse the open wound in his mouth with peroxide. After spitting, he then stuffs cotton balls in what now feels like a cavernous hole. He goes to his bedroom and slips on a pair of pants, clean shirt, and walking shoes; as he needs to be presentable when his soon-to-be savior arrives to assist him. He then unlocks the front door for his impending guest and returns to his lounge chair. Once seated, he unmutes the TV, and continues watching his show while waiting to be rescued.

Out of habit, he reaches for the wad of gum stuck on the edge of his beer can, and quickly pulls away realizing he can't chew shit. However, he reaches back again after deciding that a few swigs of beer may help with the minor pain he's feeling; besides, the alcohol can soak into the cotton balls for a slight numbing effect.

Twenty minutes later, Elsye walks through the door a little after four in the afternoon. She just finished her last pedicure. He smiles at her with a chipmunk look on the left side of his face from the cotton ball stuffing.

"What the fuck happened to you, asshole?" she asks, through an absurdly blended tone of nastiness and concern.

"Heeah's the thing, Michael CAN NOT know 'bout this!" Paps prefaces.

"Know about what? That you got in a fight with the twelve-year-old across the street and she beat your ass?" Elsye questions with heavy sarcasm while softly laughing.

"Smaht aleck" Paps bitingly responds.

"I've been called worse!" Elsye drolly admits.

"No. I cracked a tooth. Need to go to a dentist" he explains.

"So, why can't Smike know about this?" she prods.

"Cause it happened while I was eatin hahd pretzels. He's wahned me and will hang this ovah my head" Paps confides.

"What, you trust me to keep this from him? All of a sudden you trust a person of Asian descent?" she asks, then adds "My family lineage is Cambodian by the way, not Vietnamese" she touts.

Just Saying

Ignoring her comment, he confides, "Heeah's what I know. Michael has just a few friends. Those friends have always been true to him. He's a great judge of cahactah. Yaw his friend and he trusts ya. If he can trust ya, I shuahly can."

Paps' reply presents a solid and touching argument. Elsye doesn't show it, but she is moved. She knew that they have a connection between the two of them based on similar tough, no-nonsense personalities, so she acquiesces to his request for help *and* to keep it confidential.

"So, just between us, what do you need?" she asks.

"Fahst, I need a dentist. I hate dentists and haven't been to one in ovah twenty yeeahs. Think my dentist is retiahed aw dead" he clarifies.

"I don't like dentists either. My dentist, Dr. Hale, is the only man I know who has stuck his *tool* in my mouth and then told me to *spit*" she straightforwardly states with a deliberate double entendre.

Caught off guard, Paps laughs out loud and confirms to Elsye, "I *really* LIKE ya!" he says while choking back his laughter.

"Can't say that I feel the same way about you! Let me call my dentist's office and try to get you in as a new patient on an emergency basis; however, this is late on a Friday afternoon. Can't guarantee anything" she cautions him regarding any legitimate thoughts of getting a visit this quickly.

"I vahy much appreciate it, Elsye. Guessin the remaindah of the tooth needs to be pulled. I doan want anythin else done" Paps states simply with conviction.

"If you can get in for an emergency appointment, do you want me to drive and stay with you as well? They may want to gas you and not sure if you can drive in that condition or actually in *any* condition" she asserts sarcastically.

"I appreciate all that ya can do faw me. Again, Michael cannot know" Paps reiterates.

Elsye affirmatively nods and gets on her cell phone to call the dentist's office. On hold for a couple of minutes, but then Paps hears her arguing with someone that the new potential patient is a senior citizen in pain, also a military veteran, with an incapacitating injury that limits mobility. Paps isn't sure which argument sticks with the person on the receiving end, but after a couple of minutes on hold for a second time, Elsye smiles while motioning a thumbs up. Success! She came through for him, big time!

Elsye rants, "Okay, we gotta go now! Fridays are actually the dentist's day off, but he will come into the office just to address your condition. Bring your insurance and credit cards. Also, please tell me that you don't have a heart condition where you're taking meds that cause you to bleed. They asked about that."

"No haht condition, except for my immeasahble love faw ya right now Elsye" Paps proclaims in genuine appreciation for her effort.

Elsye rolls her eyes at him.

"I'll drive. Let's go" she quickly dictates to Paps.

Elsye relishes the upper hand she has with him right now.

Just Saying

"Yes ma'am, my lovely!" Paps cheerfully replies.

He obeys her command by grabbing his wallet from the side table and gets up to go, but suddenly remembers that he has beer-soaked cotton balls in his mouth. The dentist would surely notice and possibly chastise him about it.

"Wait a minute, I've gotta spit out these cotton bawls" Paps says as he goes over to the trash can and dispenses his superficial therapeutic and temporary home-made remedy.

Elsye notices and says, "Smells like beer!"

"Yeah, only good thing 'bout what happened tudday!" Paps retorts.

Chapter LXXIX   Craving

For Smike, the weekend and beginning of the week followed the same routine with Friday night's gig, Saturday morning garden work and in the evening playing new tunes for Elsye, Sunday morning band practice and afternoon music writing, and Monday driving the shredding truck. It is Tuesday now, and Smike returns home from a long bike ride he had taken on a new trail at the park that morning. As he walks into the house, he sees Paps sitting at the kitchen table drinking coffee. He calls for Smike to come over.

"Have a request faw ya Michael" Paps says, and adds, "I've been cravin sum baby goulash. Can ya pick sum up faw suppah this evenin?"

"Well, I've been craving a Greek Salad myself, so sure! Did you want something else to go with it?" Smike asks.

"Nah, gonna bake sum soft pretzels. Thought that would be good faw dippin in the goulash" he says.

Paps mentions this as if it is a novel idea, even though Michael had suggested it before.

"Okay, will do" Smike happily replies.

Paps then prods, "Do ya have any uhthah plans faw the day?"

"Not really, just working on my music" Smike says, and then asks, "Do you need anything?"

Just Saying

"I would like to visit yaw grandmuhthah's grave this ahftanoon and leave sum flahwiz, yellah roses. Hah fayvrit" Paps responds solemnly, and then adds, "Thought ya might like to go with me."

Smike suddenly realizes that it's his grandmother's birthday. She would have been seventy-four years old. Can't believe he had forgotten it until just now with Paps' request.

"Of course, Paps, I would very much like to go with you and I'll drive. I know the way" Smike warmly offers.

Paps suggests, "Let's leave right ahfta lunch. It's an owah drive each way and would like to avoid the late ahftanoon traffic."

Smike perks up with an idea, "Let me clean up and we can leave earlier and go to Chauncey's for lunch, first. If I remember correctly that restaurant is on the way to the cemetery. And lunch is on me. What do you think about that Paps?"

Paps smiles and says, "As long as we stop sumwayuh to get roses."

Smike smiles back at his grandfather and says, "I know exactly where to go for the flowers."

Smike then orders flowers over the phone "Yes, half dozen yellow roses with baby's breath and a few white lilies."

The bouquet will be ready to pick up in an hour.

A short while later, they head out for lunch at Chauncey's. The line is long, but Paps doesn't complain, actually, he is atypically quiet. After they finish their lunch, Smike stops at

Violet's floral shop to pick up the beautiful arrangement she made.

Smike hands the roses to his grandfather, and while gently grasping them, Paps says, "Nettie would love this!"

A little less than an hour later, they arrived at the cemetery. Smike worries how far they will have to walk with respect to the strain that may be inflicted on his grandfather's knee, but Paps is adamant about going to her grave, placing the flowers next to her headstone, and expressing his love for her through a short prayer.

While watching his grandfather bless himself and quietly say a prayer to his grandmother, memories of Louisa's memorial, which happened eight months prior to Grandma Nettie's passing, come flooding back.

Standing at the lectern, Smike looked out at the audience comprised of Louisa's family, friends, and many young children she counseled. Everything was a blur. Just days earlier, she passed away in his arms. Her valiant struggle against the merciless disease was over. Everyone was devastated. How could he comfort anyone when he could not be consoled himself? What could he say about her that would even come close to dignifying her virtuous life? Nothing he could possibly say would fill the emptiness of her passing. He takes in a deep breath and begins commemorating the woman he loved.

"I am selfish. All I can think about is how important Louisa was, and still is, to me. She understood me, she encouraged me, and most importantly, she inspired me. She inspired me to open up to others and give more of myself, contribute to the world, if only a small part of myself. She inspired me through graciously modeling these very actions every day of her life. Not just with me, but with her family, her friends, and the children with whom she had close relationships."

After a brief pause, he continues "I don't want to be selfish. I want to be giving, as giving as Louisa. Doubt I could ever reach that goal. But I will try. I must try to honor her. So, here goes. Nearly five years ago, I met the love of my life. Our encounter was unexpected and glorious. We were inseparable from that point on. She once said to me 'why are you always smiling Michael?' and I responded, 'because I am looking at the most beautiful woman in the world!' It was true; she was the most beautiful woman, inside and out. And, I selfishly wanted her all to myself; although, I knew fully well that sharing her with the world was what the world needed and what she needed as well. She had so much to offer and did so willingly, without question or hesitation."

Smike continues "Two and a half years ago, while feeling totally inadequate and unworthy, I proposed. Baring my soul in what I thought was a very romantic moment, she told me 'Silly, I can't marry you. You don't tie your shoes.'" (Light laughter is heard from family members and friends.)

After the laughter subsided, he resumes the memorial, "It was true; I often walked around with my running shoes untied. It's not that I'm lazy; they're just more comfortable that way. However, in a joking manner, she was telling me I needed to grow up a little before she would make that significant commitment. From my reaction, she saw I was crushed and quickly chased the rejection with, 'I love you and of course I want a future with you.' At this moment she accepted the ring, placed it on her finger, and after a passionate kiss, we were conditionally engaged. It's just the 'when' of marrying would be on her timetable. I trusted her intuition and respected her decision. I was just thrilled that someday, she would be my wife. However, that day did not come. Instead, last year she was ravaged with an unexpected illness. After the diagnosis, I pleaded for us to marry immediately. She told me that would be selfish on both our parts. I told her, 'But I am selfish! I love you!'" He stops speaking and starts crying.

Regaining his composure, he then continues, "However, she wanted to do it right. She said we should wait until after treatment and her recovery. Again, I trusted her intuition and respected her decision. And, I wanted to show her that I could be selfless . . . that I could share her with the world, even if she didn't have much longer to grace it with her presence. I understood her, I supported her, I encouraged her, and I tried to inspire her through this horrendous ordeal. I wanted to do for her as she effortlessly did for me. She will always be the love of my life, my muse, my everything."

After speaking, he steps away from the podium, walks over to Louisa's parents and hugs them. They are all consumed in weeping.

While embracing him, Louisa's mom says, "She loved you so much Smike!"

Her father, too choked up to speak, squeezed him in a hard embrace. Smike then leaves them to sit with his parents and sisters who are equally distraught in their grief.

Shaken from his stupor, Paps lightly taps him on the elbow that it's time to leave. Their drive home is shared in comfortable, consensual silence.

Just Saying

Once in Lowell, they stop and pick up a Greek salad and a large portion of baba ganoush. Arriving home, Smike turns on the oven to bake the soft pretzels. Paps goes to the family room and slides in one of his favorite movies, *Das Boot*, but waits to start it until after Smike joins him.

As he carries in the dinner trays, Paps turns on the movie and says, "This movie's so good, doan even need captions" and they silently watch the drama together while simultaneously dipping soft pretzels in the baba ganoush. After one bite, Smike thinks, *This is really good!*

Chapter LXXX   Valli in the Valley

The band organized an impromptu practice that Wednesday evening so that Violet could discuss and go over details of their next big performance at a private location in Swift River Valley. She explained how the gig is a bit of a jog to the site, but the natural setting of the location was picturesque! The theme for this gala will be *Valli in the Valley!* Apparently, the honoree for this soiree is a new retiree and she wants the musical component of her celebration to be based on the work of Frankie Valli. The baby boomer pensioner also specifically asked for particular songs. Of course, the band can easily comply, but there were songs on this list they hadn't practiced before. So, Violet wanted to go over the list and work out details for who wanted to take the lead on which songs. She began reading the list and encouraged them all to speak up; even if more than one was interested in a certain song.

Violet starts out, "Well, guess I'll do *Big Girls Don't Cry*" then explains, "You know, but with a twist on perspective. That is, from a girl's voice."

"I like that Violet, great idea!" Mitch quickly replies and then adds, "And if *My Eyes Adored You* is on that list, I want it."

"Great! And, that song is on the list." Violet responds, makes a note, and quickly makes a second suggestion, "Yeah, and I would like to sing *Working my Way Back to You* as well."

Mitch and Denny reply in agreement.

Violet then returns to the list, "*Who Loves You*" she states with a questioning pause.

Just Saying

Denny quickly responds, "That's me! I'd like that one!"

Violet thanks him, records the note, and continues, "*Beggin.*"

"Oh yeah! I'll take that one!" Mitch quickly claims.

Denny jumps in and questions Mitch, "So are these two songs you selected emotionally channeled by someone you're interested in right now?"

Flippantly, Mitch responds, "Maybe . . ." and then quickly diverts to Smike by complaining, "Come on, man, gotta pick a song. I got two, Violet got two, Denny got one! You? Zip."

This is the first time Smike had been informed of the Frankie Valli event. Once he heard the gig's theme, his spirit floated away from the band's discussion. Forced memory, hurtful and regretful feelings emerged. He once played *Can't Take My Eyes Off of You* on his harmonica for Louisa. She asked him to sing that song for her, that is, in his *own* voice and not some silly impersonation. Smike tightens from this pinching memory. He never demonstrated the courage to sing to Louisa in his *own* voice. Always gave an excuse his voice could not honor the song, or any song for that matter. He believed his excuse, but Louisa didn't. He chased his argument to her by singing something funny like a new song by a different celebrity with some type of speech impediment, style, or accent. She would laugh and appear to just blow it off, but he doubted she wasn't hurt that he couldn't trust her enough to be vulnerable in front of her. To sing to her. To openly display his fears, his inadequacies, his perceived short fallings. He should have sung to her. He waited too late. Tried on her deathbed, but never knew if she heard him or understood. He failed her. He failed himself. He failed them as a couple. He failed their love for each other.

Waving his hand to get Smike's attention, Mitch calls out, "You okay man? Think we lost ya for a bit."

Nudged back into the present, Smike joylessly and with a blank expression responds, "If it's on the list, I can play *Can't Take My Eyes Off of You* on my harmonica, perhaps one of you can sing it."

"Okay, thanks" Mitch responds with a concerned expression, and looks quizzingly at Violet and Denny like *What's going on?*

To deflect the awkwardness, Violet quickly confirms, "I'll sing that song."

Noticing something was off with Smike, Violet then says, "We have a few more songs to figure out, but what we have will work for now. Let's call it a day. Don't need to overdo it right now. Can talk more on Friday before or after our show. The Valli gig isn't for two more weeks anyway."

Chapter LXXXI   Over Did It

Paps worked on his garden all morning and then decided to cut the yard. Grass was getting tall and Michael was too busy this week to mow the yard, with his driving job and an extra band practice added to his schedule. Tuesday was an all-day outing to Nettie's grave site and it didn't help that it rained on Thursday; which was the only other day when Michael was available to complete yard work. He told his grandfather that he would cut the lawn on Saturday. Even though it was Friday, Paps just didn't want to wait another day for Michael to cut it. His impatience wouldn't allow it.

It wasn't easy, but he somehow finished cutting the grass by lunch time, leaving the lawn mower in the front yard. He then went inside to grab a sandwich and large glass of ice water. *Damn it!* he thinks as he looks in the fridge. He was out of mayo and cursed under his breath because the ham sandwich just wouldn't taste the same, especially with those fresh tomatoes from the garden. Need the mayo. So, grabbing his wallet, keys, and cane, he limped out to his car; he'll just have to drive to the grocery store. Keys in the ignition, it doesn't turn over. He keeps trying, but the battery is dead as a doornail. *Son ova bitch, muhthah aw Gawd!!!* Paps yells to himself.

Grabbing his cane, he gets out of his car and heads to the convenience store. With each step, his knee was killing him! He ignored the pain as best he could and continued to the store. Once there, he skipped his typical store tour and quickly grabbed some mayonnaise, paid for it, and slowly returned home.

Barely making it up the porch steps, he goes into the kitchen and prepares his sandwich exactly the way he likes it. He then hobbles to the front room and plops down in his lounger. The pain was more intense than he experienced in the past. In fact, he didn't even want to get up to grab some ice for his now swollen and throbbing knee. And, he didn't want to take the pills prescribed by the doctor either because that would mean no beer this evening. He felt terrible and surely didn't want Michael to see him this way, basically incompetent, let alone have Michael harp on him to take his meds or try to schedule surgery for an earlier date. And now, of course, he's already going to need Michael's help in replacing his dead car battery.

Fuck he thinks, *if it's not one thing, its anuhthah!*

He decides to call Elsye. He knows that he can trust her. Michael never found out that Paps cracked a molar and had it excised the previous week. She kept his confidence with that secret. He's just hoping that she can fit him in with her work schedule to help him out.

Chapter LXXXII   Friends Now, Forever…

"Can't make this a habit Sid!" Elsye verbalizes as a mandate when she enters the house around seven that evening.

Paps called Elsye again; this time, in pain with his knee. He explained to her that he was prescribed painkillers, but the label cautions against drinking alcohol while taking these pills at the same time. He is NOT going to give up his beer and needs a different solution to address the affliction. Before she could ask about Michael, he gave her the run down. Being Friday, Michael drives all day and has a gig in the evening. Generally, after Rally drops him off, Michael hops in his car that is pre-loaded with all of his musical equipment and rarely even runs into the house to say hello to his grandfather. Besides, if Paps shared his discomfort with Michael, he would probably only recommend a warm soak in the tub anyway. The old man is hoping that Elsye might know of some exotic Asian therapy, ointment, alternative treatment or homeopathy that could relieve his agonizing discomfort.

"Well, I recommend you ditch the beer and take the pills, but since you're against what the doctor prescribed, have you considered marijuana?" Elsye suggests.

Squelching her advice, Paps hollers "I'm not gonna smoke anythin, 'specially sumthin illegal!"

"Sid, it's 2018 and recreational marijuana is now legal in Massachusetts" Elsye elucidates to inform Paps of the current status of THC in the state.

"Damn, my genahayshun stahted the whole Mayry Jane thing befoah it was legal. That doan bothah me as much as the smokin paht. Doan wanna mess up my lungs."

Elsye adds clarification, "Don't have to smoke it. There are edibles in the form of gummies, chocolate, cookies, and drinks. A whole barrage of choices to make on how you ingest the product."

Somewhat uplifted, Paps responds "I remembah brownies. Yeah, that would be good. Do they have it as chewin gum?" he then asks.

"I believe so, not sure though" she responds, then adds, "If you're well enough to move a little, why don't you get ready and I'll take you to a shop where you can pick out a few goodies."

Elsye only makes this suggestion for him to go with her because she knows about his restlessness *and* she is concerned that he would probably complain about whatever she picked out for him. This has to be on his terms for it to work. He has to be in control and make all the decisions.

Although in a lot of pain, Paps is always willing to go somewhere, especially a new store.

He struggles to get up and says, "I'll be ready inna few minutes."

"Okay, bring identification like your driver's license and cash or credit card" she reminds him.

Once ready, they leave the house and drive to the closest recreational dispensary. After checking in and a short wait, the greeter guides Paps and Elsye to the main section of the store with the products.

When entering Paps says, "Theyah's a familiah smell to the room that no one fawgets."

Elsye responds, "So, you have indulged before, huh, Sid?"

"Like I said, my genahayshun brought national attentshun to the pot scene. But, moah so, had whiffs of this in both of my kids' rooms at some point dawin theyah teenage yeeahs."

They reach the counter and the THC barista asks, "So, what are you looking for?"

Elsye responds, "This senior citizen, Vietnam veteran, is looking for something to relieve his knee pain. It needs to be an edible."

"Well, we have edibles that contain just CBD, those that only contain THC, or a combo. If you want something that both relieves pain and promotes relaxation, I suggest the combo. We have some gummies that are very popular and effective. You get a discount for being a senior or based on your military status" the clerk shares.

Paps looks at Elsye for a suggestion as he has no idea about CBD, THC, combos, gummies, and all the rest of it. Elsye thinks that having Paps relax would be an added blessing to this situation.

He defers to her recommendation, so she says, "The combo will work for him."

"How many packages?" asks the clerk.

Elsye looks to Paps for an answer.

Realizing he has no idea, she asks, "How much do you want to spend Paps?"

"I brought sixty dollahs with me" he replies.

"Give us sixty dollars' worth, adjust for his discount and include a ten percent tip for you" Elsye directs the clerk.

Paps leans over and whispers in her ear, "Ya havta tip him?"

She snaps at him, "He gave good advice. Would you rather spend money on trying out other stuff that doesn't work for you? Besides, you're getting a discount for just being an old, cheap geezer."

"Okay, ya doan havta get nasty" Paps whines.

"Trust me, after you try this stuff, we will be friends, forever" Elsye confides.

Paps mutters under his breath, "Drug pushah!"

Elsye smirks.

They are barely in the car when Paps rips open the bag; pops open one container, removes a gummy, and throws it in his mouth.

"Slow down big boy. Just know that this will take some time to kick in" Elsye informs Paps.

"Hmmph, hopin this wawks" he skeptically laments.

Chapter LXXXIII   Fugue State

After a long Friday evening with the band's gig and a short meeting afterwards to discuss new songs for the pending Swift River Valley performance, Smike returns home close to midnight, spots Elsye's car out front, and walks in to find Paps not sitting in his lounge chair as usual, but next to Elsye on the couch with the TV turned off, and a slumbering Beauregard plopped on the floor by his grandfather. Also, Paps is barefooted with a tub of water nearby and a pair of heavy-duty rubber kitchen gloves beside it. Looks like his toe nails have been trimmed.

Paps and Elsye are both looking at Smike as he enters. He is startled at this altered seating arrangement, the appearance of a completed pedicure that Paps resisted for so long, and that Elsye is even at their house with Beauregard at this late hour on a Friday night.

Paps greets him in a loud, slurring, drawn out fashion, "Howwww ya dooin *Sssmichael*?"

Realizing that Paps is somehow incapacitated, but very surprised because even though Paps drinks beer daily, he has never really seen him drunk, so he asks Elsye, "What's up with him?"

With an unmoved look she responds, "He's toasted."

At which Paps turns to Elsye, and through a wide Cheshire grin, snaps, "Like a *mahshmallow*!"

Paps then laughs hysterically at his own response.

While chuckling, he quickly turns back to Smike wide-eyed as if he surprisingly just acquired some great revelation through divine intervention, and says, "Hey *Smichael*, that sounds good, go to the cubbid and get sum of that mahshmallow fluffy stuff in a jah and bring it to me with a LAHGE spoon!"

Elsye rolls her eyes and then darts a look and head side nod directed to the end table covered in empty snack packages all over it.

She informs Smike, "Obviously, he has the munchies."

Fumbling around, Paps mumbles, "Wayuh's my clickah?" and then leans down talking to Beauregard next to him on the floor, "Wanna watch sum TV ole boy?"

Smike looks perplexed, not clear how Paps' state of mind and altered persona happened. Elsye picks up on his confusion, turns the TV on, hands Paps the remote controller, gets up and walks into the kitchen dragging Smike along.

She explains, "Paps called me earlier to come over since you had a band gig. Said he has been in a lot of pain and didn't want to take the pain killers the doctor prescribed. Said they were poison. Plus, if he took them, he couldn't drink his beer. And you know beer is a priority for him. I suggested pot as a more natural solution, especially since it's now legal. Thought he would balk. But said he didn't want to smoke anything, even if it was legal. So, I told him about edibles, and he was surprisingly agreeable to that option. Took him to a dispensary and he picked out his goodies. Popped one as soon as we got in my car. On our way back, had to pick up Beauregard since I am watching him this evening. Paps wasn't too thrilled about that but couldn't do anything about it."

Just Saying

She continues, "When we got to your house, he was impatient that he wasn't feeling anything yet, so he ate another gummie before I could stop him. I have been with him the whole time. He's been sailing and happy for the last three hours and hasn't complained about the pain since and has also warmed up to Beauregard, loving on him and calling him *ole boy*. When he was fully relaxed, I took the opportunity to offer a toe nail trim. Remarkably, he agreed. Anyway, I grabbed some items from his bathroom and gloves from the kitchen, and violà! Done, nice and neat. And, you won't believe this, but he enjoyed it! Also, think you have a newly ordained pothead on your hands. Here's the thing, though, and this is very important; he's *much* more pleasant in this fugue state, so you'll probably both be happier with this newly discovered medicinal gem!"

Listening to every detail Elsye shares, while getting the marshmallow treat and spoon from the kitchen, Smike notes that the fluff expiration date has passed months ago. Elsye gestures a shrug like *so what?* and tells him that Paps won't notice and has probably eaten older stuff over the years. He nods in passive agreement as they exit the kitchen.

With demanded items in hand, they both return to the family room where Paps, upon seeing them, immediately reaches out his arms, fingers wiggling like a five-year-old, motioning *come on and* saying something about *'give me the pogey bait.'* Smike passes the dated sugary goop and oversized spoon to his grandfather as he and Elsye sit silently on the couch next to him and watch Paps slowly spoon out the soft treat, devouring every bite while watching in fascination a series of random commercials. Paps' normal ongoing caustic comments have silenced.

Smike leans over to Elsye and whispers, "I can live with this."

Elsye gestures an affirmative nod and smile while replying, "Thought so!"

She then asks, "Would you like some?" as she pulls out the container of edibles.

Grinning, he says, "Don't need it right now. Totally enjoying the peacefulness of the evening."

Resting her head on Smike's shoulder, she says, "Me too, but he sure is making that marshmallow stuff look good!"

They both laugh softly. Paps turns to look at them, holding up an overloaded gooey spoonful, and brandishes a sticky grin. They both laugh again, a little harder this time.

Smike mentions an additional observation, "By the way, I noticed the kitchen gloves. Understand you had to protect yourself. So appreciative! I mean, I would never go near that hazard zone of those contorted and repugnant toenails. You deserve some kind of medal for heroism!"

Elsye replies with quick wit, "Well, I guess I do have the *mettle* to *meddle* with nails not made of *metal*, so I probably do deserve a *medal*."

Smiling, Smike grabs her hand, gently raises it to his mouth, and chivalrously kisses it in a demonstrative fashion.

He then complimentarily states, "Elsye, you truly are gifted in so many ways!"

Just Saying

She jovially shares, "Just inspired by those close to me."

Paps soon falls asleep on the couch. Smike throws a crocheted blanket over him. Then, he and Elsye go upstairs to his room.

Chapter LXXXIV   French Humor

Out of curiosity, Elsye asks, "So, tell me about your grandmother. Paps lovingly talked about her while he was high. Got a little sentimental and teared up too. Never saw him this way before, seems out of his nature. Regarding your grandmother, I mean, she must've been a saint to be with him."

"My grandmother was warm, loving, and hilarious! From what she shared with me, she had a hard life growing up very poor in a depressed area of New Brunswick, Canada. Spoke French and knew very little English. As a young woman, she got sponsored for US citizenship by a doctor in Haverhill because she was known for being a hard worker, great with kids, and a wonderful, self-taught cook. She worked as a nanny, housekeeper, and cook for various families in town when she met Paps. They were introduced by a cousin of hers who said Paps was *a good guy* because he helped out at the church."

"Okay, but what did she see in your grandfather to *marry* him?"

"She told me that when they first met, she thought he was handsome. They started seeing each other and he wooed her. Never knew exactly how he wooed her, but she said he was a kinder, different person before Vietnam."

"So, your grandmother was French Canadian, did she teach you French? Parlez-vous français?" Elsye asks.

"No, not really. Just know a few dirty words" he chuckles.

"I took French in high school. So, tell me some dirty words you know in French" she requests.

Just Saying

Smike elaborates, "There is a story behind this one. When I was four-years-old, I stayed with my grandparents over the summer. Their garden was in full bloom with tomatoes, loose leaf lettuce, peppers, green beans, cabbage, whatever they could grow in the small backyard lot. Let's just say, the fresh salads were amazing!"

He continues, "Paps was mostly proud of his tomatoes. One day, and I can't tell you why, remember I was four, I decided to pee in the watering can. Guess I thought it was funny. Paps saw me and started screaming, 'Shit, shit, SHIT, Michael Alan Schrod, yaw gonna kill my t'maydah plants!' Grandma Nettie yelled at Paps to stop swearing and then firmly told me 'Michael, put your *souris* back in your pants.' I thought that was the French word for penis. She spoke in broken English quite a bit."

Elsye laughs out loud and after a short, surprised silence, explains "No, *souris* means *mouse*! Guess your grandmother had her own nickname for men's most beloved body part. That is hysterical!"

Shocked, Smike chuckles, "All these years, I never knew, just assumed I knew what she meant. Oh well, Grandma Nettie could be silly!"

"Actually, if you think about it, she was brilliant because" Elsye then gently rests her hands on Michael's hips and says "where there's mice . . ." then while slowly pulling him closer adds "there's pussy."

Both smiling, they share an affectionate gaze. He softly grabs both her hands, moves them behind her hips, pulls her close, and tenderly kisses her. The kiss is brief, but he holds the embrace as he rests his chin on her head. From this physical exchange, Elsye knew that he liked her. She knew that he was attracted to her. But she also knew he was still in love with Louisa. Smike's interminable emotional connection with Louisa would prevent their relationship from going any further. She knew that. Elsye was actually fine with this relational status. She respected him and enjoyed their friendship. He was not an idiot like so many other guys she had known over the years. She also felt confident that they could continue this playful pattern and that was acceptable to her as well because she wasn't really looking for any deep or committed relationship. She told herself, *not at this time, anyway.*

Chapter LXXXV   Turning Point

Smike's music writing continued to flow; and most recently, seemed to escalate. Louisa was no longer his sole muse, although she would always be his soul inspiration. Oddly, Paps emerged as a quirky source for both whimsical tunes as well as sentimental ones. That surprised Smike, sort of. He also experienced flashes of lyrical ideas from interactions with his closest chums Rally and Mitch, and of course, his dearest friend, Elsye. In fact, even JoJo and Slim stirred expressive thoughts and unique phrases captured in his music.

Nearly every Saturday evening when he and Elsye typically met, he played some of his budding work. She was his trusted sounding board, constructive critic, and indisputable enthusiast of his music. However, despite Elsye's vehement urging that his songs were ready to be premiered, he doubted a larger audience would be as ardently receptive.

Elsye understood his hesitancy based on an audience of one (her alone), so she encouraged him to play a few songs for his bandmates to get their take on his work. Or, at least, pitch some songs to Mitch, with whom he shared a personal as well as musical connection. He readily dismissed her suggestion.

At one point, Elsye got tired of Smike dragging his feet on her suggestion to share his music, so she created a four-point rating system based on shades of the color orange (denoting the Capote reference) for determining 'completion' of songs. 'Honey' (on the palest end of the orange spectrum) represented 'brand new or fresh' working ideas. 'Marmalade' signified 'keepers or keep going.' 'Pumpkin' stood for 'ripe, just needs final tweaks.' And, 'Vermillion' (richest shade on the color continuum) meant 'done, ready to go, and just right.' Using this rating system, she identified four of his songs as Vermillion, two Pumpkins, three Marmalade tunes, and half a dozen more Honey song drafts. This humorous but fruitful act on Elsye's part got Smike's attention and forced a turning point for him. Apparently, it *was* time to share some of his songs with others. At the band's next practice, he would play one song for them on his harmonica.

The band met Sunday morning to prepare for a very recently booked, last-minute Wednesday birthday event at Fred's, which rarely happens mid-week. However, Fred was receptive to the idea because he saw it as an easy draw of customers in the middle of the week without any expense for the band's fee. The birthday girl, who just happened to be Rebecca, would pay for the band's performance.

As they wrapped up their practice, Smike asked them for a little of their time to listen to something he had been working on. He chose to play the melody tentatively titled *Learning from Mistakes*. Mitch, Denny, and Violet were enthralled; they all loved the bluesy sound. Violet immediately asked for the lyrics and musical sheet. She wanted to sing it. Mitch was literally *singing* his praises and Denny asked if he could play it again so Granny Mabel could hear it. Astounded, but ecstatic, Smike did not expect this level of reception and encouragement. Denny then called Granny Mabel into the garage and Smike played the song a second time for her. She also loved the song and said the tune was "smoothly catchy."

Leaving band practice, Smike immediately called Elsye to thank her.

She asked, "What for?"

Just Saying

He replied, "For encouraging me to make that turn!"

His week was starting off in a new direction. A refreshed enthusiasm flowed into his music writing.

Chapter LXXXVI   Fly on the Wall

Per Paps' demand, Smike arranged for David and his boys to fix the torn-up walls from the plumbing work. They needed to replace dry wall, float and tape, texturize the surface, and then paint the walls. David informed Smike that he and his boys could complete almost everything over two days and they were available on Monday and Tuesday.

Paps liked the idea of having David around. Smike liked that this remaining work would soon be over and done with so quickly. He originally worried that his grandfather would want the two of them to tackle this project together and that would be emotionally challenging on so many levels. However, because Paps likes David and his hourly rates and material prices were so reasonable, there was no push back on scheduling the wall work.

Smike knew David was familiar with Paps' ways, so he would know what to expect regarding the elderly chap's obsessiveness in overseeing the job. Fortunately, that would just be an issue on Monday because Smike fully intended on distracting his grandfather when he was home on Tuesday. He hoped to take him on store visits as it had been a while since the two of them did that together, which would diminish the amount of time for Paps to grate on David's and his boys' nerves. They could stop at an auto shop to pick up a new car battery as well, and then later, Paps could oversee him replacing it. That would take a couple of hours. Smike felt this was a solid plan for distracting his grandfather during the wall repairs.

When he returned from work Monday afternoon, all seemed to have gone well that day. He saw David briefly, who through unspoken communication indicated that things went smoothly. Paps seemed happy too. Apparently, he felt totally in control the whole time; otherwise, Smike would have received an earful of his bitching.

Tuesday morning though, Paps did not want to go anywhere with Smike. Even though he inherently trusted David and his boys, he stayed put; wasn't going outside the walls of his own home. That also meant that Smike wasn't venturing out either. He felt that he needed to stick around and intervene in Paps' meddling on the work when possible. He could possibly divert his grandfather's attention to the garden for a short period of time in the morning, but that probably would only last so long. He then had a ridiculous thought. What if he offered to play some of his songs to Paps? How would he respond? Would he be receptive? He quickly rejected that notion based on memories surfacing from all of his grandfather's previous refusals to attend any of Smike's performances. Instead, he decided to shadow Paps like a harmless fly on the wall. Through this approach, he may be able to possibly soften or arbitrate some of his grandfather's hawking over the workers.

Smike's efforts to intervene were only partially effective. He could tell by the end of the day that David's and his boys' patience were shot with Paps' intrusive and controlling presence. However, although they were all worn down by his pestering, the work was completed late in the afternoon. Smike was certain that David and his sons were determined to finish as quickly as possible, just to be done with Paps.

As David was leaving, he quietly complimented Smike by saying, "Bless you, as I now understand what you have to deal with on a daily basis. No fun! You're a goodhearted grandson. Now, I wanna dub you Saint Michael!"

Smike thought that might be an appropriate label since it was late in the day now and he still needed to run out, pick up a car battery, and replace it so that Paps had a running vehicle.

Chapter LXXXVII   Dire Situation

After being cooped up at home overseeing the wall work for several days, Paps decides to walk to the local convenience store on this pleasant Wednesday afternoon to get some fresh air and pick up a few items. He arrives at the store and quickly gathers some products, then exits, and heads home.

Nearing his house, he sees Susan on the sidewalk holding baby Sadie, who he had not yet met.

She spots him and hysterically calls out, "Sir Sid, been looking for you! We are in a dire situation. Queen Jeanne is under a witch's spell! I couldn't help her!"

Paps responds in a calming voice, "Hold on Susan, speak a little moah slowly and tell me exactly what's goin on."

"I don't know! I tried to wake her! I tried to call for help, but the castle's phone doesn't work" she says more agitatedly.

Not sure if Susan is imagining a problem or if there is something truly wrong, concern consumes him as Susan seems distraught, in a delusional state, and does not appear stable. More importantly, she's holding this young, vulnerable baby. Walking to Jeanne's home to check on her is much farther away than his home, which is less than two blocks from where they are standing. He can call Jeanne once he gets home or if need be, get in his car and drive over to check on her.

To keep Susan and the baby safe for now, he tries to convince her to follow him.

"Susan, please come to my house. I'll call faw assistance from the kingdom wizahds. They'll know what to do!"

"Sir Sid, you are my knight in shining armor! I was walking to your castle for your help. Yes, please call the wizards" Susan gratefully replies.

As they walk to Paps' house, he asks Susan in more detail about what possibly happened. Very edgy at this point, Susan obscurely describes a situation with Jeanne on the floor, not moving. She explained how she tried rousing her to no avail and panicked when the house phone didn't work, and she couldn't find Jeanne's purse for her cell phone and car keys.

They enter Paps' house. He goes directly to the phone and calls Jeanne's cell. No response. Her phone goes to voice mail. He leaves a message for her to call him as soon as possible. He then calls her land line and it's busy. He decides to call her friend, Jean. She doesn't answer her phone either, so he leaves a message for her as well. He is very worried right now but doesn't want to raise any additional alarm in front of Susan.

Susan asks, "Are the wizards coming?"

"We need to drive ovah to yaw house, Susan. Let me get my cah keys" he responds.

Adamant in her conviction, Susan snaps "Sadie can't ride in your carriage without her royal car seat."

Paps can't take them with him, but he can't leave Susan and Sadie alone in his house either. He wants to call nine-one-one but remembers Jeanne telling him that her guardianship over Susan and Sadie was tentative. She once told him how she was worried about losing custody due to her age even though she is only in her early seventies. If he calls nine-one-one, child services may be contacted to evaluate her fitness and can possibly cause the guardianship to be lost. A real mess for her. He doesn't want that to happen. He thought to call Smike, but he already returned home after driving all day and then left to meet with band mates at Fred's Tavern for a scheduled mid-week birthday performance. Smike isn't expected to get home until around eleven that evening or later. As his reliable backup, he calls Elsye.

"Elsye, this is a *real* emahgency. How soon can ya get ovah heeah?" he pleads.

Chapter LXXXVIII   Disrupted Intervention

Elsye quickly shows up at Paps, sees a young woman holding a baby, and jokingly says to him, "So, the emergency is you've been asked to take a paternity test?"

She quickly notices the grave look on his face and shifts into a serious stance.

Now trying to support the situation, Elsye asks, "What's going on? How can I help?"

Susan urgently interjects, "Is she the wizard Sir Sid? Can she break the witch's spell on Queen Jeanne?"

Elsye looks confused and says, "What's she talking about?"

Paps says, "I'll explain laytah" then while pointing says, "This is Susan. Need faw ya to stay with hah and hah baby Sadie faw a couple of minutes while I drive ovah to theyah house to check on Jeanne. Sumthin is wrong."

"Just call nine-one-one" Elsye instructs him.

"NO! Doan want any authahities involved, trust me" Paps loudly rebuts.

Susan starts shrieking, "I don't know this Wizard Sir Sid, don't leave me and Sadie alone with her!"

Her screaming causes Sadie to start crying. Susan carefully puts Sadie down on the couch, then hastily grabs Paps' car keys from the end table and runs out of the house.

Just Saying

As she exits, she yells to Paps, "Protect Princess Sadie, Sir Sid! I need your chariot!"

Both temporarily shocked by this action, with neither one clear about Susan's intention, they just stare at each other. Quickly realizing that Susan is headed to Paps' car, Elsye runs after her. Susan had already jumped in the car and started backing out of the driveway. Elsye runs along the side of the car and pounds on the window for her to stop, to no avail. Susan pulls out and speeds down the road.

Returning to the house, Elsye starts peppering Paps with questions to find out the context of this situation. Apparently, this young woman, Susan, with an obvious mental health issue, has left a baby with them and just absconded with Paps' car.

Elsye cautions him, "Got to call the police now! This is serious!"

"No, we doan wanna draw attention to this situation with the staties. Jeanne may be fine and doan wan hah to lose gahdianship ovah what may be nothin. That would break hah haht. Let me call Michael" Paps says.

He calls, but no response. Goes to voice mail. He calls Fred's Tavern, but the line is busy.

"Whatda fuck is wrong with all the phones tudday? No connections! No one is ansahin!" Paps laments.

As Sadie cries more loudly, Elsye goes over and picks her up.

Cuddling to comfort her, Elsye says, "She's a beautiful little girl!"

"Hand hah to me. Need faw ya to drive ovah to Fred's and get Michael" Paps requests and then explains "I need to stay heeah if Susan comes back."

"You can take care of a baby Paps?" Elsye nervously queries.

"Raised two of my own. Get goin" he commands.

Elsye explains, "Here is the thing, I will not be returning after I find Smike and fill him in on what is going on. I have to work tonight, understand? That means you may have the baby by yourself for a while."

"Doan wawhy 'bout it!" Paps answers, drawing the words out in a mocking tone.

Handing Sadie to Paps, Elsye adds, "One more thing. You owe me *and* I already know what I want from you. Please agree to honor my relatively painless request that will be shared with you in the very near future."

"Okay, okay, whatevah ya need" Paps stingily agrees.

Elsye leaves. Paps holds Sadie close and sits in his lounger to rock her while waiting for Michael to show up and help out. He is now worried about both Jeanne and Susan and hopes Susan will just come back to his house. He keeps calling to get someone on the line.

Chapter LXXXIX   Connection

Heading to the bar, Elsye repeatedly tries calling Smike on his cell phone, but he doesn't pick up. After arriving at Fred's Tavern, she storms in looking for Smike. It is rather early on a Wednesday afternoon, so the place is somewhat vacant.

She spots Mitch by the bar talking with Fred and frantically asks, "Where's Smike? He's not answering his phone and I need to talk to him *now*!"

Mitch turns toward Elsye, smiles a warm visual greeting and then joshes, "Hey, slow down, don't get your panties all in a twist!"

"I don't wear panties" she snaps in all seriousness.

Startled, but pleasantly amused with her personally revealing response (which he hopes is true), Mitch grins broadly and says, "Hey, Miss Commando, did I tell you that I *like* you?"

"Well, the feeling is not reciprocated! Just where the hell is he?" She states in an annoyed and anxious tone.

Mitch responds, "He left to pick up some veggie wraps for all of us before our meeting to discuss our play list for the evening's birthday bash. Should be back in about ten minutes or so. What's going on that you so urgently need to talk with him right now?"

Bothered, Elsye summarizes "Paps had a visitor who is a little unhinged. He won't let me call the police and has tried to call Smike but got no response."

Mitch explains, "He turns his phone off when we meet for practice, but I'm surprised!"

Smirking, he adds, "Surprised that *you*, such a strong, independent thinking, self-proclaimed problem-fixer aren't able to handle an octogenarian issue!"

She snaps at him, "I manage ten-year-olds and those who act like ten-year-olds, just like *you*, all the time with ease, no trouble! Paps is not acting like a kid right now, so can't tap those skills. This is serious!"

She then adds, "By the way, Paps is not eighty yet, so he's a septuagenarian, not an octogenarian."

Mitch just smiles at her in adoration. He really likes her. She *is* smart *and* feisty!

Smike comes walking through the tavern door with several bags of food and sees Elsye and Mitch tensely talking. He wonders what is going on. Elsye spots him and quickly marches his direction. Mitch follows, curious about what will happen next.

Chapter XC Sad Sack Lullaby

Paps keeps trying to make calls while holding and attempting to console Sadie. A nasty smell starts to draw his attention. He puts the phone down and checks her diaper. Sure enough, she has delivered a specimen worthy of some ungodly behemoth creature! How could such an adorable, young child produce such a foul gargantuan mound of crap? There are no diapers in the house, and he can't keep holding her with this smell making him gag and almost pass out.

Holding her at arm's length, he balances himself on his good leg, gets up and with Sadie in one arm and holding his cane with his other arm, shuffles into the kitchen. Placing her in the kitchen sink, he removes her diaper, and while gagging, with one hand moves the soiled nappy to the side. He then lifts Sadie and uses the faucet sprayer to rinse the excrement off her body, while she cries more intensely. From the side drawer, he pulls out a couple of dish clothes to dry her. Realizing that he can't leave her naked, as another evacuation could occur, which would create a bigger mess; he grabs a couple more dish towels and duct tape from the drawer. He clumsily returns to the couch with Sadie and the makeshift diaper items. Laying her down, he arranges the cloths under her and uses duct tape to keep them in place. His project nearly completed, he picks her up and returns to the kitchen to retrieve two convenience store plastic bags. One is for the nasty, soiled diaper and the other to place over her makeshift diaper, fashioning it to be relatively waterproof. Somehow while holding her, he grabs a pair of scissors and cuts off the corners of one of the bags. Returning to the couch, he slips the plastic bag cut-out corners over her legs and uses more duct tape to keep the bag in place.

"Okay now Sadie, ya ah clean, ya ah diapahed, and ya ah wotta proof! Feel beddah?" Paps says to Sadie in a comforting manner.

She starts wailing! Paps has no idea what is wrong. He picks her up and starts jostling her for comfort. She isn't responding to any of his tactics and continues to cry violently. Doing the best that he can for at least twenty minutes or so, Paps' concern has grown while his patience has appreciably thinned.

After no productive results in calming her, he says, "Hey Sadie, doan be such a sad sack Bahjahrac!"

Desperate, he lays her on her back on the couch, takes out his gum, and starts whistling a lovely and soothing lullaby. Sadie slowly stops crying, utters a few more whimpers, and locks eyes with him as he continues to whistle. She is completely mesmerized with his impromptu musical performance. Totally focusing on Sadie, Paps continues whistling while worrying about what has happened to Jeanne, where Susan went with his car, and when Michael will get home.

Chapter XCI New Awareness

After Elsye's quick explanation of the situation, Smike says, "I had heard about Susan and her baby, but don't know details of her condition. Can't believe she took Paps' car! Also, Paps said something once about Jeanne being diabetic."

"Well, you've gotta get home. I can't join you. Dog walking and sitting Diggiddy tonight, that high energy Jack Russell Terrier, sorry" Elsye shares, and then adjoins, "and you can't call the cops. Paps was adamant about that! But call me later with an update."

Concerned, Mitch asks Smike, "How long is this gonna take? Are you gonna make it back for our show? I mean, Rebecca arranged her birthday party because of you, you know that, right?"

Smike hands him the bags of food and says, "Not sure how long it will take. Will try my best to get back quickly but got to get home and help if I can."

He then turns to Elsye and hugs her while saying, "Thank you for being there for me and Paps. You're a great friend! I appreciate everything you do for us! Will call you later with an update."

"Sure, anytime!" she replies.

Smike then quickly exits, leaving Elsye and Mitch standing there.

Mitch says to her, "So, you're a dog lover, huh? I prefer cats myself."

Elsye snidely responds, "I don't care!" then turns, and without looking back, quickly leaves.

Mitch thinks, *protests too much, she likes me.*

As Smike heads home, he tries calling Paps' landline to let him know that he is on his way. The phone is busy. Perhaps Paps is talking to someone about the situation. Within a few minutes, Smike is in the driveway and pulls up all the way to the shed. Quietly entering through the back door, he hears beautiful whistling and thinks that Paps must be playing a CD or something. Walking toward the family room, he sees Paps on the couch with Sadie. Paps is melodically whistling and the baby is cooing with delight. With his back to Smike, Paps doesn't notice him there. Smike stays behind Paps' sight and just listens. Amazed, he had no clue that his grandfather could whistle. He never whistled for him, well not that he could remember, and he definitely would have remembered. Why would Paps keep this musical talent a secret? Suddenly struck with a new awareness, Smike realizes that he needs to go to the back door and make some noise so that Paps knows he is home.

He yells out, "Paps, I'm home."

The whistling stops.

"I'm in the pahlah with the baby" Paps replies.

Smike walks in and says, "Elsye, gave me some info, but still sketchy about the details."

"Susan is a good gahl Michael. Somethin happened and she's wawhied 'bout hah grandmuhthah and we haven't been able to get ahold of hah. I think Susan took my cah to go back home" Paps explains.

"How long has it been?" Smike asks.

"Ovah an owah, I think. Listen, can ya drive ovah to Jeanne's house and check? Not fah away" Paps requests.

"Yes, I can do that, but Elsye said that Susan seems off and she doesn't know me, so how will she react to me? I'm a stranger to her" Smike says.

"Didn't think 'bout that! Yaw right, she might get scayahed" Paps responds.

"And, I tried calling you Paps, but couldn't get through. Did you hang up your phone?" Smike asks.

"Damn, let me check. Was a little crazy faw a few minutes with Sadie" Paps replies.

Sure enough, Paps had failed to hang up the phone. He quickly returns the receiver to its base.

Smike looks at Sadie in the crude and improvised diaper and smiles.

"Looks like your duct tape saved the day, yet again Paps" he jokes.

"Yeah, well, it has many pahposes!" Paps replies.

Paps' phone rings. It's Jean. Calling from the hospital, she tells Paps that she tried to return his call, but his phone was busy. She informs him that Jeanne passed out from low blood sugar and hit her head. She has a contusion and possible concussion. The doctors are in the process of regulating her blood sugar. She further explains that when Jeanne wasn't answering her phone for confirming their regular Wednesday afternoon get-together, she went over to her house. The door was wide open. Susan and Sadie were gone. She found Jeanne on the floor by the kitchen table with a head wound bleeding and unconscious. She called nine-one-one and fortunately, after being rushed to the hospital, Jeanne was doing fine now, but didn't know where Susan and the baby went. She asks if he can help find them. Paps tells her that he has Sadie, but Susan left with his car. He doesn't know where she went. He will send Michael to their house to see if she is there. Jean is relieved the baby is safe but asks to speak with Michael. Paps hands the phone to him.

Jean shares, "Michael, Susan is schizophrenic. Don't think she's been taking her medication and not sure how she'll respond to you since she never met you before, but you can't call authorities. Could cause a problem for Jeanne. Understand?"

Smike reassures her, "Yes ma'am, I understand. I have a friend in the social work field. Think he can help and will know what to do. Just need to get ahold of him. Will have Paps call you as soon as we locate Susan and make sure she is safe."

Thankful, Jean replies, "God bless ya Michael! Tell your grandfather I have to stay at the hospital with Jeanne. Have him call me back on my cell phone later. And Jeanne's house key is under the planter to the left of the front porch, if you need it."

Smike wonders if this is a common practice for hiding house keys in this neighborhood.

Just Saying

Paps provides Smike with Jeanne's address. He then advises him that if he sees Susan to tell her that he is a Wizard sent by Sir Sid and that Queen Jeanne is recovering after receiving special potions for healing.

As Smike leaves, he is on his cell calling Rally.

"Hey man, are you busy? I need your help" Smike requests with a sense of urgency.

Chapter XCII   Friend In Need

Smike gives Rally Jeanne's address so that he can meet him there. On his way, Rally takes a slight detour and picks up Tina, his mentor and longtime inspiration. He figures that her professional experience could be helpful and since retiring, she has always responded to last-minute requests. Smike arrives at the address before Rally and sits outside to wait for him. He notices that Paps' car is erratically parked on the street in front of Jeanne's house, so Susan must be inside.

When Rally arrives, he introduces Smike to Tina. Tina asks him for as much information about the situation that he knows and can share. He summarizes that Susan is in a delusional state from schizophrenia and probably has not been taking her medication. Paps shared that Susan believes her home is a castle, that she is a Lady, her daughter is a Princess, her grandmother is the Queen, and that she sees him as a Knight. He tells Tina that Susan took Paps' car and drove back to her home, probably to check on her grandmother; however, her grandmother is no longer there. She is at the hospital recovering from a head wound after passing out from low blood sugar and hitting her head, knocking her unconscious. Susan may be more upset with her grandmother now gone.

Tina understands what he is sharing and says, "She doesn't know you and doesn't know us, right? We don't want to alarm her. Was there any other advice your grandfather provided?"

"He suggested that I identify myself as a Wizard to keep up the illusion and inform Susan that her grandmother is recovering after receiving a magical potion. And, again, we are not to call the police. Need to keep this confidential so that Jeanne doesn't lose guardianship."

Providing a plan of action, Tina suggests, "Okay, Rally, stay outside, just behind us, out of her view. Smike, you and I will go to the front door and hopefully she will let us enter. Do what your grandfather directed by identifying yourself as the Wizard who helped her grandmother. You can introduce me as a Seer who can assist her. We just need to convince her to return to your grandfather's home so that she will be kept safe."

Smike and Tina go to the front door. It is slightly open.

He calls out, "Lady Susan, Sir Sid has sent me to inform you that Queen Jeanne is well and healing."

Susan comes close to the entrance and says "You look like a young Sir Sid!" then asks, "Are you a knight as well?"

Smike fabricates his response, "I'm his kin and a Wizard" and then adds, "Queen Jeanne is recovering. She wanted us to make sure that you, Lady Susan, are safe" then advised, "Sir Sid would like you to return with us to his castle. Princess Sadie is missing her mother."

Pointing to Tina, Susan asks, "Who's this?"

Extending and embellishing the fiction, he says, "This is Seer Tina. She had a vision you would be here. She is a wise woman of the land and can help you."

Tina interposes, "Lady Susan, please join us to return to Sir Sid and Princess Sadie."

Susan starts scrambling around the house and blathering as Smike and Tina, not wanting to unease Susan, slowly and cautiously enter the home.

Ambling around the room, Sarah says, "Can't leave yet. Need some things. Need diapers. Need Sadie's royal car seat" when she suddenly plops down on the floor, starts crying, and sputters, "Need to see Queen Jeanne. She needs to be alright."

Tina sits on the floor next to Susan and tentatively tries to comfort her.

Staying with the delusion, Tina gently asks, "Lady Susan, do you have any potions of your own that the Royal doctor has prescribed?"

Between sobs, Susan says, "Yeah, but I haven't been taking them. Don't have a Royal Wet Nurse and don't want any poisonous potion going into Sadie. But don't tell Queen Jeanne! Don't want to upset her" she lamented.

Through just one question, very quickly and with little effort, Tina unearthed the issue of *how* Susan was in a disturbed condition and *why* she ceased taking her medication. She was trying to protect her child by avoiding her doses but wanted to maintain a close bond with Sadie through nursing. Smike was relieved to hear Susan's response and felt that this previously unknown issue could be successfully resolved.

Tina reassures Susan, "I understand Lady Susan. That makes sense on what you are sharing with us. Let's gather everything you need and go to Sir Sid's house."

Just Saying

Susan yields to Tina's suggestion and Tina then assists her in collecting all the items for Sadie. They all exit and lock the house.

Leaving, Susan sees Rally just outside the house entrance and asks, "Who's he?"

Not missing a beat, Rally replies, "I'm the Court Jester, me Lady."

Smike smiles. His friend has delivered assistance on so many levels when crucially needed. He owes him and Tina a huge debt of gratitude. Heading to Smike's car, Susan says she wants to go in Sir Sid's royal carriage to return it to him. So, Smike, Tina, and Susan get in Paps' car. Rally follows in his car. They will return later to get Smike's vehicle.

Chapter XCIII   Somewhat Settled

The ensemble enters Paps' home and Smike notices his grandfather's immediate relief in seeing all of them there. Paps hands Sadie to Susan and she sits on the couch tenderly loving on her baby. Smike quickly introduces Paps to Rally and Tina. Tina then sits next to Susan on the couch. Smike tells Paps that Rally is taking him back to get his car at Jeanne's and he will then go directly to his gig, returning later in the evening. Rally will come back, and with Tina, will stay with all of them until he returns.

Paps informs Smike that Jean will come by later in the evening after leaving the hospital and will pick up Susan and Sadie. The visiting hours end soon, so it shouldn't be too much longer. So, Rally and Tina can leave after Jean arrives. During their phone conversation, Jean told Paps that she will stay with Susan and Sadie at Jeanne's house for as long as her friend is interned, to maintain some semblance of order for all of them. Tina comments that she feels this is a solid plan and once Jean arrives, she will fill her in on what she has learned about Susan's reason for not taking her medication.

Rally and Smike leave to get his vehicle.

As Rally drops him off, he says, "Looks like your grandfather is a soft touch for babies."

"He has his moments" Smike replies, vividly remembering the melodious whistling he secretly observed Paps use to soothe Sadie.

"Well, now I'll have some time to get to know him. Betcha twenty dollars *that I don't have*, that he will like me! Sourpusses are endeared by babies and fools. I'll act like the Court Jester and get him laughing."

"Good luck with that Rally! Thanks again and I owe you, my friend!" Smike replies as he drives off to the tavern. On his way to the bar, he calls Elsye to update her. He then calls Mitch and informs him that he should arrive just before the first song. To some extent, the crazy day has settled.

Chapter XCIV   Regrouping

Emotionally exhausted from all that has occurred, Paps gets up from his lounger and extends an offer of something to eat and drink to Susan and Tina. Shortly thereafter, Rally returns and assists Paps in the kitchen to prepare the food.

"How 'bout subs?" Paps asks Rally as he grabs sub rolls from the pantry.

"I love any meal that's *free*" Rally replies.

"So doan I! Yaw a soldjah ahfta my own haht, Rally" Paps quips, and then more seriously adds, "Least I can do faw ya. Appreciate yaw and Tina's help."

"My pleasure sir. So, you heard about my service? Smike told me, you served in Vietnam. Thank you for that Mister Schrod" Rally sincerely shares.

After opening the fridge and leaning over to grab cold cuts and condiments, Paps replies, "Long time ago" then redirects discussion with a question "So, what was yaw MOS Rally?"

Provided an opening to talk about his life, Rally did not hold back.

"Well, my Military Occupational Specialty was not so special. I was a driver. My wife, on the other hand, was a nurse. We are both using our GI Bill benefits to further our education. I'm working on a degree in social work and my wife is finishing up certification as a Registered Nurse. Tina is my inspiration for my interest in social work and a life mentor to me. She's the best but retired now."

Just Saying

Half listening while making sandwiches, Paps decides to direct Rally to help with preparing the food.

"Good faw both of ya!" Paps praises, and then requests assistance, "Grab the paypah plates ovah theyah and a knife in the drawah. I need to slice the t'maydahs."

"From your garden? They look fresh!" Rally compliments.

"Oh yeah, from the gahden and they ah joocee and delicious" Paps brags.

"Wanted to thank you for the basket of vegetables you gave us before. They were delicious! Didn't last long" Rally shares while chuckling, then adds, "And, my son Pablo LOVED those coins ya gave him. He is full into collecting now! Thanks for those as well!"

Paps nonchalantly replies, "Yaw welcome."

While gathering items, Rally prattles on and then shifting the topic of discussion asks Paps "So, didja see any action in Vietnam?"

Paps doesn't want to talk about his wartime experiences but understands that Rally asks out of genuine interest.

"Yeah, saw moah than I cayah to remembah" he blandly responds while finishing one sandwich.

He then averts, "Let's tok 'bout sumthin else. Whatcha think 'bout Michael's music?"

"Haven't heard him yet. What about you? Like his music?" Rally responds, although he already knew Paps hadn't attended any of Smike's performances. Paps asking about Smike's music surprises him.

Paps responds, "Sumthin else we have in common. Haven't hahd him play yet eithah."

"Well, guess that will have to change for both of us!" Rally suggests.

Paps doesn't acknowledge Rally's proposition.

As Paps finishes making the sandwiches, Rally takes plates out to Tina and Sarah. He returns to retrieve some drinks as Paps carries the two additional plates to the family room. As they cross paths in the hallway, Paps directs him to grab a couple of beers. Rally acknowledges with a smile. The four of them eat the makeshift meal and relax. Within an hour, Jean shows up to take Sarah and Sadie home. She shows Sarah a video on her phone of her grandmother being taken care of in the hospital. She will be coming home soon, but in the meantime, Jean will stay with them at their house. Sarah seems reassured.

Tina pulls Jean aside and reports to her what she found out about Sarah not taking her medication and the reason why. Jean appreciates the information and will help address the situation with her friend once she returns home. Sarah's doctor will be contacted as well. Rally helps Paps clean up and they soon all leave.

Chapter XCV This is Bad

Bushed, after everyone left, Paps goes to his bedroom for the evening. He will hit the sack a little early. Deserves it. Although dog-tired, he fondly thinks about the friends that came together to successfully handle the situation. He finds himself inspired by and thankful for how many helped out and how everyone played an important part in resolving what could have resulted in a not-so-pleasant situation. Smike and his friends really stepped up without giving it a second thought. Finally resting his head on his pillow, Paps quickly falls asleep with a satisfied smile on his face as dreams arise from his past.

Throughout the day and night, the woman would occasionally repeat, "điều này là xấu" when inspecting Kahn's injury. She cleaned his wound at least twice, but left Sid's alone. It had been almost two full days that Sid and Kahn received shelter and assistance from this charitable benefactress. She is saving them and they are both extremely thankful for her aid. Although nervous about what to do next, they both experience a little respite from their nagging concern of how they can return to the safety of their camp, as well as gain access to appropriate medical treatment for their injuries. In severe pain, Sid can place no weight on his right leg. Kahn is weaker from his more significant blood loss and has no vision on his left side. The woman has left them several times throughout the day for unknown reasons. They wonder why she lives alone or if she is part of a nearby village. Having no way of communicating with her, they must rely on good faith that her intentions are completely benevolent.

At a point when the woman is not in the hut, Kahn asks, "How are you feeling Sid?"

"Like shit, but grateful faw this saint who is savin us" he replies.

Kahn then says what they are both thinking, "Not sure what we can do. Neither of us is really mobile, well, that is, mobile enough to get through the rough terrain of the bush back to camp, well alone, that is. I mean, we are stronger together, but also slow each other down. And we aren't capable enough to leave the other to seek help."

"I may get strongah. And can maybe make a splint. Ya, though, have lost too much blood. Would pass out just fifty feet from heeah" Sid responds in despair.

The woman returns to the hut with smoothed-over sticks and twine braided from plant vines. It's as if she has read Sid's mind. She brings the rudimentary supplies to Sid and he quickly begins crafting a brace for his knee. If he can keep his knee stable, he may be able to move with more ease while using the rifle as a crutch. His spirit is uplifted. In his mind, he would just need a few more hours of rest before stumbling out into the jungle to seek help. Need to wait until dark.

The sun is setting as the woman serves both men a warm rice dish that they quickly devour and thank her with smiles of gratitude, which she tacitly understands and reciprocates.

"So Sid, this isn't a bowl of boogers, is it?" Kahn jokes to lighten their spirits.

"Ah ya kiddin me? This is the best meal of my life evah" he responds while blessing himself.

Kahn then suggests, "If you are up for it, you should thank her by whistling a beautiful song. Doubt that villagers have radios out here, so this might be something she would like. Can't think of another way that we can show our appreciation for her support and generosity."

"Great idear!" and Sid promptly begins whistling *You've Lost that Lovin' Feelin'* by the Righteous Brothers.

While listening, the woman squeals with laughter and claps her hands in joy! Sid is encouraged and continues whistling other common American hit songs to light-heartedly entertain her.

Chapter XCVI   Phone Call

That evening, Smike returns home to a quiet house with lights out. Paps is already in bed; no doubt weary from the eventful day. Fatigued, as well, but inspired to journal some musical ideas based on the extraordinary incident and appreciation for friendships he experienced and observed, Smike reflects on Paps' whistling. That was the most surprising element of the whole, crazy day. He figures that this is how his grandfather serenaded his grandmother by her window when he courted her. Never knew.

As he finishes jotting down some notes, he thinks that he needs to talk with Paps' oldest and closest friend, Mr. Kahn, and question him about what he observed and what it means. Of course, he doesn't want Paps to know; would appear too intrusive on his privacy. He will try to covertly call Mr. Kahn in the morning.

The next day, while Paps is in the backyard tending to his garden, Smike discreetly locates his grandfather's address book and quickly finds Mr. Kahn's phone number. He gets on his cell phone, steps out front for a walk away from the house, and calls.

When Mr. Kahn responds, Smike says, "Hello, this is Sid Schrod's grandson, Smike, who you know as Michael. I felt a need to reach out to you sir and I believe that you may be the only one who has the answers I am seeking. If you feel comfortable providing some information, I have a few questions about my grandfather's experience in Vietnam. Your responses may help me understand some of his emotional episodes I have observed."

Mr. Kahn initially resistant to openly deliver information suggests that Smike offer him insights about what he's observed regarding his grandfather's distress. Mr. Kahn clarifies that he may not be able to provide him with any recommendations to guide effective actions. Smike shares that he has seen his grandfather during what appears to be tormenting nightmares (during afternoon naps), which takes some time for him to recover physically, emotionally, and mentally. Reluctantly, Mr. Kahn explains that he believes the root of the emotional turmoil is due to Paps' perceived sense of guilt. He shares that Paps blames himself for an incident that happened during the war. When Smike prods to hear more about this incident, Mr. Kahn says that it is not his place to share. The experience is confidential between them. He adds that Smike will need to either ask his grandfather directly or ensure that he sees a VA counselor. Mr. Kahn cautions Smike that addressing post-traumatic stress disorder episodes must be handled professionally.

Smike feels compelled to tell Mr. Kahn about unintentionally observing his grandfather whistling in private to a young child to calm her. He never heard his grandfather whistle before and it was the most moving and enchanting melodious expression he ever experienced. He wondered why his grandfather hid this talent from the family and others; that is, other than to a young child who couldn't reveal his musical gift to others. He wondered more about this observation when he remembered their conversation about Paps' nickname in the Marine Corps, *Whistler's Mother*. What does whistling have to do with a potential Vietnam experience that would cause him to refrain from whistling later in his life? Smike was confounded.

Mr. Kahn replied with a strange, but pointed question, "Haven't you ever wondered why your grandfather chews gum all of the time?"

Smike pondered and quickly realized that his grandfather actively suppressed urges to whistle through gum chewing.

Smike responds, "So, the gum chewing keeps him from whistling, but I still don't understand *why* he doesn't want to whistle. Not sure why this is significant."

Mr. Kahn clarifies, "Sid once told me that 'gum fills his hole.' I believe he isn't just referring to his mouth, but also his pain. By not whistling, he is denying or avoiding emotional pain of the guilt he feels. But the horrific incident was never his fault. I can't confide more than that. The rest is up to him to share with you Michael."

Much of what Mr. Kahn revealed was both enlightening and cryptic. Smike now understood that Paps deliberately blocked inherent inclinations to whistle by chewing gum. He now knew that Paps' avoidance to whistle has something to do with war trauma; however, he has no idea of the whistling incident and its significance. His father surely had no idea. Grandma Nettie likely knew, but never shared it with the family. Paps was in his own hellish world of self-inflicted torture, unwilling to seek or accept help; possibly because doing so would unravel his denial and be some sign of fucking weakness or display his vulnerability.

Closing the conversation, Smike shares, "Thank you Mr. Kahn, I greatly appreciate your help with this matter."

Just Saying

Smike is not sure what to do with this information and definitely hesitant in approaching Paps or asking anything about what he observed. Like most other concerns about his grandfather, he will just have to wait for the right time.

Chapter XCVII   Just Right

After his conversation with Mr. Kahn, Smike collects himself and joins his grandfather in the garden. The tomatoes are at their peak of productivity and Smike guesses that many need to be picked. He spies Paps paying particular attention to one tomato plant and walks over to him.

"Does this plant need special care Paps?" Smike asks.

"Nah, just look at this one t'maydah. I mean, this will be the biggest and jooceeist of 'em awl" Paps replies.

"Actually, looks like it's ready to be picked now" Smike suggests.

"Oh no, not ready, not yet. Naychah let's ya know. It's gotta be just right" Paps cautiously advises.

Struck by what Paps claims about ripe tomatoes being 'just right' emerges as strangely familiar to Capote's orange metaphor representing the view of a finishing point to one's work. He is somehow both moved and shaken by this comparable notion of 'just right.'

Paps elaborates, "When this t'maydah is ready, want ya to make me a bacon, lettis, and t'maydah sandwich on toasted sowah dough bread with extra mayo. Make shuah the bacon is chewy and the t'maydah is a thick slice. My fayvrit."

Paps definitely envisioned how this particular tomato was fundamental to his perfect sandwich. Needed to be 'just right.' Smike inherently understood what his grandfather meant about perfection and looked forward to making this sandwich for him.

He also better understood Paps' tenacious determination to control his world, even thru small things like the flawless bite of an impeccably delicious sandwich.

Chapter XCVIII   Pre-Surgery and Other
                     Preparations

As part of Paps' pre-surgery process, he had to schedule a doctor's visit at a VA hospital different than the closer one he normally visited. This appointment also had to be conducted about a month before surgery. So, it needed to be scheduled for the following week. Also, the clinic was about a forty-minute trip one way, so Smike decided to drive his grandfather on his day off; and therefore, the appointment was scheduled for the following Tuesday. He asks Paps if they can invite Elsye to join them as she can help with navigation since she knows the out-of-town area better than either of them.

Paps agrees but states two conditions, "We go in the Plymouth since ya recently replaced the cah baddahry *and* I sit in the passenjah seat."

Smike concurs and texts Elsye to see if she is free for a short road trip next Tuesday afternoon. She quickly responds, confirms her availability, and agrees to join them. She adds a note about the two of them meeting this coming Saturday evening at her apartment. Smike welcomes this reminder and says he'll bring dinner. He's also eager to play some new tunes for her.

After Friday night's performance, Smike had several other tasks to prepare for over the weekend. He needed to practice several of the Frankie Valli songs on his keyboard for that event on Sunday. Although not a perfectionist, his high standards made him feel not fully ready with some of those songs. He planned to spend nearly all day on Saturday practicing and would play several of those songs for Elsye that evening, along with some of his new tunes he was developing.

Also, he had promised to give Pablo a harmonica lesson after work on Monday. So, at some point on Saturday, he also needed to stop by the music store and pick up some instructional information that could assist Pablo as supportive guidance. Rally invited him to stay for dinner afterward, so Smike thought on his way to Rally's house, he would pick up two small tokens of appreciation for both Marciella and Abuelita Maria. Small plants from Violet's floral shop would be nice.

Lastly, he needed to make sure to iron his clothes for the *Valli in the Valley* event. Band members were to dress semi-formally, not exactly black tie, but definitely not every day wear. Fortunately, he was riding with Mitch to the event, so that relieved any pressure about locating and driving to the venue. Over the next few days, Smike faced lots of preparation and interactions on a very tight time table.

Chapter XCIX   Lost Shoe

On the way to the scheduled doctor's appointment at the VA hospital on Tuesday afternoon, Smike picks up Elsye. Subsequently, Paps takes the helm as captain of this voyage while in the familiar area of the community; of course, annoyingly directing him where to turn at each point. Once they ventured out into new territory, Elsye took over giving directions from GPS on her phone. When she seized control of providing the travel route, Paps seemed to settle into a more passive mode of interaction by looking out the window at the sights and occasionally pointing out landmarks or other random things that sparked his interest. Smike and Elsye softly converse about his Sunday performance in the Valley and how wonderfully it all went. They were on a straight stretch of road when Paps notices a shoe on the side of the road.

As they pass it, he says, "How do shoes end up on the side of the road? How come people doan notice theyah missin a shoe? I mean, do they delibahtly toss them outta theyah cah? Why would they do that? Just seems strange."

Smike, not really interested, responds, "I have no idea, Paps."

Elsye, half-listening, while staring at her phone says, "I can Google to see what pops up."

No one responds and the topic fades as Smike turns on the radio. Paps quickly takes control and changes to his favorite station of oldies. They listen to music the rest of the trip to the hospital, with no other discussion occurring.

Just Saying

Once at the hospital, Smike drops Paps and Elsye at the front door and says he will join them inside after parking the car. Paps grabs his cane and Elsye holds on to his other arm for additional support as they walk into the hospital for his appointment. Smike later joins them in the waiting room and then accompanies his grandfather for his doctor visit, which is rather inconsequential; more procedural than anything else. As they exit the doctor's office, Paps complains that it was a waste of his time and suggests the three of them stop at the hospital lounge for coffee and snacks before heading back. They all agree.

Chapter C On the Road Again

After Paps' brief, non-eventful appointment and their coffee break, Smike retrieves the car from the parking garage and picks Elsye and Paps up at the hospital entrance. Surprisingly, Paps decides to sit in the back seat on the return home and motions to Elsye to sit in the front. He complains that the drive to the hospital took more time than the actual doctor's visit and he is tired, knowing that there is still a long drive back.

He then slouches against the backdoor as they leave and tells Elsye, "Do yaw magic on yaw phone to get us home."

He then directs Smike to put in the *Honeysuckle Rose* CD found in the glove compartment and play Willie Nelson's *On the Road Again*. Smike complies with his directive. No conversation occurs while they quietly listen to music and Paps gazes out the window in between occasionally nodding off.

At one point during this return trip, when lucid, Paps again spots the same shoe and says, "Well theyah it is, that shoe is still on the side of the road and we still doan know how it got theyah!"

Elsye suddenly shouts to Smike, "Stop, pull over, I want that shoe!"

Her request alarms both of them, but Smike pulls over about sixty feet past the shoe. Elsye jumps out, runs back, and gets the shoe.

She returns to the car and says, "Paps, you just gave me a great idea for a creative writing lesson! I'm going to use that shoe" as she tosses it back to him.

Just Saying

Paps kind of shrugs, not sure what she is talking about, while holding the weather-worn shoe. Smike though is startled and unclear of her intentions in wanting this shoe.

He asks, "What do you mean creative writing lesson?"

Elsye replies, "For my language arts class."

Smike queries, "You're taking a class?"

Elsye turns off the CD and clarifies, "No, I teach fifth grade language arts. I'll use the shoe as a prompt for a creative writing activity. Will ask the students the same questions Paps posed about *how did that shoe get on the side of the road?* and perhaps, *who was the owner?* or personify the shoe and ask *how did the shoe feel being left on the side of the road?* get it?"

"Well, no, not really! I thought you were a pedicurist and a nanny for dogs. That is what you have been doing all summer. You never told me you were an elementary school teacher!" he responds with astonishment.

"I watch dogs because I love them. I help my mother parttime at her salon on the weekends and over the summer when I'm not teaching. School starts in a couple of weeks. By the way, my brother, who cut your hair is an accountant and helps out when his business is slow. It is a family thing. We just help my mother" she explains.

"But how come you never told me you were a teacher?" he asks.

Elsye explains, "You never *asked* me much about myself. We just talk about things we have in common, like enjoying quirky and classic movies, and of course, your music. So, you really don't know that much about me or about anything I do. You also make assumptions. Didn't you ever wonder why I was at Pablo's birthday party? I'm his former fifth grade teacher."

"I didn't think about it. How would I have known? Just thought you liked roller skating. Didn't even know you were part of that birthday party" he meekly replies.

Paps jumps in and cynically chastises Smike while laughing, "Oooh, ha, ha, ha! Ya ah hah *friend* and ya didn't even know she was a teachah? That's not good!"

"You didn't know she was a teacher either Paps!" Smike retorts.

"Well, I know hah nickname and doubt ya do" Paps replies.

"So, you give her a nickname and expect me to know what you call her?" Smike responds harshly in a tit-for-tat exchange.

"I dinn't give hah, hah nickname. Hah high school friends did. It's LC" Paps counters.

"That's her name, Elsye. How is the nickname different?" Smike asks.

Paps corrects Smike with, "No, it's L . . . C . . ." he says slowly while making the signs for the letter 'L' and the letter 'C' with his hand.

He then adds with confidence, "it stands faw *Little Crazy*, which we both know, she is. She's *little*, she's *crazy*, and she's a *little crazy*. It fits pahfectly. Ya shoulda known that!"

Just Saying

A frustrated look comes over Smike's face as he wonders how the heck his grandfather knew that and wondered when he found out that information. Paps then quietly withdraws when he suddenly realizes that he learned this personal information talking with Elsye when she drove him to the dentist and he definitely doesn't want Michael to know about that!

Elsye abruptly starts laughing. They both look at her and get silent.

While continuing to laugh, she says, "I just love this! You're both fighting over who is the better friend with me. Didn't realize how much you both like me and now I'm a pawn in your family competitive chess game of who is the King and who gets checkmated!"

Under his breath, Paps trails off, "Just sayin . . . she likes me beddah."

Elsye continues, "Smike, I understand why you don't ask me questions about myself. You don't want me asking you questions. I get it. I respect that. You can share anything you want about yourself in your own timetable. But you can't assume anything about me because you haven't even asked."

Astonished, he softly states "I am sorry" and then gets quiet.

"Well, hate to say, but I am used to it. My entire life, I've been dismissed, overlooked or underestimated!" Elsye claims.

Paps quickly responds, "I nevah undahestimated ya dahlin."

"*No*, you just assumed I was Vietnamese" she meanly retorts.

"Sawry 'bout that. Shoulda known beddah" he uncharacteristically apologizes.

After brief silence, Elsye then lightly touches Smike's arm in a gesture of graceful forgiveness but in a commanding and counseling tone shares, "Get over yourself, stop making assumptions, and by nature, you are *not* a narcissist, so you need to stop being so ego-centric regarding your guarded feelings. It limits you from knowing others."

After a brief pause, Smike soberly confesses, "You're right Elsye, again, sorry."

Paps interjects, "Smike, ya needta listen to hah!"

Elsye snarls, "Hey, asshole, the same suggestions apply to you as well!"

Paps acts surprised by her response like *What? Not me!* and pulls back from the discussion while diverting his attention to the shoe, looking it over. Smike and Elsye continue talking softly while Paps cursorily listens to their conversation.

As he handles and examines the discarded shoe, Paps suddenly proclaims, "Hey, I get why this shoe was tossed; it's got a hole in the sole!"

Smike suddenly gets a serious look on his face, slightly squints as if several revelations have hit him all at once. He realizes he *has* been self-consumed. And, as insightful as he thought he was, he *does* make assumptions. He now recognizes that he is more like his grandfather than he would ever want to admit. And, more sadly, just like the tossed shoe; they both have holes in their souls.

Just Saying

Paps interrupts, "So, really, Elsye, who do ya like beddah, me aw Smike? Be honest."

In response, Elsye expels a gasp of exasperation and turns the CD back on. They quietly listen to *If you want me to love you, I will* by Amy Irving. They share the rest of the ride home in silence.

Chapter CI Orange You Glad

After arriving home, Paps grabs a beer, goes to his lounger, and turns on the TV. Smike and Elsye go upstairs.

Lying on the tiny bed next to each other in the bedroom, Smike tries to amend his mistake and strengthen his relationship with Elsye.

He asks her with genuine interest "So, what about you, elementary-teacher-who-sidelines-as-a-pedicurist-and-dog-nanny, ever been in love Elsye?"

"No" she says flatly.

"What, no high school first love?" he prods.

"I was an underdeveloped, plain Jane, Asian nerd. Never even dated in high school!" she replies.

"Okay, so what about during college?" he pushes.

"I took a full course load, worked for my mom, and waited tables to cover tuition. Didn't really have that much time for extracurricular activities. Plus, even in college I looked like I was about eleven years old" she explains.

"Well, there must have been someone you were attracted to and who felt the same way about you" Smike reasons.

"I was infatuated once. At nineteen, it felt like love, but I knew that not to be true pretty quickly" she says.

Just Saying

"Go on. I want to hear about this infatuation guy" Smike asks.

"Silly, you assume it was a guy" she scoffs.

Smike apologizes with sincerity, "Oh, sorry. But please, go on."

"Well, it *was* a guy. I was working an evening shift at this restaurant and there was this customer out with friends. He was flirting with me and I kept throwing out snarky comments and smartass responses trying to reject him. Strangely, he loved it" Elsye explicates.

"Interesting, I can see that!" Smike confirms.

"Anyway, he asked when my shift was over and that perhaps I could join him and his friends who were going bar hopping."

"Sounds a little intimidating for a teenager who didn't date, right?"

"Well, the friends were a group of girls and guys, so it wasn't that daunting or creepy. But I turned him down."

"Why?" Smike asks.

"The guy was in his thirties; I mean he was like a grandpa to me!" Elsye mocks.

"Damn Elsye, I will turn thirty-one soon. That hurts my feelings" Smike says, feigning emotional pain.

She replied with clarification, "To a nineteen-year-old he was ancient, okay?"

"Okay, he was a dog, go on. There's got to be more to this story" Smike urges.

"So anyway, he keeps coming back to the restaurant with friends, like twice a week, and every time he asks for me to be their waitress" she says.

Interjecting, Smike asks grinning, "Meant to ask you, was he good looking or perhaps rich and a good tipper?"

"He *was* good looking, well groomed, smart, and extremely well built. He was a professional, but not super rich or anything" she swiftly confirms.

"Keep going" Smike prods.

"So, like around the fifth request, I agree to go out but with the *group* of friends" Elsye replies.

"Cool . . . and?" Smike baits her to continue.

"I had a great time! Totally enjoyed the night out with his friends and these get togethers repeat weekly for a while with everyone alternating as designated driver" she adds.

"Come on, when does this guy make his move?" Smike impatiently asks.

She continues, "One night, I'm the designated driver. Every one of his friends has been dropped off and he is the last one. We get to his place; he is rather intoxicated, says he likes me, and makes a pass at me in my car."

Just Saying

"Oooh, here comes the juicy part!" Smike says in eager anticipation.

"No, I reject him and explain that I think he's just too old for me" Elsye proclaims.

"Ouch! Bet that hurt!" Smike replies.

"Actually, he was very gracious about the rejection and asked if we could stay friends and continue going out with the group. I thought that was decent of him, told him 'Sure' and then left."

"You never hooked up? How is that infatuation?" Smike queries.

She explicates, "Well, there's more. He came to the restaurant the next evening, but not to eat. He stopped by, 'as a friend,' to give me a book of prose. I thanked him and he left. That evening, after I got home, I read the book cover to cover. Loved it! It was as if he could see into my heart, soul, and head."

"So, what did you do? Did you call him?" Smike eagerly queries.

"Hold on, I am getting there. After work the next evening, I drove to his place unannounced and knocked on his door. It was late, but he invited me in. We talked for a while and then things got physical. It was amazing! From that point on, we were a couple for nearly a year. No one had *ever* made me feel this good about myself!" Elsye explains.

"So, what soured the situation and how was this infatuation and not love?" Smike quizzes.

"Well, I quickly learned that an infatua*tor* has to lead and control the infatua*tee*. I knew how much control he had over my thinking and actions because I was so emotionally high just being around him. That was dangerous for me, especially because I know that I am not one to be controlled, even when I think I want to be *with* the one who is pulling the strings."

"So, what happened?" Smike asks.

"He was moving to Connecticut for his work and wanted me to follow. I would've had to quit college. Didn't want to. He didn't understand and actually would never really understand that I had goals other than him being the sole focus of my life. He moved, it ended. No drama, just ended."

"Wow, but that was a significant loss, even if you don't call it love. You must have been hurt, right?" Smike asks.

"Yes and no. I missed him terribly but figured that if at nineteen I had met someone that I felt was this wonderful, that is, wonderful from a naïve perspective, there has to be someone else out there that I could really love and not just follow around like a puppy dog."

"That was very mature of you and pretty darn insightful! So, have you had any other less-than-perfect relationships?" Smike continues to push.

"All others have mostly been friends-with-benefits type of relationships. This will sound weird, but I figure that I will have to find someone that I *dislike* as much as I *like* to have a long-term bond. If I like them too much, it can be infatuation and I cannot or would not be myself or realize my own personal potential in that type of relational situation. I'd always defer to

Just Saying

that person and that wouldn't work, because I have to be myself to be truly happy."

Smike inserts a joking jab, "Well you dislike Mitch, so he may be a potential companion to consider."

Almost yelling, Elsye argues, "Are you kidding me? No, no, NO, he is *not* my type at all."

"Well, you barely know him. He really is a smart, good guy. Just saying" Smike replies.

"Don't need to know anything more about him. Confident about that" she adamantly claims.

Somewhat hesitantly, Smike then asks, "So, what am I in your categories of relationships Elsye?"

Elsye thoughtfully responds, "You're a friend-sans-carnal-benefits. Actually, a first for me and I like it!"

She then asks, "So what am I to you Smike?"

He doesn't hesitate in replying.

"You are one of the best friends I have ever had! I enjoy being with you, laughing together. You are brilliant, hilarious, and I truly cherish you, Elsye."

Elsye, touched by his comment, surprisingly disrupts the serious moment and breaks into a joke.

"Knock, knock" she proffers.

Smike pauses, no clue on where she is going with this and questionably responds, "Who's there?"

She states, "Banana."

Realizing he knows this joke, he continues with her gag, "Banana who?"

She repeats, "Knock, knock."

Shaking his head like she is crazy, he asks, "Who's there?"

She replies, "Banana."

He laughingly asks, "Banana who?"

Again, she states, "Knock, knock."

With emphasis he replies, "Who's there?

She replies, "Orange!"

He asks, "Orange who?"

She then provides the punch line, "Orange you glad I'm not a banana?"

They laugh as she reaches over and pulls out two oranges from her bag by his bed.

Holding them over her breasts she asks, "What do you think Truman Capote would say about these knockers?"

Laughing, Smike says, "They're perfect! Just right!"

Just Saying

After a brief pause, he then questions her, "So, you've been planning this for a while, huh?"

"Yes, yes, I have. Been carrying oranges around just waiting for the right moment!"

Both smiling, he lovingly pulls her close, bringing his arm around her as she nestles her head on his chest.

Smike then softly adds, "Got the joke from your students, huh?"

Grinning, she confirms, "Uh, huh."

Chapter CII Finally, Some Answers

Smike jumps in Rally's truck Wednesday morning and hastily explains, "I never knew that Elsye was Pablo's teacher! In fact, never even knew she was a teacher until yesterday. Thought she was a pedicurist and dog walker."

Taken aback and acting surprised, Rally replies, "Who are you talking about?"

Smike replies, "You know, that girl I had tea with after Pablo's party?"

"Yeah, so are you seeing her now?" Rally innocuously questions, thinking he will finally get some answers.

"Yeah, we spend time together. Almost every Saturday night she comes over or I go to her place and play my songs to her. In fact, she has grown close to my grandfather as well. But we are not 'dating' or anything like that. She's just a very close friend. I can always count on her to help out with different things that have come up with my grandfather. She's also really smart and witty. I enjoy being around her" Smike clarifies.

"Wondered about who you left the party with, but Marciella made me swear not to ask you about her" Rally replies.

"I mean, I didn't even know that she was at the party for Pablo. I first met her when she washed my hair before I got my hair cut, then she trimmed my beard after the haircut, then we ran into each other at the park, and then at the roller-skating rink. Have been seeing each other ever since and this whole time, I just assumed so much without asking her questions about her life. Really, I'm embarrassed" Smike sadly admits.

Rally supportively responds, "Well, I bet she understands. Pablo says she's his favorite teacher ever! Says she's funny and he learned so much from her. He also told me that she knew how to handle the tough kids too. Had a way with them."

"She definitely has a way with Paps, so her relational skills are extraordinary" Smike returns.

"Sounds like a good girl to be close to. Never know, she could be the one" Rally replies.

As they pull up to the café, Smike gets silent. He hasn't talked with Rally about Louisa, at all. Not sure if he ever will. Still just too painful. Getting out of the truck, he acts like he is in a hurry to get the drinks and just lets the conversation drop. Jojo and Slim spot him and wave as he heads to the café.

Chapter CIII Alley Cat Chat

That Friday evening, during the band break, Elsye covertly goes searching for Mitch at Fred's Tavern. She doesn't want Smike to see her or know that she has briefly dropped by before picking up Beauregard, because she wants to secretly talk with Mitch about organizing a debut for Smike's music. It shouldn't be too hard to hide from him; even during their band break because the place was bustling with patrons. Furtively asking around, she spots Violet, who tells her that Mitch is in the alley behind the bar.

"What's he doing back there? Taking a smoke?" she asks.

"Nah, he doesn't smoke. Feeding his cats" Violet replies.

"Really?" Elsye questions in disbelief.

"Yeah, has his own fan club of strays" Violet jokes.

Elsye was a little dumbfounded. She hadn't seen this aspect of Mitch before. Was he an animal lover that she didn't pick up on before? She decides to check it out. Besides, she needs to ask him about helping to plan the debut. So, she exits the bar out the door to the back alley and spies Mitch leaning against a rail, watching around eight cats eating from several tins of cat food laid out on the street while softly talking to them like you would a close friend.

"Violet told me I would find you back here. Said the only way you would get pussy is through your fan club of stray cats" Elsye jokes.

Just Saying

"First, Violet would *never* say that" Mitch confidently proclaims.

"That's true. You caught me. She didn't say that. I just thought it would be a funny line" she confesses.

Mitch doesn't seem to find it humorous.

"Second, you can call me an ailurophile. Real term for cat lover" Mitch informs her.

Elsye is impressed with Mitch's language knowledge. He's smarter than she gave him credit. Not that she thought he was dull, but he goofed around so much, just thought he was another one of those guys who wasn't serious about anything. Obviously, this is something he is serious about other than his music. She stands there silently observing him interact with the cats. He then shares information with her.

"See the white fluffy one over there? I call her Taffy. Doesn't she look like a piece of salt water taffy?" Mitch asks.

"Oh, I don't know, Blanca might be a better name for her" Elsye suggests.

Mitch quickly comments, "Oh, you are sharp! Spanish word for *white* and term for *musical half note.*"

Again, Elsye is surprised. Mitch picked up on her reference. Guess he isn't quite the idiot she assumed.

She responds, "Well, obviously, Taffy is a fan of Knead Naked's guitarist!" kindly offering a somewhat veiled compliment to Mitch.

"By the way, I do like your name suggestion, but she will always be Taffy to me, just so fluffy and a very sweet girl. Ya know, gotta go with personalities to help name 'em. And, ya gotta get to know 'em. Also, gotta respect cats . . . give 'em space. They will warm up to you when they're ready" Mitch shares, noting his affection for this particular one in the clowder.

He then tells her more about some of the other cats.

"The gray striped, short-hair boy I call Dodger. Not after the baseball team. He's a really smart rascal but keeps his distance and will disappear after the food's gone. Named him after the Artful Dodger in Dickens' *Oliver Twist.*"

Astonished, did Mitch actually cite classic literature, which infers that he read it? She is stunned into silence and totally immersed in Mitch's delightful descriptions of his adopted felines.

Mitch then points to two similar looking cats and shares, "Those two over there are probably siblings, they look like Maine Coons, and are the most vocal, so named them Prattle and Tattle."

Elsye replies, "Clever names."

"Yeah, I thought so" Mitch concurs.

While pointing to another cat, Mitch says, "The pretty Calico girl over there, I call Eliza, as in Eliza Doolittle. She is playful and makes me laugh. Does funny antics all the time. A little lazy, though, but she doesn't take any shit from the others."

Did Mitch just reference Bernard Shaw's *Pygmalion?* Definitely more well-read than she imagined. Completely captivated, Elsye contemplates this freshly emerging unknown dimension of Mitch's character.

He then adds, "Wanna help me name this new one over here, the tiny jet-black girl? I think she's a Bombay breed, not sure. Never underestimate this one, no! She's very clever, stands her ground, but a little aloof. Not a snob, just very selective of who she wants to be around. Gotta scar on her back, probably from a fight with another cat. I can tell she wants to let me pet her, but not ready yet. Ideas?"

Again impressed, but this time by Mitch's knowledge of different cat breeds and warmed by his offer to help him name one of his adopted pets from the street, she takes a stab at providing a suggestion.

"Smart, strong, and standoffish, you say? How about Lisbeth?" Elsye suggests.

"From Stieg Larsson's Millennium series? Yeah, and her scar can represent the tattoo. That's perfect Elsye, thanks. Lisbeth it is!" Mitch says warmly.

Surprisingly stirred by Mitch addressing her by her name, Elsye stays quiet and befuddled. He never did that before and she felt an immediate connection. Plus, yet again, he revealed his keen awareness of literature.

"Gotta go back inside. Should get ready for our second session. Why'dja come out here anyway? What did ya wanna talk to me about?" Mitch asks as he leans over to pet some of the cats, goodbye.

"Wanted to get your thoughts on helping Smike debut his music. He's resistant and won't listen to me. Keeps telling me he's not ready. I think he will respond to you more than me regarding his music. He has over a dozen songs written. I've heard the finished and unfinished ones and they're all great! Maybe you can help me convince him and we can organize an event? Wanna help?" Elsye asks.

"Ya mean for your *boyfriend*?" Mitch questions as a snarky remark as they both enter the bar through the back door.

"He's *not* my boyfriend, but he is a very good friend. He's your good friend, too, right?" Elsye responds brusquely.

"Okay, yeah, he's my friend. And, of course, I'll help. Actually, happy to. He played one of his harmonica songs for the band called *Learning From Mistakes* and we loved it. Didn't hear the words yet though" Mitch responds.

Elsye replies and suggests, "Yeah, that is a great one! Lyrics are rhythmical. Glad you are agreeable to help. Can you please talk to your bandmates privately to get them on board as well?"

Jumping ahead, Mitch jests, "Hey, we gotta do something a little crazy for his debut show opener. Maybe hire a stripper?"

"What? Are you looking to make a little extra cash?" she counters and makes him laugh.

Elsye adds another humorous jab, "Would probably only have rotten tomatoes thrown at you, not dollars tucked into your speedo!"

Ignoring her last comment, Mitch then openly asks, "So, how do ya wanna do this? Meet somewhere to talk about it?"

Just Saying

"That'll work. Let me give you my number and you can text me" Elsye says and then calls out her number without waiting for Mitch to write it down.

She then turns around and quickly leaves.

He yells behind her as she exits, "Good thing I have an eidetic memory" then repeats the phone number in a loud voice.

Chapter CIV Debut and Other Plans

Elsye and Mitch meet the next afternoon at *More Please Café*. While in the throes of covertly planning the premiere of Smike's music, they solidify their ideas.

"Thinking that we'll need debut flyers to hand out and post around town" Mitch suggests.

"Absolutely! My graphic software skills are so-so, would be better to have someone create it that possesses a more artistic touch" she shares.

"On it! Will draft some ideas and you can add to it and give feedback or input" Mitch confidently takes on this responsibility and then asks, "So, Smike has no idea that you are putting this together? I mean, I understand you want me to talk with him about it, but would be better if several of us were in cahoots, right? He can flat out reject everything."

"Yes, but if we frontload all the debut prep work beforehand and present it as a complete package for his approval, I think he would be more willing to follow through. He would have fewer excuses to deflect the debut idea, especially presented to him from friends who believe in him" Elsye argues.

"So, we get everything together, but when and where do we pose the idea to him?" Mitch asks.

"Yeah, and this is where I'm going to involve Paps. Smike's birthday is coming up in two weeks. Paps has already agreed to have a get-together-slash 'celebration' at his home. Of course, the real purpose will be to pose the debut to him. So, the debut work will actually be sort of our collective birthday present for him" Elsye explains.

"Super! I'll ask Denny and Violet if they wanna help with the debut, guessing they will and will wanna help with the party as well. What about his work buddy, Rally, because Smike says he has a family, takes college classes at night, and may have a tighter schedule. And hey, just thought about inviting Smike's boss. Can ask Rally to ask her" Mitch suggests in succession.

On a roll writing everything down, Elsye responds, "Great ideas! But let's keep this as simple as possible. Paps and I were talking about how Smike gets easily embarrassed with attention and Paps would appreciate keeping everything as low-key as possible. I mean, will Rally and Denny want to bring their wives? And how much food would we need to prepare? Could be easiest to have a potluck approach. Paps has already volunteered his home, paper plates, plastic utensils, and will supply the beer. I can bring wine and decorations. Rally's mother-in-law makes a fabulous tres leche cake that Smike really likes. Could ask him to bring the cake? Pretty sure that Denny and Violet would want to bring side dishes. What would you like to contribute Mitch?"

"I make a killer bean dip. Can make that and bring chips. How old will he be anyway?" Mitch asks.

"Thirty-one. And the bean dip sounds solid!" she replies.

Mitch then asks, "Howdja know about his birthday? I mean, he is tight lipped and shares so little about himself. I still don't know how he got his name Smike. I mean Paps calls him Michael, but not sure where *Smike* came from."

Elsye explains, "Well, I don't know about his nickname either and he didn't tell me about his birthday directly. Inadvertently, during a conversation, said his birthday was the same day as Truman Capote's death, so I looked it up online."

"August twenty-fifth" Mitch asserts.

"That's right! How the heck did you know that? You really are some kind of savant" Elsye praises him.

Grinning from her approval, he shares "I read a lot" then asks, "By the way, howdja get the old man to agree to have this party at his house? He's somewhat of a recluse and not a very pleasant fella."

"Let's just say, he owes me" Elsye responds slyly without revealing her tactic.

"Well, ya do have a way aboutja" Mitch says, providing her a compliment.

Somewhat embarrassed by his comment, Elsye doesn't respond well to flattery, especially unexpected praise from individuals that she is not close to. Stymied, she is briefly struck silent.

She then mutters, "Well, we don't need to make this some sort of mutual admiration society."

Mitch senses her uneasiness and flips the conversation a bit, "Wondering, is there a theme to the debut?"

Complimenting Mitch, Elsye says, "Look at you, asking about a theme. Impressive!"

Just Saying

"Not really impressive, just trying to drag this meeting out and have a little more time with you" Mitch confesses.

Taken aback by this second awkward and uncomfortable implication that Mitch *likes* her, Elsye is rendered temporarily speechless, again. He's not joking. He is serious. Her feelings about him range across the spectrum. Initially, she found him annoying, which he can be. More recently, she has noted his finer qualities and things they have in common. He is actually nerdy with literature, language, and trivia. She is as well. And, he's an animal lover, which for Elsye is a non-negotiable for acquiring close friendships. Suddenly, she takes a leap of faith.

"Well, this doesn't have to be our only get-together" she says, somewhat alarmed with the suggestion that came out of her mouth.

Mitch lights up, and questions, "Ya mean get together for something *other* than secretly planning Smike's debut?"

"Yeah" Elsye confirms with a slight smile.

"Good. Do ya bowl?" he asks oddly, and then adds "My father and I bowl on Wednesdays."

Disappointed with that offer, Elsye says, "Not really."

"Okay then, how about watching a movie at my garage loft? Have been binging movies with bowling themes. Can watch either *The Big Lebowski* or *Kingpin*" he suggests.

Suddenly animated, Elsye agrees, "How about both! I enjoy off-beat movies!"

Mitch quickly argues, "Aw, no, my new found friend. Kingpin may be an off-the-beaten-path, B-rate film, but *The Big Lebowski* is a classic. And, little side note, both films involve brother teams."

"I concede. You are correct on both film categorizations!" she replies, then adds, "Didn't think about the Farrelly brothers as co-directors for the one movie, and Coen brothers as co-authors and co-directors for the other. Are you a trivia guy?" she asks.

Mitch assertively replies, "Possess a wealth of information. Just need to get to know me to figure that out" he proudly proclaims, and then adds, "Sounds like you know your trivia as well."

"A little" she demurely discloses.

"Okay then, text me a day and time, but remember Friday nights and sometimes Saturdays are band gigs. I'll return a text with my address" he states to finalize specifics.

Totally unexpected, Elsye didn't think that meeting with Mitch to plan and discuss Smike's debut would result in a date. Flooded with a range of mixed emotions, she grins internally. She both likes and dislikes Mitch. He possesses a combination of characteristics as a partner that she has been searching for but doesn't want to consciously admit.

Abruptly, Elsye candidly shares, "I have to tell you, I love Smike."

Just Saying

With a slight hesitation and serious look forming on his face, Mitch says, "Well, I have to admit that although I'm not in love with Smike, I have very deep feelings for him myself."

They both stare at each other, eyes locked. A concentrated stare: one Massachusetts, two Massachusetts, three Massachusetts. There it is, three seconds, Mitch's theory for mutual attraction. They then simultaneously break out in shared nervous laughter.

Elsye proclaims, "You're weird!"

"Yeah, I'm weird, but you like it, right?" Mitch securely responds.

Skeptically shaking her head while beaming a crooked grin, Elsye says, "Watch for my text, you goof!"

She then adds, "Have to go now, meeting with Smike this evening. He has some new tunes to play for me. Let's tentatively plan the party for Saturday, August twenty-fifth, around seven in the evening. You check and confirm with Violet and Denny if they are available. I'll call Rally and finalize everything with Smike's grandfather."

Mitch responds, "Okay, that's a Saturday. We don't have a gig that day or night, so that should work. And, I'll see Smike tomorrow at practice. Can talk about him playing some more of his songs for the band and try to suggest he consider a debut. He won't know that we talked. Will also check with Violet and Denny about the debut party after Smike leaves practice."

Elsye gets up, turns around, and walks away. Watching her leave the café, Mitch psychically tries to compel her to turn around and look at him. By the door, she glances back and provides a hip-level, horizontal hand flip wave.

Yep, he thinks, *she likes me.*

Chapter CV Heartbreaking

Waving to JoJo and Slim while leaving the café Monday morning, Rally and Smike sip their hot drinks on their way to work when Rally breaks into an unexpected, personally intimate discussion.

Rally confides, "Over four years ago, Marciella was pregnant and we were all excited and ready to add a new member to our family. About three months after this good news, she had a miscarriage. She was devastated and for some reason blamed herself. I was crushed but told her we would try again. At that time, she couldn't even think about trying again. Instead, she focused on working full-time and taking classes to finish her schooling as a Registered Nurse. She said we might try again after both of us finished our college degrees. I don't talk about it with her, because I don't wanna be pushy on this sensitive issue, but I hope she still wants to try again. And, of course, Abuelita and Pablo want this as well. Another reason for a house and needing the room. Anyway, when we lost the baby, it was heartbreaking, the worst time for our family. Even years later, still very sad to think about, but she graduates this December. And my internship starts in January. Hoping she wants to try again in the spring or sooner."

"You're a great father Rally and Pablo is an awesome son. Another child would be a blessing to the world" Smike shares with genuine affection.

"Thanks man! You can be a surrogate uncle or perhaps godfather if we have another kid!" Rally says in appreciation.

Smike goes silent as his own sad parallel event from nearly three years ago triggers a memory and floods his thinking.

Smike received a call from Louisa. She was at the doctor's office and distraught beyond any attempt to comfort or console. Through her weeping, she couldn't articulate what was wrong, but he sadly surmised they lost the baby. He immediately sped over. Once arriving, the doctor's assistant swiftly moved him to the examination room in which Louisa was resting. Upon entering, the look on her face confirmed what he feared. No words were exchanged. He implicitly knew the baby was gone. He went over to her and held her tightly while they both cried in each other's arms.

A little while later the doctor entered the room. He had a troubled, serious look on his face and shared, "Louisa's bloodwork indicates abnormal blood counts. We need to run some additional tests. I would like to schedule a bone marrow aspiration."

Overwhelming sadness for loss of the baby was compounded when blindsided with information that Louisa had a serious health issue. They had assumed that Louisa's fatigue and nausea were due to her pregnancy, but these symptoms were most likely an early sign of leukemia. And this unforgiving illness caused the miscarriage.

"Hey Smike, ya got quiet. Still with me?" Rally asks with concern.

Surprisingly, he replies in a straightforward manner, "I was engaged to a beautiful woman who also lost our child in the first trimester. Less than a year later, she passed away from cancer. Her name was Louisa and I loved her more than life itself."

He doesn't say anything else. What he shared with Rally was excruciating enough. Shocked and stunned into silence,

Rally doesn't know how to reply from hearing about this unexpected personal information regarding his friend's past tragedy.

After a few seconds, Rally simply says, "I'm so sorry my friend."

He quickly realizes why Smike refrained from going into any serious relationship with a woman. Still grieving. Rally understands how it takes time to gain one's emotional footing after such a significant loss. He saw it in his own family, especially with his wife.

As raw as Smike feels in sharing his loss with Rally, the burden of holding all of his sorrowful feelings in has somewhat been lifted. He needed to share his grief with his friend, who needed to know what he has been carrying around emotionally and just unwilling to unload onto others. Without saying anything else, he believes and feels comforted by the thought that Rally understands.

Chapter CVI Last Perfect Tomato

During breakfast Tuesday morning, Paps proclaimed to Smike that there was another *perfect* tomato in the garden for making his favorite sandwich. He could barely control his excitement.

"Faw lunch, ya gotta fry up the bacon, just like last time. Good and chewy. This t'maydah is ready! Will be jooceeah than the last one, I'm tellin ya!" he shares with Smike.

"Well, I've got to have one of these sandwiches this time. Last time, you ate that whole tomato" Smike teases.

"Shuah, of cawse, ya gotta try it. I'll shayah this time" Paps seriously returns the joshing.

Smike was happy that Paps actually liked the way he fried bacon. One of the few things he made for his grandfather that didn't receive any critique. Funny thing, Smike didn't eat bacon. However, he would have a tomato and mayo sandwich while Paps enjoyed his BLT.

And of course, Paps was right! It was the best, most perfect and juiciest tomato he ever tasted.

After his first delicious bite, Paps commented "This is the last pahfect t'maydah this season. Gotta appreciate it."

Smike was grateful. The garden was his only unspoiled connection with his grandfather and sharing a perfect tomato topped off their transient happiness on this day.

Chapter CVII   Wrapping up Details

By Wednesday, Elsye and Mitch wrapped up all the details in preparation for Smike's surprise birthday party. Everyone was on board and happy to help out with the pending festivity.

Elsye shares with Mitch, "The only thing left is securing a date for the debut at the VFW. Violet will text us the possible days available by this weekend."

Mitch reminds her "Well, there is *one* other item to iron out. When are we going to watch those movies together? I do have the afternoon off tomorrow. Are you available?"

"Yes, but not until after one" she confirms.

"It's a date, then!" Mitch states, barely able to contain his elation.

Chapter CVIII   Books Galore

After arriving, Elsye looks around Mitch's garage loft, "Well, this certainly looks like you! Kind of cool" she demurely states.

Then, while eyeing the massive array of paperbacks and texts, asks, "How many books do you own anyway?"

"Proud to say, over eight hundred. Actually, eight hundred and thirty-eight, and still growing. Read every single one, too!" Mitch claims.

"They are all over the place! Doesn't look like you have an organizational strategy" Elsye cautiously critiques (because she loves books whether they are systematically arranged or not).

"I call this my disheveled shelves of books" Mitch jests while pointing to a ledge on the back wall.

"Smart! But, really, how do you find a book that you want to re-read or reference?" Elsye asks, and then adds, "And not all of the books are on shelves. You have some in stacks or piles and others in boxes over here" she points out.

"Yeah, so, got them organized by interests and motifs. Over here are the classics. You notice this is the largest pile" Mitch clarifies while pointing to that section.

Mitch adds, "The other pile next to it is for modern day fiction. And over here, next to that group are some graphic novels and classic comic books."

"Then, there are the technical journals and manuscripts over here on these shelves" he notes.

Just Saying

"Well, those are neatly arranged" Elsye observes.

"And I have some 'how to' and informational books in this box over in the corner. All my history and music books, my favorites, are on the shelf next to my bed. I read them the most and that's why they are together" Mitch explains.

Elsye looks a little baffled, so Mitch decides to elucidate his grouping system.

"Ya see, books in the soft sciences like literature, usually don't have answers discovered in the reading. More questions presented than answers, so they are messier, right? So, they fall in a cluttered pile. Where, content and non-fiction books generally provide answers, are straightforward; and therefore, are neatly assembled on shelves. Get it?"

"You have a complicated, but interesting, albeit, tortuous mind Mitch; grant you that! However, got to ask you, how are the books in the separate piles, boxes, and shelves organized for quick retrieval?" she asks.

"They don't need to be. I have the covers memorized by size, color, and text font" Mitch boasts.

"No way! You're kidding me!" Elsye claims.

"Nah, really. Test me!" Mitch challenges.

"Okay, I'll go for the large, messy pile of literature because that surely will be the most difficult for you to find one. How about *Oliver Twist*?" She poses.

Mitch just stares at her and with seriousness, asks, "Howdja even know that I own *Oliver Twist*?"

Elsye replies, "Your short-haired stray named Dodger gave the clue."

"Ya remembered. That's impressive!" Mitch responds while walking over, and quickly pulling the book out from the huge, unruly pile of paperbacks and hardcovers.

He then nonchalantly hands it to her, deliberately making direct eye contact.

As she grasps the book, they intensely stare at each other for a few seconds; again, one Massachusetts, two Massachusetts, three Massachusetts.

Suddenly, Mitch awkwardly discloses, "I have to confess, I love Violet."

With a crooked smile, Elsye says, "I hardly know her, but of course, everyone loves Violet."

Mitch starts to laugh and says, "You're weird!"

Elsye responds, "Yeah, but you like it."

Mitch breaks the slightly sappy moment by then asking, "So which one first? *Lebowski* or *Kingpin*?

"*Kingpin*" she replies.

"Okay, great! And would ya like a beer, soda, wine cooler, or water? I have both sparkling tonic and regular bottled water."

Elsye responds, "I'll have a sparkling water, thanks."

Just Saying

Mitch goes over to his mini-fridge, grabs the drinks, hands one to Elsye, and then starts the movie. They get comfortable on his couch and enjoy watching both shows, one after the other. Elsye notices that they mutually laugh at sections of the *Lebowski* movie that others rarely find humorous. Most others just don't get it.

After the last movie ends, Mitch asks, "Are you hungry? I can make pancakes!"

Elsye finds this delightfully peculiar, since it is in the middle of the afternoon, and says, "Absolutely!"

They both head downstairs to his tiny kitchen. She quietly watches him make the pancakes while he explains to her "You should never over beat the batter."

Mitch hands her a stack of pancakes covered in butter and syrup and then offers her a large glass of milk. She accepts the meal and drink. After taking her first bite, Elsye thinks these are probably the most delicious pancakes she has ever eaten! While sharing this homemade meal, she decides to begin some light conversation by asking Mitch a few questions.

"So, you work as a plumber with your dad. How long have you been doing that?"

"Since I was fifteen, but it's my *hobby*, not my profession. Like my father, I'm good with my hands and a pretty good problem solver and fixer-upper" Mitch responds between bites.

"Well then, if plumbing is your hobby, what's your *profession*?" Elsye queries.

"Music, of course!" Mitch exclaims.

"Oh yes, of course!" she responds, and then prods, "Any college?"

"Nah, I'm what you might call an autodidact or polymath. High school counselors recommended I go to college, but I never really learned anything from school. Waste of time. Teachers didn't get me. Well maybe two of 'em, who just let me read as much as I wanted and create my own projects. Ya know, do my own thing" Mitch expounds.

"Yes, I understand. You probably didn't know that I'm a teacher. Sounds like you are a gifted, independent thinker. Many aspects of the public schooling structure just don't do justice for some learners" Elsye confirms.

"So, you understand! And Smike told me you teach fifth grade. Why'dja want to become a teacher?" Mitch asks.

Elsye exclaims, "That's easy. I love learning! However, didn't think I had the patience to be a teacher because I grew up tutoring my younger brother and he was a real pain."

"I love learning too, but on my own terms. My older half-sister, from my mother's first marriage, tried tutoring me too, but gave up. Said I didn't need any help . . . that I was smarter than her and she was five years older. I get along with her. She has blessed my mother with two grandbabies" Mitch shares.

Elsye then asks, "Do you have any other siblings?"

"Oh yeah, an older half-brother, Miles, from my father's first marriage. Don't talk to him; he is a pussy dick who needs to grow some gonads!"

Elsye laughs and asks, "What do you mean?"

Just Saying

Mitch elucidates, "Ya know, he can't step up to the plate for anything, doesn't have the balls, always backs down, but he's a dick about it and acts like a victim. Basically, a shameless drunk, druggie, and loser. Like a pussy, points the finger at everyone else as having a problem. Disrespectful to my parents and all they try to do is help him. Never follows through on responsibilities. Can't keep a job. Can't stay in a relationship. Ya know, a pussy dick. Right now, I'm just glad that Miles lives *miles* away."

Sympathetically, Elsye shares, "Sorry to hear that, Mitch. Guess there's always at least one in the family, huh?" then tentatively adds a more personal query, "So what about your relationship history?"

Mitch doesn't hesitate in responding and shares, "Had a serious one awhile back, but that's been over a year ago" then asks, "What about you?"

Elsye says in an abbreviated response, "Had an infatuation once, but it fizzled. Just wasn't meant to be."

"Well, he must've been an idiot to let you go!" Mitch proclaims.

Elsye bashfully smiles while looking down at her plate.

Both become quiet for a bit, and then Elsye breaks the silence by requesting, "Can I have another pancake? Really delicious Mitch!"

Mitch suddenly invites Elsye to go bird watching this coming Sunday afternoon, up north near Methuen. She has never done anything like this before and delightfully accepts his invitation. He says that he can pick her up after band practice. She gives him her address as they finalize the date.

Chapter CIX Regular, Irregular Meeting

Per their regular get-togethers, Elsye met Smike Saturday evening, as usual. Not wanting to keep anything from him, she intended on telling him that she started dating Mitch; however, thought she better wait until *after* the birthday party. If she told him now, Smike would ask her how their getting together all came about and she didn't want to let on that it sprouted from her concocting his surprise debut party. Rationalizing that the party was just a week away, she would tell him later. He would definitely understand. Of course, even though she was dating Mitch now, she expected that Smike would continue to share his lyrics and play music for her. She thoroughly enjoyed listening to and giving her opinion on his developing work; that wasn't going to change. Afterall, they were very good friends.

Arriving a little earlier than normal, around six-thirty in the evening, Elsye enters and exchanges a few sardonic barbs with Paps, which was their typical give-and-take when she first arrived. On this day, she brought dessert. Well, all the fixings to make dessert, that is: graham crackers, chocolate bars, and marshmallows. She thought they could make S'mores. Smike didn't care much for sweets, but Paps loved them! It was a fitting summer treat; could be fun. However, this was not something she did before. Not even sure why she wanted to fix a sweet for them this evening. Maybe it was some kind of nervous distraction from organizing Smike's debut surprise; perhaps an activity that would keep her focused on not disclosing any information or hinting at her undercover party planning.

After setting the dessert items in the kitchen, Elsye ran upstairs to see Smike. As soon as she walked into his bedroom, he started excessive jawing; totally atypical for him.

"Nearly all week, well since Tuesday, something felt a little strange. Paps has been in a good mood and actually nice to me. And he hasn't been eating gummies, so not sure what caused his dispositional change. And the gig at Fred's last night was great, as usual, the same as before, but I mean, Denny seemed a lot chattier with me than normal. And you know, he rarely says much. And Violet, well, she kept smiling at me. She is the most serious of the group, so wasn't sure where all the smiling was coming from. Mitch, let's just say, he seems to be sailing on some kind of personal high and has been bugging me about sharing more of my songs. Incessantly suggesting I play them publicly. Everything was just off, but in a very positive way. Guess I shouldn't question it, because it's all good. It's just, all the regular interactions, well, they felt irregular. And you too, seem a little different, a little happier. Can't quite put my finger on it, not sure what's going on, if anything" Smike discloses.

Elsye immediately realizes that her covert comrades couldn't quite conceal their enthusiasm for what everyone was planning. They all loved Smike and were looking forward to honoring him and his music. Even Paps! In this moment, she thought that she was going to burst and just spurt out the entire plan. She also craved to tell him about Mitch and was holding that in as well. Elsye took a deep breath and attempted to flip Smike's loosely founded conspiratorial suspicions back onto him.

"Well, hey, something is going on with you too! My goodness, haven't heard you this loquacious before. Guess that is a good thing, because normally I have to knock you over the head to get you to talk!" she nervously rebutted, hoping it would divert his pondering rationalizations.

Just Saying

Smike seemed to quiet after her spiel. They then relaxed into their normal routine of him playing his music and her intently listening, until Paps yells at them from downstairs.

"Hey, I'm ready faw my Smawz. Gonna fix it faw me Elsye?"

Smike asks, "What's he talking about?"

Elsye confesses that she brought a treat this evening; wanted to make S'mores for everyone.

Smike loudly and confidently responds, "See? Something is up! You don't bring desserts over. What's that all about?"

Quick on her feet, Elsye argues, "Well actually, wanted to play off of Paps' new found love for marshmallows, get it? I mean, even if he's not eating gummies, he's still a self-proclaimed pogey bait hound!"

Smike just stares at her with a questioning look on his face. He's not completely convinced with her argument. They head downstairs and she makes the dessert for them. Smike requests a half portion. Paps says he'll take Smike's other half in addition to his own. They all sit in the family room watching Paps wolf down the gooey confection. Smike and Elsye clean up and she hugs him good-bye. Paps gives a wave and smile to thank Elsye. He then furtively winks at her as a subtle reminder of their quiet arrangement. It *was* a rather irregular night, but still a good one.

After leaving Smike's house, Elsye texts Mitch,

Smike's spider senses have been raised. He thinks something is up but doesn't know what. We gotta tone back our excitement about his surprise party; otherwise, he may figure it out.

Chapter CX Hard, Hearty Laugh

Before band practice on Sunday morning, Mitch let Denny and Violet know that Smike sensed something was up regarding their secret birthday plot. He had somehow noticed that they were treating him a little differently. They didn't realize they were displaying any variance in their interactions with him. Mitch suggested they conduct practice like all previous weeks. Fortunately, during their practice session, they all pulled back and tamped down their anticipation for the following week's surprise event. For Mitch, this was harder to do than he thought. He was euphoric for another reason; his newly formed relationship with Elsye.

After practice that afternoon, Mitch picked Elsye up, fully prepared for the bird watching date with snacks, drinks, and two pairs of binoculars. Their outing proved to be spectacular! Elsye couldn't remember a time so relaxing when her normal ruminating thoughts, that constantly plagued her, lifted so easily where she actually got lost in the moment. She was 'present' with him. It was nice.

Near dusk, when they started heading back to Lowell, Mitch took a short detour to a location nearby where he said there was a fox den by this hill and they might be able to catch some baby fox frolicking, which kits often did at the end of the day. Amazed that he knew about this location and the nature of the foxes, she was completely smitten when they observed kits come out and start playing with and chasing each other. Observing the pure and vibrant beauty of these animals in their natural environment proved to be a delightful and memorable experience.

Just Saying

As the sun began to set, they were getting hungry. Mitch suggested they join his parents for dinner. This would be the first time for her to meet them. Mitch and Elsye saw each other only a couple times (other than planning Smike's birthday party and debut), so it seemed a little strange of an invite. Actually, it might be more awkward if she held off formally meeting his parents since they had already seen her arrive and leave Mitch's garage loft earlier in the week. She self-consciously waved but never really noticed if they waved back. Elsye hesitantly agreed to the dinner invitation.

Mitch said, "Great! Let me call my mother and let her know to set another plate. Think dinner will be soup and salad and she makes the best soups!"

Elsye's anxiety kicks in and increases as they get closer to Mitch's house. This is so impromptu; she has no idea what to expect.

They arrive and walk through his parents' front door, where his matronly mother eagerly greets them.

After Mitch makes a formal introduction, his mother clarifies, "Just call me Livi, rather than Olivia or Misses Monroe."

"Yes, Livi! Thank you so much for having me over for dinner" Elsye politely responds.

She takes a relieving breath and thinks, *Okay, that's not so bad.*

Livi then guides them to the kitchen because dinner is ready and by this time, already on the table. Curtis, seated, rises to greet Elsye. They all sit down and begin eating their salads.

Mitch tells his parents that the two of them enjoyed bird watching and he named a few breeds that they spotted. He added that they saw some kits playing around their den as well.

Livi, a mild-mannered woman, innocuously responds, "Well, that's nice."

Curtis just quietly eats while occasionally eyeing Elsye. Elsye actually met Curtis before at Paps' house when he was working on the plumbing problem, but the man never said one word to her; didn't even acknowledge her while they all shared a pizza. She's not even sure if he remembers her. Essentially, she has no idea how to chitchat with either of Mitch's parents and doesn't have a clue what to talk about. They are both much quieter and more reserved than Mitch, so ambivalence sets in Elsye's thinking on what to talk about regarding what interests them. Then she remembered Mitch and his father bowl.

Elsye awkwardly interjects, "So Curtis, Mitch told me that you like to bowl and that Wednesday is your bowling night."

With little affect, Curtis responds by simply repeating some of Elsye's segue, "Yeah, we bowl on Wednesdays."

Mitch notices the conversational uneasiness and takes the opportunity to brag on his father by sharing, "He has a one eighty-eight average right now!"

Everyone remains clumsily quiet as they finish their salads and begin eating soup.

After one taste of the hot broth, Elsye says, "Livi, your soup is delicious!"

Just Saying

Livi responds, "Why thank you Elsye, it's one of my mother's recipes."

Through their cordial exchange, Mitch flashes a childlike smile at both of them.

The discomfiture is nearly unbearable for Elsye as she considers what to say next and tries to muster some nerve to impart another small talk prompt.

Suddenly, Curtis speaks up in a rash, almost interrogative style probe.

"Why do ya like my son?" he asks Elsye directly.

Dumbstruck, Mitch and his mother look up from their meals and stare at Elsye. Startled, she wasn't prepared for this type of question and just thought of the first thing that popped in her head.

"Well, he makes great pancakes!" she responds in an honest, uncomfortably excited tone.

Curtis furrows his brow in a concerned and puzzled look as if he didn't really understand her response or was not expecting it. After a couple of seconds, his tense look unfurls into a huge smile and he starts laughing, that escalates into a real belly laugh! Mitch and Livi join him in soft, forged laughter but only because Curtis is laughing. No one is really sure what he's laughing about.

Curtis' hard genuine laughing builds, like what happens when someone can't stop nervous laughter that is suddenly unleased in unusual situations or settings like a funeral where one isn't supposed to laugh. They all just stared at him. Livi seems confused. Mitch appears baffled as well. Curtis tries to calm and stop laughing to continue eating, but each time he tries to suppress his laughter, it rages harder. Doesn't help that he sees all of them just staring at him. While still laughing, he suddenly gets up and heads to the bathroom down the hall, waving his hand behind him like he'll be right back. They hear him in the bathroom catching his breath trying to control his cackling, but erupting in waves every couple of seconds with loud snorts.

Livi looks at Mitch and softly says, "Your father hasn't laughed that hard since Uncle Lawrence dropped his dentures in his beer while giving a toast at your cousin's wedding."

Mitch responds, "Yeah, I know. Weird. He rarely laughs at all, ever!"

They sit there at the kitchen table for a few more minutes listening to Curtis continue to laugh, but now sounds of loud choking chortles reverberate through the house.

In a soft voice, sounding worried, Livi urges Mitch, "Go check on your father Mitch to see if he is alright. Don't want him to have a heart attack."

Mitch gets up from the table and walks over to the bathroom. He finds his father sitting on the toilet, looking down, and running water to wet a wash cloth. He watches as his father wipes the sweat from his forehead with the damp rag.

With serious concern, Mitch asks, "You alright?"

As his father looks up at him to respond, he stares for a second and then bursts into another heavy round of uncontrollable laughter. Mitch just stands there until his father, completely consumed in laughter, waves Mitch out of the bathroom. Mitch exits and while returning to the table with a perplexed look on his face, shrugs his shoulders to his mother and Elsye like he has no idea what is going on.

After a few more minutes, they hear Curtis catching his breath as the snickering subsides. He leaves the bathroom to return to the table, but midway to the table he sees all of them just staring at him, he breaks into another round of laughter and immediately turns around and heads back to the bathroom. Mitch drops his spoon, totally confused about his father's reaction to Elsye's response. Somehow, the three of them finish their soup with little discussion while Curtis continues to try and calm himself in the bathroom.

At the front door as Mitch and Elsye get ready to leave, Livi warmly cups Elsye's hand in a kindly and tender fashion. Curtis suddenly shows up at the door, smiling and without saying anything, gives Elsye a bear hug embrace. Although surprised, she welcomes it. Mitch and Elsye then walk to his car as they converse about the day.

"I really had a good time today, Mitch! Thanks for taking me bird watching and really loved seeing the baby foxes playing. Dinner was lovely as well. Your mom is a gentle spirit. She made me feel comfortable. Not sure, but guess your dad likes me or thinks I'm funny. I wasn't sure about his reaction. What's your take on it?" Elsye effuses, hoping for validation on Mitch's father's opinion of her.

"Have to tell you, my father doesn't laugh. I mean, I can count on one hand how many times I've heard him laugh, except for when he would chuckle while watching the *Roadrunner* cartoon with me as a kid. He's a serious kinda guy. But I think he likes you. He hugged you and he's not a hugger either!" Mitch honestly shares.

"Well good, just wasn't sure" Elsye replies with relief.

"Now, if he had a heart attack from laughing, you would be on the family's shit list, you know that, right?" Mitch jokes.

They both laugh.

Mitch then adds with some apprehension, "Wonder how your parents will take to me?"

Elsye quickly kids, "Well, you're more likely to make my mother cry than laugh!"

Mitch stares at her for a few seconds with a soft smile and then gently moves both of his hands to cradle her face. She gives him an approving and welcoming look. Moving closer, he kisses her. Elsye feels like *this is the most sweetly perfect kiss*. Their first kiss. It lingers, like perfect first kisses should.

Then Mitch pulls away, rests his cheek against hers, and seductively whispers in her ear, "You have to hear me play my guitar."

Swooned in the moment, Elsye murmurs "Yes, definitely! Just make me pancakes afterwards."

Chapter CXI Favor Ruse

After Smike returned from work on Monday afternoon, Paps called him over to the family room.

"Hey, I ran into Andy Schatzah at the stoah this mawnin. Ya met him awhile back at one of yaw consawts. Anyway, he invited me to watch the Red Sawx game at the VFW this Sattahdee and drink sum beeah. Need a favah. Can ya drop me off and pick me up? Doan wanna drive if drinkin beeah" Paps asks in a stretched-out request topped with a reasonable rationalization.

Surprised, but very pleased that his grandfather wants to socialize outside of his home (extremely rare for him), Smike responds, "Of course Paps, would be happy to! What time does the game start?"

Paps responds, "Stahts a little ahfta six, but wanna get theyah eahliah cause we ah gonna eat sum wings togethah too. Pahhaps ya can join us faw suppah? Doan need to stay faw the game cause I know the *little crazy one* comes ovah on Sattahdees, but not until laytah, right?"

Smiling inside, Smike thinks about how Paps calls Elsye *little crazy one* and warmed that his grandfather wants to enjoy a meal with him and Andy.

Smike replies, "Sure Paps, would love to join you and Andy for some wings. So, when do you want to leave Saturday?"

"Let's leave by five cause will need to ohdah the wings and they take a little time fryin 'em" he replies.

"Got it! We'll leave by five" Smike confirms.

"Ya should be back by seven to play music faw ya gahl. Can bring sum wings back faw hah! Can pick me up laytah, round ten. Game should be ovah by then" Paps suggests.

Then he adds, "One moah thing, wanna be shuah to get a basket of vejtibles togethah faw Andy. Doan let me fawget that. Tail end of the gahden's produce, but awl still good."

Smike acknowledges Paps' generosity as a wonderful idea.

Paps has successfully pulled off the preliminary ploy for his 'favor' ruse. Filled with high-charged energy, Paps self-anoints himself as the ultimate scam artist, prankster, con man, hoaxer, swindler, trickster, charming charlatan, and premiere deceiver! He internally snickers while virtually rubbing his hands together like some evil villain who has orchestrated a supremely sinister plot. The grandest satisfaction of this whole shenanigan is that Smike is totally clueless! Paps revels in his glory; there is nothing better than executing a well-orchestrated secret mission. It takes a team to pull off, but his part of the surprise party is fundamental to the final outcome.

After his conversation with Paps, Smike thinks this has been a strange week; especially with how his grandfather has been acting differently and actually wanting to go out into a public venue. Can't quite put his finger on it, but everyone has been so pleasant and kind; especially Paps, the normally reclusive, ornery, and crabby codger! Guess you can make lemonade out of lemons, but Smike hasn't even been trying to squeeze the rotted fruit for juice.

Chapter CXII   Premiere Pitch Party

Paps kept the surprise party a secret but knew that if he didn't mention *anything* about Smike's birthday on Saturday, the boy might be suspicious. So, at breakfast, Paps gave Smike a present wrapped in duct tape with a bow made out of the seventies tie that Smike borrowed awhile back.

Smike, grinning ear-to-ear at the wily gift wrapping, expressed to Paps how the packaging alone fully captured Paps' personality. Opening the box, Smike found inside a coin collector's folder filled with older, collectible coins. Deeply touched by this thoughtful gift, he then read the birthday card,

To Michael,

Will attend your Veteran's Day performance. My knee should be healed by then.

Love, Paps

Beaming, Smike imparts appreciation with sincere sentiment.

"Thanks Paps! This is one of the best Birthday presents I've ever received!"

"Thought ya'd like it" Paps responds in a casual manner.

Then Paps tells Smike that another gift for his birthday would be the wings meal at the VFW. Smike thanks him again. They spend the rest of the day doing their own thing. Paps stays downstairs watching television. Smike retreats upstairs working on his music, interrupted only by phone calls from his parents and sisters wishing him happy birthday.

Five o'clock rolled around and Paps was spiffed up ready to go to the VFW. Smike was impressed.

"Paps, you're going to draw attention with your clean shave and that sharp outfit!" Smike remarks with sincerity.

"Well then, pahhaps ya should clean up a bit too, so I doan outshine ya!" he replies.

This was his way of prompting Smike to be a little more presentable for the forthcoming party, which he knew nothing about.

"I can put on a nicer shirt, but it's just the VFW. Don't think they even have much of a dress code" Smike gently joked.

Smike changed his shirt, grabbed the basket of vegetables for Andy, and they left for the VFW.

Soon after they left, Elsye and Mitch arrive at Paps' house. She swiftly locates the backdoor key where she was told she would find it and they bring in all the decoration materials, wine, Mitch's famous bean dip with chips, and the designed debut flyers. The party was to be set up in the kitchen, so they got busy with placing the streamers and balloons. Denny shows up next and sets his appetizer on the kitchen counter. They begin conversing about how surprised Smike was going to be and how he would realize through their support that his musical debut is inevitable. Violet soon knocks on the front door and Denny lets her in. She brought flowers from her shop, which per Elsye's direction, presented orange ribbons. Violet seemed so excited. She loved surprise parties. Then, escorting Vicki, Rally walks right in, proudly carrying a huge tres leche cake. Elsye introduces Rally to everyone and then Rally introduces Vicki. Vicki, of course, does not hesitate to ask about the decorations.

"Orange is a unique color for a birthday party! I am assuming it's because Smike went to the University of Texas, which is their school color" Vicki surmises.

That wasn't the reason for the orange balloons and streamers, but Elsye didn't want to explain the long Capote backstory, so playing off this convenient coincidence, she fibbed, "Uh yeah, you nailed it!"

As Mitch was leaving to park his car down the corner at David's house, he asked that everyone follow him as well. It was getting close to the time of Smike's expected arrival.

Meanwhile at the VFW, Smike and Paps were well into polishing off the chicken wings while conversing with Andy. Paps was right, Andy loved to talk about baseball and knew so many details and statistics about all of the Red Sox players. Smike couldn't follow everything he was sharing but was actually having a good time. Paps seemed to be enjoying himself as well.

With Paps being so pleasant, Smike thought, *what a nice birthday*. Then, abruptly, in the middle of the first inning, Paps starts to complain about his stomach. Said he thinks the upset is caused by the wings being too greasy.

"Hate to cut this shot, but yaw gonna havta take me home Michael. Need my own private tahlet faw what's brewing in my bowels" Paps announces.

It was an Academy Award winning performance and Smike was totally convinced that he needed to get Paps home as soon as possible. Andy feigned his concern, as he knew this was part of the deception to get Smike home for the party.

Andy gives his bogus blessing, "Do what you gotta do, I understand Sid. Have been there before regarding these wings!"

Smike intently drives Paps home and pulls into the driveway. He quickly unlocks the back door to let Paps in.

After they enter, everyone jumps out and yells, "Surprise!!!"

Bewildered by this totally unexpected event, with everyone smiling at him, Smike finds himself overcome and temporarily shocked until gaining his bearings on what was actually going on. As they all exuberantly yell out 'happy birthday,' he soon breaks into a smile and begins hugging and shaking hands with each of his close friends. He then turns to Paps with his arms outstretched, calling him in to come closer, while Paps stares at him and doesn't budge an inch.

Forcing an appreciative gesture, Smike goes over to Paps and gives him a demonstrative hug, as he compassionately shares, "You really fooled me, Paps! I'm impressed. Have to tell you, that was a De Niro-level performance!"

"Well, I was shootin faw Nicholson, but I'll take the compliment" Paps haughtily replies.

Rally then gains everyone's attention and while holding his phone up, says, "Have something to share with Smike. Pablo learned how to play happy birthday on the harmonica."

Rally then proudly shares the video of Pablo playing the song while everyone listened and tried to watch on the phone's small screen. Once the song was completed, everyone applauded and again, wished Smike a happy birthday.

Smike shakes Rally's hand and says, "That was the ultimate gift from Pablo! Please thank him for me."

Paps is already by the cake directing Elsye to start cutting slices for everyone. Smike goes up to her while she places wedges of cake on plates and side hugs her.

Leaning over and whispering in her ear, he says, "I know you set this all up, or at least started it. Not sure how you knew my birthday, but this was very thoughtful of you my dear friend. I love you!"

Elsye temporarily stops serving portions of cake and on her tippy toes, whispers back into his ear, "I love you too! Capote was the clue to your birth date. This is just the beginning. We all have something special to share with you."

Everyone finds a spot to sit, as they all begin eating appetizers and cake, and enjoying cold drinks. Carefree chit chat exchanges occur over the next couple of minutes. During a slight lull in the conversation, and after gaining everyone's attention, Elsye makes an announcement.

"Dear Smike, our friend and musical inspiration, who we believe will be a national star in the very near future, we have a collective gift" she broadcasts.

Mitch then stands up and hands Smike the expertly designed debut notice.

"Just read it" Mitch dictates.

The flyer, on an orange background and various shades of brown text, reads,

Smike Schrod
Extravaganza Debut

Sunday, November 25
1:00—3:00 pm
Veterans of Foreign War Hall

Join in the launching of Smike Schrod's new collection of bluesy ballads. His harmonica and keyboard performance will be accompanied by the band Knead Naked. Song titles include:

Learning From Mistakes
Found Love, Lost Words
Don't Leave Me on the Side of the Road
Perfect For You
Give the Boot to the Cranky Old Coot
Just Saying
(and many others)

Smike first reads the card silently, swamped in mixed emotions of incomparable happiness, foreboding anxiety, and extreme love for his friends. This flyer is a definitive statement, validating that his work is now ready and he must move forward in sharing his music publicly. No stalling, no excuses, no waiting. He is now forced, in a very supportive manner, to take the next step. It was time. The right time.

He then reads the flyer out loud to everyone who all cheer at the end. He stumbles to find the right words to say and form an appropriate response of gratefulness.

~ 408 ~

Just Saying

Before he can utter one syllable, Paps interjects, "Yeah, so evahyone knows, now is the time faw ya to shit aw get off the tahlet Michael!"

The group laughs warmly.

He simply responds, "Yes, you are all right. It's time to do this. Thank you, everyone! I am humbled by this honor, deeply appreciate your support, and love you all!"

Still in a state of shock, Smike hugs and personally thanks everyone as the party slows down and his friends start to leave. Paps says goodnight and departs to his bedroom for the evening. Elsye remains.

Without saying anything to each other, she and Smike walk upstairs. Once in his bedroom, he gives her another thankful hug and personalized recognition.

"Thanks for believing in me, arranging this party, and pushing me to move to the next level with my music" he says.

Elsye responds, "You've been ready for a while. I knew when you thanked me last month for encouraging you to *make that turn*, and you did that by sharing a song with your bandmates. I was just following your understated, subtle cues."

Smike then coyly shares, "What you didn't know is that I have written a song about you, inspired by you, and was planning to play it for you tonight. So, now that song will have to be added to my debut performance."

"Really! I am honored! What's the title?" she asks, barely able to wait to hear it.

"Paps gave me the title, *Little Crazy One*" he blissfully shares.

An enormous smile appears on Elsye's face as she says, "I'm so flattered and thrilled! Please play it for me now!"

Smike plays this song to her delight and shares a few others, including one in draft form about Mitch. At that point, Elsye shares that she is now dating him and explains how their friendship transpired regarding the party plans.

"Of course," she countered, "this is all very early in our relationship. But I do like him."

Very happy for both of them, Smike confirms, "See, I told you he's a good guy. Very smart too! And, he loves animals. Figured that once the two of you got over you initial bumpy meeting, you might connect. You have more in common than you first realized. And, you are both two of my favorite people."

Chapter CXIII   Unquestionable Purpose

The party basically forced unquestionable purpose in finalizing Smike's songs and practicing them over the next three months. Additionally, his bandmates wholeheartedly agreed to extra practice sessions in preparation for his debut. He had to forge ahead, ensure this happened, make everyone proud, and realize his dream. This would be a true trial of his musical conviction that could potentially synthesize all of his work to this point.

Regarding Paps' surgery the following week, his resistance to the procedure had lifted since his garden was now cleared out and the season ended. Also, informal discussion with Denny at the party helped appease some of his concern regarding post-surgery physical therapy. Paps' emotions were no longer leading his reluctance as he fully accepted the logical purpose of the surgery, which was to increase mobility and relieve his pain.

Chapter CXIV   Double Whammy

As Paps slowly comes out of his anesthesia-induced grogginess, the doctor shares with Smike his post-surgery report.

Dr. Brandt informs him, "The surgical procedure took a little longer than expected because there was an arthritic section to clean up, but everything went well. After therapy, your grandfather is going to be significantly more mobile and should experience no pain."

Smike responds, "That's wonderful to hear! Thank you doctor! So, it's my understanding that he will be discharged some time on Saturday, right?"

"Yes, that is the most likely discharge date. I don't expect any complications. You can stay the night with him if you choose. Tomorrow, physical therapists will have him up and around with a walker. He will be informed of what he can do over the next few weeks and will be provided with a physical therapy schedule. You will want to make sure he comes in twice a week for rehabilitation. Of course, I will want to see him after his release as well" Dr. Brandt shares.

"Again, thank you doctor. Thank you, very much!" Smike responds.

The doctor exits and Smike sits down next to his grandfather's bed.

Paps rouses and asks for water. Smike grabs a plastic cup, fills it, raises the bed into a more upright position, and then

Just Saying

attempts to assist him in drinking the water. Paps grabs the cup and forcefully pushes Smike's hand away.

"I can do it myself. Not an invalid Michael" Paps barks meanly.

After a minute, to lighten the mood, Smike asks, "How are you feeling Paps? The doctor said everything went well and that you'll be chasing me around the house before you know it."

"I'm okay. Just doan like hospitals. Yaw gonna get me out soon, right?" Paps responds, slightly slurring.

"Looks like you will be discharged after tomorrow. So, you'll spend tonight and tomorrow night here. I'll stay the night with you tonight, to get you things you might need" Smike confirms in an attempt to comfort his grandfather.

Unexpectedly, Elsye is at the hospital room door.

She walks in and in a serious tone asks, "So, was the lobotomy successful?"

Not missing a beat, Paps responds, "Smahtass!"

Elsye glibly responds, "Well, I've been called worse!"

She then hands him a wrapped present that she had been holding behind her back.

"Not sure you're strong enough to unwrap and open it but brought you a little something that I think will *raise* your *spirits*" Elsye satirically shares.

"Shit, ya know I'm strong enuf to open anythin that's free" Paps replies.

He then rips off the wrapping and opens the box. Inside is a can of beer. Paps gets really excited.

"Ya know I love ya Elsye!" he exuberantly exclaims.

Smike, looking concerned, responds with caution and a complaint, "You can't bring that in here. He can't drink beer in the hospital! He just had surgery!"

"Oh, don't worry about it. Don't be such a worry wart Smike!" Elsye snaps, in a Paps' mocking fashion.

Paps laughs and says, "Theyah's my gahl!" as he pops the top and takes a sip.

Suddenly, he spits it out and says, "What's this shit? Tastes like lukewahm wotta!"

Elsye starts laughing and removes the can from Paps' hands. She lifts it up and shows him that the bottom of the can had been doctored. Without either of them knowing it, she punched a pencil-size diameter hole in the bottom, drained the beer, refilled it with water, plugged the hole with a cork and then placed a piece of silver duct tape over the cork.

"That's just not funny Elsye! Wahmed my haht and then broke it!" Paps harshly replies, but then starts chuckling.

Smike should have known better. Elsye was just playing with Paps and pulled a good one on him. He was surprised that she didn't let him in on the joke though, but she probably wanted this double whammy. She got both of them pretty good with her fitting, personalized prank.

Chapter CXV Scheduled Goals

The next six weeks, Paps routinely attended physical therapy twice a week. At home, he diligently followed the directives of the therapist and responsibly exercised based on the regime prescribed. He was like the ideal patient; making great progress with his therapy sessions as he religiously and obediently followed all of the physical therapist's strict suggestions. Smike never saw his grandfather listen to anybody this closely before, other than Grandma Nettie. Of course, Paps was in full control of following through on his exercises. And, Smike thought that his grandfather had something to prove regarding his recovery. He would be stronger, more mobile; and therefore, after recuperating, would be completely independent from family assistance. He had his recovery goal and focused on it.

Smike also noticed that Paps hadn't experienced any bouts of bad dreams lately, not in months that he could tell; so, he had refrained from asking him about them. It could be that his previous nightmare episodes were triggered by his concern over surgery or a result of the pain he experienced; Smike just wasn't sure. And Paps' therapy kept him busy and very productive in increasing his movement and mobility, which now appeared unimpeded. After successful surgery, all of Paps' exercise efforts bundled together may have been all that he needed to yield productive results and dissolve his recurring nightmares. His pain was gone. He was much more agile. He seemed happier as well.

Like Paps, Smike too, meticulously worked toward his individual goal in September and October by persistently journaling his song ideas, finalizing them, and practicing every note. He even found time writing his music while waiting in the lounge during Paps' twice-a-week physical therapy sessions. They were both so focused on their individual goals during the early autumn months, little else played into their daily interactions.

Chapter CXVI   Appreciation Letter

Paps' recovery progressed nicely. By the end of October, even though it was chilly, he had re-established daily afternoon walks to the convenience store. After one of the walks, and as part of his afternoon ritual, he retrieved his mail. He noticed an envelope addressed to him from an unfamiliar company. Probably junk mail from some business soliciting money, he thought, and would toss it, but not before opening the envelope since he was curious to read what it was about. Once inside his house, he walked to the kitchen table to sort and open the postal deliveries.

This letter addressed to S. Schrod, reads,

Dear S. Schrod,

Your generous gift of a lock of hair has made a significant and loving tribute to individuals who suffer from hair loss due to trauma or cancer treatment. We are able to make wigs for many . . .

Paps stops reading. He suddenly realizes this letter is for Michael, not him. It is not a solicitor scamming for money; rather, it's a letter of appreciation, of thanks. He quickly surmises that Smike gave his hair as a gift to this organization. He instantly realizes Michael grew his hair as a selfless act, to honor Louisa. He had harassed his grandson for no good reason and now he was embarrassed by his actions. Why didn't Michael just tell him? Now he was pissed!

Chapter CXVII   Trick *and* Treat

When Smike came home from work, expecting trick-or-treaters later in the evening, he made sure to prop the front gate open since the latch was still sticking. He thinks that's something else he needs to fix.

As soon as Smike enters the house, Paps, reclined in his lounge chair, immediately asks, "Ah ya gonna pass out treats faw Halloween?"

"Sure, will be home all evening" Smike replies.

"Good. I went to the dollah stoah eahliah tudday and got sum candy. In the cubbid in a lahge plastic punkin. Doan give to any kids tahlah than me! I'll be in the pahlah watchin my shows all evenin" Paps states.

Smike already figured he would be joining Paps in the family room listening for the doorbell to ring, or knocks on the door, or sounds of kids bustling outside. He would be the one to repeatedly get up and pass out candy. It would be a little too rough for Paps since he was still recovering from knee surgery.

Standing by the stairs, Smike asks "What time do you think kids will be coming by?"

"When it stahts gettin dahk" Paps answers.

"Okay, have just enough time to heat up the leftover casserole that I made yesterday" Smike says.

"Put sowah cream on my portion" Paps commands.

"Of course!" he replies.

Smike turns on the oven, and then goes up stairs to quickly change out of his work cloths and freshen up. Returning downstairs, he throws the casserole in the oven, and then goes to the family room to visit with Paps.

"How's your knee feeling today?" Smike asks.

"Beddah" he replies in a somewhat curt manner.

It seemed to Smike that Paps was not himself, but he wasn't quite sure what was going on.

Expressionless, Paps says, "Mail came faw ya. It was mahked *S. Schrod*, so I thought it was faw me and opened it. It's on the kitchen table."

Smike gets up, goes to the kitchen, and sees the envelope, top torn, on the table. It was an appreciation letter from *Loving Locks*. He sits down, reads the letter, and feels warm contentment that in some way he has helped someone. Paps must have read the letter and now knows *why* he grew his hair so long. He suspects that Paps wants to talk about it, but not sure who will be the one to initiate the conversation. Perhaps Paps is feeling a little pride for him. Or, perhaps he's a little irritated because Smike never told him his intention for growing his hair. Perhaps, it's a combination of both. He returns to the family room.

Smike informs Paps, as if he didn't already know, "The letter is from a company that makes wigs and hair pieces for people who lose their hair."

Just Saying

Paps responds in a soft and understanding tone, "Really nice of ya Michael. Nice ahnah to Louisa."

"Thanks Paps" Smike replies.

While rubbing his bald head and softly laughing, Paps says, "Wish I could do sumthin like that."

Smike laughs. The two of them have established their own way of facing the elephant in the room. They understand each other a little better with each passing day. Nothing else is said about the matter.

"Think the casserole is almost ready. Want a beer, Paps?" Smike asks.

"Shuah, thanks!" Paps says.

A few minutes later, Smike serves a bowl of the casserole with a dollop of sour cream on top and hands Paps his beer. He joins his grandfather on the couch to eat prior to trick-or-treaters arriving. First knock occurs before Smike finishes his bowl of food. It isn't even dark yet! He goes to the door and it's Jeanne with Susan and baby Sadie, who is dressed like a little princess. He invites them in.

"We can't stay long. Just wanted Sid to see Sadie in her princess costume" Jeanne says.

Susan, carrying Sadie, walks over and hands the baby to Paps. Smiling, he welcomes her into his arms and jovially starts talking to her.

"She had to see Sir Sid, her knight in shining armor" Susan cheerfully claims.

Watching Paps melt into this kind, normal grandfatherly mode by doting on and sweetly interacting with the baby girl, Smike feels a warmth come over him. His grandfather seems like a totally different person. Guess babies trigger something in him to drop his cranky demeanor. Infants must be his weakness. Paps does tend to protect and stand up for the defenseless. Those who he perceives need guardians. Just tough on everyone else.

After a few minutes, Jeanne, Susan, and Sadie leave to make their rounds in the neighborhood. They intended to visit early, before the main stream of trick-or-treaters started to raid the area and intrude on their visit. They wanted a little uninterrupted time with Paps.

Returning to his dinner, he notices Paps still smiling after their visitors left. Smike thinks, *Yep, he definitely has a soft spot for babies.* Like expected, costumed youngsters start pounding on the door and Smike is ready for them. As he greets and dispenses candy, he directs them to step all the way up to the entrance so that Paps can see different costumes and the display of various caricatures. Not sure if his grandfather would even care, but he seemed to be enjoying the parade of young guests in silly getups and made cornball comments to many of them.

About mid-evening, while still by the front door handing out treats, two young boys, one dressed as a shark, the other as Captain Hook, come up to the door yelling *Trick or treat?* with their mother following at a distance behind them carrying a young girl dressed as a witch.

Smike leans down while handing out the candy and the boy dressed as a shark warns him, "Better watch out, I'm a shark and might bite your hand off. See what I did to my brother!" while pointing to the false hook on the end of his brother's arm. Smike starts laughing, bearing a huge smile.

Suddenly, the older one points and says, "Hey, see his gold tooth! It's the thumb whistler" and throws his fake hook off his hand into his candy bag, clasps his hands together, and attempts to make the whistling sound that Smike had previously modeled to him months ago.

The mother, by the door at this point, asks, "Smike? Didn't know you lived in this neighborhood."

He looks at the mother and says, "I'm sorry, I don't believe I know you."

Seeming to understand why he doesn't recognize her, while holding her daughter next to her face, she grabs the end of her daughter's black wig, places it over her forehead and presents a glum pose.

Smike suddenly realizes it's one of his co-workers, and says, "Shannon! I didn't recognize you. You aren't in your Gothic garb and dark make up. Wow, you look totally different!"

She replies, "Yeah, I know. Every day is Halloween for me at work. Like role playing to be any character other than a tired, worn-out mother of three young kids! Plus, in a Gothic persona, most people just leave me alone. I need a little solitude, ya know?"

Smike gets it; however, he assumed Shannon's dark look he saw at work was her normal guise and didn't realize that her regular look was actually as an exhausted mom.

Paps sees the interactions and becomes curious, especially after hearing something about Smike whistling, so he gets up and walks over to the entrance.

The older kid recognizes Paps too and loudly proclaims, "Hey, it's the gum contest grandpa! Remember when he had us balance it on our heads? I won!"

Shannon says, "So this is your grandfather Smike? We know him! Ya know, you both have a way with kids. You both saved me on two separate occasions. I just didn't know either of you then. Guess it runs in the family. Having a touch with kids."

Smike had no idea what they were talking about regarding their interactions with Paps and some contest. And, Paps was clueless on what the kids were describing about the thumb whistling. Obviously, there was some strange coincidence in how their actions overlapped.

Shannon continues, "You both are ultimate tricksters in how you handled my kids. Both gave me a treat too! So funny, huh?"

Smike and Paps just look at each other a little astounded. Later in the evening they will have to exchange stories about the incidents that they both had forgotten until this moment. Didn't seem like a big deal back when the events happened, so they were easily forgotten. But the kids didn't forget. Smike thinks he was wrong about kids' short attention span. Guess they both made a difference in some small way.

Chapter CXVIII   Benefactor

The beginning of November roared in with chilling air! Smike noticed that JoJo wasn't with Slim the last time he and Rally stopped for coffee on Friday, and not this Monday morning either. Weather could definitely be the reason.

Because it was so cold, Rally dropped Smike off at the main entrance of the shredding business this morning. A finely dressed man in a suit and tie greets him at the door and asks, "Are you Michael Schrod, known as Smike?"

"Yes" he replies, surprised by this man seeming to know him.

"I'm Ken Cranston, executor of Jonas Jordan's estate. You have been named as a beneficiary in his Will," said the man.

"Who? I don't know a Jonas Jordan" Smike claims.

"You probably know him as JoJo" he reports.

Startled, Smike says, "Yes, I have a casual acquaintance with JoJo from the café but have had only fleeting discussions with him. This must be some kind of misunderstanding" he counters, then quickly adds, "When did he pass?"

"We figured that you might be surprised with this information. He passed last week. Come to my office sometime this week and we can discuss this further" the man says while handing him his business card with contact information.

Perplexed, Smike shares, "This is very confusing."

Elaborating, the man says, "I understand. For now, let's just say that Mr. Jordan viewed you as a compassionate individual who would do right by his wishes. More will be explained once we meet. At that time, I will share the Will with you and explain the conditions. Let's schedule a time to meet this week. Just call or email me."

"Okay" Smike replied softly, still stunned from this unexpected news and not sure what it all meant.

The man left before he could ask about Slim. He wondered, *does Slim know about JoJo's death?*

Chapter CXIX   The Will and the Way

Later in the week, during his day off on Thursday, Smike arrives at Mr. Cranston's office, still reeling about this inheritance situation. The secretary escorts him into the conference room. Mr. Cranston gets up and shakes his hands, offers him a seat, and a drink. Smike sits down but declines the drink. Mr. Cranston then pulls out the Will and gives Smike a copy. He goes on to explain some context of the situation.

"Mr. Jordan had a heart condition and knew that he didn't have much longer to live. He came to me to serve as executor and rewrite his Will. It is the most unique Will I have ever crafted" he pauses briefly, and then continues, "So, you may know Slim or have seen him at the café" he queries.

Smike responds, "Yes, I know him. Sometimes JoJo was standing beside him and talking; and other times, Slim was sitting alone in front of the coffee shop, usually later in the day."

Mr. Cranston continues, "Yes, Slim is an elderly mute, homeless man and we have been unable to identify him, find out his real name or where he's from. Mr. Jordan didn't even know. Anyway, a few years ago, Mr. Jordan befriended Slim after meeting him outside the café and just started talking to him. Slim would kindly listen, but of course, never respond. At some point, Mr. Jordan started buying coffee and pastries for Slim and they would conduct a seemingly one-way visit outside the café. It became a regular event and they developed this unexplainable friendship and connection. Anyway, a few years ago, before a pending bad winter storm, Mr. Jordan was concerned about Slim's safety and suggested that he stay in his garage. Mr. Jordan was surprised when Slim got up and without saying anything, followed him home, which was just a short walking distance away. Slim stayed the night in the garage on a cot with sleeping bags covering him and a portable heater nearby. From that night on, Slim continued to return and stay the evenings in Mr. Jordan's garage. No one but the two of them knew about this arrangement. Really, hell of a story! Mr. Jordan was a sympathetic and charitable individual."

"JoJo's generous nature is clear, but I don't understand how I play any part in this situation" Smike says, still blurry about what was going on.

"Mr. Jordan told me that you, unsolicited, regularly bought them coffee and pastries. He said that you often stopped and talked with them as well. He shared that you exuded an unconditional acceptance for both of them. Through your actions, spoken and unspoken, he saw you as a kindhearted, thoughtful, humane, and non-judgmental person. Mr. Jordan prided himself on being intuitive about others."

"I appreciate those kind words, but really, didn't do much of anything" Smike replies.

"Well, Mr. Jordan thought your actions revealed the perfect candidate to serve the purpose of his wishes" Mr. Cranston discloses.

He continued, "Mr. Jordan was a childless divorcee. He retired a decade ago, had substantial savings, and owned his home. His only family is a nephew, a successful stockbroker in New York City. Mr. Jordan had discussed with his nephew the conditions of his Will. Basically, he would inherit all the funds and any items in the home that he wanted. But, to own the home, which the mortgage was fully paid off years ago; he would have to agree to allow Slim to stay in the garage each night, until his eventual passing. This meant that the nephew would either have to live in the home until Slim's death or he would have to find someone agreeable to rent the home with the condition of housing a homeless man. The nephew respected his uncle but told him that he was unwilling to interrupt his career to live in Lowell, even if for only a year or two. Mr. Jordan appreciated his nephew's honesty. Basically, the nephew gets all the funds, except for twenty thousand dollars, and all the items in the home that he selects to keep. The home goes to you, if you agree to allow Slim to stay in the garage in the evenings until his passing. Twenty thousand would be funds allocated to feed Slim. Other than breakfast, Mr. Jordan gave him a meal each evening, like a bowl of soup, a sandwich, or another light meal. Whatever Mr. Jordan fixed for himself; he would give a serving to Slim. Really quite simple with little inconvenience."

Mr. Cranston provided details that Smike was trying to wrap his head around, so he began to ask a barrage of questions.

"So, how did JoJo even find out my last name? Why didn't he talk to me directly to verify my willingness to follow through on this situation? Is this even legal? Could funds have been provided to care for Slim rather than having someone take care of him via a proxy? You do understand my uncertainty about all of this, right? Besides, I am not planning to stay in Lowell and will probably be moving back to Texas in a few months."

The attorney explains, "Mr. Jordan shared with me that he noticed the business logo on your work shirt, so he visited that business to give the owner a compliment about your cordial actions. Inadvertently, while he was praising you, either the owner or a co-worker shared your full name. Mr. Jordan then gave me your name to add to the Will, explaining that he didn't want to wait to get you on the Will since he saw you only intermittently. He fully intended on talking with you the next time he saw you. Unfortunately, he passed away that same week."

Smike truthfully responds, "That is a lot of responsibility. I have to tell you sir that I don't want to benefit from this situation. And, I don't need a house."

"Mr. Jordan understood this would be a huge obligation; however, he said that Slim doesn't have that much longer on this earth. He just didn't want him to die on the streets. He also knew that Slim appreciated the familiarity of his garage as a safe and secure location. And he knew that Slim liked and trusted you. Listen, you don't even need to live in that house. You just need to make sure that Slim has access to the garage in the evenings and receives a small meal each night. After Slim passes, you are free to sell the home and keep the funds from the sale or donate to a homeless shelter; it really doesn't matter" Mr. Cranston says as encouragement for him to consider the option.

Still skeptical, Smike asks, "How long do I have to think about this? And, if I decline, what will happen with the home and with Slim?"

"The sooner you decide, the better. Right now, I go by each evening, make sure the garage is accessible, and provide Slim with a meal. Can't do this for much longer. The nephew will be coming by to gather memorabilia from the home but has informed me that he plans to leave large utilities such as, washer, dryer, refrigerator, and other furnishings, like the couch, television, dining room furniture, beds and bedroom furnishings, and other items intact. He doesn't have room for those items in his New York apartment. And, he doesn't care to take the time to sell them. What he leaves will stay with the house. If you decline to accept the conditions set forth, the home and furnishings will be sold and the funds will go to a homeless charity. However, we won't be able to do anything formally to help Slim since we don't even know his true identity. Going down that rabbit hole in the courts would also be costly and take a lot of time. Slim would likely pass before any resolution. Seems very strange, I know. But again, Mr. Jordan was an insightful individual and thought this would be the best scenario for Slim. He also had great faith and trust that you would assist fairly and honorably for Slim's benefit" Mr. Cranston responds.

"I need some time to think about all of this. I promise to give you an answer soon, just need to figure out what to do. In the meantime, if you will give me the address of JoJo's home and keys, I can take over providing Slim with evening meals. I cook every day for my grandfather anyway, so that is not an issue at all. And Slim knows me" Smike replies.

Mr. Cranston shares, "Mr. Jordan was spot on about you. Will also give you some money for the food as it comes directly from the funds set aside for Slim. By the way, Mr. Jordan bequeathed his belt buckle to Slim. When I gave it to him, he wept and understood the significance of the act. If you see him, you will notice him wearing it."

Chapter CXX   So Much Going On

Besides being sad about JoJo's passing, Smike was emotionally disturbed by the whole situation of being named a beneficiary of a Will for a man he barely knew. Until he worked everything out in his head, he wasn't going to talk about it with Paps. Actually, he didn't want to talk to *anyone* about it. Of course, he would inform Rally that JoJo passed away, but wouldn't share any information about the Will. He would tell Rally that the barista informed him about JoJo's death rather than a lawyer, because Rally's inquisitive nature would spew a slew of questions that he didn't want to address at this time. The whole situation just felt really strange.

Smike had so much going on this week with work, news of the Will, and two musical performances. Plus, his thoughts kept returning to the Veteran's Day performance at the VFW this coming Sunday; Paps would attend for the first time ever to hear him play. He had anticipated this event for months. Regardless of so much going on, after his meeting with the lawyer on Thursday, Smike delivered an evening meal to Slim. Slim was appreciative and without saying a word, pointed to the silver buckle he was wearing as tears streamed down his face.

He didn't know what to say to him, but he kindly shared, "You had a great friend in JoJo. He made sure that you would be taken care of and you can stay here in the garage as long as you like."

With this statement, in good faith, Smike committed to following through on the Will's directive. He just wasn't sure how he would enact that commitment.

Just Saying

Slim reached out his hand for a shake. Smike warmly obliged.

Before picking up coffee Friday morning, Rally mentioned how JoJo had not been seen with Slim for over a week now. Smike pretended that he would ask the barista about it.

Before returning to the truck, Rally watched Smike outside the café, lean over, hand Slim his food and drink, and say something to him.

Entering the truck with their drinks, Smike shares, "Found out very sad news. JoJo passed away."

Rally replies, "Damn! That stinks! Does Slim understand that he's gone?"

Smike speculates, "I think so. He's wearing JoJo's belt buckle."

Rally offers a suggestion, "We should do something for the family."

Sharing half-truths, half fibs, he says, "I agree and asked the Barista about plans for his burial. Apparently, JoJo has only one surviving nephew and there will be a memorial next week. He will give me details once he hears about it. I was thinking that we could take Slim to the ceremony if he is agreeable to ride with us."

"Yeah, find out! I wanna go and taking Slim is the least we can do" Rally replies.

Suddenly, Smike gets an idea. He knows how he can address one pressing issue but will need to iron out some details. Again, another task added to everything else that was going on; however, this action could yield a plausible resolution to a nagging problem.

Friday evening, before Smike's gig, he made Paps dinner and set up a second plate of food to go. Of course, Paps asked him about it. Smike explained that for the next couple of weeks, he would be providing evening meals to an older gentleman who needed some assistance. Paps unquestionably accepted his explanation. He knew Michael was a giving individual and he respected his grandson's act of kindness in attending to the needs of a senior citizen. He always believed everyone should help those less fortunate.

Chapter CXXI   Itch That Just Couldn't
Be Scratched

On this day, Veteran's Day, as promised, Paps would hear Smike perform for the first time. However, despite all of Smike's efforts, Paps remained the *Itch that he just couldn't scratch*. Somehow, he couldn't quite reach this *itchy spot* and worried that even if he did, the actual scratching could likely cause bleeding. Such a challenging conundrum with a prickly old codger. He hoped through the performance, his grandfather would understand and support his musical passion and ambitious pursuit.

As the band set up, Smike spotted Elsye arriving with Paps. He also saw Andy join them at the back of the hall, bringing several beers to their table. Rally arrived as well, waving wildly to get Smike's attention. As Smike waved back, he felt overcome with a flush of exhilarating emotions, which ran a continuum from intense anxiety to supreme joy. He always played music for his own pleasure but still felt some sort of generational debt in meeting familial expectations. This sense of *owing* had slowed his entry into music, as he sensed others, well actually, specifically Paps, felt a musical career, *just wasn't good enough*. Now, to make his stand and fully identify as a musician, he was past the point for releasing this self-imposed obligation. He was a musician, whether Paps accepted it or not.

The band and audience were charged! Smike occasionally looked for Paps' reaction to different songs. He appeared to be enjoying himself, which inspired Smike's full release of his musical self to this audience-of-one naysayer.

After performing several applauded songs, Denny and Mitch start a duet of a mid-60s song by Peter and Gordon, titled *A World Without Love*, accompanied by Smike on keyboards. Within the first couple of minutes of this veterans' song favorite, Smike watched Paps suddenly get up as Elsye reticently aided him in exiting the hall. Andy and Rally stayed seated at the table, looking slightly surprised. Paps' early departure seemed strange, but Smike was at least pleased that his grandfather stayed through several songs of the full performance. He couldn't contemplate a reason for his premature exodus but had no real concerns about it because Elsye was with him. Besides, Paps attended like he said he would, which was the most Smike could expect. He needed to be satisfied with his grandfather's partial attendance.

Chapter CXXII   Sparked Memory

"Looked like you were enjoying the music and the beer, so what's with leaving early?" Elsye asks Paps as he hurries out of the VFW and tramps toward her car.

"Doan wawhy 'bout it. Just get me home" Paps barks.

"Hey listen, if you aren't feeling well, just tell me. We can stop and get some gummies at a dispensary if needed" Elsye suggests.

"Nah, have plenny at home. Just tyuhd" Paps falsely claims.

"You don't seem tired at all. Seem pissed or upset for some reason. What's going on?" Elsye pushes for a real explanation.

Short on patience and not feeling he needed to account a reason for leaving to anyone, Paps curtly snaps, "None of yah bizness!"

Elsye doesn't appreciate his brusque reply to her. Something was definitely off with Paps and for the first time, she didn't know how to respond with appropriate effect, so she kept her response short and simple.

"Okay asshole, taking you home" Elsye replies.

She drops him off out front without saying anything and doesn't bother walking him to the house. As she drives away, Paps enters his home and goes directly to his bedroom. Sitting on his bed, he starts to weep. *That song. That fuckin song. Why'd they havta play <u>that</u> song?*

After a few minutes of crying, emotionally distraught, Paps composes himself, undresses, and gets into bed. Before long, he falls asleep. As what occurred in the past spurred a hurtful memory, he was soon dreaming about his most traumatic war experience.

Chapter CXXIII   No!

The sun has set, and Sid is still whistling while the woman continues to demonstrate appreciation for the music he has brought into her life. He then starts whistling another song, one that was popular at the time, *A World Without Love*. The woman gleefully claps in appreciation!

Abruptly, three soldiers burst into the hut. One quickly slams his rifle butt into the woman's head as she lifelessly collapses like a limp rag doll, falling to the side of Sid.

Seeing this horrific act, Sid screams out in terror, "NO!!! What ah ya dooin?"

He begins wailing and continues to scream, "No, no, NO!!! What ah ya dooin, ya fuckin idiots?!? She was helpin us" as he fought two soldiers attempting to lift him up and assist him out of the hut.

A third soldier gets Kahn up and moves him out directly behind them.

During this sudden and shocking event, neither Sid nor Kahn recognizes that the soldiers attempting to rescue them are their squad comrades, Caldwell, Thomas, and Romanoli.

In an angry confused fit, Sid yells at them, when one grabs his face to look directly in his eyes and says, "It's me, Romanoli. You're safe now Schrod. It's gonna be okay. Just need to get you medical assistance."

Broken-hearted, Sid continues to cry, collapses in their arms, and becomes despondent as they whisk both of the injured soldiers to a Huey in a nearby clearing.

During the transit, Sid hears Caldwell say, "We heard whistling in the distance and just followed it. As we got closer, we knew Schrod was in the hut. Probably would not have found you guys otherwise."

Rather than feeling relief from being rescued, Sid felt incessant rumination through burdened thoughts of guilt, 'That woman is dead now because of my whistling. I caused her needless death.'

This nameless woman, charitably and unexpectedly, provided him with a tangible, existential understanding of humanity. In a blink, her brutal slaying swiped that away; ravaging and robbing his soul of a sense of justice, virtue, and morality in the world. His soul was raked raw. He internalized this guilt and condemned himself to never whistle again.

Chapter CXXIV   Shaken

Smike arrived home around ten in the evening, still swelling with exhilaration from the performance and fully expecting Paps to still be up. He hoped to hear his grandfather's opinion about his music; good or bad, just wanted to get some take on his grandfather's position regarding his musical goal. Weird, but as he walked in, all the house lights were off. Apparently, Paps was already in bed, which was early for him. He wondered if his grandfather wasn't feeling well and that's why he left the session early. He trudges upstairs to his room and calls Elsye to find out.

"Hey, what's going on with Paps? Just got home and he's already in bed. Was he not feeling well?" He asks her.

"I have no idea! He appeared to be physically fine, just seemed emotionally shaken and didn't want to talk with me about it when I asked. What was odd about the whole thing is that he was really enjoying the music and then it was like an agitation switch was flipped quite suddenly. Like he went to the dark side or something. I did not push him to explain anything because he got downright bitchy. I mean, more than I've ever seen him get with you or with me in the past. So, I dropped the angry son of a bitch off and left. Figured you would call me to talk about it" Elsye explains.

"Well, guess it will have to wait until the morning because he is asleep and would get ticked off if I woke him up just to talk. Elsye, thanks for attending the performance with him and thank you for trying to appease his crotchety nature. Will call you tomorrow once I find out what this whole issue is about" Smike shares.

Elsye replies, "My pleasure, and by the way, the performance this evening was AMAZING! Rally was so jazzed to hear you play; I'm guessing that he will talk your ear off tomorrow morning and give you endless praise!" she replies.

"You mean, talk my ear off more than normal?" he jokingly queries.

Laughing, she honestly shares, "No really, he was so impressed and was kicking himself for not attending one of your performances earlier!"

"Nice to hear! I have a few things to share with him tomorrow as well!" Smike imparts.

They end their conversation, share their good-byes, and Smike gets ready for bed, soon falling asleep after a long, prolific day.

Around three-thirty in the morning, suddenly awakened by Paps' loud screaming, Smike jumps out of bed.

"No, no, NO!!! What ah ya dooin, ya fuckin idiots?!?" Paps yells repeatedly.

Smike hears him screaming and runs downstairs, his anxiety heightened with the prospect of intruders in the house.

Scrambling to Paps' bedroom door, he turns on the lights, and sees his grandfather thrashing about, still yelling, but now saying something about *She was helping us!*

As he grabs his grandfather's shoulders to waken him from this apparent nightmare, Paps fights him, takes a swing, and while opening his eyes filled with tears and crying out, he repeatedly shouts, *I killed hah! My whistlin killed hah!*

He tries to comfort his grandfather and says, "You're dreaming Paps, need to wake up!"

Still highly disturbed as he begins to gain consciousness, Paps slowly realizes he was asleep and it was a bad dream, very bad dream, his worst!

Smike being there, seeing him in this state, and trying to calm him, does not soothe Paps' irritation. While sitting on the bed next to him, Smike unknowingly asks his grandfather what he assumes is a benign question.

"Who are you talking about Paps?"

Paps recoils, while still somewhat not fully conscious, pushes Smike away, mumbling and crying "I killed hah! My fuckin whistlin killed hah!"

In a calming tone, Smike responds, "Paps, it's a dream. You're in your home, in your own bed. Everything's alright."

Paps continues to yell, "It's not alright! Will nevah be alright! Ya just doan know. Just doan get it. Ya wuhrn't theyah!"

Smike leans toward his grandfather and again tries to physically comfort him.

Paps shouts out while swinging his arms, "Get yaw hands off of me!" and then harshly commands "Get the fuck outta my room! No, get the fuck outta my *house* NOW!!! I mean it Michael, get OUTTA MY HOUSE!"

Shaken by seeing his grandfather emotionally overwrought and visibly violent towards him, Smike runs upstairs, grabs a change of clothes and his keys, and leaves. He thinks it is probably best that he does *exactly* what his grandfather directs him to do since he doesn't appear to be able to help calm his disoriented grandfather at this time.

Outside in his car, in the cold, he wonders where he should go. It's four in the morning, and not like he could just call Elsye, Mitch, or Rally and wake them up. I mean, he could, but that would be a huge inconvenience for them and he really didn't want to trouble them with this situation. He could just get a hotel room and then remembered that he had keys to JoJo's house. He would go there for the rest of the night. Early in the morning, he would call Rally and fabricate an excuse for needing to drive to work in his own car, would say something about some previously scheduled afternoon appointment that he had just remembered. Rally would accept that reason.

Arriving at JoJo's house, it felt bizarre for him to just enter, but he did. He decided to sleep on the couch, since it would be even stranger for him to sleep on one of the beds. He doubted that Slim even noticed him pull up, but he would be sure to go out to the garage at sunrise to talk with him and explain the temporary situation. For now, he needed to get some sleep. It was going to be a long day to follow.

Chapter CXXV   More Serious

On his drive to work, Smike calls Mr. Kahn. This call was more serious than the previous one. He was intensely upset about the event that transpired in the early morning hours and just didn't know what to do.

"Mr. Kahn, I am so sorry to bother you. This is Smike Schrod, Sid's grandson. I'm concerned about a terrible nightmare my grandfather had last night, where he kept repeating 'I killed her, my whistling killed her!' When I tried to comfort him and asked what he was talking about, he cursed at me, and ordered me to leave his house, so I did" Smike confesses.

"This is critical Michael. Has he had many dreams like these lately? Are they increasing in number?" Mr. Kahn asks.

"No, actually, he hasn't had any bad dreams that I can tell, for nearly two months. I assumed that the nightmares were triggered by his knee pain and his perseverating worry about the pending surgery. The surgery was successful and he is getting around very easily now with no pain. Just doesn't make any sense. I'm confused and concerned. What should I do?" Smike asks, hoping Mr. Kahn knows of an intervention process for veterans suffering from post-traumatic stress disorder.

"First, I will call him this morning. Hopefully, he will answer the phone. I need to come to Lowell and talk with him in person but can't leave until tomorrow morning when my wife can drive me. I think he will welcome my visit. However, not sure how long I can stay; we have family arriving over the weekend for a week-long Thanksgiving visit next week" Mr. Kahn explains.

"You coming for just tomorrow would be greatly appreciated. What should I do in the interim?" Smike asks.

"Call the Veterans Hospital and ask to talk with a specialist. You'll want a professional with you when you return to your grandfather's home. Hopefully, they can have someone available to assist you later today or early tomorrow" Mr. Kahn suggests.

"Thank you, sir, I greatly appreciate your suggestion and will call the hospital this morning. I can call you back later today and let you know the status of any assistance they provide as well as an update on how Paps is doing at this point, that is, if I can. Right now, not sure if he will even let me back in his house" Smike shares.

"Michael, he's very angry and emotionally raw from reliving the trauma. He may lash out at anyone who he fears to be a threat, including you. Reality is a little warped in his head right now. I suggest you stay away unless a specialist is with you or until I arrive" Mr. Kahn cautions him.

"Yes sir, I understand. Again, thank you for all of your support and suggestions. It really helps" Smike gratefully acknowledges.

They end their conversation and Smike immediately calls the VA. His call is kept on hold as he pulls into the shredding business parking lot.

Chapter CXXVI   Friend Indeed

Rally sees Smike at his locker and immediately starts praising him about his performance at the VFW hall the day before. Then he notices Smike talking on the phone.

While covering the speaker on his cell phone, Smike responds, "Thanks my friend, but confidentially, there's some shit going down with Paps."

Rally asks, "Does this have something to do with him leaving the performance early yesterday?"

While still on hold, he quickly shares, "Not sure what is going on, but he had a horrible nightmare last night. Its PTSD related, and I am not trained or equipped to help. The VA hospital has me on hold right now. I'm hoping to get a specialist to join me to talk with Paps when I return home from work this afternoon."

Rally suggests, "I'll call Tina. She knows a lot of psychologists. Perhaps she can drive over there and talk with him. He knows her."

"You have always been such a good friend Rally! But, don't trouble Tina. I know this isn't really her line of work. And, Paps may get doubly pissed off if someone he perceives as an outsider becomes involved" Smike says.

Rally then offers, "Okay, how about, I join you when you talk with Paps?"

"But you have class on Monday evenings this semester, can't ask you to do that. I will call Elsye and see if she's available this afternoon. I swear, between the two of you, I feel so fortunate to have you both as friends. You know that saying is true, *a friend in need is a friend indeed*" Smike acknowledges with sincere appreciation.

Rally then asks, "So, when you called me earlier this morning, you already knew you would get an appointment with a VA specialist this afternoon or you were hoping too?"

"That was a convenient white lie. Didn't want you to know about this issue until I talked with you face-to-face. I figured you would understand" he confesses.

Suddenly, someone on the other end at the VA responds. Smike answers.

Rally notices and whispers "Good luck" as he exits.

Smike explains the situation to the responder on the phone and requests assistance. His call is transferred to another representative who also places him on hold. He puts the call on speaker and jumps in his truck to conduct his daily run.

The VA call basically went nowhere since there was no specialist available to help address Paps' emotional situation for at least *another week*! Smike thinks *What the fuck?!?*

He then texts Elsye; she was teaching and he knew she couldn't talk on the phone at this time. In his message, he requested she meet him later in the afternoon to talk about what was going on with Paps and his nightmare. Between the two of them, they could devise an approach to address the distressing situation. Elsye texted back that it would be easier for her if he could come to her apartment when he got off of work.

Chapter CXXVII   Tragic

While meeting with Elsye, Smike received a call from Mr. Kahn. Over the phone, Mr. Kahn finally shared more information about the tragic event that happened in Vietnam over fifty years ago. He explained that they were both injured through a downed helicopter and assisted by a native Vietnamese woman who provided safety in her hut and tended to their wounds. To show appreciation for her altruism, Sid whistled some songs for the woman, who enjoyed the music tremendously. The whistling was heard by the rescue troops who barged into the hut and with the butt of a rifle, caused blunt force trauma to the woman's head, killing her. Sid was mortified and fought his comrades who were attempting to extract him from the site. It was a horrible injustice. Sid felt responsible and blamed his whistling; his musical gift, which since that event, he has viewed as a curse.

Mr. Kahn shared that he spoke with Sid and learned that this scenario was what Sid dreamt about when Smike entered his room and attempted to calm him. From his conversation with Sid, he also unearthed what triggered his grandfather's painful memory: a song from the Veteran's Day performance the day before. He revealed that the song played by the band just happened to be the same song he was whistling when the woman was assaulted. Agitated and emotionally raw from hearing the song, after Sid returned home and fell asleep, he relived the traumatic experience as a nightmare, as if the event was actually occurring. No one could have known. However, for Smike, everything was horrifically falling into place and making sense about his grandfather.

Mr. Kahn added that through their conversation, Sid's disturbed state seemed to slowly diminish. However, he cautioned Smike that his grandfather still needs professional help. Smike shared that he would go to the VA hospital in the morning and attempt to personally make a counseling appointment, but was told over the phone earlier that day, that no one could see his grandfather until the following week.

Mr. Kahn informed him that he would arrive the next day to support his friend and assist with whatever counseling services can be accessed. Lastly, Mr. Kahn advised Smike not to return to his grandfather's home until after he arrives in Lowell. He believes that Sid's pride plays a huge part in not wanting to reveal his vulnerable feelings to his grandson or any other family member for that matter. Mr. Kahn's plan is to enter first, talk with his grandfather for a bit, and then call him into the house after Sid agrees to him being there. Smike confirms he will follow Mr. Kahn's suggestions and thanks him again for being such a supportive and loyal friend to his grandfather. Smike hangs up and just stares in a daze.

Reeling in myriad, highly-charged, intense emotions, he attempts to process all the information by sharing with Elsye. She sits quietly beside him listening intently. And, although seriously worried about Paps, Elsye is more concerned about how this family disturbance will impact his pending debut in less than two weeks. She urges him to not let this incident derail all his debut work to this point.

Elsye tenderly shares, "Smike, you are not responsible for what has happened to your grandfather. He will receive help, the emotional support he needs. You will be a part of that, but others with more experience need to step in and guide him through this rough, emotionally jarring episode. You need to stay focused on your debut. Please! All the work that you and the band have put into preparing for your premiere and all the practice you still need to complete; just can't let that go. Got to move forward. Got to do it. Use your feelings to feed your music, like you always do."

Logically, she was right, but he still felt he needed to help his grandfather as much as possible.

"You can stay with me tonight if you need to" Elsye offers.

"Thanks, but I have that covered" Smike replies, not informing her where he would go.

Smike decided that until Mr. Kahn arrives, he will stay at JoJo's house; since apparently Paps is not ready to have him back into his house. All of his possessions are still at his grandfather's house and he needs clean clothes and his instruments, but he will just make do for now in this whole problematic situation. Tomorrow morning, he would go to the VA and find someone who would listen. No, he will demand that someone listen and assist with this troubling situation.

Chapter CXXVIII   Futile Efforts

Time at the VA hospital Tuesday morning was mostly wasted. All representatives appeared overwhelmed with too many responsibilities. And, they all stated the same thing; Smike's grandfather needed to be present to receive assistance. Fucking futile effort! However, he did manage to schedule an appointment with a PTSD specialist, but for the *following* week. Whether Paps would actually show up for this appointment was a more pressing concern.

Smike wondered, should he call David and ask him to check on his grandfather, like through a neighborly visit? Or, should he ask Jean and Jeanne to perhaps call and say they would like to drop off a cake? On what pretense could any of them provide a logical reason for stopping by? Perhaps, these actions would just be more futile efforts that would go nowhere. And, he hadn't run these ideas by Mr. Kahn, so really shouldn't act on them. Not right now, anyway. Inviting others to intervene could complicate things as well. It just felt like everything he had done so far felt futile and pointless.

Then, he received a text message from Mr. Kahn that he arrived at his grandfather's home. He will receive another text for when he can join them. Smike confirms that an appointment with a counselor has been scheduled for his grandfather for the following week and he is standing by to hear when he can return to Paps' house and talk with him.

Chapter CXXIX   Brothers of Anguish

Mid-morning, Paps lets Jonathan in. Neither says anything to each other as they walk into the kitchen. Paps makes a pot of coffee and offers Jonathan a cup. They sit there for a few minutes just sipping the hot brew.

"Brother, it's time . . . time to get some help for what you went through. You have carried this anguish long enough" Jonathan gravely counsels.

Paps asks, "How havya done it Jonathan? I mean, ya handled it so much beddah. How? Howdja do it?"

"You know I had my own trials with the trauma, Sid. Part of me was delusional for a while. I hoped, and falsely believed, that the woman who cared for us was only injured and later fully recovered. Of course, that was some type of deflection or denial tactic used early on just to deal with the inhumanity of what we observed. Reality then kicked in regarding what I had to personally deal with: losing my eye, all the surgeries, and being labeled 'disabled' which really ticked me off. To tell you the truth, I think being seen as handicapped spurred more anger, where I felt I needed to prove something" Jonathan confides.

"So, ya just let it go?" Paps quizzingly queries.

"No, never let it go. Never could. And, you know that. But, had to move past it all. Proving myself was a doable goal, something tangible to keep my mind focused on being productive. Wallowing in dung would never make things right, and for whatever reason, I thought, things could be better and I wanted to be part of making things better. Probably sounds idealistic. Basically, I stayed busy on learning about the world and improving myself" Jonathan openly shares.

"Nah, I get it. Workin was my therapy and Nettie, my counselah. Ahfta I retyuhd, found prahjects to keep me busy. But, ahfta Nettie passed; the nightmares came back moah frequently. And my damn knee pain reminded me daily 'bout what we saw. Tried to shake the memahries, but like a sticky boogah, couldn't fling 'em away" Paps divulges.

Jonathan thoughtfully responds, "Neither of us will ever be able to just fling those memories away my friend, but there are smart individuals, some who have gone through similar experiences, who can help you talk through your recurring thoughts and nightmares. They will know how to help you. I mean, I will always be here for you, but you need a knowledgeable counselor, hopefully someone as smart and as insightful as Nettie."

"I hate tokkin to kids who think theyah expahts and wanna lecchah me. Doan like it when priests do that too!" Sid replies honestly.

"I understand, but you've got to at least try to see someone. Promise me that if an appointment is scheduled, that you will attend" Jonathan pleads.

"Ya set it up, I'll go. But, can't promise I'll keep goin. Doan have patience faw fools!" Sid replies.

"That doesn't explain your patience with me Sid!" Jonathan lightly jokes.

Just Saying

Sid chuckles and then says, "But I'm the Jokah in life's deck of cahds, not ya, one-eyed Jack. Ya wuhr nevah a fool!"

Jonathan then asks if he can text Michael and invite him back to the house. Perhaps, they can all talk a little bit over a sandwich. Sid feebly agrees to this arrangement.

After texting Smike, Jonathan adds, "Michael reminds me of you Sid. He's a good-hearted person and an individual with strong conviction. He wants to help you, please let him. Well, at least don't close him out of your life. I think he wants to help, not because he thinks you need him, but perhaps because he needs you. He needs something from you. Probably your approval or blessing. Not sure. And, not sure if you realized that previously. But like I said before, family helps family. Not going to get around that."

A short time later, Smike walks through the door. He sees Paps and Mr. Kahn at the kitchen table and joins them. Mr. Kahn informs them that he will return to visit the Friday after Thanksgiving and at that time plans to stay for a few days over the weekend. Smike gets up and makes them a couple of sandwiches. Light conversation is exchanged. After completing their meal, Mr. Kahn gives Sid a warm hug and leaves.

Chapter CXXX   Somehow

Somehow, after Mr. Kahn's visit and his reassuring conversation with Paps, Smike was invited back into his home. Paps looked scruffy, wouldn't talk much or make eye contact with him. Elevated tensions between them generated an edgy, uncomfortable atmosphere. They both just went through the motions of living in the same house, but intentionally stayed away from each other. Smike really wanted to talk with his grandfather, but like all of his other experiences, any conversational exchange would have to be initiated and controlled by Paps. That hadn't changed.

Somehow, despite all the turmoil, Smike was able to concentrate on his music and continue practicing with the band. He remembered learning about natural instincts, how when faced with a threat, there are three typical responses of fight, flight or freeze. He froze when first experiencing his grandfather's violent nightmare and then flew out of the house to run away from the situation. Now, he found himself in the fight mode. He was fighting for both of their survivals; his grandfather's treatment for trauma and his own to establish himself as a musician. Somehow over the next two weeks, Smike stayed the course. He prepared for his debut, perhaps with a little more intensity due to the emotional weight he carried. Fortunately, his bandmates Violet, Denny, and Mitch as well as his close friends Elsye and Rally, provided daily support and encouragement.

Smike and Rally took Slim to JoJo's memorial service. Somehow Slim understood what they were doing for him and how they were all honoring JoJo. Slim proudly wore JoJo's belt buckle to the service. JoJo's nephew and Mr. Cranston personally thanked them for bringing Slim. Somehow, nothing else was said.

As days passed, somehow, Paps seemed more responsive to Smike. Mr. Kahn had been supportively calling him daily, which was definitely helpful. Paps also agreed to make the scheduled appointment with the PTSD specialist. Mr. Kahn apparently played a role in Paps following through with this first counseling meeting. Surprisingly, Paps scheduled additional appointments; of course, always on his own terms. Somehow, Paps was no longer fighting those closest to him, no longer fleeing his self-inflicted torment (but rather facing it), and no longer frozen in his mental state. However, further actions and choices he might take to heal were all on him.

At one point, Paps informed Smike that they would not be going to Aunt Vera's for Thanksgiving, a typical holiday get-together in Connecticut shared with his daughter, her husband, and their grown children. He didn't want to be around family and didn't want to eat turkey; just wanted Kielbasa bologna on toasted pumpernickel bread, daubed with hot, spicy mustard, and dill pickles on the side. Somehow, he felt this was a better holiday meal and staying home, more practical. Smike concurred and called his aunt to provide an inoffensive excuse for them not attending the family gathering and shared meal.

Smike knew that Mr. Kahn had a settling presence on his grandfather and hoped, although he thought this was a long shot, that somehow during his return visit after Thanksgiving, he might convince Paps to attend his debut. Of course, his musical premiere was coming up very quickly and no one was really sure about Paps' current, vapid emotional state.

A few days before his debut, Smike arranged to meet with Rally and settle a bet they made earlier. Somehow, Rally actually followed through on a real bet with Smike but lost. So, after work, the Wednesday before Thanksgiving, Rally was directed to meet with him at an unfamiliar location.

Smike shared, "Bring your family Rally, since they need to be there to experience your embarrassment in losing your first real bet!"

Rally mournfully replied, "Can't believe you're doing this!"

Smike responded, "Just teaching you a lesson my friend."

Chapter CXXXI   A Real Bet

Standing on the sidewalk in the cold, just staring at each other, Smike seriously asserts to Rally, "Come on man, this is the real deal, you got to pay up. Twenty dollars. Hand it over" while holding out his hand for receipt of payment.

In disbelief Rally says, "Can't believe you're doing this" as he reaches into his pocket to pull out cash that he then reluctantly hands over to him.

Receiving the funds with a grin on his face, Smike matter-of-factly states "Well, you know, a bet is a bet, and you lost this one."

Rally just continues to stare at him, doubting that this is really happening. For the first time ever, Rally is speechless, almost in shock.

Running up behind Rally, Pablo screams with excitement, "I've got my own room dad and there's this huge backyard! Can we get a dog now?"

Beaming, Rally turns and says, "Maybe, but that's up to your mother."

Exiting the home in the background, Abuelita Maria soon follows behind Pablo, comes over to Smike and gives him an appreciative cuddle while repeating "Eres un santo, eres un santo, Smike!"

She then pulls away from the hug, reaches up to embrace his face and with tears in her eyes, kisses him.

Abuelita then turns to Rally and says, "Cocina enorme . . . mi sueño" before she starts softly weeping in thankful happiness.

A short time later, after fully surveying the house, Marciella joins them on the sidewalk.

Speaking directly to Smike, she says, "I *never* approved of Rally gambling, but so grateful he lost this bet!" she then adds, "especially to the generous godfather of our expectant blessing."

He responds, "Well, Rally should never have doubted me when I told him he would have a house by Thanksgiving. He is the one who placed the real bet, for the first time, and lost!"

Handing the keys to Marciella, Smike says, "It's cold outside, let's go in your new home and warm-up."

A few weeks back, Smike determined the perfect resolution to the dilemma placed on him with JoJo's Will. He would give the house to Rally and his family just before Thanksgiving. The gift was a true pay-it-forward arrangement. In his eyes, it would not only support Rally, his family, and his educational pursuits, but also promote Rally's future patronage to the community as a social worker. Of course, Slim would also be devotedly taken care of with this arrangement. It was a win-win-win situation. A real bet that would benefit all.

Chapter CXXXII   Do It. Become . . .

After two heavily taxing weeks, and highly anxious about the debut the next day, Smike couldn't fall asleep. Thoughts of Louisa both comforted and tortured him. Will his songs serve as a worthy tribute to her?

He remembered holding her in his arms for the last time. The doctor explained how near the end, her breathing would become labored. She may lose consciousness but could possibly still hear him and understand what was going on around her. After her family said their painful good-byes, leaving him to be alone with her, he felt numbed in complete sadness. She, however, pulled together a sliver of remaining strength to whisper her last words to him.

"Just breathe Smike. Do it. Become. . ."

Louisa didn't finish her sentence. He burst into tears, and in his own voice, started singing *Can't Take My Eyes Off of You*. He kept thinking, *Please Louisa, hear me. Please hear me sing! Please!* while singing the song to completion. She was gone. He hoped but didn't know if she ever heard him sing. Now, he would sing tomorrow, in his own voice, and finally honor her. She deserved that.

Chapter CXXXIII   Debut

Violet, front and center on stage, announces through a microphone, "Welcome everyone! We have a special treat this day as our keyboardist and harmonica player extraordinaire, Smike Schrod, will honor us with the debut of his new songs. *Knead Naked* feels privileged to serve as the back-up band in this tribute. Please join me in a welcoming round of applause for introducing Smike Schrod and his musical debut!"

The crowd claps loudly as the band wastes no time playing the first song *Learning From Mistakes* with Mitch as lead singer. Elsye stands near the front of the stage, filming the entire event, capturing all band members shining in full glory.

Mitch begins singing the first stanza,

Learning from mistakes, that takes me to new places.

Learning from my past, that passed up promising chances.

Learning to be me, from some place I yearn to be.

Learning from mistakes, to help me sense some serenity.

After completion of this song, the band continues with an exceptional performance of eight additional songs. The audience's appreciation grows as the band's momentum builds.

They pause before the last song when Violet informs the audience that Smike will sing this song and she will assist on her violin.

Just Saying

The crowd erupts into additional cheering! Unexpectedly, Paps, Jonathan, and Abby enter at the back of the hall and find seats near where Curtis and Livi are sitting. Paps had made tremendous gains in his therapy sessions the previous week; and apparently, Jonathan had supportively convinced him to attend the debut.

This will be the first time he has ever sung in his own voice to anyone, and the audience is a full crowd, which now includes his grandfather who he just saw enter. His nervousness consumes him as Elsye, still near the front of the stage, nods to him that she is ready to video his performance.

Smike hears Rally in the audience yell out, "We love ya man!"

Encouraged, Smike softly shares with the audience, "This is dedicated to Louisa."

While closing his eyes and envisioning her, he channels her energy to begin playing a melody on his keyboard.

Sweeping resisting thoughts away, he starts to sing in a slow tempo and gravelly timbre, emotionally focused on how every note is a memorial to Louisa.

Just saying...

Can't say how much I want you

Can't say how much I need you

Can't say how much I love you

Can't say how much I miss you

Just saying…

What remains is…

A hole in my life

A hole in my heart

A hole in my soul

A hole that will never be filled

What remains is…

My love for you

My need for you

He pauses slightly and shifts to an instrumental section of the song where he plays his harmonica, accompanied by Violet on her violin. They play multiple stanzas that poignantly resonate with the enthralled spectators. Upon completion of their instrumental duet, Smike returns to his keyboard and gains momentum in singing the final stanzas. Finding his voice, with more confidence at this point in the performance and fully channeling Louisa's spirit, he continues, his heart brimming with emotion.

Just saying…

Can't say how much I want you

Can't say how much I need you

Can't say how much I love you

Just Saying

Can't say how much I miss you

Just saying…

What remains is…

A hole in my life

A hole in my heart

A hole in my soul

A hole that will never be filled

What remains is…

My love for you

My need for you

As his voice trails off, the audience explodes into applause, several members yelling out praise and some even whistling. Violet comes up and warmly hugs him. Mitch slaps him on the back. Denny gives him a high five. Elsye, grinning with happiness, waves to him while still video-taping. Smike has found his voice! His real voice! His voice as the musician he has always been. He then looks at the audience, waves his appreciation, scans the room, and sees Paps with Jonathan and Abby at the back. Surprisingly, he sees Paps clapping in celebration of his performance!

While applause continues, Smike gets up. He walks to the back of the hall, goes over and shakes Paps' hand. Paps stands up and hugs him. They stay embraced while Violet says, "Let's give it up again for Smike's premiere performance! We have all just witnessed a rising star my friends!"

Pushing away from the embrace and facing Paps, Smike says, "Thanks for coming Paps! I really appreciate you being here."

Paps responds, "Proud of ya Michael. Yaw music makes people happy and me too!"

Smike replies,"Couldn't ask for a greater compliment Paps!"

Smike then turns to Jonathan who is seated nearby and shakes his hand.

Abby, standing next to her grandfather, says, "That was the most beautiful song that I've ever heard!"

Smike stares at her. She returns the gaze. One Massachusetts, two Massachusetts, three Massachusetts. Their stare is unbroken for several seconds as he starts smiling at her. He notices her long flowing auburn hair is not tied in a sloppy bun. And her genuine smile takes over her entire face. He doesn't remember ever seeing her smile before. She is striking.

Chapter CXXXIV   Knotty or Anise?

"I know you think it might be too early being the first week in December, but gotta finalize our Christmas song list. So far, we have *Jingle Bell Rock, Winter Wonderland, Feliz Navidad, Rockin Around the Christmas Tree, Silver Bells, It's Beginning to Look a Lot Like Christmas, O Holy* Night, and my duet with Mitch *Baby, It's Cold Outside*. Need to know your solo pieces" Violet asks.

Denny quickly replies, "Sticking with *Little Drummer Boy*."

"Perfect" Violet confirms as she writes it down. "Guess you'll be dressing up as a soldier from the Nutcracker?"

"Yeah, just like last year" Denny acknowledges.

Smike interrupts, "Wait, so, we also dress up for this particular Tavern holiday gig?"

"Oh yeah, this event is huge. Even patrons come in dressed up. But, no one can be Santa except for Fred" Mitch explains.

Smike asks, "So, who are you dressing up as Mitch?"

He eagerly responds, "The Grinch. Gotta be the naughty one, ya know? Everyone thinks it's hilarious!"

"Actually, that's quite comical! So, what Christmas song solo complements that persona?" Smike asks him.

Mitch replies, "I get a little help with my solo from Fred, who dressed as Santa, helps me with *Santa Claus is Coming to Town*. He doesn't sing or anything; he just walks around while I am singing about being naughty or nice, with a bag slung over his shoulder and passes out random gifts to those on his 'nice' list. Mostly paper coasters with the bar's logo on them but also a few gift cards. And, at the end of the song, I have a stocking filled with rubbers and pass them out for those on my 'naughty' list."

"You're a sly one, Mr. Grinch!" Smike cleverly responds.

They all chuckle.

Violet then asks, "So, Smike, what about you? Gotta a song picked out for your solo?"

A little apprehensive, he shares, "Was thinking about *All I Want for Christmas is My Two Front Teeth* and sing as Mike Tyson. I would wear a covering over my teeth while singing. I have the Tyson lisp impression nailed down pretty good. Was also batting around the possibility of *Marshmallow World* as Dean Martin. This one would kind of be like a private joke about my Paps who has reacquired an appreciation for marshmallow fluff after imbibing in some inspirational gummies. Elsye is in on the gag and would find it pretty funny, too. However, my Dino impersonation isn't great, still working on it, so need the band's input and preference. Also, have no idea what holiday character to dress up as. Didn't know that was part of the holiday gig until now, so hadn't thought about it."

Mitch replies, "A couple years ago, we did the *Two Front Teeth* song and some seniors pulled out their dentures at the end. Was a huge hit! We were all laughing our asses off. But, would prefer you sing the *Marshmallow* song, especially if Paps shows up because he hasn't come to a show at Fred's Tavern before. And we haven't done that song before. Regarding what to wear, can just put on some fake antlers and be a reindeer or dress like an elf with hat and pointy ears. If you wanna waggish look, go with the antlers. Can claim you're 'horny' to the fans."

Mitch then queries, "So, is Paps actually coming to this Christmas performance?"

Smike responds, "Thanks for your humorous input, Mitch. And yes, Paps is planning to attend. Elsye agreed to escort him. You know she has her way with him."

Smike then solicits input from Violet and Denny, "Other thoughts on song and garb?"

Violet shares, "I agree on the *Marshmallow* song. Great selection to add to our list. Think you would be a handsome elf, but whatever you choose to dress up as will work."

Denny then quickly adds, "So yeah, the *Marshmallow* song. Costume, can go as chimney sweep maybe or Frosty the Snowman. To keep it simple, can just wear a top hat."

"Appreciate everyone's input! Dino it is then and I'll dress like Rudolph with lit-up red nose and antlers. That character can be both naughty and nice" Smike shares to finalize his decision for the song and costume.

Violet concludes, "Okay, thanks Smike! And, like in the past, I'll dress as an angel, wearing a halo, and end our session with my solo *All I Want for Christmas.*"

Mitch adds, "Violet rocks this song! It's her signature work and the ultimate ending to our Christmas session."

"I have no doubt. Can't wait to hear you sing it Violet" Smike says.

"You won't hear it until the performance. I don't practice it with the band" Violet clarifies.

Violet then adds, "Also, remember, after the session, we'll share our yearly Christmas shot of anisette for good luck! This is one of our traditions as a band."

"I am game, but what's anisette?" Smike asks.

Denny explains, "It's a liqueur made from anise that tastes like licorice. Something like Sambuca. Can take it straight up or on the rocks."

"Got it!" Smike responds.

Violet then apologizes to everyone that she needs to run some errands. After she leaves, Mitch asks Smike and Denny to stick around for a couple of minutes. He has something he wants to share about their Christmas gig.

Mitch informs them that "Beau is gonna formally propose to Violet at the end of the Christmas performance as she is singing the last song. He wants us to assist setting it up. He's ready to finally tie the knot."

Denny responds, "About time! How can I help?"

Smike adds, "Yeah, of course, count me it. This will be my introduction to Beau. Can't believe I haven't met him yet."

Mitch adds details on how the proposal will go down.

Just Saying

"So, here's the plan. Violet thinks that Beau won't be home until the day after the gig. He will be staying with his sister so Violet won't know he's back in town. Everyone in her family knows this is going down, except for Scarlett. Family didn't want her spilling the beans, so she doesn't know about it, but will be there. Anyway, they will ALL be there and will probably video-tape the proposal. So, Beau will stay outside by the bar's back door until Fred cues him when Violet is about halfway through the song. During her last stanza, one at a time, we will come over in front of Violet, drop down on one knee and hold out a diamond ring pop. You know, those lollipops shaped like diamonds that kids wear as rings to suck on. And, we'll act like we're proposing."

A little concerned, Smike asks, "Violet will be surprised by us doing this, right? I mean, she organizes everything and this isn't in the script."

"She knows how to improvise and will figure we are just goofing around. Trust me. She won't miss a beat" Mitch explains.

For clarification, Denny asks, "And this is when Beau will walk through the audience to the stage and propose?"

"Exactly! Of course, as she spots him moving through the crowd, we will move out of the way" Mitch adds.

"That is a grand idea for his proposal to her. But, guessing that as serious as Violet is, she will cry, especially with family, friends, and fans in the audience" Smike shares with concern.

"Oh yeah, she will lose it. I know it! She will cry. She'll cry hard! But she told Beau that whenever he got around to proposing, that it had to be a real surprise. No typical dinner out at a fancy diner, bistro or restaurant. He's supposed to catch her off guard" Mitch explains.

"She'll definitely be caught off guard. Glad it will be part of our last song. Don't think she would be able to continue after that!" Smike adds.

"After the proposal, the audience will toast them with shots of anisette that I'm springing for. Fred and I suggested that to Beau, and he loved the idea."

Smike confirms, "This is going to be something to see! I am so happy for Violet, Beau, and her entire family!"

Mitch says, "Yeah, the whole proposal scheme is gonna be both naughty and nice!"

Chapter CXXXV More Than One Surprise

Two weeks later, the Christmas performance at Fred's goes just as expected, with tears flowing during Violet's ending solo and her acceptance of Beau's surprise proposal. It was a beautiful, truly moving moment. The whole event even tugged at Paps' heartstrings as he and Elsye sat at the band's table near the front of the stage and shared a shot of anisette. Mitch meandered around the bar, blissfully pouring shots to patrons.

After this main event, a man from the audience comes up to Smike, pulls him aside, and asks to talk. Paps and Elsye see them conversing from a distance and wonder about their discussion.

"I had to see you perform in person Smike. Watched the video posted online from your debut last month and was very impressed with your harmonica performance. Also, your songs were wonderful. Did you really write all of them?" the man asks.

"Well, yes, I did! Thank you for the compliment" Smike shares, not knowing who this guy is or why he wants to talk with him.

The man continues, "I would like to offer you more than a compliment. I would like to offer you an opportunity to play with an up-and-coming band named *Beholden* based in Nashville that needs a harmonica player and back-up singer. They begin touring nationally for concerts in January and recently signed a contract with a major recording studio" the man shares.

In shock, Smike asks, "Not to sound rude, but who are you?"

"I'm sorry, should have introduced myself. My name is Howie Anderson and I'm an agent for bands and musicians. I shared your videos with all members of *Beholden* and they would like to fly you to Nashville for an audition, but quite frankly, from what I have seen, that will only be a formality. You will probably spend most of your time negotiating a contract and discussing possibly recording some of your songs. Are you interested?"

Astounded, Smike responds, "Well this is a complete surprise" then asks, "What kind of music does *Beholden* play?"

"They play blues, ballads, a little soulful country. How about I show you some of their songs on my phone?" Howie suggests.

"Sure, I would like to hear their work" Smike responds.

Howie pulls out his phone and accesses some clips for viewing. Smike watches with intense interest. He likes what he sees on the videos. The two complete their discussion and shake hands. Mr. Anderson leaves as Smike, in a pleasant daze, walks over to Paps and Elsye.

Paps asks, "Who was that? And what did he wan?"

Momentarily ignoring Paps' question, Smike asks, "Elsye, so you posted videos of my debut online?"

Admittedly, she states, "Yes, yes, I did. Never know who may see your performance, hear your music, and love it like the rest of us."

Smike replies, "You're right! That man wants to be my agent. Looks like I'm going to Nashville!"

Chapter CXXXVI   Fixed Gate

Standing by Paps' front porch, Smike fondly hugs Elsye. She has been a dear friend and he will miss her terribly. He appreciates that she looks after his grandfather and is the only local who can effectively handle his flashes of acerbic remarks. More importantly, Paps values his bond with her. They share a unique kinship that transcends generational and cultural gaps.

Unobtrusively, Paps patiently waits nearby for his farewell embrace. Smike goes in for a full-frontal hug that differs from their previous side hugs.

Paps welcomes it and mumbles, "Take cayah of yawself in Nashville. Come back to see me in the summah aw soonah. Will need help with the gahden."

"Of course, Paps!" Smike responds, feeling a surprising sadness emerge.

Unceremoniously, Smike then turns and walks towards his car parked on the street and fully loaded with all of his possessions. He gets to the gate and is surprised how easily it opens.

Turning around to Paps, he asks, "When did this get fixed?"

Paps responds, "My naybah David and yaw friend Mitch helped me fix it. Woan stick anymoah. Can easily open it now whenevah ya return."

Smike instantly realizes that the three of them secretly conducted the gate repair. Like a message to him. He can always visit with no resistance, no hitch to him returning home. Paps would always welcome him.

Smike waves to both of them, jumps in his car, and drives away. Once out of the neighborhood, he turns on his radio to an oldie station and sings along with songs that are playing. Heading south, miles away on the Interstate, up ahead he spots a worn running shoe on the side of the road. Without hesitation, he pulls over, jumps out of his car, retrieves the shoe, and tosses it in the passenger side of his car. He then gets back into his car and drives off. Continuing south, he glimpses at the shoe. *Some lost souls get found*; he thinks.

Chapter CXXXVII   Nailed It

"He's not gonna like this" Mitch quietly cautions as Elsye stealthily slathers Tahitian Pink polish on Sid's beastly toe nails. He had fallen into a satisfying slumber after a taxing shopping spree that morning after Smike's departure, followed by a huge homemade spaghetti meal that Mitch prepared for the three of them.

"That's the point, ya goof!" she snips while flashing an impish grin.

In deference to Elsye's unspoken scheme, Mitch shrugs, clueless to what she's up to, but confident that Sid will not find this remotely amusing.

"Okay, so I'm going to the kitchen to get everything ready. Give me a couple of minutes and then make noise to wake him. Be ready for explosive and combative bitching!"

A short time later, Mitch fakes a cough. The old man remains motionless. Mitch then intensifies and exaggerates his forged hacking. Sid rouses with eyes half open, unmistakably irritated.

"Damn Mitch, gotta take cayah of yah bahkin. Doah wanna get us awl sick" Paps grumbles.

"Yeah, sorry 'bout that" Mitch replies to continue the ruse.

Sid then clumsily shifts in his lounger, looks down at his propped feet, and briefly wonders why he's sockless. Spotting his painted toes, he quickly realizes the underhanded action taken while he was snoozing.

"Yah in on this, Mistah co-conspiahtah?" Sid meanly asks.

"I told her it just wasn't your shade" Mitch teases.

Sid then violently screams, "Elsye, get in heyah and take this shit off my toes! Not fuckin' funny!"

Without verbally responding, Elsye slowly enters the family room sporting a vintage military gas mask, a school crossing guard safety vest, and long rubber gloves up to her elbows, while carrying a bucket in one hand and a large utility-grade steel file in the other.

Briefly dumbfounded, Sid suddenly bursts into laughter.

After regaining his composure, he taunts, "I see yah ready fah battle!"

Matter-of-factly, Elsye replies, "It's time for your unconditional surrender."

Mitch drolly quips, "Guess she nailed it, Sid."

They share a laugh that only family understand.

Epilogue (October 3, 2025)

Part I

Elsye looks out the window at trees filled with leaves lightly rustling in the breeze; just starting to change into myriad hues of color. She treasures the fall season; always felt comforted by the crisp air that awakened her senses and memories. As she contentedly stares out the window on this exquisite morning, she reminisces about an old friend and wishes he knew about her good fortune and rich life. Looking down at the floor, she smiles at the serene source of her opulence; her young daughter quietly playing on a thick comforter with a hound puppy curled up on one side and two cats sprawled on the other side, peacefully snoozing.

She calls out, "Mitch, can you watch Alysha for a bit. I need to drop something off just outside of town. Will be gone a little over an hour or so."

Mitch walks into the kitchen where Elsye has been washing dishes and says, "Sure! Just finished putting in another set of book shelves. Need a break."

He then plops down next to the child and pressing his forehead against hers, says, "Ya wanna help your father feed the chickens, my beautiful girl?" The child starts patting him on the head, giggling.

Elsye beams looking at them both. She then grabs her jacket, goes to the dog's toy box, retrieves a chewed-up shoe, and exits the kitchen door.

Driving away from the farm house on a gravel road, she heads towards town.

Part II

It's a cool breezy afternoon, leaves swirling in the trees, as Smike walks through the cemetery, advancing toward the headstone. As he nears it, he smiles broadly, noticing that others have previously visited and left mementos and symbolic tokens to honor the deceased.

"Daddy, mommy is too slow pushing Grandpa Jon. I want to be with you" a child yells while running behind his father.

He hears the mother calling, "Sidney Jonathan Schrod, slow down and wait for me" as the young boy runs up to him, away from his mother's calling.

Smike replies to the child, "Of course son, and you can help me place the gift. You don't remember, but when you were a baby, Grand Paps would whistle a lullaby to comfort you."

The young boy looks up and grins at his father.

Abby soon arrives behind them, pushing Jonathan in a wheelchair.

Seeing the items surrounding the headstone, Jonathan notes, "I see that others have shown their respects recently. The beer can adds just the right touch. A tomato, although slightly rotten is appropriate. Curious to see this little plastic figure that looks like a knight with a sword raised; however, not sure what the old shoe means."

Just Saying

"I'll explain the story of the shoe later Grandpa Jon. It comes from a close friend of both of ours when I lived with Paps" Smike responds.

"Did you want some time alone?" Abby thoughtfully asks while sweeping her hair away from her face and then resting her hand on her largely protruding abdomen.

"No, that's okay; in fact, Sidney is going to help me" Smike says.

He reaches into his pocket and pulls out a pack of Juicy Fruit.

He hands it to Sidney and says, "My Paps used to offer me gum all the time. When I was your age, he would balance it on my head. I want you to place it here." He points to the section of the headstone that reads, *Soldier of life, always ready for a fair fight.*"

Sidney places the pack of gum where his father pointed and then asks, "Do you have some for me?"

Smike replies, "Yes, sure do. But your mom is in charge of when you get it. Don't want to spoil your appetite."

Abby smiles and says, "Doubt that's ever going to happen. The boy eats like a horse."

Smike responds, "Runs in the family . . . Just saying."

About the Author

Denise McDonald, Ed.D., Professor Emerita of Curriculum and Instruction, University of Houston – Clear Lake, has published academic research and practitioner articles, positional pieces, books, book chapters, and even a poem. She is founding editor of the journal *BRIDGE – Bringing Research In Direct Grasp of Educators*. Recently retired, *Just Saying* is her first novel. Other than writing, Denise enjoys long, daily walks and making jewelry for family and friends. However, her favorite activity is spending time with her granddaughters. Denise lives with Chris, her husband (and muse), in Seabrook, Texas.

JEBWizard Publishing
Books with Character